Fergus's smile hid the pain he felt on her behalf. 'I wasn't ashamed of you on that day, Becky, and I never will be.'

'It's easy to say that now, Fergus Vincent, but one day you're going to be famous. You won't want a Lewin's Mead brat hanging round you. Mary Carpenter's right. I should stay here. There's no other way to shake off the dirt of Lewin's Mead. I'll learn everything she can teach me, and I'll learn it well. You'll never have to be ashamed of me, I promise you.'

'Cross your heart?' Fergus managed a grin, although he felt closer to tears.

'Cross my heart and hope to die.' Becky grinned, too, and it cost her even more. The woman who had brought Becky to the garden was advancing down the garden steps towards them now. It was time for Becky to return to the house.

'I'll need your help sometimes, Fergus.'

'You'll have it, I promise you.'

Becky nodded briefly but she was unable to prevent tears from welling up in her eyes. Cuffing them away angrily, she said: 'It's all right. I don't cry . . . never.' Then, as her eyes filled again, she whispered: 'But I still wish I was coming home with you.'

Becky

E.V. Thompson

sphere

SPHERE

First published in Great Britain by Macmillan London Limited in 1988
First published in paperback by Pan Books Ltd in 1989
Published by Warner Books in 1999
Reprinted by Time Warner Paperbacks in 2002
Reissued by Sphere in 2010

A CIP catalogue record for this book
is available from the British Library.

ISBN 978-0-7515-4571-5

Printed in the UK by CPI Mackays, Chatham ME5 8TD

Papers used by Sphere are natural, renewable and
recyclable products sourced from well-managed forests and certified
in accordance with the rules of the Forest Stewardship Council.

Mixed Sources
Product group from well-managed
forests and other controlled sources
www.fsc.org Cert no. SGS-COC-004081
© 1996 Forest Stewardship Council

FSC

Sphere
An imprint of
Little, Brown Book Group
100 Victoria Embankment
London EC4Y 0DY

An Hachette UK Company
www.hachette.co.uk

www.littlebrown.co.uk

To Celia
for her help and understanding

CHAPTER ONE

WHEN FERGUS VINCENT first saw Becky she was lying amidst accumulated rubbish on the cobbled footway of Lewin's Mead, the worst slum in the busy port of Bristol, and he could not decide whether she was alive or dead.

No road-sweeper wielded broom or shovel in these streets, nor were there house-servants to clear a space in front of each tall half-timbered house. Prosperous merchants had once lived here, but that had been in the early years of the eighteenth century, more than a hundred years before. Now the tall unsymmetrical houses leaned drunkenly towards each other across a maze of narrow dingy thoroughfares, hiding the dank rubbish-strewn alleyways from the revealing light of the sun.

Stooping, Fergus prodded the rag-clad figure. It sat up immediately.

'Here! What d'you think *you're* doing? Leave off!'

'I didn't expect to find anyone sleeping in the street at this hour. It's hardly evening yet.'

'What's it to *you* when I sleep?'

The girl's voice carried a broad Bristol accent, and Fergus had an overpowering urge to sketch her as she sat scowling, surrounded by rubbish. The girl's pinched face was as dirty as any he had ever seen, but dirt could not hide the wary expression in her eyes. It was an expression Fergus had seen in the slums of half a hundred cities.

'Do you know Back Lane?'

Rising to her feet, the girl peered up at him suspiciously.

The light was poor, but Fergus could see she was older than he had first thought. Small for her age, she was probably about thirteen.

'What do you want in Back Lane? If you're looking for a tart, I know a young dollymop who'll serve you well – or you can have me for a guinea.'

Fergus had met younger girls than this one selling themselves and he was more amused than shocked.

'If I had a sovereign to spend on a woman, I'd want more for my money than a bundle of skin and bones wrapped in rags. That's not why I'm here. I'm seeking a friend.'

'A friend of *yours* in Back Lane?' The girl studied Fergus from head to toe. She saw a slim thin-faced young man with unfashionably long hair who must have been in his early twenties. From the way he moved it was evident he limped quite badly. His clothes were hardly those of a gentleman but, like Fergus himself, they were *clean*. This alone set him apart from the residents of Back Lane.

'What's your friend's name?'

'Henry Gordon.'

'*Jock* Gordon? The artist?'

'That's right. You know him?'

Fergus was both delighted and relieved to know he had found the right place. In the letter received by Fergus some months before, Henry Gordon had been overflowing with enthusiasm for the many subjects just waiting to be painted in Lewin's Mead. But Henry Gordon was a man of rapidly changing moods. It would have been in character for him to move on only a few days after telling Fergus of all he hoped to achieve in Lewin's Mead.

'I *did* know him.'

'He's gone? Damn! I wrote and told him I'd be here soon. . . . He couldn't have got my letter.'

'It wouldn't have made any difference.' The girl spoke almost nonchalantly. 'He's dead. It was probably the drink, though some think he caught something that came in on one of the foreign boats, down at the docks. Couldn't really say, myself. One day when I spoke to him he seemed as right as rain. The next, he was dead.'

Fergus felt deep shock. Henry Gordon had been his best friend – his *only* friend in earlier days, when Fergus had no one else to whom he could turn. He had known Henry Gordon for as long as he could remember. The artist had been more of a father to him than Fergus Vincent senior.

When Fergus had returned to Edinburgh from one of his sea-trips and learned his dying mother had been taken to an asylum for the chronically insane, it was Henry Gordon who helped Fergus to have her moved. Fergus still had nightmares about those terrifying nights when he had sat beside his mother's bed in a locked ward, as demons in every conceivable guise moved in to torment the unfortunate inmates of that uncaring and degrading place.

It was Henry Gordon who stood with Fergus at the graveside while his mother was lowered into the ground of a chilly and fog-shrouded churchyard, while Fergus's own father was accepting consolation – and drinks – from friends in the smoky warmth of an Edinburgh tavern.

From early childhood days, too, it had always been Henry Gordon who encouraged Fergus to sketch, offering his own artist's materials when there was no money in the Vincent household to indulge what Fergus's father scathingly dismissed as his son's 'nonsense'.

Even in later years when Henry Gordon developed a liking for the bottle and lost his teaching post at the Edinburgh academy, he had always worked hard to encourage the young sailor-artist.

'You won't be wanting Back Lane now?' The girl broke into Fergus's unspoken grief.

'What? No. . . . Not unless Henry's left any of his work behind. But it will be long gone by now, I expect. When did he die?'

'Must be a week ago. Ten days at the most. But if you're talking about his paintings they're still in his room.'

'The room hasn't been let?'

'Whores who work the docks are the only ones with money in Back Lane, and no drunken sailor's going to risk a broken neck climbing stairs to Ida Stokes's attic in the dark. Give me a penny and I'll take you there. For two I'll carry your bags.'

Fergus had a small kitbag slung over his shoulder and a large slim canvas satchel tucked beneath his arm. The two bags contained all he owned in the world. He had no intention of trusting either to an unknown Bristol street-urchin.

'What's your name?'

'Becky.'

'Becky what?'

She shrugged. 'I ain't never had no other name.'

For a moment Fergus softened. It was a fleeting emotion. Children who begged for a living were convincing liars.

'I'm Fergus Vincent. I'm an artist, too. Show me where Henry Gordon lived. If his work is still there, I'll give you *three* pence. If it's gone, you get nothing.'

'All right.' If Jock Gordon's belongings were still in the house, Becky would be three pence better off. If they weren't – well, the cobbles were no harder in Back Lane than here. 'His stuff will be there. Ida Stokes gives away nothing that comes her way, and no one with any money's come to Back Lane since Jock died.'

Fergus did not doubt her words. Little would happen in the closely packed Lewin's Mead slums that did not quickly become common knowledge. Much of the city's crime originated here. Any one of the residents of the narrow streets could have quoted time, place and the villains responsible for every unlawful incident. But none would. It was the same in the slums of every city in the land. Such close-mouthed silence had nothing to do with loyalty. A poor man lived by his own laws. Often crude, they were always effective. The secrets of a slum were kept where they belonged.

Becky led Fergus through narrow streets and narrower alleyways that became progressively dirtier as they climbed the hillside away from the quays and docks of the city centre.

As they neared a cheap beer-house which had more sacking than glass at its windows, Fergus could hear the sounds of a noisy argument. He and Becky had almost reached the door when a woman's screams rose above the din. Suddenly women and children spilled out of the beer-house doorway into the cobbled alleyway. In their midst was a scowling thickset man whose face was black with coal-dust and

4

streaked with rivulets of perspiration. The man's fists were flailing, and he drove a woman ahead of him.

The crowd parted, and Fergus saw that the object of the coal-heaver's attentions was a thin scarecrow of a woman, no more than five feet tall. It was she who was screaming as she staggered back before the assault of the angry bully. Around them other women shouted obscenities at the man, while a couple of small children tugged at his clothes and begged him to stop.

Halted by the crowd, Fergus watched in growing horror as the coal-heaver hit the woman yet again. She fell backwards, her head striking the cobblestones with a sound that reminded Fergus of a hen's egg falling on a hard surface.

The woman lay on the ground unmoving, but her angry assailant had not finished with her. He began to kick her with heavy-booted viciousness, each kick accompanied by an angry oath.

Fergus had seen enough. He was too slightly built to be a fighter, but he would not stand by and watch a woman being kicked to death. Pushing through the futilely shouting crowd, he charged at the coal-heaver just as he aimed yet another powerful kick at the woman.

Caught off-balance, the coal-heaver slipped on the cobblestones and fell heavily to the ground. He was up in an instant, looking to see who had the temerity to take him on. His glance found Fergus, and with a roar of anger he lunged forward, big coal-blackened fists swinging.

Most of the wild punches missed – but not all. One caught Fergus in the mouth and knocked him to the ground, and now it was his turn to be on the receiving end of the heavy-booted kicks.

As Fergus tried desperately to roll away, a small ragged figure leaped at the coal-heaver and clawed his face, jumping clear before he could retaliate. Taking heart from such unexpected support, the screeching women in the crowd began pummelling at the coal-heaver, the sheer weight of their numbers forcing him to back away along the cobbled alleyway.

Fergus climbed awkwardly to his feet and found Becky standing waiting for him, holding his bags.

'Come on!'

'The woman. . . . She might be badly hurt.'

'Her friends will take care of her. It's best to mind your own business when you're in Lewin's Mead.'

Fergus dabbed at the corner of his mouth, and his fingers came away sticky with blood. His lip was cut, and it felt as though one of his teeth was loose. But things might have been a great deal worse.

'Yet you stopped that coal-heaver from giving *me* a hiding.'

'If he'd knocked you out, your pockets would have been emptied in seconds. I wouldn't have got the three pence you've promised me.'

Becky thrust the bags at him, then turned and walked away. Smiling wryly, Fergus limped after her.

Minutes later they reached a cul-de-sac that was overshadowed by tall leaning houses. This was Back Lane. The cobblestones here were broken and uneven, and there was more accumulated rubbish than they had encountered in any street or alleyway through which they had passed. It would have been far worse had Back Lane not been on a hillside. As it was, rain pouring from the roofs washed much of the household filth into lower, less fortunate thoroughfares.

Becky led Fergus to a house at the very end of the narrow lane. A nondescript mongrel dog lay inside the door, feebly scratching at a tattered ear with a rear paw. It paused to growl when Fergus stepped over the threshold, but at an admonishment from Becky the sound died in the animal's throat, its tail beating a tattoo on the stone floor.

Their arrival had not gone unnoticed. Fergus had seen a shadow behind the dirty glass and brown paper of a downstairs window as they came in from the street. Now a door off the hall opened and a woman peered at them through the gloom.

'Who's that? If it's a catchpoll, you're too late. Irish Molly's gone back to Ireland. Sailed yesterday from the docks.' The old crone's voice was cracked and hoarse.

'It's not a constable, Ida. His name's Fergus. Fergus Vincent. He's a friend of the artist. The one who died.'

Ida Stokes advanced across the hall. She was an untidy, heavily overweight woman with indifferent eyesight. When she leaned closer to peer into Fergus's face he smelled cheap gin on her breath.

'He's bloody. What happened to him?'

'He tried to stop Joe Skewes beating his woman.'

'Joe Skewes? That man will kill someone one day, you mark my words.' Ida Stokes shook her head disapprovingly. She suddenly snapped at Fergus: 'Are you here to pay the rent your friend owed when he died?'

'No. I've come to see if he's left any paintings.'

'You're taking nothing until I'm paid what's owing to me. It's the law. I'm within my rights. . . .'

'I'm here because I'm Henry Gordon's friend, not his executor. Anything I take will be paid for. Where's his property?'

Fergus's manner was curt. The news of Henry Gordon's death had come as a great shock, and he was fighting hard to hide the grief he felt. He had no intention of wrangling with this woman about his friend's effects.

Surprisingly, Ida Stokes's manner underwent an immediate change. The Back Lane landlady had an ignorant woman's respect for learning — and Fergus's words branded him as an educated man. He had also mentioned he would pay for anything he took away. . . .

'The things are in his room at the top of the house. Wait here. We'll need a candle; the stairs are dark.'

When Ida Stokes disappeared into her room, Fergus dipped inside a pocket and produced a silver fourpenny piece. Handing it to Becky, he said: 'Here, use it to buy some food to fill that skinny belly.'

Becky snatched the money as though she feared Fergus might change his mind. The coin disappeared beneath her raised skirt a moment before Ida Stokes reappeared, the landlady's hand protecting the flame of a candle-stub against the draught coming through the open street-door.

Ida Stokes set off up the stairs without a word, and Fergus followed, Becky coming with them.

Three young women stood talking together in a doorway

on the first-floor landing. They looked curiously at the candlelit procession, and one of them, a thickset, dark-haired girl, hooted with mirth.

'Will you look at this! Ida's showing Becky and a young gent to a room. Becky's finally realised she's been sitting on an untapped fortune all these years.' The woman spoke with a strong Irish accent.

Rounding on the speaker, Ida Stokes snapped: 'Becky's doing nothing of the sort. She brought this gentleman to the house to check the belongings of his poor dead friend. So start showing some respect – and if any of you idle slatterns have laid your thieving hands on anything from his room you'd better return it now. Then you can get dressed and go out to earn some money; especially you, Irish Molly – you owe me a fortnight's rent. If I've had no money from you by the morning, you'll be out on the street.'

'You wouldn't do that, Ida. You know the beaks are after me because of the misunderstanding about that sailor's purse. . . .'

A loud and derisive snort from Ida Stokes interrupted the lament, but only for a moment.

'If they find me and bring charges, it'll be Australia this time for sure. Transportation, and me not a well woman.'

'And I'm not a *rich* one. Pay your rent tomorrow or there'll be someone else in your room by nightfall.'

Leaving the Irishwoman grimacing after her, Ida Stokes led the way up another flight of dark stairs. Wheezing laboriously, she said to Fergus: 'I should never have let that girl inside my house. She's trouble. All these Irish girls are alike. I'm too soft-hearted, that's what I am. Always been the same.'

There were several rooms off the next landing, but only one had a door. In one of the rooms a low fire was burning in the grate and a smell of unwholesome cooking pervaded the air. By the light of the fire Fergus could see a motley collection of men, women and crying children, sitting or lying on the bare floorboards. To Fergus's surprise Becky entered this room and was greeted with a shrill-voiced flow of Irish invective from a woman crouched by the fire.

'Does Becky live here?' Fergus asked the question as the landlady gathered herself to tackle yet another flight of stairs, this one narrower and more uneven than the previous two.

'Live here?' Ida Stokes echoed his words. 'Only when she has money to pay for a place in the room. I let it to an Irishwoman, O'Ryan. Never told me her first name. Not that there's any reason why I *should* know, not as long as she pays her rent regular. The less I know of them as stays here, the better it is for everyone. If I don't know names, I can't tell 'em. Can't be stood up before the magistrate for what they call "harbouring", neither. Becky comes here when she can pay her way, like the rest of 'em in there. When she can't she's out on the street. There's no shortage of company for her *there*, I can tell you.'

'Has she no family?' Fergus asked the question even as he was telling himself that Becky was none of his business.

'None as would admit to being "family". One of the sailor's women was once pointed out to me as her mother, but she's been dead these six or seven years — could even be longer.'

The wheezing old landlady's words conjured up memories for Fergus of his own childhood. He, too, had lived in a slum — an Edinburgh slum, where families were crowded into tenement buildings, as many as forty people occupying a flat originally built for two.

The cramped overcrowded conditions had bred disease, depravity — and frequent violence. There had been times when Fergus had gone hungry, too, but the one thing that had never been lacking in his life was the love of his mother. This was the thing he remembered most of all about those childhood days. It had provided him with the strength to fight free of his surroundings when an opportunity arose for him to join the Royal Navy.

Ida Stokes laboured up the last few protesting stairs and shook a key free from the jangling bunch worn on a cord about her neck. Inserting the key in the lock of the door at the head of the stairs, she turned it and said: 'Here you are, young sir. Everything's exactly as your friend left it — may God rest his poor soul.'

The attic room was long and narrow, with a sloping ceiling and a deep alcove at the far end. It also had two windows and was surprisingly light, even at this hour of the evening. The old house was taller than most of its neighbours, and there was a view from the windows over the adjacent rooftops. Fergus began to understand why Henry Gordon had been content to live in such an insalubrious area. Fergus wondered why the money-conscious landlady had not relet the room. When he put the question to her Ida Stokes was momentarily discomfited.

'Some mischievous gossip put word about that your friend died of cholera. It's a wonder I didn't lose *all* my tenants. There was no truth in the tale, but I'll not be able to let the room again until all such foolish talk's ended.'

'What *did* cause Henry's death?'

Ida Stokes kicked one of the many bottles strewn about the floor. 'Here's your answer – but as his friend you'll know all about his drinking habits. He reached for a bottle as soon as he opened his eyes. Mind you, he never woke before noon on most days. . . . But that was *his* business, as I often told him. I don't go prying into other folks' affairs. You'll find his paintings and the like in the alcove, just around the corner.'

Crouching on the floor in the small extension to the room, Fergus sorted quickly through the paintings leaning haphazardly against the wall. One or two had been painted on canvas, but most were on stiff pasteboard. There were portraits of sailors and dockside workers, one or two of inns and taverns – and a number of Becky.

'Well, what are they worth to you?'

Fergus shook his head. 'Very little, and I know of no one who'd buy them.'

He looked around the room as he spoke. Paint and pencils lay in untidy profusion on the single grubby table and also about the floor. There were paint-stained rags lying among them, and brushes were crammed inside an old pot on the window-sill. There was also an unfinished portrait on an easel standing close to the window.

'You might get a pound or two for everything, but no more.'

Fergus did not see Ida Stokes's disappointment. He was thumbing through a sketchpad which had been thrown carelessly on to the floor. There were many sketches here. Realistic *live* scenes drawn inside inns, or on the quays of the busy port. There were more sketches of Becky, too. Some were good.

'Will you give me two guineas for the lot?'

Fergus shook his head. 'I do my own sketches.'

He looked about him at the room. The walls were grubby, and the bed sagged in the middle like a first-day sailor's hammock. The bare floorboards were warped and rotten, and the floor sloped at an alarming angle. Above him dark mould-patches on the lath-and-plaster ceiling indicated where rain came in. But the light during the day would be exactly what an artist needed.

'If I decided to stay in Bristol, how much would you charge me for this room?'

Recovering quickly from her depression, Ida Stokes's expression resumed its natural cunning. 'It's a good room. Folks in Bristol are falling over themselves for places like this. I'd a mind to let it to a ship's bos'n, or a mate, perhaps.'

'How much?'

'I could get four and sixpence for it, easy. Five shillings if I let it to the Irish. They'd sleep twelve here with room to spare. . . .'

'I'll give you two shillings.'

'Two? That will hardly pay for the wear on my stairs. *Four* shillings – and I'll wash your bed-linen once a month, free of charge.'

'Two and sixpence, paid in advance – and my bed-linen washed once a fortnight. Agree now and I'll give you a guinea extra for the bits and pieces lying about the place.'

'I should know better than to dicker with a Scotsman – and mad to consider having another artist in my house. Make it *two* guineas for the things and the room's yours when you show me the colour of your money.'

Five minutes later Fergus was alone. Opening the windows to clear the smell of cooking that seeped up from the floor below, he sat on the sagging bed and looked about him with mixed feelings. Henry Gordon had spoken to him many times of living in just such a place as this and of using his talents to show how so many of the subjects of Queen Victoria lived in the mother country. Both men had agreed it was far more worthwhile than painting the dull and overweight wives and children of the more 'solid' citizens, as did so many artists of the time.

From the bustling port of Bristol, Henry Gordon had written to tell Fergus he had discovered a slum where he could put his ideas into practice. From Lewin's Mead he would produce a true and enduring record of the life and times. Not for the first time, he had suggested Fergus should leave the Navy and use his own considerable talents to help in Henry Gordon's self-appointed task.

The suggestion had raised a smile at the time. The letter had arrived while Fergus was serving on board a British man-of-war in the Mediterranean, with a promising naval career ahead of him. Taught by his mother to read and write, Fergus spent his off-duty hours studying in the narrow confines between decks. He was already an 'upper yard man', one of the lower-deck élite, and he had a thirst for learning.

Then Fergus's career was brought to an abrupt end. Boarding a suspected Arab slave-ship in rough seas off the North African coast, he slipped, and his ankle was crushed between the two vessels. At first the ship's surgeon feared he would need to amputate the foot, but fortunately decided Fergus should be taken instead to hospital in Gibraltar.

Hospital surgeons were able to save Fergus's foot, but he would have a serious limp for the remainder of his life. His sea-going days were over.

Convalescing, Fergus transferred the energy he had given his studies to his sketching. He wrote to tell Henry Gordon he would come to Bristol as soon as he received his discharge.

Fergus had limped down the gangplank of a small naval frigate in Bristol's docks only an hour before, with money and a discharge certificate in his pocket, and his sketchpad beneath his arm – only to learn he was ten days too late. Fergus felt like crying his anguish out loud. Henry Gordon was dead – but his dream could live or die with Fergus.

Reaching out, Fergus picked up his late friend's sketchpad again. It fell open at a sketch of Becky.

Fergus wondered whether she and the other residents of Lewin's Mead would accept him if he moved in and painted them as they went about their daily lives. He remembered something Henry Gordon had once told him.

'A good artist is accepted *wherever* he chooses to work, but in a slum an artist must observe the rules of the people who live there. *Their* code. Break it and he might as well pack up his things and leave. . . .'

CHAPTER TWO

FERGUS WAS AWAKENED by sunlight streaming in through the windows of the attic. Easing himself from the uncomfortable bed, he pulled on some clothes and made his way across the room to a window. A number of sparrows were chirruping happily on the roof outside, and Fergus watched them for a while as he planned the day that stretched ahead of him. He would start by checking how much work Henry Gordon had done. He picked up one of the sketchpads and looked through it yet again, marvelling at the enthusiasm which escaped from Henry Gordon's pages.

Fergus was still examining the pad when the door opened and Becky walked in. She asked no permission. Did not even greet him. Crossing to where he squatted on the uneven floor, she stood at his shoulder and looked down at the pad in his hand.

'I'm in there.'

'I know.'

He allowed the pages to fall back slowly, stopping when he came to a sketch which showed Becky peering in at a bakery window. Looking up at her, he said: 'It doesn't look as though you've washed since this was sketched.'

Becky ignored his comment. 'Can you draw as good as Jock?'

'He taught me.'

'Let's see *you* draw me, then.'

'Go and stand over there by the window.'

As Fergus picked up his own pad and a pencil, Becky

walked to the nearest window. She struck a stiff self-conscious pose – and then suddenly her attention was captured by three baby sparrows. Perched on the guttering of a nearby roof, they were noisily demanding food from their attentive but overworked parents.

'Look! Come and look at this.'

Fergus moved to the window and pretended to take an interest in the birds. His pencil moved swiftly over the paper as he worked to capture Becky's expression. He sketched the face of an innocent young girl, far removed from the product of the slums who had offered to prostitute her body to him for a guinea.

Enthralled, Becky watched the sparrows for many minutes, until a flock of pigeons arrived to take over the gutter in rapidly increasing numbers, their strutting and cooing eventually causing the protesting young sparrows to take to the air in nervous unpractised flight.

When Becky returned her attention to Fergus the moment of uncomplicated innocence had passed – but he had captured it on his sketchpad. Fergus continued sketching for some minutes more, perfecting the shape of an ear, shading in Becky's high cheekbones, and correcting the angle of her jaw. But the *essence* of the portrait had been transferred to paper in those first few moments.

Fergus put down his pencil, and Becky looked at him questioningly.

'It's done. It's a sketch, not a full-size portrait.'

Doubtfully, Becky left the window and took the sketch from his hands. She looked at it intently for a long while.

'Is that me? *Really* me?'

'*I* think it is.'

Becky looked back at the sketch. When she spoke again there was a strangeness in her voice.

'Jock never painted me that way.'

'Perhaps he never saw that particular expression on your face.'

She looked up at him again, and there was something in her eyes that made him want to paint her again. Then she shook her head. 'It's more than that. You've drawn the me that's *inside*. Not the me that other people see.'

'It's what an artist *should* do.'

'I'm not sure I like it.'

Handing back the sketchpad, Becky walked to the door. Pausing with her hand on the latch, she looked back at Fergus. 'But you're a good artist. *Better* than Jock.'

Then she was gone, the door swinging shut behind her.

Fergus spent the remainder of the day tidying the attic room and examining more closely the paintings and sketches produced by Henry Gordon during the last months of his life.

There was a small grate in the room, and Fergus found kindling and coal at the bottom of a nearby cupboard. He lit a fire and at noon stopped to make himself a brew of weak, sweet, but milkless tea, using ingredients he had brought with him in his bag. Afterwards he removed his own drawings and materials from his bags and laid them out on the table.

By the time evening began darkening the room Fergus was feeling hungry. He needed to eat. He would also have to earn some money. He had cash in his pocket, but it would not last for ever. Paying for the room and for Henry Gordon's effects had made a hole in the money the Navy had paid to him.

Arming himself with pencils and a pad, Fergus made his way down the rickety stairs. They seemed steeper and even more dangerous today. On the first-floor landing he stood aside to allow Irish Molly to pass. Behind the Irish prostitute a middle-aged sailor laboured up the stairs, his face dark-tanned. The Irish girl gave Fergus a cheerful wink, and he knew she would soon have the money to satisfy her debt to Ida Stokes.

It was almost dark outside, and Fergus did not see Becky standing in the deep shadows beside the doorway until she spoke.

'Where you off to, Fergus? Had enough of your new ken already?' She used a slang word to describe Ida Stokes's disreputable house.

'I've a living to earn. I'm off to the quayside. If I'm lucky, I'll find a few homecoming sailors willing to pay for a sketch to take home with them.'

'I'll take you to the Hatchet inn,' Becky said eagerly. 'Jock went there sometimes. He made good money, too ... but he drank it all.'

Fergus shook off the thoughts her words conjured up of his friend's lonely death.

'Lead on, Becky. If I do well, I'll pay for your supper tonight.'

Fergus fell in beside his ragged companion and they walked in silence for a while. Becky seemed to be deep in thought and suddenly she said: 'You don't need to pay me for doing things for you. You're living here now. You're one of us.'

Thinking of those residents of Ida Stokes's house he had seen so far, Fergus was by no means certain he wanted to be 'one of them', but he kept such thoughts to himself.

'That's very generous of you, Becky. But, then, you don't need pennies from me when you can command *guineas* from fine gentlemen.'

Becky looked at Fergus quickly and caught the tail-end of his smile. 'I *could* get a guinea. More, if I wanted. There's one girl I know who's taken to the houses of posh gents and earns *three* guineas a time.'

'But not you?'

'No.'

The admission was given after only the slightest hesitation.

'What would you have done had I taken you up on your offer?'

They had left Back Lane behind. The houses they passed were still part of the slums, but some showed lighted oil-lamps in their windows, casting a yellow light on the cobbled footway. As they passed through one of these pools of pale light Fergus glanced at his companion. Her clothes were more ragged than he remembered from their morning meeting, and he was quite certain no water had touched her face since then.

Becky intercepted his glance and, as though reading his thoughts, she pushed a strand of hair back from her forehead.

'If you'd said you wanted me, I'd have asked to see your money, of course. Then I'd have snatched it and scarpered quick.'

Fergus did not doubt her. Becky had already impressed him as being a straightforward child, even in her dishonesty.

Suddenly the lighted windows were behind them and they were passing through a narrow arched alleyway. When they came out on the other side Becky led him across a steep and narrow street before plunging into yet another maze of dark alleyways.

When they emerged the next time they were in a busier thoroughfare, indifferently lit by an insufficient number of gas-lamps.

Fergus stopped and looked about him. The cries of street vendors vied with the rattle of carriage wheels on the cobblestone road surface, and here and there a few bold pedestrians took their lives in their hands as they ventured across the busy street.

Suddenly Becky put her hand on Fergus's arm and pointed to a figure standing a little way back from the nearest gaslamp, his face barely discernible.

'Who's that?'

'It looks like a constable. . . .'

Before Fergus could say more Becky had gone, darting back into the maze of alleyways from whence they had just come.

The man who had caused Becky to take to her heels crossed the circle of gas-lit footpath and approached Fergus. Exceptionally tall and powerfully built, he wore the high black hat and blue frock-coat of a police constable.

'Good evening to you, sir. I think we're in for a surprisingly cold night.'

'I hope you're wrong, Constable. I've come out without my coat.'

'Few folk hereabouts own a coat. But they don't have far to go before they're home. You'll be a stranger here?'

'I arrived yesterday – on discharge from the Royal Navy.'

'Ah! Then, you won't have had time to learn about the places where it's wiser for an honest man not to walk alone. The Lewin's Mead rookery is one of them.'

' "Rookery"? I'm sorry, Constable . . . I don't understand.'

'The area from where you've just come, sir. Thieves,

vagabonds and cut-throats all have their nests there. It's as bad a slum as you'll find in any city – and I should know. Before coming here I was a constable in Whitechapel, in London. A nasty incident occurred in the rookery only yesterday evening. A young woman was viciously assaulted and had her head broken. She'll be lucky to live.... But didn't I see a young companion with you a minute ago? She darted back to the rookery a bit quick when she clapped eyes on me.'

'It was just a young ragamuffin,' Fergus lied. 'She was guiding me to the Hatchet inn. Yes, she did go rather quickly.'

'Then, you'd best check you've still got your purse, sir. There are some clever young dips in the city, and young girls is the worst of 'em.'

'My purse is hidden away safely at home, Constable. I've no more than two pence in my pocket. It's hardly worth the attentions of a pickpocket.'

'Indeed, sir.... But you said you was going to the Hatchet inn. I'm acquainted with the landlord. Charlie Waller's not a man to serve ale to young gentlemen unless they've money to pay for it.'

Fergus smiled ruefully. He was being subjected to a polite but insistent inquisition by this constable.

'I'm hoping to *earn* money at the inn, not spend it. I'm an artist. I want to sketch a few of the Hatchet inn's customers.'

'Ah!' The constable released a satisfied sigh, leaving Fergus with the distinct impression he had just passed some form of test. 'Well, seeing as how I've frightened off your guide, the least I can do is show you the way to the Hatchet inn.'

Limping along beside the other man, Fergus felt very small. The police constable was a big man and, with his top-hat, he towered almost two feet above Fergus. The constable was also talkative.

'There was another artist painting in these parts recently. As I recall, he was a Scotsman, like yourself.'

Fergus explained about Henry Gordon and of his own reason for coming to Bristol.

Clicking his tongue sympathetically, the constable

declared: 'It's always sad to lose a friend, especially one who's been kind to you in the past. But did you say you'd taken his room? That would be in Ida Stokes's house, along with Irish Molly and some of her friends?'

Remembering his first meeting with Ida Stokes, and her conversation with Irish Molly, Fergus believed the big constable was questioning him again, albeit rather cleverly.

'Mrs Stokes is my landlady. I don't know who else stays in the house. Mrs Stokes seems to have a great many lodgers.'

It was the second lie Fergus had told to the constable, without quite knowing why. He owed no loyalty to anyone living in the house in Back Lane. ·

The constable did not pursue his line of questioning. Instead, he said: 'There are houses in the rookery more crowded than Ida Stokes's. The whole place is like a stew, bubbling away in a great cauldron. Every so often I and my colleagues need to skim some of the scum off the top to stop the whole thing going bad, if you understand me. But I don't think I caught your name, sir.'

'Vincent. Fergus Vincent.'

'I'm Constable Ivor Primrose. If you ever need help, or have anything you think I might like to hear about, call on me at the police station opposite the Bridewell. Here we are at the Hatchet inn, now. Charlie Waller is the landlord; tell him I've sent you – but whatever you do don't offend him. Charlie was once a prizefighter, and his temper's a bit uncertain at the best of times.'

Fergus arrived at a rapid decision. Constable Primrose could prove to be a great friend in the future. In the light from one of the inn windows Fergus made a rapid sketch. Holding it closer to the light, he added a couple more details, then tore out the page and handed it to the constable.

'You mentioned a girl who was badly beaten yesterday. I witnessed the incident. I'm reluctant to give evidence while I'm living in the "rookery", as you call it, but this is a fair likeness of the man who did it.'

Constable Primrose held the sketch up to the light. 'Joe Skewes! I thought as much. He's never far away when there's violence in the rookery.'

Folding the paper carefully, Constable Ivor Primrose unfastened two of the buttons on his coat and carefully placed the sketch inside. When his jacket was buttoned again, he said: 'You can leave this with me, Mr Vincent, but I won't forget your help.'

Touching a finger to the brim of his tall black hat, the policeman turned and walked slowly away.

It was still early in the evening, but the main tap-room of the Hatchet inn was crowded. There were many sailors here, and a number of women – women like those Fergus had seen talking together on the first-floor landing of Ida Stokes's house in Back Lane. One of them accosted Fergus as soon as he stepped inside the tap-room door.

'Hello, my lover. You a sailor? Looking for a good time ashore? I'm just the girl for you. What's your name, then?'

Fergus shook his head. 'I'm not a sailor any more, and I'm not looking for a girl. I just want to find a quiet corner, near a lamp.'

As the girl walked away across the smoke-hung room she passed a broad-shouldered bald-headed man. He had just deposited a number of overflowing pewter mugs on a table occupied by four sailors and two untidy women. The man jerked his head in Fergus's direction and spoke to the girl. She shrugged and gave a brief reply.

Wiping the palms of his hands on the short leather apron tied about his waist the bald-headed man frowned and made his way across the room to where Fergus stood.

'Can I help you, sir? Fetch you a drink?'

'Are you Mr Waller?'

The man's frown deepened. 'I'm Charlie Waller. Who's asking?'

'Fergus Vincent. I'm an artist. I'd like to sketch your customers . . . sailors.'

'So long as you're buying my ale you can do what you like – if it doesn't annoy my other customers. Now, what can I get you to drink?'

'I'll have a porter . . . but I won't be drinking much. I'll be sketching – and selling to your customers, I hope.'

'So that's your game! I thought it might be something like that. Well, you're not welcome in my inn. One of your sort was in here a while ago. I let him stay at first because he spent good money. Trouble was, when he'd had too much he'd start making sketches that my other customers objected to. I put up with him for a while – like I said, he spent money – but he had to go in the end. If you've no intention of spending, you'd best leave now. It'll save us both trouble. Out you go.'

Backing towards the door with the burly landlord in close attendance, Fergus managed to say: 'I'm a *good* artist. I might prove an attraction. . . .'

Charlie Waller seemed unimpressed, and Fergus continued to retreat. He was convinced that, should he come to a halt, the landlord would throw him out. Then, as his feet found the step that led to the street, Fergus spoke in desperation: 'Constable Primrose said I should tell you I'm here on his recommendation. . . .'

The menacing advance of Charlie Waller slowed, then stopped altogether. 'Ivor Primrose sent you?'

'That's right.' Fergus moved aside to allow three noisy sailors to stumble in through the door at his back. 'I left him outside your door only a few minutes since.'

'Why didn't you say so in the first place, instead of wasting my time? I'm always happy to do a favour for Ivor Primrose. Have you seen him fight?'

Fergus shook his head.

'Likely you will if you come here often enough – especially when there are Yankee sailors around. It's sometimes necessary to crack a few heads at such times – and there's no one does that better than Ivor Primrose. He'd have made a dandy prizefighter had he taken to "the fancy". Personally I can see no sense in putting on a constable's uniform and becoming a target for anyone with a mind to punch a Peeler. But Ivor seems to enjoy it. He's honest, too, and that's more than I can say for some other constables we've had about here. A quart of ale and some meat pie in the back room when they come on duty, then they disappear before trouble starts, in case they're asked to do anything about it. Here. . . .'

The landlord jerked a thumb at a painted-faced woman who was seated at a small table beneath an oil-lamp which hung from a dark-wood beam. She rose without a word, and Charlie Waller motioned for Fergus to take her place.

'This is the best-lit seat in the place. It's not much, but you'll find there's enough light to work by. How much do you charge for a sketch?'

'A shilling. Less if I find someone with a particularly interesting face and he'll let me make a sketch for my own collection.'

'I'll expect a penny ha'penny from each shilling, for the house. You can begin by sketching me, so I can see how good you are.'

Charlie Waller had features to delight any artist, but Fergus took care not to reproduce too many of the symptoms of advancing age he saw there. The landlord was elated with the resulting sketch, and the exercise aroused much interest among the customers. Soon there was a pint of porter on the table before Fergus and he was working on his first paid commission of the evening.

Fergus returned to Back Lane that night with his evening's work. He had sold eleven sketches and there were more in his sketchpad. Two would one day be transferred to canvas. It was a good beginning to his work in Bristol and boded well for the future.

A noisy quarrel was going on in one of the first-floor rooms of Ida Stokes's house; but the door was closed, and Fergus passed by to climb the complaining stairs that led to his own room.

Moonlight shone through the attic windows, and Fergus had no difficulty in finding a candle and putting a light to it. He was placing it on the table when he caught a movement in the shadows at the far end of the long narrow room.

'Who's that? Who's there?' He held up the candle and peered into the gloom.

'It's me. . . .'

A small figure sat up from the floor. It was Becky.

The candlelight fell on her face. There was a bloody graze at the corner of her left eye, and the skin about it was beginning to discolour. There was a bruise lower down on her face, too, and the ragged dress had been ripped from one shoulder.

Crouching beside here, Fergus asked: 'What's happened to you, Becky? Who did this?'

'Joe Skewes.' Becky mumbled the name, and Fergus saw there was blood on her lip, too. Becky had taken a beating. 'He came to the house. Told me to keep my mouth shut about the fight he had with his woman.'

'*Told* you? Joe Skewes has a strange way with words. Come over here.'

Leading Becky to the table, Fergus soaked the corner of a thin threadbare towel with water from a chipped jug and dabbed it on her dirty injured face. She tried to pull away from him, but he made her stand still and persisted in his efforts.

'I know you're a stranger to water, but your face needs cleaning.' There was a deep scratch on Becky's cheekbone, as though Joe Skewes had been wearing a rough-surfaced ring on one of his fingers.

Becky winced when the area about her bruised eye was touched, and Fergus felt sudden anger well up inside him. 'Joe Skewes ought to be put away. The man's worse than an animal. First his own woman, and now you.'

To his surprise, Becky shook her head. 'She deserved a drubbing. She spends time in beer-houses with sailors while Joe's at work. She must have known what he'd do when he found out.'

Gently, Fergus began to dry her face. 'That doesn't excuse what he's done to you.'

'It's said his woman will die. If she does, and Joe Skewes is taken, he'll be topped, sure enough. He's protecting himself.'

'I doubt whether the hanging of Joe Skewes would stop the world,' retorted Fergus. 'I'm surprised he hasn't tried to find *me*.'

Becky's sudden silence expressed more than words. Pausing in his task, Fergus said: 'He *was* looking for me, wasn't he? Did you take a beating for not telling him where *I* was?'

'He was more interested in knowing *who* you were,' replied Becky. 'I told him you were some gent from Clifton way who'd come to Lewin's Mead looking for a woman. I said I was taking you to Irish Molly, but that you'd run off after the fight.'

'Did he believe you?'

'He didn't ask me again. Just hit me around a bit, then left.'

'If he went away again, what are you doing up here now?'

'He'll be drinking again tonight, and I *know* Joe Skewes. When he's got enough ale in his belly he'll be looking around for someone to beat. Folks keep clear of him then. His woman isn't at home, so he might come looking for me again. Can I stay here tonight?'

'Stay as long as you like. If it hadn't been for me, you wouldn't be in this mess now. Have you eaten? I've brought back some ale and half a pie from the Hatchet inn. The landlord gave it to me for sketching his wife.'

'I haven't eaten all day.'

Fergus looked at her disapprovingly. 'What have you done with the four pence I gave you?'

'I had to give it to Mary O'Ryan. She lives in the room downstairs. I owed it to her. She guessed you'd given me a few coppers to bring you here. She said if I didn't give it to her she'd get her latest man to strip me to the skin and look for it. He'd have done it, too. He's tried before now – and he wasn't looking for money then.'

Fergus shook his head despairingly. 'God! What sort of place is this I've come to?'

'It's Lewin's Mead, Fergus. I don't suppose it's any different from anywhere else. Not that I know. I haven't ever *been* anywhere else.'

CHAPTER THREE

WHEN FERGUS WOKE and heard breathing in the room it startled him. Then he remembered that Becky was sharing his attic.

She had been wise not to spend the night in the overcrowded room rented by Mary O'Ryan. Joe Skewes *had* returned to the house in the middle of the night. Fergus and Becky had listened in apprehensive silence as the bullying coal-heaver lurched from room to room, shouting for Becky to show herself. Once it seemed he might climb the stairs to the attic, but the steep stairway defeated him and he made a noisy descent, much to the relief of the two listeners.

This morning Becky slept as though she did not have a care in the world. She lay spread-eagled inside a folded blanket, much of the top half thrown back to reveal her thin arms and upper body. Her head was lying to one side, hiding the bruising around her eye. Fergus stood looking down at her for a few minutes before reaching for his sketchpad.

He was on his sixth sketch before Becky stirred. Opening her good eye, she saw him standing over her and she showed a brief moment of fear before realising what he was doing. Then she smiled and made a move to rise, but Fergus said hurriedly: 'Not just yet. Don't move for a few minutes.'

'Why . . .?'

'Don't ask damn silly questions. Just stay still while I finish this. . . . No! put your arm back where it was.'

Becky pouted, but did as she was told.

Frowning in concentration, Fergus worked for another ten

26

minutes while from her makeshift bed Becky studied him with great interest.

When he was satisfied, Fergus relaxed and placed his pencil and pad on the room's small and unsteady table. Smiling at Becky, he said: 'That's enough to be getting on with. I'll not be paying you a model's fee, but I promise that you'll have the first canvas I paint of you. For now, you'll have to make do with a cup of tea. Start the fire while I fetch some water from the yard.'

The pump was in a dark yard hemmed in on all sides by tall buildings. It was shared by at least fifty families, and Fergus joined on the end of a line of bucket-carrying men, women and children, all shuffling towards the pump. There was little conversation. Most of those in the line appeared to be suffering from the excesses of the previous evening. Fergus wondered how they earned the money they spent on drink.

By the time Fergus returned to the attic room Becky had a cheerful fire crackling in the grate and a soot-blackened kettle was already rattling noisily on the coals. When Fergus asked Becky where she had obtained the water, she grinned.

'From the O'Ryans', downstairs. They were cleaning up after Joe Skewes's visit. He fair took the room apart. Fifteen of 'em was in there when he arrived, four of 'em men. Joe had every one out in the street for an hour – except for the one he put to the wide in the hall.'

The smile suddenly left Becky's face. 'It's a good thing I wasn't there, though. Mary O'Ryan said he'd have killed me for sure.'

'Is he likely to come looking for you again?'

Becky shrugged. 'No one knows what Joe Skewes is likely to do next. He ain't like other men. He's got a son who lives in Lewin's Mead, too. The pair of 'em have terrified the place for years.'

'I think you'd better stay up here with me for a while.'

Becky's face lit up with pleasure. 'Can I . . .?' She hesitated and the smile left her face. 'You know what the others will think?'

'They can think what they like. As long as I'm paying the rent for this room I'll do as I wish here. Can you cook?'

Becky shook her head. 'I've never learned.'

'Then, it's about time you did.' Fergus flicked a bright silver florin through the air towards her, and Becky caught it instinctively. 'Go out and buy some things. Eggs, bacon, bread – tea and sugar, too.'

Becky tested the coin between her teeth before replying: 'You must have had a good evening's work at the Hatchet. But there's no need to spend your money. I can pinch what you want. It might take me an hour or two —'

'I'll not have you stealing for me. You'll *buy* what we need. It'll be a unique experience for you.'

The proprietor of the first shop Becky entered chased her out through the door without giving her time to prove she had money. It would have been a similar story in the second shop, too, had Becky not opened her hand quickly and showed the proprietor the silver coin clutched in her palm.

Only partly satisfied, the suspicious grocer grumbled that he'd had girls like Becky in his shop before. If he hadn't turned them out promptly, he would swear they'd have stripped his shop of goods in no more than ten minutes. Indignantly, Becky informed the grocer that just because *she* had ragged clothes it did not mean she was dishonest.

Unimpressed by her indignation, the grocer kept Becky under close scrutiny while he weighed and wrapped her purchases. Even so, she managed to slip a two-ounce packet of tea into the pocket of her ragged dress without the grocer seeing.

Her shopping completed, Becky handed over the two-shilling piece with a degree of pride. She had never spent so much money at one time before. The grocer was not an unkindly man and he was aware that this was an unusual occasion for her. The purchases totalled one shilling and tenpence halfpenny. Before handing her the penny halfpenny change the grocer took down a sweet-jar from a shelf behind his wooden counter. From inside he lifted out a large, striped, pumpkin-shaped sweet. Handing it to her, he said seriously: 'Here you are, miss. I always like to give something a little extra to my best customers.'

If Becky felt any pangs of conscience in respect of the two ounces of stolen tea in her pocket, she did not allow it to spoil this moment.

'I expect you'll remember me next time I come shopping here,' she said, with all the ragged dignity she could muster. The shopkeeper held open the door, and she swept from the shop without a backward glance, clutching the groceries tightly to her.

Becky's feeling of self-importance lasted until she turned the last corner leading to Lewin's Mead. Not thirty yards ahead of her she saw two men talking. One looked uncomfortably like Joe Skewes. Becky never waited to confirm the rapid identification. Clutching the groceries even more tightly, she turned and ran.

Becky's intention was to enter the Lewin's Mead rookery by another alleyway, farther along the street, but her luck ran out when she was halfway there. Passing a doorway, she cannoned into a burly, black-hatted, blue-coated figure. The next moment her thin arm was taken in a strong and painful grip.

'Not so fast, young lady. Who are you a-running from?'

'No one. I . . . I'm in a hurry to get home.'

'I don't doubt it. Anxious to get this little lot tucked out of sight, I'm sure.'

The constable lifted a packet of sugar from the pile of groceries. Weighing it in the palm of his hand, he asked: 'Where did you steal this lot from?'

'It isn't pinched. I bought it.' Her cry was half indignation, half pain as the constable tightened his grip on her arm.

'Oh, yes?' There was heavy sarcasm in the constable's voice. 'No doubt you pawned the family silver to get the money. You'd better tell me which shop it's come from, my girl.'

Becky was about to tell him when she remembered the two-ounce packet of tea hidden inside her pocket. 'I don't remember.'

'Now, there's a surprise,' said the constable with heavy sarcasm. 'All right, young lady, you come along to the police office with me. Perhaps your memory will return along the way.'

'No!' Becky screamed the word, at the same time kicking out at the constable. Had she been wearing shoes, her struggles might have been effective. As it was, the constable tightened his grip on her arm until she cried out in pain.

'Struggle as much as you like, you're coming along with me, young lady. . . .'

A loaf of bread fell to the ground, and as the constable stooped to retrieve it Becky's thin bony knee came up and struck him on the nose.

'You little trollop! I'll see to it you're charged with assault as well as with thieving.' Tucking the loaf beneath his arm, the constable pulled out a handkerchief and held it to his nose. It came away stained with blood, and the constable hooted in anger. 'You'll regret this, you mark my words. No one makes my nose bleed – especially some ragged urchin who ought to be thrown in gaol and forgotten.'

His words only made Becky struggle all the more, but the constable retained his tight grip on her arm and Becky was handicapped by the groceries, which she was determined not to lose.

By the time they passed through the doorway to the Bridewell police station Becky was sobbing with anger and frustration, but she was more upset by the thought that she had failed Fergus than by the predicament she was in.

Fergus had found a new canvas among Henry Gordon's possessions. Setting it up on the easel, he began a painting of Becky, based on the sketches he had already made of her. While he was working, time had no meaning for him. Not until his stomach began to complain of hunger did Fergus put down his brush and wonder for the first time what was keeping Becky.

Squinting out of the window. Fergus looked up at the sky. It was overcast, but as far as he could tell it must have been early afternoon. Becky should have returned long ago.

He frowned as he wiped paint from his hands with a cloth kept by his late friend for the purpose. Becky must have found something to do that was more interesting than shopping. She was a young girl, and time would mean little to her.

She was probably using her visit to the grocer as an opportunity to see what the other shops had on display. He would go to the Hatchet inn and have something to eat while he worked.

Before leaving the attic Fergus moved the partially completed portrait closer to the window and gave it a critical appraisal. It was going to be good. *Very* good. Probably the best painting he had ever produced. Becky's sleeping pose was entirely innocent and natural. The thought made him smile ruefully. Here he was, living in the heart of one of the most notorious slums in the country, earning a precarious living sketching sailors and their women – and he had found innocence! Taking a last look about him, Fergus closed the door of the attic and set off for work.

The smoke-filled interior of the Hatchet inn quickly brought Fergus down to earth. Three large ships from the West Indies had entered the Bristol docks that day. The inn was crowded with sailors, all of whom had money burning holes in their pockets. Charlie Waller, perspiring heavily, suggested Fergus should forget his sketching and return when business was not quite so hectic. Just then one of the prostitutes saw Fergus and called for him to come to the table where she sat and 'do a likeness'. Shrugging his shoulders in resignation, Charlie Waller hurried off to fetch another order for the noisy and thirsty sailors.

Fergus had sketched the prostitute the previous day, but now she was with a new 'friend' and insisting that he pay for another.

It was the beginning of a busy but lucrative few hours for Fergus. When he eventually left the inn and gratefully gulped in comparatively pure, cold air there were twenty-seven shillings jingling in his pocket and he had drunk more than he was used to.

Entering Ida Stokes's house, Fergus found Irish Molly arguing with a man in the ground-floor hallway. The Irish prostitute was insisting that her prospective client pay for his pleasures in advance. The man was reluctant, but he grudgingly agreed to part with the Irish girl's fee as Fergus pushed past the couple and began to climb the stairs.

He had almost reached the first-floor landing when Irish Molly called after him.

'Have you heard about the po-lice arresting Joe Skewes?' She pronounced 'police' as though it were two words.

Fergus replied that he had not heard the news, but he was relieved for Becky's sake and he promised to tell her.

'I'm thinking she'll know all about it already. She was seen this morning being taken off by a constable.'

'This morning . . .?' Fergus had been so busy at the Hatchet inn it had slipped his mind that Becky had not returned with the shopping she had gone out to buy. He hurried upstairs much speedier than was prudent. His crippled ankle failed him on the uneven attic stairs, and he received a skinned shin for his foolhardiness.

'Becky?' He called her name in the darkness of the attic room, but there was no reply. When he found and lit a candle its pale yellow light showed him that the room was exactly as he had left it that afternoon.

Fergus sat down for a few moments to gather his thoughts. Irish Molly's news might mean nothing at all. Becky could be anywhere. Perhaps she had lost the money he had given to her – or even had it stolen. She might have spent the money and was afraid to return to Ida Stokes's house and tell him. If so, she could be sleeping anywhere. He knew she did not always spend her nights in the crowded house.

All these possible explanations for Becky's absence went through Fergus's mind as he sat in the attic room. Finally he admitted to himself that he believed none of them. The answer to Becky's whereabouts lay in the news Irish Molly had so casually imparted to him.

It was some minutes before Irish Molly responded to the insistent banging on her door. When she did appear she stood in the doorway, having dressed hurriedly, her lank untidy hair hanging about her shoulders. She carried a lighted candle in one hand and there was fear on her face before she recognised Fergus.

'What the hell d'you think you're doing hammering on my door like that at this time of night? Are you wanting to wake the whole house?'

'You said someone saw Becky with a constable this morning. What exactly did they see?'

'You got me out of bed to ask about that little urchin? Look, here Whatever-your-name-is, I've got a man in my bed and a living to earn. If you're feeling lonely upstairs by yourself, try Iris in the next room. She's only had a short-timer tonight. She'll be free by now. . . .'

'Who's that out there? Get rid of him! I've paid you good money. . . .' The grumbling voice of the seaman Fergus had seen arguing with Irish Molly came from inside the room.

As Irish Molly began to close the door Fergus said hurriedly: 'I believe Becky's been arrested. She might be sharing a prison cell with Joe Skewes right now. Where would the police take her?'

'Becky arrested . . .?' Irish Molly opened the door wide again, at the same time turning back to shout at her unhappy client: 'Will you shut your gob for a minute! You'll get your money's worth when I'm good and ready!'

Returning her attention to Fergus, Irish Molly asked: 'Why would the po-lice want to arrest Becky?'

'I don't know, but I'm certain that's what's happened. I sent her out to buy groceries for me this morning and I haven't seen her since. Where would a constable take her?'

'To the police station opposite Bridewell prison. Oh, the poor girl. It's a terrible place. Haven't I been there myself – and more than once? A child like her shouldn't be put inside such a place as that – especially if Joe Skewes is there, too.'

'How do I find the Bridewell?' Irish Molly's words had alarmed Fergus.

'It's hardly more than a few hundred yards from here, but in the darkness —'

'Will you take me?'

'I'm sorry. . . . I'm too well known to go poking my head inside a police station, and there's a little misunderstanding about a sailor that's not cleared up yet. But I'll tell you how to get there. . . .'

By the time Irish Molly had given Fergus directions to the Bridewell the sailor in her bed was grumbling once more.

'I must go now. Do what you can for Becky. She's a good

girl really. . . . Oh, for goodness' sake stop your bleating, man. I'm coming back to bed now — and you'd better have something to be making such a fuss about. . . .'

The door closed, and Fergus was left standing alone on the draughty landing.

CHAPTER FOUR

FERGUS FOUND HIS WAY to the Bridewell police station, but not before he had run the gauntlet of pimps, prostitutes and would-be pickpockets who lurked around the fringe of Lewin's Mead's alleyways even at this hour of the night. At the police station he needed to convince the watchman who sat outside that he had a good reason for entering the building.

There was a sergeant on duty in the police office, and behind him the police gaoler sat making a laborious entry in a huge cloth-bound ledger. Fergus quickly established that Becky *was* being held in the cells, but he was less successful in ascertaining what crime she was supposed to have committed.

'We're keeping her in custody pending certain enquiries,' declared the sergeant enigmatically. 'May I ask the reason for your interest? Are you a relative of this girl? If you are, perhaps you'll be kind enough to supply us with her surname. All she'll tell us is that her name is "Becky". Short for "Rebecca", no doubt.'

'Probably, but "Becky" is the only name she's ever known, and I doubt if there's anyone left alive who knows any more about her. As for the rest – I'm a friend, I sent her out to buy groceries for me this morning and I haven't seen her since.'

Just for a moment Fergus thought the sergeant looked disconcerted, but the policeman recovered quickly. Crossing the room, he returned carrying the huge ledger. Turning back a couple of pages, he studied one of the entries. Eventually he looked up at Fergus and said: 'The young lady *did* have certain victuals in her possession when she was arrested, but she refused to tell us the name of the shop where she obtained them.'

'*Wouldn't* tell you – or *couldn't*?' queried Fergus. 'She doesn't read.'

'That will all be looked into, sir, don't you worry. But she couldn't give us an acceptable address, so we had to keep her in the cells. There's also the matter of her assaulting Constable Fitzpatrick, of course.'

'Assaulting a constable?' Fergus was incredulous. 'She's a *child*. A mere scrap of a girl. The very idea is laughable!'

'I doubt if a magistrate would share your view, sir. But since you're here perhaps you'll be kind enough to give me *your* name and address. It seems you might be a material witness in this matter.'

When Fergus gave the address of Ida Stokes's house in Back Lane, the police sergeant frowned. 'It's the address the young lady gave.'

'It's a lodging-house. A great many people live there. How do I set about having Becky released?'

'There's no question of her being released just yet, Mr Vincent. Unless she appears before a magistrate in the meantime, I suggest you call again in a couple of days. I might be able to allow you to the cells to see her then.'

'But she's done nothing! Why should she have to remain locked up?'

'If she's done nothing, you can rest assured she *will* be released, Mr Vincent. No one is held in custody without due cause. Now, I have a busy police office here. If your business is over . . .?'

'Is there a chance of seeing Becky tonight?'

'She'll see no one until it's been decided what will happen to her. Good night, Mr Vincent.'

The sergeant's impatience was beginning to show, but Fergus had one last question that needed an answer.

'I believe you arrested someone else from Lewin's Mead today – Joe Skewes? I hope he's not in the same cell as Becky. He's already given her one beating.'

The police sergeant gave a sigh. 'Mr Vincent, most of our prisoners are from the Lewin's Mead area and most have fought each other in the past, or will do so in the future. As it happens, tonight we have both Joe Skewes and his son Alfie in the cells. Alfie's in the cells with this girl and some others, but his father isn't. Joe Skewes is likely to face a murder charge if his victim dies. In view of the seriousness of the charges against him he's been placed in a cell on his own. If that's all, I must ask you once again to leave. *Now*, if you please.'

Outside the police station Fergus felt both angry and helpless. Becky was still incarcerated in the police cells, and no one seemed anxious to establish her innocence. Just then someone walked between Fergus and the gas-lamp attached to the wall of the police-station entrance. Glancing up, Fergus saw the figure of Ivor Primrose looming above him.

'Well, well, if it isn't the young artist. What are you doing here at this time of night? Are you sketching policemen instead of sailors now? Charlie Waller tells me you've been doing good business at the Hatchet. He also says you're a fine artist.'

'I came here to get a girl released from custody. She's been wrongly arrested.'

Ivor Primrose's eyebrows drew closer for only a moment. 'Why, bless you, sir, I doubt if anyone's ever been shut away in a cell without someone coming along and saying the very same thing. It's all part of the game, you might say. But liberty is a very precious thing and it's neither given nor taken away lightly, I can assure you. What has this young lady-friend of yours done?'

Fergus repeated what the sergeant had said to him, adding his own explanation.

'Well ... mistakes *can* be made, but if it has in this case you can rest assured it will be righted when she comes before a magistrate.'

'But she's only a child. She shouldn't be locked away with *criminals*.'

'I doubt that any more harm will come to her there than has already been done during a lifetime spent in the rookery.'

Constable Primrose hesitated and appeared to be trying to make up his mind about something. Eventually he said: 'I owe you a favour for the sketch you gave me, Fergus. I can't do anything about having this young girl released from custody – or even help you to see her – but there's someone I know who *can*, if she's a mind to. She's a Miss Tennant. Miss Fanny Tennant.'

'Where can I find her?'

'Nowhere at this time of night. But tomorrow morning she'll be at the ragged school, in St James Back.'

' "Ragged school"? What's that?' The expression was new to Fergus.

'It's exactly what it sounds to be. A school for children who are too shabbily dressed for them to be accepted elsewhere. It's early days to say whether or not it's working, but the youngsters from Lewin's Mead are better off there than wandering the streets getting into mischief.'

'Thank you. I'll call on Miss Tennant first thing in the morning.'

'You do that, Fergus. Meanwhile I'll make it my business to visit this little friend of yours in the cells. She'll come to no harm, don't you worry.'

For Becky, the hours that followed her arrest were a nightmare. Inside the station she complained bitterly and loudly about being arrested 'for nothing'. When the constable who had arrested her cuffed her ear and ordered her to be quiet, Becky promptly grabbed his hand and sank her teeth into the fleshy part of his thumb.

Howling with pain, the constable shook Becky off as though she were a tenacious terrier. He cuffed her again and might have gone further had not the station inspector put his head round the door of his office and demanded to know what was happening.

'It's an urchin from the rookery,' replied the constable. 'I've brought her in for stealing. She's just bitten me.'

'Put her in the cells,' ordered the inspector. 'She'll soon quieten down there. Don't take her yourself; I want to speak to you in my office.'

Becky was relieved at the departure of the constable who had arrested her, but the feeling was short-lived. The constable whose task it was to search her was coarse and foul-mouthed. When he found the two-ounce packet of tea and a penny halfpenny in the pocket of her ragged dress he forced her to strip and seemed to enjoy the sight of her standing naked before him.

When she was eventually allowed to slip her dress on once more the police gaoler led her down a narrow corridor to a heavy iron door which had a small steel-barred grille for a window. Peering inside first, the gaoler turned a large key in the lock, then swung the door open with some difficulty. Grasping Becky by the shoulders, he propelled her roughly through the doorway.

'Here you are, Alfie. I've brought you something to keep you warm. There's not much of her, so keep the others away or there'll be nothing left for you.'

With this the constable gave Becky a violent shove that sent her sprawling in the straw covering the cell floor, and the door clanged heavily shut behind her.

There was a sudden movement in the straw not far from where Becky had fallen. Suddenly a shadowy form rose from the ground, grotesque and malformed in the scant light that shone through the grille of the iron door. A woman's voice screeched in anger, and the figure launched itself at Becky.

It seemed nothing could save her from the clutches of the demented woman, but as Becky tried to scramble clear there was the sound of a chain snapping taut and the woman jerked backwards and fell heavily to the ground.

As Becky sat up, hardly more than an arm's length from the woman who now lay moaning at the end of a stout taut chain, she became aware of laughter in the cell about her. There must have been upwards of twenty prisoners, of both sexes, in the cell.

Suddenly someone was kneeling beside her, and she smelled stale alcohol. 'Now you've met Annie come on over here with me. I've got a jug of good porter and I'll share it with you if you're a good girl.'

A hand reached for her arm and began caressing her skin.

'You need friends in prison, young 'un, and none will serve you better than Alfie Skewes.'

As Becky flinched back in sudden fear, a woman's voice called from across the cell: 'Don't you take no notice of him, dearie. Alfie Skewes has never given nothing but trouble to anyone. Him *and* that father of his.'

The hand stopped stroking Becky's arm, and Alfie Skewes jabbed a finger in the direction of the unseen speaker.

'Keep that gin-trap mouth of yours shut, woman, or you'll part company with your tongue long before you can perjure yourself in a courtroom.'

Becky took advantage of the diversion to scramble clear of Alfie Skewes. Giving the moaning madwoman a wide berth, she made her way towards a group of women who sat with their backs against the far wall of the cell. As Becky reached the place a woman moved over to make room on the straw beside her.

'What you in here for, dearie?'

'Nothing. I've done *nothing*.' Becky spoke indignantly.

'Of course you haven't. None of us here has done anything.'

In the gloom someone tittered nervously, and the woman asked: 'What will *they* say you've done? When you're brought up before the magistrate?'

'Pinched some groceries – and I *didn't*. I bought 'em with money that was given to me by Fergus. He's an *artist*. He's drawn pictures of me.'

'You don't draw pictures of *ordinary* people. Who'd want to see pictures of the likes of *us*?' The question came from across the dark cell.

'He probably mistook 'er for the bleedin' queen.' The sarcastic comment ended in a coughing fit.

As the laughter subsided, another voice said: 'Can't be much of an artist if he can't tell who he's painting, I says.'

'He's a *good* artist,' declared Becky defensively. 'He draws sailors in the Hatchet, and they pay him for doing it.'

'*I* draw sailors in the Hatchet,' retorted the sarcastic voice of another woman. 'That's what I've been brought *here* for.'

Again there was laughter, and the woman who had first spoken to her put a hand on Becky's arm. 'Take no notice of her, dearie. She'll not be laughing when she stands up in court tomorrow. Her and her ponce robbed one sailor too many. She'll be for the boat this time. For life, I don't doubt.'

Soon after midday there were the sounds of activity in the corridor outside the cell, then the door was opened and a constable stood in the doorway, calling out names.

When 'Rose Cottle' was called the woman next to Becky struggled heavily to her feet. 'That's me, dearie. Brought here for buying a handkerchief from a poor starving child like yourself. How was I to know it was stolen?'

'Will you be sent to gaol?'

'Bless you, no, dearie. It'll be a fine at the most – but they'll have to prove me guilty first. Come and see me when you get out of here. You and me could do business together. I've got a dollyshop on the corner of St James Street. You might know it.'

Becky *did* know the dollyshop. Unauthorised pawnshops, where the poor and thieves parted with goods for no more than a fraction of their value, dollyshops were recognised outlets for stolen goods. Becky had seen a dress she admired inside the dollyshop owned by Rose Cottle and was in the habit of returning to the shop time after time, merely to look at it through the window.

Rose Cottle was talking again: 'Watch that Alfie Skewes, dearie. He does some little favours for me sometimes, but he and that father of his are both "bludgers" – footpads. They're not above poncing, cheating, or anything else that might pay a shilling or two. Alfie's no respecter of young girls, either. Keep clear of him and come and see me when you get out of here.'

The constable standing in the doorway called her name again, impatiently this time, and Rose Cottle waddled to the doorway, grumbling for the gaoler to 'show a bit of consideration for an old lady what's shaky on her pins'.

It proved to be a long day for Becky. She expected someone to take her to the police office and ask her questions about the groceries, but no one came for her. Whenever the door opened it was to call someone else or, on more than one occasion, to admit new prisoners.

By evening there were only five prisoners left in the cell — six, if the madwoman was included in the number.

Three of the prisoners were men: Alfie Skewes and two men who might have been sailors. The other prisoner was an old woman who had been found with a number of forged coins in her possession. She claimed to be as baffled as the police by their presence in her purse.

Late in the evening a pot of weak soup and a mound of bread was brought to the cell and placed just inside the door, together with a pile of pewter bowls and spoons.

The men and the old woman were the first to help themselves, each doing their best to elbow the others out of the way. Becky waited until the others had left the pot before serving herself. Then she saw the madwoman looking at her. The woman was not old; she could not have been more than twenty-three or twenty-four, but there was something in the crazed eyes that made Becky shudder. However, she could not see the chained woman starve. Filling a bowl with soup, Becky pushed it cautiously across the floor to the madwoman.

'You're wasting your time, girl.' The observation came from Alfie Skewes, but Becky ignored him. Pushing the bowl closer to the chained woman, she suddenly jumped back in alarm as the madwoman screamed and sprang at her.

Becky avoided the outstretched arms, but the soup was a casualty. The bowl spun across the cell, its contents lost among the straw.

Alfie Skewes hooted in merriment. 'What did I tell you? You should have listened to me, girl. Here, this is how you feed a lunatic. . . .'

Picking up a chunk of the hard bread, Alfie Skewes hurled it with considerable force at the tethered woman. It hit her on the head and bounced off into the straw. The woman screamed and put up an arm to defend herself as another rock-hard crust came her way.

Alfie Skewes and his two companions continued the barrage until their missiles were exhausted. All the while the madwoman's screeches brought hilarious laughter from the three men, while the old woman cackled with laughter at the 'fun'.

The whole incident made Becky shudder. It reminded her of something that had happened when she could have been no more than six years of age. A gang of boys had cornered her in a muddy gully where the River Frome flowed into Bristol's harbour. Pelting her with mud and stones, they had shouted and taunted her, driving her before them into the water. Before a passer-by came to her aid she was waist-deep in mud and filth and quite hysterical.

The one-sided barrage over, the madwoman scratched about among the straw, seeking the bread. When she found a piece she sat crunching it and growling like a dog with a bone whenever one of the men pretended to dispute her possession.

The cruel tormenting continued for almost an hour until two more diversions occurred in quick succession. The first was the arrival of another prisoner. Loud-voiced, boastful and half-drunk, he informed his fellow-prisoners that he had been arrested for attempting to rob a sailor in the yard of a dockside alehouse and had 'changed the face' of the first constable who tried to arrest him. He claimed it had taken four constables to subdue him and bring him to the Bridewell police station.

The next diversion was the arrival of a great pewter jug filled with porter for Alfie Skewes. When the newcomer commented with envy on Alfie Skewes's good fortune he was invited to join Alfie in a drink and informed slyly that it was the price paid by friends for his silence.

Becky was also invited to drink with them, but she preferred her own company on the far side of the cell and sat dejectedly with her back against the cold stone wall. She had hoped Fergus would come looking for her when she did not return to his attic studio. There was no reason why he *should*, she told herself, but he must have wondered what had become of her. Gloomily she admitted he was probably the only one who could extricate her from the mess she was in.

Sunk deep in her thoughts, Becky was not aware that the old lady on a counterfeiting charge and Alfie Skewes were having a long whispered conversation, casting frequent glances in her direction. When the furtive whispering came to an end the old woman crossed the cell and crouched in front of Becky, holding out a tankard of porter towards her.

'Here, child. Have some. It'll cheer you up. Alfie sent it across specially for you. We all need to help each other in here. It's the only thing that makes life bearable. . . .'

'I want nothing from Alfie Skewes. Give it to *her*.' Becky jerked her head in the direction of the madwoman, who rocked back and forth in the straw in the centre of the cell, her knees drawn up to her chin. As she rocked, the woman made a noise that might have been either singing or weeping.

'You should be grateful that someone's taking an interest in you, girl. Many a time in here I'd have given my soul for an important friend like Alfie Skewes.'

'Important? Because someone brings him a jug of porter? Or is it because he throws stale bread at a madwoman? Alfie Skewes can keep his porter and his "importance". I've got a friend who'll come looking for me soon. When he finds me you'll learn that importance is more than a threepenny jug of porter.'

Her voice carried clearly to where the men squatted close to the doorway, drinking. Alfie Skewes scowled his displeasure then rose to his feet. Making his way to where Becky sat, he stood above her for almost a minute. When Becky refused to look up he kicked the sole of her outstretched foot none too gently. She drew the foot back.

'Why are you being so rude to me? What have you got to be so stuck up about, eh? You say you're sorry and be nice to me, you hear?'

When Becky did not reply Alfie Skewes reached out towards her. Taking a fistful of hair, he jerked her head back painfully, forcing Becky to look at him.

'I'm talking to you. Answer me. . . .'

When Becky still said nothing the man released her hair. Straightening up, he drew back his leg to kick her. This was the moment for which Becky had been waiting. Reaching out, she pushed him, utilising all her strength.

Caught off-balance, Alfie Skewes staggered backwards.

Halfway across the cell he tripped over the softly crooning madwoman. Her transformation was as sudden as it was frightening. Screaming incoherently, she leaped upon the fallen man and looped her chain about his neck. Then, leaning back, she pulled the chain tight.

The ensnared prisoner tried to shout, but only succeeded in mouthing strangled sounds that were lost in the madwoman's fury. The other prisoners watched in silent horror until suddenly Alfie Skewes's arms dropped to his side and his heels began to beat a muffled tattoo on the straw-covered floor.

'The mad hag's killing him.' One of the sailors was the first to recover his senses. Snatching up the quarter-full pewter jug, he ran to where the struggle was taking place and brought the jug crashing down upon the madwoman's head. She dropped to the floor without a sound, and as she lay motionless her attacker removed the chain from about Alfie Skewes's neck.

Enough porter remained for some to be poured down the throat of the near-strangled man, but it served only to make his choking worse. However, it was soon apparent that the madwoman's victim would not die, although it was by no means certain he would ever recover his voice.

When the gasping man had been propped against the cell wall his rescuer rose to his feet and glared at Becky. Meanwhile the madwoman began to twitch spasmodically and moan, for all the world like some wounded animal.

'She's the one who caused all this trouble. She pushed Alfie. . . .'

There were growls of agreement from the other prisoners, and the second seaman said: 'She ought to be taught a lesson.' The men looked across the cell towards Becky, and she suddenly felt very, very frightened.

'You should have listened to Alfie. He said you needed a friend in here. I ought to know; I've been in here often enough. . . .' The old woman's cackling ceased to register with Becky as the men prisoners advanced upon her, skirting the moaning madwoman.

With her back against the cell wall Becky looked desperately about her for a means of escape. There was

45

nowhere. She saw the slop-bucket in a corner. If only she could reach it, she might use the bucket as a temporary weapon. . . . Even as she prepared to dart across the room one of the seamen lunged forward and grabbed her by the arm. Before she could fight him off her other arm had been taken.

'What shall we do with her?'

The question was asked by the sailor who had saved Alfie Skewes. It was answered by his companion.

'You've been to sea for a twelvemonth and you ask a question like that? Keep a tight hold of her and I'll *show* you what to do with her. The rest of you can have a turn when I'm finished.'

Fumbling with his trousers, the sailor advanced upon Becky. When he was no more than a pace away from her she screamed and kicked out with all the force she could muster.

There was sudden bedlam in the cell. Shouting in pain, the sailor staggered away. Doubled over and holding his groin, he tripped on the madwoman's chain. The sudden jerk brought her to her knees screaming. Meanwhile Becky fought with all her young strength against the man who held her, while the old woman screeched advice to him.

The only one to see Constable Ivor Primrose enter the cell was Alfie Skewes, but he was unable to warn anyone. The others became aware of his presence only when one prisoner was sent reeling by a backhand blow from the fist of the giant constable. Then he grasped each of the men holding Becky. As they released their hold on her Constable Primrose brought their heads together with a crack that sounded painfully loud in the sudden silence that fell upon the cell.

It took Constable Primrose no more than two minutes to ascertain the cause of the rumpus. After satisfying himself that none of the injured parties was actually dying, he turned his attention upon the male inmates of the cell. He warned them in no uncertain terms of the consequences should Becky be molested again, promising each man a flogging, with the maximum number of lashes allowed by the harsh laws of England.

Whether or not Constable Ivor Primrose had the power to

ensure that such a punishment was meted out did not matter. The imprisoned men believed he would carry out his threat.

Satisfied that no harm would befall Becky for the remainder of her time in the cell, Constable Primrose told her of Fergus's visit to the police station and his attempt to secure her release.

'He'll be back again tomorrow. Likely he'll be able to see you then. Don't you fret, my girl. If you've done nothing to break the law, that young man will have you out of here in no time at all.'

When the door slammed shut behind Constable Ivor Primrose, Becky lay down in a corner farthest away from the others and covered herself with straw. There was a warm glow inside her that even the squalor of her surroundings could not extinguish. The other prisoners had heard what Constable Primrose had said to her. They had heard him say that Fergus would soon have her out of the cell.

Even more important to Becky was the knowledge that Fergus *had* come looking for her, after all.

CHAPTER FIVE

FERGUS MADE HIS WAY to St James Back as soon as he thought there was likely to be someone in the ragged school. He had no problem finding the premises. So much noise emanated from a disused and neglected chapel that it had to be a school.

It was a surprisingly large building, and Fergus wandered around inside for many minutes before meeting someone who looked as though she might know what went on there. He approached her intending to ask where he might find Miss Fanny Tennant, but the girl did not wait for *his* question.

'Who are you? What is your business here?' Her manner was as brisk and crisp as her appearance. No more than five feet two inches tall, she was about Fergus's own age and was dressed in a neat white blouse and a long coarse-weave brown skirt. But it was her hair that attracted immediate attention. Had Fergus been painting it, he would have used more red than yellow, but no doubt she would have preferred to have it called 'tawny'. Obviously very long, it was drawn back severely and pinned up with great care at the back of her neck.

'There's a back door for tradesmen, but if you are seeking Miss Carpenter you'll need to return another day.'

Her clothes might have been those of a servant, but servants were rarely allowed to keep their hair quite so long. Fergus finally decided she was probably a lady's maid to an indulgent employer.

'I'm looking for one of the teachers here. Fanny Tennant.'

The girl's manner changed from brisk officiousness to cold hostility. 'I am *Miss* Tennant. Do I know you? I can't recall meeting you before.'

'You haven't....' Aware that use of her first name had offended her, Fergus did his best to rectify his grave error. He had need of her. 'My name is Fergus Vincent. I was told you might be able to help me.'

'Indeed?' Fanny Tennant was unbending. 'If you have a child you wish to attend our school, you need only bring him, or her, along. We will expect you to contribute to the child's education if you have the means. If not ... We rarely turn needy children away. The same applies to the provision of a meal. We only provide soup and bread – but for many of our children that is the bridge between starvation and survival.'

'I'm not here to discuss a child's schooling. I've come to ask your help for a friend. A young girl who's been arrested by the police.'

Fanny Tennant's manner remained one of uncompromising disapproval. 'We are not here to provide a prison visiting service for wayward girls, Mr Vincent. There are other organisations who involve themselves in such activities. I don't doubt that your church will provide you with details to assist your lady-friend.'

'She's not a lady. She's a mere child. An orphan.'

Fanny Tennant succeeded in looking more disapproving than before, and Fergus added hurriedly: 'The child befriended me when I arrived a couple of days ago. I'm new to Bristol, and she guided me to the house where my friend had died. I sent her out yesterday with money to buy groceries, and she never returned....' Fergus shrugged sheepishly. 'At first I thought she'd probably spent my money on something she wanted – she has *nothing* of her own – but last night I discovered she'd been arrested. She's in the cells at the Bridewell police station. I've been there, but the sergeant won't allow me to see her. Constable Primrose suggested I should find you and ask your help.'

'Ivor Primrose made such a suggestion, after his sergeant said you *couldn't* see her?'

'I assisted him soon after I arrived in Bristol. I think it's his way of saying "Thank you".' Fergus found encouragement in the fact that Fanny Tennant knew Constable Primrose's first name.

Fanny Tennant studied Fergus for a few moments. She saw a slightly built young man with overlong hair and a face dominated by a pair of alert and intense eyes. She had also observed his limp.

'Are you in employment, Mr Vincent?'

'I'm an artist. I make a living.'

Fanny Tennant raised her eyebrows in surprise. 'Are you a *good* artist?'

Fergus grinned. 'Becky thinks I'm the best.'

'Becky?'

'That's her name. The girl who's been arrested.'

Once again Fanny Tennant gave Fergus a searching stare. 'Do I have your assurance there is nothing improper in the relationship between you and this young girl?'

'Of course. She's a mere child.'

'We have children in this school who have earned a living by prostitution since they were old enough to be taken on the streets by their mothers. I try not to pass moral judgements. My duty is to teach and try to show them there *is* a better way of life. However, I would be failing in my duty were I to help this girl to return to immorality.'

'You have my word there's nothing like that between us.'

'Very well, I'll come to the Bridewell police station with you and we'll learn why the girl is there. But I am no miracle-worker, Mr Vincent. If the girl is guilty of dishonesty, she will have to suffer the consequences — no matter how much I disagree with sending children to adult prisons. Now I must ask you to wait outside the building while I fetch a coat. I fear some of our impressionable young girls find your presence a distraction.'

As Fergus made his way to the door he passed a knot of giggling bold-eyed young girls who could not have been any older than Becky. A few minutes later he was joined by Fanny Tennant.

It was not far to the Bridewell police station, but as they walked along together Fanny Tennant questioned Fergus closely about his previous life and his reason for coming to Bristol. He told her about the Royal Navy, and Henry Gordon, and explained his reasons for living in Lewin's Mead. By the time they arrived at the police station Fergus felt he had satisfied the ragged-school teacher that he did not intend leading Becky into a life of debauchery when she was released from police custody.

Fanny Tennant marched into the police office and demanded imperiously to see the inspector in charge. Much to Fergus's surprise the sergeant on duty hurried away immediately to find his superior officer. Fergus was even more surprised when the inspector appeared a few moments later. After greeting Fanny Tennant respectfully by name, the senior policeman invited Fanny and Fergus to his office.

Pulling out chairs for his two guests, the inspector enquired first after Fanny Tennant's father, and then her uncle.

Replying that both men were well, the ragged-school teacher made it clear she had not come to the police station on a social visit.

'You have a young girl in your cells. She's called Becky. I don't think she has another name.'

'The urchin from Back Lane? Yes, she's in the cells on suspicion of stealing groceries. Is she one of your pupils?'

'No.' Fanny Tennant looked quickly at Fergus. 'Not yet. But Mr Vincent can throw some light on the matter. He gave her money to buy groceries for him. Your constable arrested her before she could return with them.'

The inspector frowned. 'I have a report here from Constable Fitzpatrick . . .' He shuffled through a pile of documents and pulled out a single sheet of paper filled with neat handwriting. Scanning through it quickly, he said: 'Constable Fitzpatrick reports that the girl behaved in a highly suspicious manner. She tried to run off when she saw him, and then refused to say where she'd purchased the goods. She also kicked and bit Constable Fitzpatrick when she was arrested and faces a secondary charge of assault on police.'

'Have you *seen* Becky? There's no more meat on her than on a slice of belly pork. A charge against her of assaulting a constable will be laughed out of court. She was *frightened* of your constable, as all the children from Lewin's Mead are. *That's* why she ran.'

The inspector maintained a dignified silence, but Fergus felt his response would have been very different had Fanny Tennant not been present. Fergus wondered why she was treated with such cautious respect here in the Bristol police office.

'You must agree there is a possibility the girl has been unlawfully arrested, Inspector. I would like to see her.'

After only a brief hesitation the inspector said: 'Of course, Miss Tennant. I'll have her brought here. Would you like some refreshment while you wait?'

Before Fergus could reply, Fanny Tennant said: 'I have work to do at the school. I wish to waste no more time than is absolutely necessary.'

'Of course.'

The inspector rose from his chair and hurried out. When he had gone, Fergus said: 'You seem to have a great deal of influence here, Miss Tennant.'

When Fanny Tennant smiled her whole face relaxed, making her look years younger, and far less formidable. '*I* have no influence. In fact, the inspector and many of his constables would be delighted to see the ragged school closed down. However, my father is a city alderman and chairman of the Watch Committee, which controls the police force. I take unashamed advantage of the fact that I am his daughter.'

'And your uncle – the one mentioned by the inspector?'

Fergus was treated to the smile again. 'Oh, he's a Member of Parliament for Bristol.'

Fergus was still speechless when the door opened and Becky was ushered into the room. The neatness of the police inspector's office served to accentuate her dirty unkempt appearance, but the delight on her face when she saw Fergus made those in the room forget her raggedness and Fanny Tennant looked sharply at Fergus.

'I knew you'd come to get me out. I told them in the cell you'd be here before long.'

'We'll have you out of here soon,' promised Fergus. 'Just as soon as one or two small matters are cleared up. Miss

Tennant has come with me to help you.'

It was a moment or two before Fergus's words sank in, and Becky's new-found happiness changed to dismay. 'I'm *not* going off with you? I've got to go back to that cell again?'

'Not for long.'

'But I've done nothing — and I don't want no help from *her*.' Becky jerked her head defiantly at Fanny Tennant. 'She's a busybody who tries to run other folks' lives for 'em.'

'You need someone to help run *yours*, that is quite certain,' snapped Fanny Tennant. 'Inspector ... leave us alone for a few minutes, if you please.'

It did not please the inspector at all, but he obediently backed out of the room, closing the door behind him.

When he had gone, Fanny Tennant turned her attention to Becky. 'Now, young lady, Mr Vincent has been to a great deal of trouble on your behalf, and *I* have many other things I should be doing, so we'll have no more nonsense. The inspector says you refuse to say where you purchased the groceries you were carrying at the time of your arrest. If we are to secure your release, we *must* know where they were bought.'

Becky looked from Fanny Tennant to Fergus uncertainly, then her mouth clamped tight shut.

'I see. Such reluctance can mean only one thing. You *did* steal the groceries. All the same, I suggest you tell us the name of the shop immediately. The police will find out sooner or later, and I would rather *we* spoke to the shopkeeper first.'

'I *didn't* pinch 'em,' declared Becky vehemently. 'I paid for everything with the money Fergus gave me. . . .' She hesitated a moment before adding reluctantly: 'There might just be a couple of ounces of tea extra.'

'Is that all?'

Becky nodded, meeting the ragged-school teacher's stern look which dared Becky to lie to her.

'That's all. Honest.'

Fanny Tennant's nod of acceptance surprised Fergus. She surprised him still more when she spoke again.

'I know when a girl is lying to me and I'll not see a child thrown into prison for a few pennyworth of tea. Which shop did it come from?'

'The one in Broad Street.'

'That's only just around the corner from here. We must waste no more time. It's probably one of the first shops the police will visit.'

Fanny Tennant rose to her feet, and Fergus followed suit.

Becky's face registered dismay. 'Can't I come with you? I don't want to go back to the cells again.'

'You'll need to stay here a while longer, Becky. Don't worry, we'll have you out of here just as soon as we can – probably by midday. I promise.'

Fergus took hold of Becky's hands in a bid to reassure her, and once again Fanny Tennant's questioning look encompassed them both.

'There will be a condition attached to your release, Becky.'

Fergus dropped Becky's hands, and they both turned towards the speaker.

'A condition?' Fergus was puzzled. 'I don't understand. . . .'

'I intend keeping an eye on Becky. She'll commence classes at the free school – the ragged school – on Monday.'

'I don't see why I should . . .!'

'Becky! Miss Tennant's been a great help. Without her I wouldn't have been able to *see* you, let alone secure your release. The police might yet bring charges against you. I agree with her. You *should* go to school. It's a wonderful opportunity for you.'

'School is for *kids*.'

'We have older children than you, Becky. Anyway, I *insist*.'

Becky would not look at Fanny Tennant. Her eyes went to Fergus, and he nodded.

'Oh . . . all right, then. But I don't see why I *should*. I've not done nothing. . . .' Becky's voice faltered as she remembered the two ounces of tea.

Fergus had to resist an urge to hug Becky to him. She looked more childlike and vulnerable than at any time since he had first met her.

'Good girl. Don't worry about anything now. We'll have you out of here just as soon as we can.'

*　　*　　*

Walking from the police station with Fanny Tennant, Fergus brought up the question of the assault charge being made against Becky. The ragged-school teacher shrugged the matter off.

'Given the circumstances of her arrest, the police will not want to proceed with any other charges. I'll see to that. I only hope the grocer will be equally accommodating.'

Fortunately the grocer had no wish to press charges against Becky. He remembered her well and even suggested that *he* might have included the extra tea in the purchases, by mistake. The grocer recognised the alderman's daughter as soon as she entered his shop, and Fergus had no doubt this accounted for much of the man's generous and forgiving manner. It was a great relief. Now there was no reason why Becky should not be released from police custody before the day was out.

Fanny Tennant agreed with him. She had work to do at the ragged school in St James Back, but she suggested Fergus should return to the police station and tell the inspector what they had learned.

When Fergus tried to thank Fanny Tennant for her assistance, the teacher silenced him immediately, saying: 'I wouldn't be working in a ragged school if I didn't care about children like Becky. There are far too many of them. We *all* need to do everything we can to help them.'

Fergus murmured polite agreement – and immediately regretted such unthinking rashness.

'I am pleased to know you are equally concerned. The children I teach are not as amenable to discipline as children from more – shall we say *stable* home backgrounds? In order to teach them anything at all we need to make their lessons *interesting*. To hold their attention. You can be of very great assistance to us in our work, with your sketches. It need only take up a couple of hours of your time each week. Shall we say Wednesday afternoons, about two o'clock? Good. Now I can return to the school with a clear conscience and tell Miss Carpenter it has been a very satisfactory morning's work.'

CHAPTER SIX

IT WAS THREE O'CLOCK in the afternoon before the police inspector released Becky. A constable had checked Fergus's story with the grocer, but then the inspector had to listen to a complaint from the disgruntled Constable Fitzpatrick, his red and swollen nose a testimony that Becky's assault was a determined one.

By this time Fergus had spent some hours in the police station, and his patience was wearing thin. When he announced he was going to fetch Miss Tennant to help settle the matter, the inspector ordered that Becky be brought up from the cells.

The inspector gave her a stern warning about running from constables when ordered to stop, but Becky did not even pretend to listen. Instead she grinned happily across the office at Fergus.

'Do you understand what I'm saying to you, young lady?' The inspector was aware his warning had fallen on deaf ears.

Becky nodded, not shifting her gaze from Fergus.

The inspector gave up. Shrugging his shoulders, he said to Fergus: 'Take her away. I hope she pays more attention to Miss Tennant than she has to me.'

In the busy street outside the police station Becky took Fergus's hand in a spontaneous gesture of relief and happiness. 'I *knew* you'd come and get me out, Fergus. Even when the others said no one would want *me*, I knew you'd come.'

Becky's happiness was contagious, and passers-by smiled at the young cripple and his ragged companion.

'Who else was in the cell with you?'

The happiness left Becky, and her hand dropped away from his. 'I don't want to talk about them. For all I care, they can all "get the boat".'

Fergus wondered what had happened to Becky while she was in police custody, but her face had assumed the stubborn expression he had seen there before; he knew better than to question her right now.

When they arrived at the house in Back Lane, Becky had to run the gauntlet of well-wishers who crowded around to offer their congratulations on her release from police custody. It was rare for a resident of the Lewin's Mead rookery to be arrested by the police and released without having served a prison sentence.

As it happened, not one but *two* Lewin's Mead dwellers had been freed from the cells of the Bridewell police station.

Irish Molly was among the well-wishers, and while Becky was chatting to the numerous occupants of Mary O'Ryan's room the prostitute took Fergus aside. In a low voice she said: 'Try to keep Becky with you as much as you can. Joe Skewes also got out of gaol this morning.'

'You mean . . . he's escaped?'

'No, he was released. His woman died, but before she did she gave the police what they called a "dying declaration" and swore her injuries were the result of an accident. She said Joe Skewes had been trying to *help* her after she'd fallen downstairs.'

'But I *saw* what happened. So did Becky, and a couple of dozen others.'

'We *all* know what happened. The fact remains that Joe Skewes is free and he thinks Becky narked on him.'

'But she *didn't*. Becky would run a mile the other way rather than talk to a constable. That's what got her in this lot of trouble.'

'It's what Joe Skewes *thinks* that matters. Just be careful for a while. Joe Skewes is celebrating his release right now and in another day or two he'll probably not even remember Becky. Until then he's dangerous.'

When they eventually reached the attic room, Becky

started a fire in the hearth while Fergus prepared something for them to eat. Afterwards, as Fergus cleared away, Becky looked through the sketches he had made for himself at the Hatchet inn. One of them made her chuckle, and in answer to his question she held up the sketch. It was of a sailor dancing a 'hornpipe' with one of the women at the inn.

'This is good, Fergus. What will you do with it?'

Fergus shrugged. 'I'll turn it into a proper painting one day – but there's a painting over there that's much better.' He pointed to the canvas resting on the easel, close to the window.

Becky crossed the room and when she saw the incomplete painting her eyes opened wide in delight. 'It's *me*, when I was sleeping the other morning.'

Fergus stood beside her and looked down at the canvas. 'It's probably the best thing I've done, and I have other sketches of you that will one day make even better paintings. You're an inspiration to me, Becky.'

Becky beamed happily, but at that moment the lid of the kettle began rattling noisily as steam set it dancing and they both rushed to move the kettle to one side of the fire.

Becky asked suddenly: 'You going to paint that Tennant woman?'

The question took Fergus by surprise. 'I haven't thought about it. I doubt if she could spare the time to sit long enough for me to paint her.'

'Would you like to?'

Fergus thought of Fanny Tennant's face with its high cheekbones and her long, unusually coloured hair. 'Yes, I think I would.'

Becky pouted. 'She's *bossy*.'

'Fanny Tennant was a great help to you, Becky. If it hadn't been for her, the story of your arrest might have had a very different ending.'

'Oh, it's *Fanny* Tennant, is it? Perhaps *you* ought to go to her old ragged school, instead of me.'

Fergus grinned. He knew how the thought of having to attend school rankled with Becky. 'I *am* going to the ragged school. She's asked me to spend a couple of hours each week teaching there.'

Becky did not share his amusement. After glaring speechlessly at Fergus for a few long moments, she turned away and headed for the door.

'Where are you going?' Fergus remembered Irish Molly's warning about Joe Skewes.

'Not that it's any of your business, but I'm going downstairs to talk to Mary O'Ryan and the others. *They* don't try to run my life for me.'

Becky had not returned to the attic by the time Fergus gathered together his sketchpad and pencils and set off for the Hatchet inn, but as he passed the door of the Irish family's room on the next floor he could hear her voice dominating the conversation.

The sound gave Fergus a sad pleasure. There could not have been many occasions in Becky's young life when she had done something to warrant so much attention. It was a pity it had come as a result of being arrested. He shrugged off the thought. The reason did not really matter. Everyone needed to feel important occasionally.

It was another busy evening at the Hatchet inn, and Fergus did not return to his attic room until the early hours of the morning. Although tired, he was well satisfied with his evening's work. Sketching sailors and their women was proving a profitable business. Nevertheless, Fergus realised the port of Bristol would not always be as crowded with ships as it was at present. He needed to take full advantage of the situation for as long as it lasted.

Becky was not in the attic room, but Fergus was not unduly concerned. She lodged with the Irish family when she had money — and her credit would be good in view of her current popularity.

Fergus was awakened earlier than he would have liked by the sound of a crackling fire and the smell of frying food.

Sitting up in bed, he saw Becky crouched by the hearth. One hand was holding a skillet over the flames while with the other she tried unsuccessfully to push back a recalcitrant tress of hair which hung dangerously close to the fire.

Becky gave Fergus a sidelong glance and she said defensively: 'I'm making you breakfast.'

'I thought you couldn't cook.'

Her chin came up defiantly. 'I watched Mary O'Ryan doing it this morning. It's easy.'

'Hold that pan straight,' said Fergus hurriedly. 'If you tip the fat on the fire, you'll burn the house down.'

Becky levelled the skillet hurriedly.

'It smells delicious,' Fergus volunteered, hoping he had not offended her.

Her delighted smile gave him his answer. 'Does it really?'

'I've never smelt a better meal.'

Reluctantly rising from his bed, Fergus pulled on shirt and trousers and walked the length of the room to stand beside Becky's crouching figure.

'Do you think it's nearly done?' Becky looked up at him anxiously.

Fergus gazed down at rashers of streaky bacon foundering in a sea of broken-yoked eggs and grubby dripping, all evidently placed in the skillet when the fat was still cold.

'It looks delicious,' Fergus lied. He wished he had drunk less at the Hatchet the night before. 'But it might need a few more minutes' cooking. I'll have a quick wash while I'm waiting.'

Breakfast looked no more appetising when it was transferred to a plate, together with most of the melted dripping, but a thick chunk of bread soaked up most of the greasy excess, and a glass of water helped wash the whole meal down.

'Becky, you're a wonder.' Fergus's gratitude was tinged with relief at having successfully cleared the plate. He only hoped his breakfast would *stay* down. 'I hope you're as quick at learning school lessons.'

Much of the happiness escaped from Becky's face. 'I don't want no schooling. Do I *really* have to go?'

'Yes.' The breakfast lay in Fergus's stomach with the weight of a cannonball. 'You've promised, and a promise should always be kept.'

'All promises – or only those made to Miss Tennant?'

'*All* promises.'

'Did you go to school?'

For just a moment Fergus forgot the rebellion in his stomach as he thought about the lessons given to him by his mother. It all seemed a lifetime ago.

'I bet you went to a *proper* school, one chosen by your mum and dad.'

'No, my mother taught me to read and write.'

'Is she still alive?'

'No, she died a few years ago.'

'Your pa, too?'

Fergus nodded. His father *had* probably drunk himself to death by now.

'So we're *both* orphans?' It put an immediate bond between them.

'Yes, Becky. We're both orphans – but I can read and write.'

'All right, then, I'll go to her rotten old ragged school.'

Suddenly the breakfast he had just eaten began an assault on Fergus's stomach, and he winced. Fortunately Becky did not notice.

'Do you fancy her?'

'Fancy who?' Turning away, Fergus placed a hand to his stomach. He felt very peculiar.

'*Her*. Fanny Tennant.'

'I've hardly spoken to the woman. If you hadn't got yourself arrested, I'd never have met her.'

'Honest?'

'Honest. Now, run off and find something useful to amuse yourself. I have work to do.'

Becky smiled happily, unaware of Fergus's discomfort. 'I didn't *really* believe you fancied her. Jock used to say that painters prefer their women with some meat on 'em.' She hesitated. 'I ate with Irish Molly last night. She said that the way I eat she don't doubt I'll be bigger than her in *no* time. She put on a special spread because I'd not been sent to prison. Got it from the butcher in St James. His wife's away with her sick mother, and Irish Molly calls in there at night. We ate more'n two pounds of belly pork between us. . . .'

Fergus groaned. 'Becky. . . . Go away now. Come back and talk later.'

'All right, I won't keep you from your work any longer. I'm glad you ate a good breakfast. Irish Molly says you're the sort who'd probably starve to death if no one fed you. At least I know you've got something in your stomach today.'

Becky's statement was not accurate for long. From the doorway of the attic room Fergus waited until Becky entered the room occupied by the O'Ryan family. The moment the door closed behind her he fled down the stairs and just made it to the communal privy in the yard behind the house before he was violently ill.

When Becky returned to the studio in the early afternoon Fergus was working. He feared she had come to offer to cook him lunch, but much to his relief she made no mention of food. After she had wandered about the attic in a desultory manner for some minutes he wiped his brushes on a rag and asked: 'What have you been doing this morning?'

Becky shrugged her shoulders carelessly. 'I went to St James Back to see who went to the ragged school. It's like I said before, they're all *kids*.'

Fergus smiled wanly. His stomach had not yet returned to normal. 'Then, you can feel superior when you're with them.'

'No, I can't,' Becky rounded on him fiercely. 'It may be called a *ragged* school, but there's no one there as ragged as *me*. I'm not going, Fergus. I won't go there to be laughed at.'

Becky turned to run from the room, but Fergus caught one of her arms and pulled her around to face him.

'No one is going to laugh at you.' Even as he spoke Fergus was looking at Becky's dress. Dirty and torn, it was in reality little more than a tattered piece of rag. It was also much too short for her. Designed as an ankle-length dress, it hardly covered her knees.

'Come here a minute.' Leading Becky to a chair by the table, Fergus sat her down. She looked up at him wide-eyed, as though fearing he might be about to strike her.

Releasing her arm, Fergus said: 'You're quite right. The dress you're wearing is a disgrace. Do you know any place nearby where you might buy a dress that's half-decent?'

Becky remembered the dress she had admired so much.

'There's a dollyshop in St James Street. I've seen a dress there – but it costs three and six.'

Fergus withdrew a soft-leather, draw-string purse from beneath his shirt and took out a bright silver coin. 'Here's a crown. Go and buy it. Then I want to hear no more about not going to the ragged school. Is that clear?'

Becky looked up at Fergus in an awed silence. He had given her a *crown* – a *whole crown* – and asked for nothing in return. She frowned. There *had* to be a catch. No man gave a girl so much money for *nothing*.

Returning to his painting, Fergus had picked up a paintbrush before he looked up and saw her indecision.

'What are you waiting for? Go and buy the dress before it's sold, or before I change my mind. Get some ribbon while you're there, too, and I'll wash your hair when you come back. By the time I'm finished with you you'll be the *best*-dressed girl in Fanny Tennant's school, not the worst.'

Clutching the silver coin, Becky left Ida Stokes's house with mixed feelings. She was on her way to spend more money on herself than she had ever possessed before. She should have been the happiest girl in Bristol. She *would* have been, had she been certain Fergus was doing it for *her* and not in order to impress Fanny Tennant.

CHAPTER SEVEN

ROSE COTTLE'S 'DOLLYSHOP' was an ordinary house on the corner of St James Back — and the dress was still there, hanging from a pole placed inside the window, where it could be seen by passers-by. A grey woollen dress with red tape edging, it had probably been stolen from a washing-line in one of Bristol's more fashionable suburbs.

Becky thought it the most beautiful dress she had ever seen, but she walked past the house three times before venturing in to spend the coin that lay warm and safe in the palm of her hand.

'What do you want?' In the passageway of the dollyshop a big woman wearing a faded black dress emerged from the shadows and blocked Becky's path. It was Rose Cottle, the dollyshop-owner. 'If you've been dipping, I don't want to know about it, or you ... unless you've got a fine fogle or two.'

'I'm no pickpocket, and I'm not here to sell anything.'

Rose Cottle moved closer and peered into Becky's face. 'Why, bless my soul! It's the child from the cells. Come in, girl, come in. So you got off, too, eh? Good. I knew you was a bright girl as soon as I clapped eyes on you. A girl like you can earn a lot of money with some help from me. *Easy* money.'

'I've not come to work for you. I'm here to buy a dress. The red and grey one hanging in the window.'

Taken aback, the dollyshop proprietress looked suspiciously at Becky. '*You?* Buy a dress? Let's see the colour of your money first.'

Becky opened her hand to reveal the large silver crown given to her by Fergus. The suspicious attitude of Rose Cottle underwent an immediate change.

'Well, who'd have believed it! Come inside, child. You've got good taste. At five shillings that there dress is a bargain. I bet there's not another like it in the whole of Bristol.'

'It was a bargain at three and six when I last looked at it,' retorted Becky. 'A young gent gave me this crown to buy more than just that old dress.'

Rose Cottle looked again at Becky. She was as dirty as any young urchin the dollyshop-owner had ever seen, and the dress she wore was no more than a filthy rag, yet there *was* an appeal about the girl. Enough, it seemed, to captivate a young man who could afford to spend a crown on clothes for her. Well, she might as well spend it in the St James Street dollyshop as elsewhere.

One day the 'young gent' would tire of her. Rose Cottle had seen it happen to young girls many times before. When it occurred Becky would not want to return to a cold hard bed among the rubbish of Lewin's Mead. She would be desperate for money – and there was only one sure way for a girl from the rookery to earn a living. When this day arrived Rose Cottle wanted to be the one to whom Becky would turn for help.

The signs would be easily read. When a young mistress was abandoned by her lover the first things to go were her clothes, bought back by a dollyshop-owner at a greatly reduced price, and then . . .?

Rose Cottle received a considerable income from ragged young prostitutes who came to her for nice clothes with which to entice sailors and the young men of Bristol. The dollyshop-owner hired out clothes to them and also rented out 'short-time' rooms above the shop, thus ensuring that most of the young girls' earnings came her way.

'If you think the dress should be three and sixpence, then three and sixpence it shall be, dearie. Rose Cottle ain't one to go back on her word, even if it means I make not a farthing profit because of it. The dress is yours. What would you like to go with it? A shift? Some ribbons? How about shoes for those pretty feet? I've got a lovely pair at the back of the shop. If they've been worn at all, I swear it must have been by a lady who 'ad a carpeted floor. There's hardly a sign of wear on 'em. She had them made at a cost of *guineas*, I don't doubt. For you, four *shillings*. No, because you're such a pretty little thing, *three*. You tell your gentleman friend about them – but don't forget to tell him they're *five* shillings, you understand me, dearie?'

The advice was accompanied by a wink and a chuckle, both lost on Becky. She walked past the dollyshop-owner to where the dress was hanging. Quite unselfconsciously she shrugged her own dress from her shoulders and allowed it to fall to the floor about her ankles. Stepping out of the ragged circle, she reached down the red-trimmed grey dress and slipped it over her head.

Becky had trouble fastening the unfamiliar buttons, but she refused Rose Cottle's offer of assistance and eventually succeeded. Standing in the centre of the room with the dress on, she hardly dared to breathe.

'*Lovely*, dearie. You look *lovely*.'

For once Rose Cottle meant what she said. The ankle-length grey dress had transformed Becky. Hugging her slim body, the red-trimmed bodice hinted at budding maturity.

From the rear of the shop Rose Cottle produced a badly stained and dirty dressing-table mirror, and she held it so that Becky might see her new dress from every angle.

Fearing that at any minute she might burst from pride and sheer delight, Becky nodded and held out the crown.

'I'll have the dress. But I'm not paying more than three and six, so I'll have some change, if you please.'

Becky's pride was, if anything, heightened by the time she returned to Ida Stokes's house. With her new dress on she had been able to go in shops without the proprietor coming out from behind his counter and chasing her off, or hovering nearby to ensure she stole nothing.

She had bought ribbons for her hair – and soap. Real 'lady's' soap. She had also bought a present for Fergus. A beautifully shaped clay pipe, and three pennyworth of tobacco. The fact that Becky had never actually seen Fergus smoking a pipe caused her a moment's pause for thought, but she quickly shrugged off her faint misgivings. *All* the men she had ever seen smoked pipes. Fergus had probably not had an opportunity to buy one for himself since his arrival in Bristol.

Clutching both happiness and purchases close, Becky entered the house in Back Lane. She needed to lift her long dress well clear of her ankles in order to climb the stairs, and it delighted her.

When she reached the first landing Becky became aware of the aroma of cheap gin. It became stronger as she crossed the large dark landing – and suddenly a figure rose from the shadows beside the second flight of stairs and loomed over her.

'I've been waiting for you. . . .' The man's voice was slurred and thick with the effects of heavy drinking, but Becky recognised it immediately as belonging to Joe Skewes.

Becky turned and made a dash for the stairs leading to the ground-floor hallway but, drunk as he was, Joe Skewes was too fast for her. He grabbed and caught her by the collar of her new dress. Screaming as a number of buttons parted company with the front of her dress, Becky dropped her purchases to the floor.

The scream owed as much to fury as to fear and, twisting in his grip, she kicked out, her foot catching Joe Skewes in the groin.

Grunting in pain, the drunken man released her, but he still barred Becky's escape. He recovered quickly, and for some minutes the relentless pursuit continued, with Joe Skewes crashing into doors and walls, and Becky shrieking loudly whenever he had her cornered.

By now all the doors leading off the landing had been thrown open and the occupants were adding their voices to the din, shouting for Joe Skewes to leave Becky alone.

Working beside an open window in the attic, it was a couple of minutes before Fergus realised that the din he could hear came from somewhere *inside* the house. He recognised Becky's voice and, putting down his palette and brush, he set off in search of the source of the noise.

He pushed his way through the gathered residents of the second floor in time to see Joe Skewes corner Becky yet again on the landing below.

As Fergus gained the stairs to come to Becky's aid, Irish Molly ran from her room brandishing a heavy iron skillet. The Irish prostitute swung the pan in an awkward back-handed swipe that threw her off-balance, but the result was quite spectacular. The flat bottom of the heavy iron pan struck Joe Skewes on the side of his head and knocked him back to a sitting position at the top of the stairs leading down to the ground floor.

Irish Molly swung the skillet again. This time she missed, but the result was no less effective than before. In contorting to avoid the blow Joe Skewes leaned too far backwards. Fergus watched in speechless awe as the violent coal-heaver executed a series of backward somersaults down the steep stairs.

By the time Fergus reached Becky, Joe Skewes was lying spread-eagled on his back in the hall at the foot of the stairs. Coming from the doorway of her room, Ida Stokes stood over him, shrieking abuse at the prostrate man.

Fergus's concern was for Becky. She kneeled on the floor of the landing making strange, unintelligible, animal-like noises that resembled the whimpering of a small hurt puppy.

Dropping to his knees beside her. Fergus asked anxiously: 'Becky ... are you badly hurt? Where ...?'

Becky put her hands to her throat, and her wail of anguish was directed at the skillet-wielding Irish Molly.

'He's torn the buttons off me new dress. I've only just got it. ...'

Irish Molly lowered the skillet and put a comforting arm about Becky. 'It's all right, my love. You come with me. We'll have it fixed up in no time at all.'

As she helped Becky to her feet, Irish Molly spoke to the bewildered Fergus: 'Don't worry yourself; I'll take good care of her. Go and look at Joe Skewes. God forbid I've killed him – although, so help me, no man deserves it more.'

Irish Molly led Becky away, her head close to the younger girl's, talking comfortingly to her. Moments later the door to

Irish Molly's room closed behind them. Still baffled, Fergus turned his attention to Joe Skewes as the haranguing from Ida Stokes reached new heights.

The coal-heaver was on his hands and knees. Looking up at Ida Stokes, he shook his head and tried to gather his scattered wits. The effort was too much. Giving up the task, he crawled on hands and knees across the hallway and out through the open door, pursued by Ida Stokes's shrill voice.

The O'Ryan family was carrying out a loud-voiced conversation entirely in Gaelic as Fergus made his way past them and climbed the stairs to his attic room. He was concerned about Becky and was hurt that she had turned away from him to Irish Molly when she was in trouble. He tried to shrug off the feeling. After all, he had come into Becky's life only a few days before. Irish Molly had been around for a long time. No doubt there had been other occasions when Becky needed help. All the same, he wished he had been successful in his clumsy attempt to comfort her.

Fergus had been painting for an hour when he heard footsteps on the creaking stairs outside before the door opened. He was completing a detail of a sailor he had sketched the previous day and did not look up immediately. When he did, his brush fell slowly away from the canvas, all thoughts of painting gone.

Becky stood in the doorway wearing her new dress, the buttons sewn back into place. But Irish Molly had not stopped with the buttons. Becky's hair had been washed and brushed, the dark tresses tied back with a red satin ribbon. Her face had been washed, too, and at her throat she wore a narrow chain, from which dangled a cheap red glass pendant, loaned to Becky by Irish Molly in a moment of generous understanding.

Becky entered the attic room in shy anticipation of Fergus's reaction to her new image. Irish Molly had told her she looked 'positively ravishing'. Not entirely certain of the meaning of 'ravishing', Becky had some qualms. As Fergus gazed at her in silent open-mouthed astonishment, Becky's uncertainty grew.

'My new dress . . . you don't like it?'

As Becky's face began to crumple, Fergus gathered his wits together rapidly.

'Like it? Of course I like it. . . . *More* than like it.'

Fergus meant every word. The dress could have been made for her, and Fergus made a rapid mental reassessment of Becky's probable age.

His reaction delighted Becky. She was watching his face closely, and his changing expression revealed far more of his thoughts than Fergus would have wished.

'I've brought *you* a present, too.' Handing him a small package, Becky added an apology: 'The pipe got broken by Joe Skewes.'

Opening the package, Fergus held the tobacco and broken-stemmed pipe in his hand. 'That's all right, Becky. It's still usable — and the thought is more important than anything else.' Fergus's face screwed up as though he was in pain, and then he leaned forward and kissed her on the cheek. 'I can't remember the last time I was given a present. Thank you.'

Suddenly Becky was clinging to him, her cheek against his chest. 'It's me who ought to be thanking *you*, Fergus. I've never had a present from *anyone* before. It's a *lovely* dress. Irish Molly says she thinks it's the best she's ever seen. I *know* it is.'

Becky's hair smelled of the 'lady's' soap she had bought. When he brought up his hand to touch it Fergus felt the hair still damp beneath his touch.

Suddenly Becky pushed away from him, concern on her face. 'I've been so busy thinking about my dress I've forgotten to get you something to eat.'

'It doesn't matter,' Fergus said hurriedly. 'I have to go to the Hatchet now. I'll get something to eat there.' He lifted a hand to touch her hair again, but dropped it to his side uncertainly. 'You'd better sleep up here tonight. . . .'

Fergus deliberately avoided meeting Becky's eyes. Somehow it had seemed so natural for her to sleep in his room before. Something — the dress, her hair, or perhaps her new-found cleanliness — had come between them. 'We don't want to risk having Joe Skewes spoil your new dress again.'

Fergus smiled, hoping that if he treated the ugly incident as a joke he might be able to break down the barrier of awkwardness that had suddenly come between them.

'If that's what you want.' Becky, too, sensed the barrier, but she was more puzzled than embarrassed.

'I think it would be the most sensible thing to do.'

Becky nodded agreement. 'I'll walk to the Hatchet with you.'

Becky walked as far as the main road where they had seen Constable Primrose on an earlier occasion. Ivor Primrose was not here this afternoon, but posted to the door of a deserted house nearby was a large coloured poster on which was a drawing of a paddle-steamer, and Fergus stopped to read it.

'What does it say?' The question from Becky reminded Fergus that she was unable to read.

'It's advertising a boat-trip from the docks tomorrow. It's to give people a chance to have a trip on a real ocean-going paddle-steamer. It says there will be a band and refreshments on board as well.'

'Can we go and watch it set off?' Suddenly Becky was a child again. 'I *love* boats.'

After only a moment's hesitation, Fergus said: 'We can do better than that. I'll take you on the trip. It should be fun.'

'You'll take me for a trip on a paddle-steamer? Honest?'

'Honest.'

Her enthusiasm was contagious, and Fergus found himself grinning. '*And* I'll buy you some of those refreshments.'

Suddenly Becky was hugging him again. 'It sounds wonderful! Can I tell Irish Molly?'

'After a hugging like that you can tell the whole world – but be sure to get to bed early tonight. You don't want to be late rising. The paddle-steamer sets off at nine o'clock sharp.'

Becky did as Fergus suggested and went to bed early – but she did not sleep. Covered by a single blanket she lay on the straw-stuffed mattress in Fergus's bed, her new dress neatly folded on a chair nearby. The room was warmed by a low-burning fire, and Becky lay drowsily gazing through the windows as a sickle moon harvested the star-spangled sky.

She felt thoroughly contented. In the space of less than a week her whole life had undergone a dramatic change. Gone was the ragged urchin, kicked from underfoot by every drunken man who staggered along the footways where she lay most nights, or reviled by 'honest' traders when she lingered near their shops and stalls.

Becky felt she *belonged* – belonged to Fergus Vincent. She gave herself a mental hug. It pleased her merely to think about him. Fergus made her feel safe – and he *cared* about her.

For as long as Becky could remember she had never considered anyone but herself. Selfishness was an essential requirement for life in the Lewin's Mead slum. Every day was a new and desperate battle for survival, especially for a small abandoned child. A *constant* battle. Winners took all in the rookery. Losers rarely had a second chance.

There *had* been good days, of course. Days when a woman might include Becky in a family meal, or allow her to sleep among her own children. But such occasions had been infrequent, and they never lasted for long. A day would come when generosity was forced to give way to expediency, and Becky would return to pick over rubbish in the street with a steadily growing band of fellow-urchins. Sometimes she would join a group of them to follow a drunken man, hoping he might fall in the gutter where his pockets would be emptied in seconds.

Later, as Becky grew older, she received more frequent offers of victuals and a night's lodgings – but there was always a price to be paid for such 'benevolence'. It was a price Becky had not been prepared to pay.

Caught between thinking of Fergus and of the boat-trip he had promised her for the next day, sleep seemed a long way off, yet suddenly Becky started up, disturbed by a sound, and she realised she had been sleeping.

At first Becky thought it might have been Fergus's return that had woken her, but then she heard the sound again. There was an argument going on in the room occupied by Mary O'Ryan, and Becky remembered it was Saturday. It was the night Mary O'Ryan's man was paid and returned home. The latest in a long string of men who had lived with the Irishwoman before moving on, this one was a navigator – a 'navvy', employed on a railway line being built to link up with Brunel's 'Great Western'.

Becky was glad she was not in the downstairs room tonight. This latest man became argumentative after a bout of drinking. If another of Mary O'Ryan's many lodgers was similarly inclined, it usually led to an hour or two's dangerous violence.

Rising from the bed, Becky made up the dying fire. It was late spring, but the nights were still cold. She wondered what the time was. She had heard a church clock strike a great many times, but had not thought to count the chimes.

Pulling the blanket about her again, Becky snuggled down and nurtured her thoughts of Fergus. She hoped he would not be too long in returning home.

CHAPTER EIGHT

'COME ON, SLEEPY HEAD. The boat will be long gone if you don't move yourself. This is what comes of taking over my bed while I'm out working for a living.'

Becky woke with a start and sat up. She tried to focus on Fergus through heavy-lidded eyes but gave up and let her head fall back to the pillow.

'What time did you get home . . . and where did you sleep? I stayed awake waiting for you as long as I could.'

'Three ships came in on the evening tide, and the Hatchet was full of sailors. It seemed as though every one of them wanted me to sketch him. When I came in I slept on the floor by the fire. If things continue as they are, I'll be a rich man by the year's end. Come on now, out of that bed. It's a lovely morning, and we need to be at Cumberland Basin before nine o'clock.'

Cumberland Basin was part of the Bristol dock complex almost a mile from Lewin's Mead, and they would have to walk there.

Forty minutes later they were at the quayside and Fergus was paying their fares to a crewman who stood at the foot of the gently sloping gangplank that linked ship to shore. The sailor frowned when he saw Becky approaching with Fergus. Barefoot and hatless, she contrasted greatly with other young girls boarding the ship. Well shod and wearing hats, most had come pale-faced and newly-freed from sin, direct from celebrating Communion at one of Bristol's many churches.

But Becky's obvious delight and anticipation when she

74

reached the gangplank and gazed wide-eyed at the sheer bulk of the paddle-steamer brought a smile to the face of the sailor, and the shortcomings of her attire were immediately forgotten.

'This your first voyage, missie?'

Becky nodded, overawed by the size of the great steamer which Fergus was hastily sketching on the pad that was his constant companion. Smoke trickled from the vessel's two tall yellow funnels, and dirty brown water was being gently churned to froth by the huge paddle-wheels, one on either side of the vessel.

'Don't you worry about a thing. By the time we get back here this evening we'll have made a sailor of you.'

Becky smiled at him and then reached nervously for the comfort of Fergus's hand as they stepped from the quay to the gangplank.

Once on board, Becky gripped Fergus's hand even tighter. The deck stretched away for a seemingly vast distance both fore and aft of the gangplank. There were ample green-painted seats, but most of the passengers were promenading along the deck, the ladies enjoying the opportunity to show off their Sunday-best dresses.

Fergus led Becky to a seat by the guard-rails, close to the stern of the paddle-steamer. Unusually subdued, Becky's eyes missed nothing that was going on around them. After a while she whispered: 'Fergus, why does everyone look at me all funny-like as they walk past?'

'There's nothing "funny-like" about their interest. They're looking at you because you're the prettiest girl on the ship, and they're envious of me because I'm sitting with you, holding your hand.'

Becky squeezed his fingers gratefully, and all her doubts were forgotten when loud orders were shouted from the canvas bridge spanning the long deck. Sailors hurried all about them, and minutes later the gangplank was heaved ashore. Mooring-ropes followed, and with the paddles beating the muddy water to a frenzy the steamship edged away from the quayside.

This was the signal for the red-uniformed band assembled

near the bow of the ship to strike up a catchy tune. In that moment Becky became a child again. Dragging Fergus to his feet, she hurried him to where other passengers were gathering about the bandsmen. Displaying a determined energy, Becky forced her way between them. Dragged along in her wake, Fergus mumbled apologies to surprised and indignant fellow-passengers.

Not until she had an unobstructed view of the band did Becky come to a halt. Releasing Fergus's hand at last, she absentmindedly cuffed her nose as she stood watching the musicians.

During a brief lull between tunes, Fergus asked: 'Have you ever heard a band playing before?'

' 'Course I have!' Becky looked at him scornfully, before adding: 'I've never *seen* one, though. Not close like this, I haven't.'

Becky continued to watch the band long after most other passengers had drifted away, men to the below-decks saloon with its alcoholic comforts, women and children remaining on deck. Soon young girls were squealing in mock-terror as small boys on the high cliffs beside the gorge lobbed balls of mud towards the paddle-steamer as it navigated the river flowing through the gorge, far below.

Becky did not tire of the band until the paddle-steamer had successfully negotiated the last bend in the River Avon and was gathering speed towards the Severn estuary.

Meanwhile Fergus had gone to the rail to watch a large sailing ship being positioned for its trip up-river by a diminutive and fussy little steam-tug. As Becky joined him at the rail two children, a young boy and a girl of about Becky's own age, moved along to make room for her. As she took her place the two children tittered and, in a loud whisper that carried to both Fergus and the object of their amusement, the girl said scornfully: 'She has no shoes on. . . .'

The boy made a sound for his companion to be quiet, then he, too, giggled.

Fergus saw the blood drain from Becky's face and he gripped her arm, fearing she was about to faint.

In a strained voice, she said: '*That's* why everybody's looking at me. It's because I've got no shoes on.'

76

'Take no notice, Becky. They're just unthinking children. . . .'

His words were wasted. Becky's eyes were searching among all the passengers on deck.

'I'm the *only* one with no shoes.'

'It doesn't matter, Becky. I doubt if anyone else has even noticed. You're wearing a prettier dress than any other girl on the boat.'

Fergus silently cursed the insensitivity of the two young children, but they had already moved off to rejoin their mother and an older woman who might have been a grandmother.

'I want to sit down, Fergus. Let's go and sit down.'

'All right, but you mustn't let the foolish chatter of a young girl spoil your day.'

Becky made no reply, and Fergus followed her to a seat that faced outwards on the starboard side of the ship. Here Becky sat down with her feet tucked beneath her, hidden under the seat.

As the paddle-steamer heeled over to make the turn into the wide waters of the Severn estuary, Fergus pointed to the far side of the estuary. 'See that land over there? That's Wales.'

Fergus had last looked at this view when he was on his way to Bristol on board a naval frigate, a week before. The realisation startled Fergus. It seemed he had known Becky for years.

'Enjoy your day, Becky. Tomorrow I'll take you out and buy you the best pair of shoes in Bristol. I promise.'

Becky turned her head to look at Fergus, and for a brief embarrassing moment he thought she would cry. Instead her hand sought his once more. 'You don't have to buy no shoes for me, Fergus. You've spent too much of your money on me already. But I'll make it up to you. Honest.'

'That's better. Now, you just sit here and enjoy the view and the fresh air. I'll go and find some of those refreshments we've been promised.'

Fergus returned carrying a tankard of ale and a glass of ginger beer in one hand, and balancing a plate piled high with a variety of cakes and pastries in the other. Unused to such rich fare, Becky temporarily put the misery of having no shoes behind her, but she did not go unnoticed.

Becky's eating habits reflected the environment in which she had fought a fierce battle for existence for as long as she could remember. Each cake she ate was snatched from the plate, crammed in her mouth whole and swallowed in the manner of a puppy bolting a stolen delicacy.

Among the passengers who watched her in horrified fascination were the boy and girl who had called attention to her bare feet. When Becky looked up and saw them watching her she quickly drew her feet back beneath the seat, at the same time giving them such a fierce look of crumb-embroidered ferocity that they scuttled away and went in search of their mother.

When the last cake had vanished from the plate, Becky mumbled through a mouthful of pastry that they had been 'lovely'.

'They should keep you going until lunch-time,' observed Fergus. 'Come on now, there are guides all around the deck pointing out landmarks and taking parties on guided tours of the ship. Neither of us has ever been on a paddle-steamer before. Let's make the most of it.'

Still self-conscious about her unshod feet, Becky was reluctant to leave the seat, but Fergus insisted. Soon they were in the midst of a crowd of passengers gathered about one of the sailors who pointed out landmarks in the Somerset countryside, on what he insisted upon referring to as the 'larboard' side of the paddle-steamer.

They remained with the same group as the sailor moved to the starboard side of the vessel and gave a vivid and probably inaccurate description of the industries of Cardiff, whose smoking factory-chimneys could be seen on the Welsh coast.

There followed a tour of the ship, from the cramped officers' quarters to the boiler-room, a hot hissing hell-hole filled with coal-dust, escaping steam and gleaming brasswork. In the engine-room they both watched in silent fascination as oiled steel rods that drew their power from the heart of the steam-powered engine elbowed great wheels into perpetual motion.

When they returned from the heat of the engine-room to the chill of the deck it was immediately evident that a change of weather was in the offing. Fergus had been aware of increasing movement in the ship while they were below decks. Now he could see the horizon heaving and falling, and the waves about the paddle-steamer carried white lace on their curling crests. The vessel had emerged from the Severn estuary into the Bristol Channel. There was no land between here and America to hold back the vast power of the Atlantic Ocean.

At first the passengers treated the movement of the ship as a huge joke, laughter greeting each roll of the ship which caused them to stagger drunkenly about the deck.

As the paddle-steamer ploughed on its course and the uncomfortable motion continued, the laughter died away. Passengers sought a place to sit in silence, pretending not to notice the pale drawn faces of their neighbours. Soon the band stopped playing and the musicians filed below deck, carrying their instruments with them.

When a white-coated steward came on deck and called in a loud voice that a midday meal was being served from a buffet in the ship's saloon his announcement provoked groans and hardly anyone moved. Becky was an exception. Turning eagerly to Fergus, she asked: 'Does it mean *we* can eat now?'

Fergus was also unaffected by the ship's movement and he looked at Becky with new respect. 'Of course. Come with me and choose what you want to eat.'

In the saloon Becky worked her way along a long table, pausing at each white-hatted chef for more to be added to the increasing pile of food on her plate. The steward spoke to Fergus in an awed whisper: 'Bless me, sir. It's a good job there aren't too many like her on board. We'd be out of food before we fed half of you.'

'There's not much fear of that today,' commented Fergus. 'Most of the passengers seem to have lost their appetite.'

'Can't say as how I blame 'em, sir,' confided the steward.

'I've no stomach for food myself when the weather plays up. Mind you, there's really no need for us to be out here at all. It's not as though we're going anywhere in particular. Cap'n Clegg could have kept everyone happy by staying close to the Welsh coast instead of coming out here. But "Let 'em get some good sea air in their lungs," he says when the mate suggested we should turn back. "Do 'em good and put colour in their cheeks." He should come down from the bridge and have a look at some of them up on deck now. Not much colour on *their* faces. . . . They ain't breathing any too well, neither. But you can't tell Cap'n Clegg anything. Not when he's had a few drinks, you can't. Begging your pardon, sir, you'd better help your young lady. She'll never carry that lot up on deck by herself – and if she eats it all someone ought to give 'er a bleedin' medal!'

Fergus followed Becky up on deck. She had helpings of every kind of meat – pork, ham, roast beef, boiled beef, chicken, game pie and tongue – all buried beneath mounds of mashed potato and salad, heaped with pickles and topped with a hunk of fresh bread.

A few passengers followed the progress of Becky and her gargantuan meal with unconcealed amazement. For most, food was the last thing they wanted to think about and they turned their pale faces in other directions.

Impervious to the misery of her fellow-passengers, Becky attacked her huge lunch with the same gusto she had shown towards her morning snack. It was more than many of her observers could bear. Among those who rushed for the guard-rail was the girl who had commented upon Becky's lack of shoes.

By the time Becky was ready to sample a dessert, some of the male passengers were beginning to gather in small angry groups, their glances turning frequently towards the canvas-enclosed bridge where the captain stood surrounded by a number of his officers. The buffeting of ship and passengers had gone on for long enough. What had begun as a pleasurable Sunday outing had become a miserable uncomfortable ordeal. It was time to bring the voyage to an end. The ship's captain must be asked to turn his ship around and return to calmer waters.

By the time Becky had consumed a sizeable portion of plum pudding and another glass of ginger beer the conferring passengers had elected three men to approach the ship's captain and ask him to turn his ship about and return to calmer waters.

Seated beside the now replete Becky, Fergus watched with interest as the three gentlemen appointed by their fellow-passengers climbed the ladder to the ship's skeletal bridge and put their request to the black-bearded captain. Fergus could not make out the words used in reply, but no one on the long deck of the paddle-steamer missed the captain's bellow of anger. With the irate commanding officer pointing the way, the passengers' deputation beat a hasty retreat down the ladder to the deck.

Now the knots of passengers grew larger, women making themselves heard among them now. When one of the ship's officers left the bridge he was immediately surrounded by noisy gesticulating passengers, and soon they were joined by another of the ship's officers. Meanwhile, on the bridge, the bearded captain stared straight ahead, ignoring the altercation on the deck beneath him.

Eventually the two ship's officers returned to the bridge, and now it was their turn to experience their captain's anger. He ranted and raged at them while the crowd of passengers beneath the bridge grew larger. Then other officers came to stand beside their colleagues in open opposition to the captain.

Suddenly, with a final dramatic gesture the paddle-steamer's captain pushed the other officers aside and clattered down the ladder to the deck below. Walking with an unsteady gait for which the movement of the ship was not entirely to blame, he strode along the deck pushing passengers aside with the same disdain he had shown for his officers.

When he reached a companionway at the stern of the paddle-steamer the heavily bearded captain clattered noisily down the ladder and disappeared from view.

'What's happening?' Becky had been so engrossed with her meal that she had missed the whole drama involving captain, officers and passengers.

'I think we're about to turn back.'

'So soon? I thought we was out for the whole day.'

Her loudly voiced dismay was overheard by one of the three passengers who had been in the delegation to the bridge. Pausing briefly beside their seat, he said pompously: 'There is no need to upset yourself, child. We are only returning to calmer waters. There is no reason why we should return to Bristol just yet.'

Dropping his voice to a far from confidential level, he addressed his next words to Fergus. 'The captain should never be in command of a passenger-vessel. He's been *drinking*! One of the officers told me in confidence that he is more often drunk than sober during a voyage. It's *disgusting*. I intend taking the matter up with the ship's owners tomorrow. . . .'

At that moment the ship heeled over and began a wide turn in the rough waters. The movement caused the man to side-step away from them, and he continued his progress at an unsteady angle along the long wooden deck.

'Why do we need to turn around? I'm quite happy out here.' Becky spoke indignantly. The rough weather did not trouble her, and it meant that the other passengers were far too preoccupied to concern themselves with the way she was dressed.

'Everyone doesn't have your wood-lined stomach. Come here a minute; you've got gravy streaked halfway to your ears. . . .'

Becky obediently thrust her face forward and allowed Fergus to wipe it clean with his handkerchief.

When he had done she beamed at him. 'I *am* enjoying myself today, Fergus. It's the best day I've ever spent. Can I have another ginger beer now?'

'You're just a belly on legs. If you're not very careful, you'll be bursting out of that dress. All right, stay here and I'll go and fetch you another drink.'

Looking back as he made his way to the hatchway leading down to the saloon, Fergus saw Becky anxiously examining the seams of her dress. Fergus smiled. Becky was a confusing mixture of worldly-wise young woman and innocent child. He had grown very fond of her.

CHAPTER NINE

TWO HOURS AFTER TURNING BACK, the paddle-steamer splashed its way into calmer waters in the lee of the Welsh coast and an anchor was dropped. Soon afterwards the band came on deck once more and colour began to return to the wan faces of the paddle-steamer's passengers.

Before long the crew began to gather children for a game of Musical Chairs. Becky refused an invitation to join in, even though it looked as though it might be fun. She likewise refused to be drawn into a game of charades, or any of the other games being organised for the passengers, declaring she was quite content to sit and watch the merry-making.

Fergus knew it was because Becky had once more become conscious that she had no shoes, but he made no comment. Instead, he sat beside her making sketches of the passengers as they enjoyed themselves.

The games and music continued until a ship's officer announced it was time for the paddle-steamer to get under way and return to Bristol. The announcement was greeted with howls of disappointment. The outing that had so nearly foundered in uncomfortable misery had become an experience the passengers were reluctant to have brought to an end.

So loud and prolonged was the passengers' reaction that the ship's officers had a brief consultation among themselves. A few minutes later it was announced that the games could continue for another hour. The passengers were also reminded that drinks were still being sold and snacks were available in the ship's saloon. This last piece of information caused Becky to brighten considerably and she prevailed upon Fergus to fetch more food for her.

Commenting that the sea air was turning her into a greedy seagull, Fergus set off for the saloon. There was so much happening on deck that he decided to use the nearest hatchway in a bid to find a short-cut there.

Once below decks he could hear the sound of raised voices along a passageway leading towards the stern of the ship, in the opposite direction to the saloon. After listening for a few moments, Fergus set off to find out what was happening.

The noise came from the part of the ship where the officers' cabins were situated, and Fergus turned a corner in the passageway in time to see the black-bearded captain trying to force his way past four seamen. After a violent but unsuccessful attempt, the captain began cursing his men.

'You'll regret this, every one of you. If ever you get out of gaol, I'll make damned sure you never work in a ship again. This is mutiny, you hear me?'

'Sorry, Cap'n. The mate has taken command of the ship now and he says you're not to go to the bridge. Go and lie down, sir. You'll feel better by and by, I dare say.'

'Don't you tell me what I should do, mister. Dammit, twenty years ago I'd have strung you up from the yard and made an example of you. . . .'

At that moment two officers hurried along the passageway behind Fergus. When they reached him he recognised them as having been on the bridge when the captain's authority was unsuccessfully challenged.

One of the officers paused to ask Fergus to leave the officers' quarters, adding: 'Don't worry about what's happening down here, sir. Everything is in hand. If you care to go forward to the saloon, you'll find food and drink there.'

Murmuring his thanks, Fergus moved away, but only a few paces. He was curious to see what would happen next.

One of the officers took hold of one of the captain's arms and tried to lead him away, but the deposed commanding officer shook the hand off angrily. In so doing he staggered and fell heavily against the bulkhead.

'Keep your hands off me. You've taken over my ship; don't

add assault on your captain to your crimes – and crimes they are, as you'll find out soon enough. You can be sure of that, mister. I'll have you in court before you're a day older.'

'You've been drinking, Captain Clegg. Please return to your cabin and remain there until we're back in Bristol.'

'Until . . .? We're never going to *get* to Bristol. It's seven o'clock now, time we were entering the Avon and riding a rising tide to Bristol. Leave it any later and all the pilots will be engaged. I suppose you damn fools have forgotten it's Sunday? Half the pilots are Wesleyans. They won't work Sundays. It's first come, first served to get to Bristol today, mister – and *my* ship ought to have been first in line.'

There was enough logic in the captain's words to concern the officers, but the mate who had assumed command said: 'You let *me* worry about that, Captain Clegg. You return to your cabin peaceably now, or I shall have to ask these seamen to take you there forcibly.'

'Forcibly? *Forcibly?* Why, I'll have your guts for halyards, so help me if I don't. . . .'

At a signal from the mate the seamen closed in upon the furious captain. After a brief scuffle he was bundled away, shouting oaths after the man who had assumed command of the paddle-steamer in his place.

Fergus did not wait to hear any more. Hurrying back along the passageways, he located the saloon and took another heaped plate on deck for Becky.

The paddle-steamer weighed anchor and set off across the Severn estuary no more than half an hour after the incident witnessed by Fergus, but it was another hour before Gibbet Isle at the mouth of the River Avon was reached. It was immediately apparent that, drunk or sober, Captain Clegg had been right. Many ships were gathered here and there was a noticeable dearth of tugs and pilot boats.

With steam-whistle shrieking, the paddle-steamer eased its way into the tidal river before it was brought to a halt by three sailing vessels anchored in the main channel. Then there began a battle of words between the acting commander of the paddle-steamer and the masters of the sailing ships.

The argument ended when the officer on the bridge of the

paddle-steamer telegraphed 'slow ahead' to his engine-room. Paddles thrashed the water to foam as the steamer nosed forward. Only now did the master of one of the sailing ships order his seamen to slacken the anchor chain and allow the sailing vessel to drift clear of the oncoming steamer.

There were other sailing ships anchored in the main channel of the river, and the paddle-steamer proceeded cautiously up the narrowing river until it was opposite Pill, the small steep-sided creek from which the pilot cutters plied. On most days the pilots would be waiting at the mouth of the River Avon, vying with each other for business, but not today. As Captain Clegg had reminded his officers, it was Sunday, and many of the pilots were men of strong religious convictions.

As an anchor rattled down from the paddle-steamer, the acting captain paced the bridge and waited for a pilot to come out to him.

He waited in vain. Pilots for excursion vessels were always arranged well in advance – but no arrangements had been made for the paddle-steamer. Captain Clegg was himself an ex-Pill pilot and he had no need of anyone else to guide his ship through the winding Avon gorge.

By now the tide was on the turn and darkness was approaching. Time was crucial. If the paddle-steamer did not set off up-river very soon, its acting captain would be stranded miles from Bristol with a couple of hundred irate passengers on his hands. He ordered the dinghy lowered in order that two of the ship's officers might be rowed ashore, their mission to find a pilot and persuade him to take the paddle-steamer up-river.

The officers were gone a long time, during which darkness fell. So did the tide. The ship's lights showed glistening black mud on either side of the narrowing channel, and the passengers became as apprehensive as the acting captain who paced the bridge incessantly.

The dinghy returned from Pill creek, and the passengers raised a hearty cheer when they saw there was an additional man in the boat. Their enthusiasm waned when the 'pilot' was helped on board. White-haired and frail, he was as stooped and gnarled as a stunted wind-sculpted winter blackthorn.

It seemed the paddle-steamer's acting captain also entertained doubts about the old man's ability to guide the big ship up-river. After some discussion on the ship's bridge the pilot turned away and was halfway down the ladder to the deck before he was called back again. Time had run out. Responsibility for taking the great paddle-steamer up-river to Bristol *had* to be given to the crippled old pilot.

With whistle shrieking the paddle-steamer was got under way, churning up mud as well as water before finding the centre of the channel. The band was ordered to strike up again, and the upper deck was festooned with lanterns, but the passengers had lost their festive spirit. Crowding the ship's rails, they peered anxiously into the darkness, and when they spoke it was in low nervous voices.

Becky echoed the fears of the majority of passengers when, caught up in the apprehensive mood of those about her, she asked Fergus: 'Do you think we'll make it to Bristol?'

'Of course we will.' Fergus put a reassuring arm about her shoulders. 'I don't doubt that our pilot is the most experienced man on the river. He's probably taken *thousands* of ships through the Avon gorge.'

Fergus was right. The old pilot had spent forty years guiding ships along the winding river that linked Bristol's docks with the Severn estuary. But he had rarely attempted the feat in the dark, and *never* with a ship as large as the paddle-steamer. What was more, he had been retired for eight years because of crippling arthritis. He had been taken on for this trip solely because he was the only man available who knew the river at all.

Even so, the old pilot might have succeeded where few younger men would have dared, had not a small sailing vessel being towed by a fussy underpowered little tug not also attempted to beat the falling tide and reach Bristol that night.

The two vessels were just ahead of the paddle-steamer at the notorious Horseshoe Bend when the sailing ship swung wide. In a bid to correct his course the coxswain of the sailing ship swung his wheel hard over. The vessel veered away from the northern bank – and promptly grounded on the other side of the channel. Straining at the other end of the tow-rope like a terrier on a lead, the tug did not have the power to pull the sailing vessel free and, swinging as though on a pendulum, it, too, grounded on the mud of the south bank of the river.

Faced with the unexpected double grounding, the ageing pilot of the paddle-steamer had to make an immediate decision. It was a bold one. By increasing speed there was a chance that the steamer might hold the channel and squeeze past the other vessels. The great bulk of the paddle-steamer would cause some damage to the rigging of the listing sailing vessel as it scraped past, but this was the least of the pilot's worries.

Calling for full speed, the pilot shouted instructions to the helmsman. The paddle-steamer churned past the sailing ship, snapping off spars and ropes. Moments later it ploughed past the grounded tug, too – but this was the last piece of good luck the pilot would experience. He was a product of the age of sail. His last few working years had brought him into contact with steamships, but never anything as large or as powerful as the passenger-carrying paddle-steamer. Before he could reduce the still increasing speed of the ship it was upon an acute right-hand bend. The sharp iron bow sliced into the mud as efficiently as a knife sliding through butter. The vessel rose in the air, tilting alarmingly, and came to an abrupt halt, scattering passengers in all directions.

The great wooden paddles were still turning at high speed, and above the violent juddering of the stranded vessel the passengers could hear the splintering of wood as one of the paddles fought a disastrous battle with the heavy Avon mud.

The paddles were eventually brought to a halt by the initiative of the ship's engineer, and the ensuing silence was broken only by the sound of steam escaping from a broken pipe.

As the passengers picked themselves up there was a babble of voices expressing anger, shock – and terror.

Half the lanterns had been thrown from their hooks by the force of the grounding, and in the gloom Fergus could not see Becky. He called her name repeatedly and felt great relief when she rose from a pile of sprawling passengers who had been thrown together against the guard-rails.

'Are you all right?' he asked anxiously.

'I think so.' She clutched his arm, seeking reassurance. 'What'll we do now?'

'Stay here and wait for someone to come and rescue us, I suppose. There's nothing else we *can* do.'

'But ... won't we sink, or something?' Becky's grip tightened on his arm. She was genuinely scared. Capable of coping with most things that happened in the rough harsh world of Lewin's Mead, she was lost outside the confines of its narrow streets and alleyways.

'I expect a tug will be sent to tow us back to Bristol when the tide turns. Until then we'll just sit firmly on the mud. . . .'

As though in determined contradiction of Fergus's words a sudden judder ran through the ship. Then a shout went up that the small tug had broken free of both tow and mud. As his small vessel wheezed past the stranded paddle-steamer, the tug-boat captain called out that he would send help from Bristol.

More lanterns were found, and the angle at which they hung indicated that the bow of the paddle-steamer was high on the mud, with the stern well down in the channel. But no one was in any immediate danger, and as their fear seeped away the passengers began to enjoy the unexpected experience of being 'shipwrecked'. Soon the band began playing once more and the ship's officers announced that food and drink were once more available in the ship's buffet.

The party atmosphere lasted for about two hours, until an ominous sound began to make itself heard. The paddle-steamer's structure began creaking and groaning as though bemoaning its own fate, and a whispered rumour went round that the ship was breaking up. The officers were quick to move among the passengers and reassure them, but uneasiness had descended upon the ship once more.

Some four hours after the grounding, lights were spotted on the bank between the ship and Bristol, and as they drew closer many men and horses became discernible. A rescue force was on the way.

A great cheer rose from the passengers – but they soon learned that rescue was still some way off. When the Bristol men reached the bank nearest to the paddle-steamer a shouted conversation began with the ship's officers, and the truth of the situation emerged for the first time.

The hull of the great ship was twisting under the strain placed upon it by the grounding and the angle at which it was lying. Water had flooded the after bilges, adding to the weight. Far from floating clear of the mud when the tide rose, it was feared the ship would sink!

The furore caused by this unexpected disclosure rendered further conversation between ship and shore impossible for many minutes. When he could once more make himself heard, the leader of the shore party assured those on board they need have no fears. He had sent for long ladders. These would be laid across the mud and up the side of the ship. All the passengers would be safely on dry land long before there was any danger.

The news was greeted with mixed reactions by the women, but the men agreed it was better to be *doing* something about their predicament than to remain on board all night in the hope that things *might* be all right.

It was close to three o'clock in the morning before ladders reached the stranded paddle-steamer. Large wooden rafts had been hastily constructed on the bank, and with the aid of ropes stretched between shore and ship the rafts were hauled into position on the mud. Then ladders were laid across them and lashed together, the final ladder extending up the side of the ship to the deck. A rescue could now commence.

Some difficulty was experienced by the women with their long and impractical dresses, but gradually more and more passengers reached the bank, loud in their relief at having safely negotiated the unusual gangplank on their hands and knees.

By the time it was the turn of Fergus and Becky to go ashore the wooden rafts had sunk deep into the mud, causing the centre of the long sagging ladders to touch the surface of the black evil-smelling ooze, and making them dangerously slippery.

By a coincidence, the two children who had commented upon Becky's naked feet were immediately ahead of Becky on the ladders. It had been Fergus's intention to cross ahead of her, but at the last minute Becky pushed in front of him.

When they were well out on the long sagging ladder the well-dressed young girl in front of Becky screamed and there was a heavy *plop* as she fell from the ladder in the darkness. All became immediate confusion as the girl's mother screamed and men from both ship and shore shouted conflicting advice.

It was Becky who saved the day by lying on her stomach and gripping the other girl's hands. Then, with Fergus helping, the girl was hauled back to the ladder.

Instead of being grateful, when the girl regained her breath she accused Becky of deliberately knocking her from the ladder.

'I did *not*!' Becky spoke indignantly. 'You'd stopped. If I'd knocked you into the mud on purpose, I wouldn't have stopped to pull you out again.'

'Come on, we'll get you to the bank and dry you.' The girl's father had crawled along the ladder from the shore to her assistance. 'If you fall ill because of this, I'll sue the steamship company. Why I agreed to bring you all on such a foolish adventure I'll never know. . . .'

'But I've lost my shoes. They're stuck in the mud. . . !'

'*Damn* your shoes. Come on, girl. My God! You stink like a dockyard sewer. Don't *touch* me. . . .'

Fergus smiled secretly in the darkness. For the sneering young girl to have lost her own shoes was an ironic twist of fate.

For a long time Becky lay on her stomach in the darkness, not moving forward. Realising she might have exhausted herself pulling the other girl from the sticky mud, Fergus let her rest for a while, but then the passengers behind him began complaining at the lack of movement on the ladder, and Fergus asked: 'Are you able to go on, Becky?'

'Just a minute.' Her voice sounded muffled, but not particularly weary.

'What are you doing?' Fergus spoke irritably, increasingly aware of the growing number of passengers waiting impatiently on the ladders behind him.

'I'm going now.' Becky sounded suddenly cheerful, and the ladder began shaking as she scrambled ahead.

There was much confusion on the river-bank. Rumour and counter-rumour swept the ever-growing crowd of rescued passengers. Transport to Bristol was being arranged. . . . Passengers were expected to make their own way home. . . . They were to await a boat from Bristol. . . . Fergus and Becky joined the steady trickle of passengers who decided to walk back to Bristol.

It was dawn by the time they reached the city, and Fergus was beginning to feel the strain of the last twenty-four hours. Not so Becky. With her arm linked through Fergus's she skipped beside him as he limped along. Chattering happily about the great adventure they had just experienced, she occasionally hummed some of the songs the band had played – and frequently reminisced happily about the food they had eaten.

As it grew lighter Fergus could see that Becky was covered from head to toe in black mud. He supposed it must have happened when she pulled the young girl to the ladder and he commiserated with her on the state of her new dress.

'Oh, *that* doesn't matter. It'll wash off easily enough.'

Fergus was surprised by her cheerful reply. He had expected her to be upset – angry even. Then he noticed a suspicious bulge beneath the dress, held surreptitiously in place by her free arm. Coming to a halt, Fergus demanded to know what Becky was hiding.

'Nothing!' Becky was indignant, but she tried to work the lump to the side farthest from him.

'Let me see what it is.'

Fergus put on his sternest no-nonsense voice. Reluctantly Becky reached beneath the muddy dress and pulled out a pair of lady's satin ankle-boots that were even muddier than her dress.

'Where did you get them?' Even as he asked the question Fergus realised he knew the answer. 'You *did* push that girl from the ladder!'

'No, I didn't,' Becky defended herself indignantly. 'I didn't pinch these shoes, neither. She left 'em there in the mud, too

93

scared to search for 'em. I wasn't, though ... so that makes them mine.'

Fergus opened his mouth to argue with her – but closed it again without saying anything. Discussing the legal niceties of ownership with Becky would get him nowhere. 'Lewin's Mead Law' weighed heavily in favour of the possessor of disputed property, whatever else the laws of the land might suggest. Moreover, there was a certain wry justice in the situation.

Suddenly Fergus grinned. 'If their late owner is having to walk home, I doubt if she'll ever again mock anyone without shoes.'

CHAPTER TEN

FERGUS AND BECKY made their way quietly up the stairs of Ida Stokes's house and met Irish Molly in the act of letting an all-night client out from her room. Client and prostitute stared in amazement at the homecoming couple, Becky coming in for special attention.

'What the hell have you been doing? I thought you were away on a boat-trip down the river somewheres.'

'Looks like it was low tide and they've walked back....' Even as he spoke the client was bundled down the stairs by Irish Molly, who quickly returned to Becky.

'You'd best come into my room and let me clean you up. You can tell me what's happened while I'm doing it.'

Becky hesitated, reluctant to leave Fergus, but Irish Molly snapped: 'He can clean himself up. I've had enough of sorting out the problems of men for one night. I haven't had an hour's sleep with him who's just gone. I should be looking for tired old merchants at my age, not healthy young sailors just back from six months at sea. Come on, young lady. In there with you and let's get you cleaned up. Holy Mother! You smell worse than the backyard!'

Fergus went up to the attic and cleaned himself up before lying down on the bed to wait for Becky. It had been a strange twenty-four hours. A day and night like no other he could remember. He grinned as he remembered Becky and the way she had behaved on the boat. He had enjoyed being with her....

When Becky entered the room wrapped in a large dress

that belonged to Irish Molly, Fergus was sprawled on the bed snoring loudly.

Becky was disappointed. In her mind she had been practising a special 'thank you'. The boat-trip had been a wonderful treat, in spite of its disastrous ending. She wanted Fergus to know exactly how she felt.

Fergus did not stir when Becky covered him with a blanket. After laying her newly washed dress on the flat window-sill to catch the sun, Becky lay down in a corner of the room. Within a few minutes she, too, was fast asleep.

Heavy knocking at the door brought Fergus awake with a start. As he struggled from the bed the knocking was repeated.

'All right! All right! I'm coming.'

Few callers came to the attic room, and Fergus thought it must be Ida Stokes. Anyone else in the house would have knocked only once, if at all, before walking in. But what could the landlady want? The rent was paid up. . . .

He opened the door and was confronted by Fanny Tennant. Aware he was wearing no shirt, he stuttered: 'I . . . I'm sorry. I didn't know it was you. If you wait a minute, I'll finish dressing.'

'Don't bother, Mr Vincent. I came to find out why Becky hadn't come to school this morning, but I can see the ragged school has slipped *both* your memories.'

Frosty-voiced, Fanny Tennant was staring beyond Fergus. Looking round, Fergus caught a glimpse of Becky's naked body before it disappeared inside Irish Molly's loaned dress.

'You have been less than honest with me, Mr Vincent. I should know better, but I confess to being disappointed. Very disappointed. Nevertheless, I expect to see Becky at school tomorrow.' Turning away, Fanny Tennant started back down the stairs.

'Wait! Let me explain. I'll dress and walk through Lewin's Mead with you.'

'Explanations are unnecessary, Mr Vincent. I told you once before, I try not to pass judgements on people. As for walking with me through Lewin's Mead, I venture to suggest I am safer here than you.'

Having made this observation, Fanny Tennant lifted her skirts above her ankles and disappeared from view around an angle of the stairs.

'Damn!' Scowling furiously, Fergus turned back into the room. 'She's gone away with entirely the wrong idea. That woman is too full of her own importance even to consider she might be wrong.'

'Does it matter what she thinks?' Becky asked the question casually. 'What we're doing here is nobody's business but yours and mine.'

'That's not the point. I don't want her thinking . . . Oh, it doesn't matter!'

'You don't want Fanny Tennant thinking you might care enough to have me living with you. Is that what you were going to say?' Becky looked at Fergus defiantly, but there was just the hint of a tremor in her voice.

'That's *not* what I was going to say at all. She *knows* I'm fond of you. If I weren't, I wouldn't have gone to her for help in getting you out of the police cells. But before she would agree to help me I had to give her my word we weren't living together. I don't like her — or anyone else — thinking I'm a liar.'

Suddenly Fergus grinned. 'Although how anyone might believe I would fancy you in that dress, I don't know. There could be two of you in there without either one ever meeting the other. Get a fire going; I'll go out and buy some food for us.'

Becky smiled, but it had nothing to do with Fergus's humour. He had admitted he was *fond* of her. No one had ever told her that before.

That evening in the Hatchet inn Fergus saw a face he immediately recognised. It was the black-bearded captain of the paddle-steamer, the man whose removal from authority had indirectly resulted in the grounding of the vessel.

Fergus attempted to speak to him, but there was no sense in the man tonight. The only time he was briefly rational was when Fergus mentioned he had been on board the grounded vessel.

'*Grounded*, you say? *Wrecked* is what you mean.' The captain's voice boomed out above the sounds of the inn, and heads turned towards the speaker. 'My officers mutinied and then wrecked my ship. One of the finest vessels ever to sail out of Bristol – and what do the owners do? I'll tell you. They've dismissed *me*. Me who's never so much as lost an anchor in thirty years of command. Dismissed on the evidence of a gang of *mutineers*. It's *them* the owners should have dealt with. Strung 'em up, every lying mother's son. Made an example. Made an example. . . .'

Obadiah Clegg's voice dropped away to an incoherent mumble as he stared down into his tankard. Fergus backed away, leaving the befuddled former paddle-steamer captain alone with his drunken misery.

Returning to his seat, Fergus sketched a portrait of Captain Clegg as the seaman sat motionless, hunched over his tankard of ale. It was a good sketch and captured the utter dejection of the black-bearded man.

Soon afterwards Fergus was asked to make a sketch of an East India crewman for the man to take home to his family. When it was done Fergus looked across the room to where he had last seen Obadiah Clegg, but the sea-captain had gone.

It was not a very busy evening, and as he was still tired as a result of the previous evening's shipwreck Fergus left the Hatchet inn and returned home earlier than usual.

There was light showing beneath the attic door, and when Fergus entered the room he found Becky there. She was wearing the dress Fergus had bought for her, together with the newly scrubbed shoes she had 'acquired' from her unfortunate fellow-passenger on the paddle-steamer. She stood beside the table, her hands hidden behind her back. On the table was a bottle of brandy, a pewter tankard, a small ham and a loaf of shop-bought bread.

Fergus looked at the items on the table with some surprise.

'They're for you. For taking me out yesterday.'

'Where did the money come from?'

'I saved it . . . from the money you gave me to buy the dress.'

It was a lie, Fergus knew it; but Becky was happy, and he was reluctant to spoil the moment for her.

'It's a wonderful surprise, Becky. Just what I fancy right now.' This at least was the truth. Fergus was hungry, and bread and ham were a great improvement on Becky's fried eggs.

'I've got another surprise for you. Here. . . .' Becky brought her hands from behind her back, and he caught the gleam of gold. Then she was holding his hand and placing something in his grasp.

In his hand Fergus held a finely scrolled gold pocket-watch, complete with a heavy gold chain. Becky was watching him with eager anticipation, but the eagerness disappeared when she saw his expression harden.

'Becky, where did you get this?'

Her chin came up in a characteristic expression of defiance. 'It's a present. I bet you wouldn't ask Fanny Tennant where it came from if *she* gave you a present.'

'She's not likely to give me a present, Becky. Certainly not one like this. This is real gold. Where did it come from?'

'You don't *have* to keep it if you don't want to. There's lots of others I can give it to.'

Becky tried to snatch the watch back from him, but Fergus closed his hand about the extravagant present.

'I asked a question. Where has this come from?'

Becky tried to slip past him to the door, but Fergus was too quick for her. He was certain now that the watch had been stolen.

'You'll not leave this room until you've told me where it came from.'

'I thought you'd be pleased with the watch. You *need* one; you've said so more than once.'

Becky was close to tears, and for a moment Fergus weakened. Then he looked at the watch and hardened his heart. It was a valuable time-piece. Someone would report its loss.

'The thought that you *wanted* to give me a present touches me very much, Becky, but I'll not have you stealing for me – and there's no other way you could have got this.'

As he was talking Fergus flicked open the back of the watch. Engraved inside was the name 'Aloysius Tennant' and the date 'October 1821'. Fergus looked at Becky sharply. 'Where *did* you get this? The name in here is Aloysius Tennant. Could it be one of Fanny Tennant's relatives?'

'What if it is? Are you going to tell her I pinched it from him?'

'Of course not – but it will have to be returned to its rightful owner.'

Becky met his gaze unashamedly and shrugged her shoulders. 'Then, I've done you a favour, haven't I? Given you an excuse to go and talk to her. To make your peace.' Suddenly she said: 'I wanted you to have a present, Fergus. Something *special*.'

'You don't *need* to give me a present – and certainly not *steal* for me.'

Becky gazed at him in hot-eyed accusation. 'You don't understand, do you?'

Fergus moved across the room towards her, but with a sudden unexpected movement she slipped past him and reached the door. Flinging it open, she paused for a moment on the top stair.

'You're no different from anyone else. Whenever I try to do something nice it's always spoilt. I hoped you'd be different. . . .' Becky choked on her words, then turning she fled noisily down the stairs to the street.

Some time later Fergus enquired for Becky in the room on the floor below. Mary O'Ryan was drunk and aggressive. She informed Fergus that she had not seen Becky for days, and doubted if her life had lost any of its colour on that account. In the room behind the woman a man crooned tunelessly to himself while two companions quarrelled and a child cried monotonously and fretfully. It was easy to see why Becky was eager to find a place away from the overcrowded O'Ryan room, but it did nothing to help him find her.

It would have been foolhardy to go out and search the

maze of streets and alleyways that formed Lewin's Mead at such an hour, and Fergus returned to the attic, hoping she would return when her anger and hurt had worn off.

Becky did not return that night or the next day, and Fergus spent many of the daylight hours searching for her without success. She seemed to have disappeared off the face of the earth, and no one to whom he spoke would admit to seeing her.

Irish Molly listened sympathetically to his guarded explanation for Becky's disappearance, but she shrugged off a suggestion that Becky might have run off.

'Where would she go? Like most of the urchins around here she's lost outside the alleyways of Lewin's Mead. No, she's here somewhere, but if she doesn't want to be found, then she won't be. She knows this place better than anyone you'll ever meet. Go about your business, Fergus. She'll come back in her own time — if she wants to.'

CHAPTER ELEVEN

THE GOLD WATCH weighed heavily in Fergus's pocket on his way to the ragged school to give his first art lesson to Fanny Tennant's pupils. There was still no news of Becky, although he and Irish Molly had made enquiries throughout the rookery.

The cool reception Fergus received from Fanny Tennant did nothing to make him feel better. She met him at the entrance to the converted chapel, and her eyebrows rose in an expression of exaggerated surprise.

'Mr Vincent! This *is* an unexpected pleasure. I assume you *have* come to give an art lesson to our pupils?'

Brushing aside his mumbled affirmation, Fanny Tennant snapped: 'What of Becky? It was agreed she would attend school. . . .'

'You'll have to ask her yourself – if you can find her. She went out on Monday night, and I haven't seen her since. To tell you the truth, I'm very concerned for her.'

'For *her*, Mr Vincent? I doubt it. I doubt it very much.'

'I haven't come here to argue with you. I'm here to sketch for your pupils – and also to ask if you recognise this.' As he spoke Fergus pulled the gold watch from his pocket and handed it to her.

Fanny Tennant took the watch, and her expression told him immediately that she *had* seen the watch before. 'Yes. It belongs to my father.' She looked up at him suspiciously. 'How did it come to be in your possession?'

Fergus shook his head. 'That doesn't matter. Let's say I'm

pleased to be returning the watch to its rightful owner.'

Fanny Tennant was watching him carefully. 'Becky stole it, didn't she? My father missed it after coming here to inspect the school. He lost his purse, too. He said a young girl bumped into him outside. A girl wearing a grey and red dress.' Fanny Tennant held up the watch. 'Did she leave you because of an argument over this?'

'Becky has never lived with me. She stayed in my room when she had nowhere else, that's all.'

'Be that as it may, my father will be grateful for the return of his watch – but don't expect a reward.'

'None was asked for. Now that's over with . . . I came here to do some work.'

Fergus knew Fanny Tennant did not believe his version of his relationship with Becky, but it did not matter for the moment. It was far more important that she did not pursue the matter of who had stolen her father's watch. Aloysius Tennant was an alderman and chairman of the Watch Committee. A Bristol judge would ensure that Becky received the maximum sentence for the theft of *his* watch. She might even be transported. . . .

He became aware that Fanny Tennant was talking to him.

'You'll be teaching a class of older children, some of the first to attend our school. You'll find them surprisingly bright, but we haven't been able to instil a great sense of discipline into them. It might be better if I remain in the classroom with you for today.'

Fanny Tennant's caution proved unnecessary. The ragamuffins from the Lewin's Mead rookery maintained an air of indifference until Fergus sketched a couple of hastily executed but good likenesses of a few of them. Then the ragged youngsters clamoured to be shown how to sketch one another. Soon they were hunched over their tables, laboriously producing crude sketches. Fergus moved among them as they worked, guiding their primitive efforts and occasionally adding a few lines of his own to make a sketch appear more lifelike. A couple of the boys possessed a raw elementary talent, and Fergus spent extra time showing them a few basic techniques.

Thoroughly absorbed in what he was doing, Fergus was startled when a bell rang somewhere inside the school. Fanny Tennant said: 'That will be all for today, boys and girls. Mr Vincent will be here again next week to give you another lesson, and I'll see you all tomorrow morning. Try to be on time, if you please.'

As the last of the pupils disappeared through the classroom doorway, Fanny Tennant gave Fergus a rare smile. 'Your lesson was a great success, Mr Vincent. It's the first time I have ever been greeted with a groan when I have sent them home from school. I must congratulate you.'

Gathering up his materials, Fergus said: 'A couple of the boys show some talent. They should be encouraged.'

'I have never believed talent to be lacking in Lewin's Mead – only opportunities. But while we're on the subject of talent . . . Don't you think yours is wasted in Lewin's Mead?'

'No.' Fergus tucked his folder of drawings beneath his arm and took up the bag in which he carried his materials. 'We're both educators, in our own way. You're teaching the children about the present, in order to prepare them for the future. I hope that one day my sketches and paintings will show the children of the future what life is really like in Bristol during our lifetime. I want them to realise there's more to it than well-dressed men and women, and tidy Clifton street scenes.'

'You're a strange man, Fergus Vincent. Would these views you hold prevent your from *visiting* tidy Clifton? We're having an informal dinner-party at my home on Friday night. I would like you to be one of our guests.'

The unexpected invitation took Fergus by surprise. Since their first meeting he had felt that Fanny Tennant disapproved of him and his way of life, yet here she was inviting him to an informal dinner with her family.

Fanny Tennant realised something of what he was thinking. She smiled as she explained: 'Not all city aldermen are Tories. My father is a nonconformist in both politics and religion. He enjoys meeting those who choose their own path through life. You'll come?'

Fergus's first inclination had been to decline the invitation, but he surprised himself by nodding his head.

'Good. We will expect you at about seven-thirty.'

Not until he was in the narrow street outside the ragged school did Fergus realise he had not asked Fanny Tennant where she lived. Shrugging the collar of his coat up about his ears as protection against a heavy shower, he thought that the home of Alderman Aloysius Tennant should not be difficult to find. Certainly not as difficult as the present whereabouts of Becky.

Fergus had intended spending the evening painting in his attic studio, but the disappearance of Becky had left him strangely unsettled. The thought of keeping his own company held little appeal. He decided to go to the Hatchet inn and earn himself some money.

As it happened, the Hatchet inn was unusually quiet, and Fergus made only three sketches during the whole of the evening. Soon after ten o'clock he decided to return home. He was about to enter an alleyway that led to the rookery when a tall figure stepped from the shadows of a nearby doorway. It was Constable Ivor Primrose.

'It's a little early for you to be heading home, Fergus.'

'There's no business about. The Hatchet's so empty the "girls" are buying their own drinks. Even the regulars seem to have gone elsewhere tonight.'

'They'll be at the Chartist meeting up on the Downs, together with all but three of the Bristol police force. Tomas Casey's come down from the north to make a speech, and trouble has a nasty habit of travelling with him.'

'Tomas Casey? I don't think I've heard of him, but I must confess I know very little of Chartism.'

Ivor Primrose snorted. 'Ask twelve Chartists what it is they're seeking and you'll have twelve differing answers. For Dr Tomas Casey it's just another means of stirring up trouble for the Government. He's been imprisoned in Ireland for his views, but it hasn't prevented him from being elected to Parliament by his countrymen.'

'He sounds an interesting man.'

'He's an agitator – a *dangerous* agitator. We can do without his kind here in Bristol. . . .'

The tall policeman changed the subject abruptly. 'You must have well-nigh filled your sketchpad by now. Mind if I have a look at what you've done?'

Fergus passed over the sketchpad and waited patiently as Ivor Primrose leafed through the pages, chuckling when he found sketches of characters he recognised and occasionally putting a name to a face.

'You have many drawings of that young lady who got herself into trouble a while back. Is she behaving herself now?'

'She ran off a few days ago. I haven't seen her since.'

Still turning over pages, Ivor Primrose gave Fergus a shrewd glance. 'She's a product of the rookery, Fergus. Expect too much of her and you're doomed to disappointment.'

Suddenly the constable stopped talking and stared down at one of the sketches. Jabbing a heavy finger down on the paper, he demanded: 'Where did you draw this?'

Moving with the pad closer to the gas-light that illuminated the entrance to the alleyway, Fergus stared down at the portrait of Captain Clegg.

'He was in the Hatchet a few nights ago, drinking to drown his sorrows.'

'He drowned more than his sorrows. Someone saw him jump into the dock, but by the time we got to him he was dead. He'd had his pockets rifled at some time, too, and there was nothing left to identify him. He's in the mortuary now.'

Visibly shaken, Fergus said: 'His name was Clegg. *Captain* Clegg. He was in command of the paddle-steamer that ran aground coming up the Avon. At least, he *should* have been in command. His officers relieved him and put him under arrest in a cabin for being drunk.'

'It would seem he got drunk once too often.' Handing back the sketchpad, Ivor Primrose pulled out a pocket-book and began writing. 'I'm obliged for your help, Fergus. If I see or hear anything of your young waif, I'll get word to you.'

CHAPTER TWELVE

FERGUS'S ORIGINAL INTENTION had been to go to dinner at Alderman Tennant's house dressed in his 'everyday best', but at the last minute he gave way to his own misgivings and bought a suit from a tailor's shop not far from the Hatchet inn.

He felt uncomfortable in his stiff new clothes walking the alleyways of the dockside slum. Fortunately the residents of Lewin's Mead had come to accept his presence among them and were even showing proprietary pride in his talents.

So wrapped up was Fergus in thoughts of his appearance that he failed to observe a small figure who watched him intently from the shadows of a Back Lane doorway. When he turned the corner from Back Lane, Becky slipped quietly into Ida Stokes's house. Had he seen her, Fergus would have happily forgone the uncertain pleasure of an evening in Bristol's most fashionable suburb.

The spacious and elegant houses of Clifton were far removed from the crowded slums of Lewin's Mead. Each house stood in its own gardens, occupying a space that might have housed a thousand rookery residents. Built on a hill high above the city they also commanded an attractive view over the surrounding countryside. Having grown accustomed to the narrow streets of Lewin's Mead, Fergus felt uncomfortably conspicuous.

A neatly dressed maidservant opened the door to Fergus, and a moment later Fanny Tennant came into the hall to take him to meet her father and the other guests.

Fanny was a very different girl from the one Fergus had last seen at the ragged school in St James. Gone was the neat austere look. Her long hair hung loose, reaching almost to her waist, and she wore a long pale green dress that was deceptively and expensively simple.

The change in her appearance was accompanied by an apparent shift in her attitude towards Fergus. After greeting him warmly she led him along a high-ceilinged corridor towards a room from which there came a loud buzz of conversation. It seemed a great many other guests had been invited to the 'informal' evening at the Tennant home.

At the doorway to the room Fanny Tennant paused. 'Don't be overawed by my father. He occasionally forgets he's at home and not in the council chamber. You and I are probably the youngest people here, so I will be looking to you for support.'

Fergus realised immediately they entered the crowded room that he was underdressed for the occasion. In spite of the wording of Fanny's invitation most of those present wore formal evening wear – including the host, Alderman Aloysius Tennant.

When the two men were introduced, Aloysius Tennant shook Fergus's hand enthusiastically, saying: 'So you are Fanny's young artist friend. She's told me a great deal about you.'

As Fergus tried to digest this surprising statement, the city alderman's eyes were searching the crowded room. Finding the guest he sought, Aloysius Tennant took Fergus's arm and led him towards a curtained alcove, explaining as he went: 'There's someone here who's dying to meet you. You'll get on well together. Lady Hammond is a great supporter of the arts, as well as being a well-respected expert in her own right.'

Alderman Tennant pushed his way through the crowd gathered in the alcove, murmuring polite apologies along the way. At their centre was a large-bosomed lady of advanced years dressed in a brown velvet dress with a stole to match. Perched on the edge of a hard-padded settle, she turned lively blue eyes on the newcomer.

'Lady Hammond, I would like to introduce a young man to you. Mr Vincent is an acquaintance of Fanny. He's an artist.'

Fergus took the hand that was extended to him and bowed over it, acutely aware that Lady Hammond was casting a critical eye over his clothes.

'What do you paint, young man? Landscapes? Portraits?'

'Portraits, mainly.'

A cynical half-smile crossed the face of the seated woman. 'But of course. Clifton has become a Mecca for portrait-painters seeking commissions.' Her comment brought a ripple of amusement from some of the guests behind Fergus. 'Very well. Bring some of your work to my house and leave it with my butler. I can't guarantee a commission, but you'll have an honest criticism of your work, at least.'

Painfully aware of the amused derision of his fellow-guests, indignation welled up inside Fergus.

'I doubt if my portraits would be of any interest to you, Lady Hammond. I don't paint flattering portraits of Clifton society – or any other society. I live and work in Lewin's Mead, sketching drunken sailors and their women, and dirty-faced urchins who grub in the gutter for food. I paint *life*. Real down-to-earth life as it's lived by thousands of people in your city.'

Inexplicable anger had replaced indignation, and the shocked expressions on the faces of his fellow-guests told Fergus his outburst had gone too far.

As he pushed his way from the alcove someone started applauding and a loud voice called: 'Bravo! Bravo, sir! That's telling them what they should hear, and no mistake.'

Looking up, Fergus saw a diminutive figure dressed as casually as himself elbowing his way across the room towards him. Reaching Fergus, the beaming and perspiring newcomer grasped Fergus's hand in both his own. 'I'm delighted to make the acquaintance of such an outspoken young man.' The Irish accent and his disdain for the company about him gave the man away even before he introduced himself. 'Tomas Casey at your service, young sir. Tell me, are *you* a Chartist? If not, why not?'

At that moment Fergus saw Fanny Tennant hurrying

towards him. Freeing his hand from the Irishman's strong grasp, he braced himself to meet his hostess.

'I'm sorry if I upset Lady Hammond, but —'

'Upset her? My dear Fergus, you've made her evening. I should never have allowed Father to make the introductions. He's dedicated to making money and he thinks everyone else is the same. He believes people only have parties to meet those who might prove useful to them. He forgets some people come to parties simply to enjoy themselves. He honestly thought he was doing you a favour by introducing you to Lady Hammond. She is a very generous patron of the arts. Were you to take some paintings to her house, she would give you an honest appraisal of them and probably buy some, too, even if she didn't really like them.'

'I don't need anyone's charity.'

'*I'm* aware of this; so, too, are my father and Lady Hammond — now. Please, come back with me. Lady Hammond really does want to speak to you.'

'Don't you retract a single word, my boy. Remember those "real" people you were talking of — the ones you and I know all about.'

'No political speeches, Tomas. Lady Hammond has been very generous to you and your cause.'

'That's because she recognises it as a *just* cause. She hasn't bought my soul with her money.'

Fanny Tennant led Fergus back to the alcove, the guests making way for them. Lady Hammond was aware of their approach but she did not look up until Fergus had halted before her. For a moment her glance held his, but he could read nothing in her eyes. Then she patted the empty seat beside her.

'Sit down, young man. Come along, I won't attack you.' She shifted her position slightly as Fergus obeyed her command.

'That's better. I don't know why today's young men feel they have to be rebellious in order to be noticed. Tell me something of your work. Do you *really* live in Lewin's Mead?'

Gradually, with patient and sympathetic questioning, Lady

Hammond drew Fergus's story from him, while Fanny Tennant listened with many of her interested guests.

After hearing details of Fergus's proposed series of paintings about the men, women and children who frequented the rookery, Lady Hammond asked: 'Is it really necessary to *live* in this slum in order to complete this "record of life", or whatever it is you intend calling your sketches? Could it not be carried out just as well from Clifton?'

'No. By living there I become one of them. They behave naturally when I'm around. I also see what's happening and *feel* it for myself. It's important if I'm to put real *life* into my sketches and paintings.'

Some of the intensity of Fergus's feelings came out in his explanation. Lady Hammond was watching him with great interest and she asked: 'How good are your sketches, young man?'

Before he could reply, Fanny said: 'He's very good, Lady Hammond. Very good indeed.'

Fanny Tennant's remarks took Fergus by surprise. He had not realised she had studied his work in any detail.

'Then, I must see some for myself. You have taken on a noble project, young man, but not one to make your fortune. Certainly *not* while you're living in Lewin's Mead.' She gave a faint shudder. 'Bring some of your sketches to my house and we'll discuss the matter further.'

Fergus realised he was once more dismissed, but Lady Hammond had expressed a genuine interest in his work and suddenly it seemed everyone wanted to talk to him. It was a long time before he was able to break away and find a drink.

Tomas Casey was standing at the drinks-table. The Chartist leader had not been without a glass in his hand for many moments during the course of the evening.

'Well, well, well! So they've made you the "belle of the ball" after all, eh? Beware of sudden fame, my young friend. It's no more enduring than a butterfly in a rainstorm. If Lady Hammond hadn't called you back when she did, all you'd have been given would have been the toe of someone's boot kicking your backside through the doorway. But now it'll be "No, Mr Vincent," and "Yes, sir, Mr Vincent," and "You're a bloody genius, Mr Vincent". Hypocrites, every one of 'em. Soft over-privileged hypocrites.'

'Aren't you worried the "hypocrite's" gin you're drinking will choke you?'

Tomas Casey lowered the glass from his mouth and smiled ruefully at the clear liquid there. Swirling it about and allowing the fumes to escape from the tiny alcoholic whirlpool, he said thoughtfully: 'Since I became a Chartist I've choked on far worse. I used to love my fellow-men, Mr Vincent. It's only since I began fighting half the world on behalf of the other half that I've become a cynic.'

'Why do it?'

Tomas Casey shrugged, and then grinned. 'I'm an Irishman, Mr Vincent. I was *born* fighting.'

'Is that all Chartism means to you? A fight?'

Some of the fire that had made Tomas Casey a formidable leader of men cut through the alcoholic barrier he had put between himself and the world, and the Chartist leader became suddenly serious. 'If that were *all* it meant, I could spend a happy life in any dockside town. No, Mr Vincent, what Chartism means to me is fighting to give a working man the dignity that God intended he should have. After all, *he's* made in God's image, too. He should have the dignity to decide his own future. The dignity to play a part in that future and be treated as a man. But before he can achieve any of this he must be given the vote. The *vote*, Mr Vincent, the all-important vote.'

'I know little of Chartism.'

'That's a sad admission from a man who claims to be recording the life of the working classes for posterity.'

'You're right,' agreed Fergus. 'I'll come to your next meeting. When is it?'

'We'll be meeting on Durdham Downs on Thursday evening at about six o'clock. You'll have no problem finding us. Just follow the constables. They'll all be there. If I visit Lewin's Mead in the meantime, where will I find you?'

Fergus gave Tomas Casey his address in Back Lane; then, after thanking Fanny Tennant for inviting him to the party, Fergus left.

On the way home he stopped for a moment on the heights of Kingsdown and looked down at the jumbled moonlit roofs of Lewin's Mead. Huddled close together they seemed to shut out the world about them. He could not help comparing the abject poverty of its residents with the luxuries he had just enjoyed. Champagne and fine foods, consumed in vast quantities by the families of plump and complacent merchants who dressed in expensive clothes and bedecked wives and daughters with a fortune in jewellery.

Then his thoughts turned to Becky. She was somewhere in the crowded slum below him. But where . . .?

CHAPTER THIRTEEN

NOT UNTIL HE WOKE THE NEXT MORNING did Fergus notice that Becky's few miserable possessions had disappeared from the attic room. He clattered down the uneven stairs, and his persistent knocking brought a bleary-eyed Irish Molly from her bed.

'Oh, it's you.' Irish Molly's fingers made a futile attempt to bring some order to her tangled hair. 'I thought it might be.'

'Becky's been back. Her things have gone. Did you see her?'

'I did. Now you've woken me you'd best come in. Get the fire started, and I'll brew a cup of tea. What time is it? It feels like the unholy crack of dawn.'

'It's after nine – but Becky? Where is she? What's she doing? Why didn't she stay?'

Irish Molly groaned. 'Will you keep your tongue still between your teeth for a while? I have trouble thinking of the answer to *one* question at this time of morning. Me poor head's reeling. Make a start on that fire, will you?'

'Tell me of Becky.'

'The child's all right. She's not happy, but there's nothing in the Good Book to say the poor are entitled to happiness. My mother used to tell me that – and there's nothing happened in *my* life since to teach me any different.'

'Where is she staying?' Fergus stood back as flames attacked dry tinderwood in the grate and smoke rolled into the room from an unswept chimney.

'She wouldn't tell me, but she can't have left Lewin's

Mead. She knows too much of what's been going on here.'

'Damn!' Keeping his face turned away from the billowing smoke as much as was possible, Fergus used his foot to push the blackened kettle farther into the fire. 'If only I'd been here to speak to her.'

'She only came to the house because she knew you'd gone out.' Irish Molly eased a grubby slip down over her large hips. 'I told her you'd searched everywhere for her. Said you wanted her back.'

'What did she say?'

'She snorted loud enough to drive the cork back in a bottle of Hollands. She'd watched you going out all dressed up like a dog's dinner and guessed you was off to see your fine fancy-girl at Clifton.'

'Where do *you* think she's staying, Molly?'

The Irish prostitute's head emerged from a rough-spun dress that covered the grubby slip. 'There's a hundred places to hide no more than a stone's throw from this very house. My guess would be that she's in one of the old houses backing on to the river. I've heard that a boat-load of my people came in from Ireland this week and have moved in there.... Hey! Aren't you even stopping for a cup of tea?'

But Fergus was gone. Irish Molly shrugged at the closing door and picked up a dirty cup. Flinging the previous night's grouts in the fire, she ran a finger round the rim to remove a couple of tea-leaves, then spooned sugar into the cup.

The area adjacent to the River Frome was avoided even by the unfastidious residents of Lewin's Mead. The river was little more than a sluggish open sewer, and the stench from it was overpowering. The houses backing on the river were a hotchpotch mixture of Tudor and early Georgian, all in an advanced state of decay. They were occupied by the city's vagrants, their numbers recently swelled by the arrival of immigrant Irish families, driven from their homeland by unemployment and yet another failure of the potato crop.

The Irish reacted with suspicion when Fergus began asking after Becky. Few spoke English, and those who did were reluctant to admit to it. Fergus persisted in his questioning until a large number of ragged and silent men joined the group about him. No one made an overt move against him, but they were becoming suspicious, and their very hopelessness posed a threat. Uprooted from their homes by a combination of outdated feudalism and unbalanced husbandry, starvation had brought them to the brink of despair. They had fled from their homes with death never more than half a pace behind them, and the restraints of a law-abiding society meant little to them. Fergus deemed it wiser to end his futile questioning and leave them to their misery.

It was doubtful whether Becky was here and, settling down at a safe distance, Fergus spent a while sketching the listless Irish children who sat in silent misery about the houses.

When Fergus returned to the attic he sat looking at the sketches. He wanted to commit them to canvas immediately, yet somehow he could not bring himself to begin. In some way the children still *lived* while they were on his sketchpad. Re-creating them on canvas seemed in some strange way to be an acceptance of the fate that would inevitably overtake them in their squalid surroundings.

Fergus was fighting his indecision when Irish Molly came up the stairs to the attic. She entered the room without knocking and saw him hunched in his chair in front of an empty canvas.

'Did you find her?'

Fergus brought his mind back to thoughts of Becky and shook his head.

'You came back more quickly than I expected. I hoped you might have had some luck. . . . Holy Mother! Where have you seen children like these?'

Irish Molly was looking down at a sketch of two young children, one sitting, the other lying. Surrounded by filth and rubbish, both had dull dark eyes too large for their pinched skull-like faces. The prostrate child had bones that seemed intent on breaking through his taut skin.

'They're Irish children. I saw them at the houses by the river. . . . Molly, are you all right?'

The Irish girl had suddenly begun to shake, as though she were about to fall in a fit. 'I'm all right. . . .' Irish Molly's voice was hoarse with the emotion she was feeling. 'But *they're* not. They're dying. I . . . I've seen it all before. We were put out of our cottage when I was ten, and came here, to Liverpool, with some others. My father thought he'd find work to do in England. There was no work, and we were all of us moved on from one place to another, even when the smaller ones began dying. Every place we went to the folks were concerned that we'd become "a burden on the parish". They wouldn't feed us and they didn't want to have to bury us. They just wanted us to move on, to go somewhere else. Their consciences could stay untroubled so long as they didn't have to *watch* us die. I had two brothers die just outside Liverpool, and a sister is buried right here in Bristol. My father disappeared somewhere on the road in between. Ma thought he'd run off to look for work. I didn't. I believe he threw himself in the river because he couldn't bear to watch his family starving to death before his eyes.'

'You were the only survivor?'

'Survivor? Oh, yes, I'm a "survivor". I was ten years old when I became a whore – but I survived. I thought times had changed since then – until I saw these sketches.'

Abruptly Irish Molly turned away and ran from the room, clattering at a dangerous speed down the uneven stairs from the attic.

Fergus felt he should follow her. Then he looked again at the sketch that had upset the Irishwoman so much. He stared at it for a long while. Then, standing before the empty canvas, he picked up a brush and began to paint.

CHAPTER FOURTEEN

BECKY WAS DEEPLY HURT and bewildered by Fergus's refusal to accept her 'gift'. True, she *had* stolen the watch, but *everyone* in Lewin's Mead was a thief when the opportunity arose, and she had stolen the watch especially for *Fergus*. He had been kind to her, and she was desperate to give him something in return. She had no money, so the present *had* to be stolen. How was she to know that the man from whom she had taken it was a relative of that Tennant woman? It would not have made any difference to anyone had Fergus *accepted* the gift.

Becky felt that life was unfair. All she had succeeded in doing was to give Fergus an excuse to go and see Fanny Tennant. All right, *let* him go to her. They could have each other. He didn't belong in Lewin's Mead, anyway. He was more. Fanny Tennant's kind, whatever he said to the contrary.

Becky spent that first night in a doorway. There was one ugly moment when a drunken man fell into the doorway and landed on her. He made a nuisance of himself when he realised she was a young girl, but she sank her teeth into one of his exploring hands and then used a bony elbow to great effect on his face.

Cuffing a bleeding nose, the unhappy drunk staggered to his feet and weaved his way homewards. Behind him Becky drew up her knees and rested her forehead on them. She was very unhappy — but stubbornly refused to contemplate returning to Fergus and his attic studio.

The next morning Becky was abroad at daybreak. She stole a loaf of newly baked bread from a basket inside a bakery doorway, then wandered about the dockside until it grew busy.

By mid-morning she was hungry again. She returned to the bakery, but the proprietor was more alert now. He told her to 'clear off', emphasising his words with a menacing broom. Becky felt better after giving him some cheek, but she was still hungry.

She passed close to the ragged school and heard the monotonous sound of a lesson being repeated, parrot-like, by a class of children. Perhaps the lesson was being given by Miss Fanny Tennant. The thought reminded Becky of Fergus, and she felt more miserable than ever.

Becky wandered aimlessly round a corner looking down at the ground when a voice said: 'Hello, dearie. It's Becky, isn't it? I thought I recognised that dress. It suits you, dear.'

It was Rose Cottle, the dollyshop-owner, standing in the doorway of her premises. She had seen Becky turn the corner and noticed immediately the dirty downcast face, the unbrushed hair, and the creased dress stained with dirt from the doorway where she had spent the night.

'You're looking tired, dearie. It's this spell of hot weather we're having. Makes us all hot and irritable. What we need is a good storm to clear the air. Come inside the shop: I've got a nice hot cup of tea, fresh made. You look as though you can do with one.'

It was just what Becky needed. Her mouth felt as though she had been eating dry sand. She followed Rose Cottle inside the dollyshop.

'Sit down and take the weight off your feet.'

Rose Cottle knocked a mangy-looking cat with ragged ears from a chair. Taken by surprise, it crashed heavily to the floor, registering an indignant protest. The dollyshop-owner's response was to hook her toe beneath the animal and send it on its way to the door, at the same time saying to Becky: 'Another of me strays. Animal or human, they all find their way to Rose Cottle. I'm a soft touch, dearie. My husband always used to say: "You'll never be a rich woman,

Rose. Never have a penny, you won't, 'cos you're all heart." I don't mind. We're on this earth to help one another, I say. Ain't that the truth, Becky?'

The tea was stewed and barely warm, but it was wet and sweet. Swallowing a large mouthful, Becky nodded. 'Is your husband still alive?'

'Him? No, he was dead before you was born, I dare say. They strung him up outside the New Gaol, down in Cumberland Road. Drew as big a crowd as any of the rioters. There was hardly room to move between the river and the gaol that day.'

Becky looked at Rose Cottle open-mouthed. 'He was hung? What had he done?'

'He'd done *nothing*, dearie. Nothing at all – and I should know. I lived with him long enough. He'd barely got enough "go" in him to get out of bed for his dinner. But they said he'd been waylaying gentlemen riding into Bristol, down Stokes Croft. He was still swearing his innocence when they gave him the drop and he was just as dead as if he'd owned up and told me what he'd done with all the goods he'd pinched. Talking about menfolk, them's a fancy pair of "runners" you're wearing. Did that gentleman of yours buy 'em for you?'

The sudden tightening of Becky's expression confirmed the dollyshop-owner's suspicions. Becky was once more fending for herself.

'I got the shoes myself.'

'That's best, dearie. Look after yourself and you're beholden to no one. I says it all the time to the young girls who come to me for advice when they're in trouble. I've always got a spare bed for them as needs it. Nice little room it is, too. Small enough to feel cosy, but large enough to entertain a gent if you need to earn a shilling or two. It would just suit you.'

'I don't entertain no gentlemen.'

'I never thought for one minute you did, dearie. I was just letting you know as how I'm broad-minded about such things, that's all. A girl needs to earn a living the best way she knows how, these days. Times are 'ard and no mistake – and there's worse ways of earning money. I should know; I've tried 'em all! Have a look at the room, dearie. You'll like it; I just know you will.'

'I've got no money to pay for a room, but thanks for the tea.' Becky stood up to leave.

'Who's asking for money? Have you heard me so much as mention *money*?'

Looking about her quickly, as though someone else might have crept into the room without being observed, Rose Cottle leaned towards Becky and dropped her voice. 'As a matter of fact I was hoping you would take the room in return for a little favour.'

'What sort of favour?' Becky viewed the offer with suspicion, but the dollyshop-owner chose not to notice.

'All the girls around here aren't as trustworthy or high-minded as yourself. They come begging me to let 'em have nice clothes to catch the eye of young dandies in the arcades. Of course, I can't loan 'em such fineries for nothing now, can I? So, to make sure I get my money and the return of my clothes, I make 'em bring the young gents back 'ere. It's only fair, I'm sure you'll be the first to agree. But some of the girls are *greedy*. They're taking men to *other* places, then coming back telling me business is bad and they've had no customers at all. It's not the money I'm concerned about, you understand. But one of these days a girl will meet a careless young man who has a purse full of gold. He'll lose his money, and I'll never see her or my clothes again.'

'What could *I* do to stop it happening?'

'Follow the girls around for me. Make sure they don't take their young gents off somewhere else. You'll be doing us *both* a favour, really. Stopping them from getting into trouble, and looking after my interests at the same time.'

'That's all I'd need do to have a room of my own? Nothing else?'

'Nothing at all, dearie. Of course, if you wished to do some "business" yourself, start earning money, I'd expect you to pay me *some* rent. That's only fair.'

Rose Cottle's wheedling manner was not in keeping with what Becky knew of her character, but she could see very little wrong with such an arrangement. The opportunity to sleep with a roof over her head – in her *own* room – appealed to her.

'Show me the room.'

'Of course. You'll love it, I know. It's one of the best rooms in the house.'

The room was somewhat less than the dollyshop-owner had claimed. Tucked beneath the eaves at the back of the house there was no ceiling between the occupant and the tiles of the roof, and Becky had room to stand upright only within an area an arm's length from the door. She would have rats for company, too. One scampered across the room as Becky entered with Rose Cottle, but rats were nothing new to her. Rats and mice abounded in the gutters and doorways of the narrow streets outside. The room was dirty and had no window, but it had a mattress, a table and chair, and a fireplace – and Becky would not be sharing it with *anyone*. It was undreamed-of luxury.

'Well, dearie, what do you think?'

Becky nodded. 'All right, I'll come and live here.'

'Good! First time I clapped eyes on you I knew you had a wise head on your shoulders.'

For just a moment Becky wondered why Rose Cottle was so pleased, when it was the dollyshop-owner who was doing *her* a great favour.

'When do you want me to start watching the girls who borrow your clothes?'

'This evening. Young Maude Garrett will be along here for certain. Always works the arcades on a Tuesday. Spends all her money over the weekend, I expect. Mind you, she's working most other evenings as well, these days. But you settle in, dearie. Make yourself at home. I'll call you when I want you.'

Becky's call came at seven o'clock that evening, when her stomach was complaining noisily about being empty. Rose Cottle came swiftly and quietly to the small room. 'Maude Garrett's downstairs now, getting dressed. Go outside and wait for her to come out, then follow her – and don't lose her.'

Becky had never seen Maude Garrett before. Had Rose

Cottle not come to the doorway of the dollyshop and gesti-culated wildly in the girl's direction, Becky would never have taken her to be a part-time prostitute. Dressed in a ground-length gingham dress, with a light shawl draped just off her bare shoulders, and a demure poke-bonnet covering her mousy-coloured hair, Maude Garrett could have passed her-self off anywhere as a respectable middle-class girl.

Others were not so easily misled. Maude Garrett had saun-tered half the length of Bristol's upper arcade, not far from the dollyshop when a smartly dressed young man stopped and engaged her in conversation. Minutes later the couple were returning to Rose Cottle's establishment.

Fifty minutes later Maude Garrett 'hooked' another client in exactly the same spot. Once more they returned to a room above Rose Cottle's dollyshop.

On this occasion Maude Garrett did not emerge from the dollyshop until some twenty minutes after her client had departed. By now it was growing dark. Gas-lamps in the arcade were spilling their yellow hissing light on the pave-ments below, while in the shadows high up in the glass roof pigeons ruffled their feathers and cooed softly as they settled down for the night.

Maude Garrett found her next man in the lower of the two arcades. An older man this time, there was some discussion before Molly nodded her head and led the man away. But she did not take him in the St James direction. Instead, she took him to Broadmead, at the other end of the arcades. At a door beside a shuttered ironmonger's shop she paused, glancing along the street in both directions before ushering the man inside and closing the door behind them.

The young 'dollymop' catered for the needs of her latest client with astonishing speed. No more than fifteen minutes after taking him to the rooms above the ironmonger's shop Maude Garrett was back in the street. The man seemed dis-gruntled, but Maude Garrett wasted no time placating him. Leaving him standing in the street, she returned to the gas-lit shelter of the arcades.

Twenty minutes later Maude Garrett was leading yet another man up the stairs of Rose Cottle's dollyshop.

When Becky followed the girl through the door, Rose Cottle came out of the room that served as her shop.

'Maude says there was a constable patrolling the arcades and she needed to stay out of his way for a while. Is she telling the truth?'

Becky shook her head, feeling strangely guilty about informing on the other girl. 'She took a man to a place in Broadmead. She wasn't there long, though.'

'Long enough for her to earn a couple of easy shillings, no doubt. I *thought* this was happening.'

'Do you want me to follow her again when she goes out?'

'No, dearie. You go up to bed now. Maude won't be bringing any more men back tonight.'

When Becky hesitated, Rose Cottle said sharply: 'Off you go. I'll deal with Maude Garrett. You've done your part.'

'I'm hungry. I've had nothing to eat since this morning.'

For a moment Rose Cottle's expression might have been one of triumph. 'I've provided you with a room and bed, dearie. You can't expect me to *feed* you as well. Food costs money, and we all have to work for that. I've told you, I don't mind what you do in your room. I'll even lend you nice clothes to wear when you go out – on the same generous terms as I've given Maude Garrett, her as is abusing my generosity.'

Becky shook her head, and Rose Cottle said hurriedly: 'You don't need to make up your mind straight away. But if you don't want to go hungry . . .!'

As Becky turned away the dollyshop-owner said quicky: 'I can't see a young girl go to bed with a complaining belly. There's a tasty stew cooking over the fire in the back room. Help yourself to what you want. Take as much as you can eat to your room; you could do with a bit of fattening up. Think about what I've said. When you're good and ready, I'll find some gentleman who'll treat you nice – and put a gold coin or two in both our purses. Don't you forget now.'

Carrying a bowl filled with stew up the stairs to her room, Becky *did* think of what the dollyshop-owner had said. She had no qualms about getting money in any other way, but for some reason she had always drawn the line at allowing some man to make use of her body. It was the one thing no one had ever been able to take from her. It was also something she could offer to Fergus that had never belonged to anyone else.

CHAPTER FIFTEEN

FERGUS FOLLOWED UP Tomas Casey's suggestion that he attend his Chartist meeting. As the Chartist leader had predicted, the Bristol police were there in great numbers. 'The Downs' were a wide expanse of meadow and scrub overlooking Bristol city, and the police travelled there in black-painted enclosed vans, parking them close to the meeting-place.

There were a great many Bristol residents here. Men and women from Lewin's Mead, St Pauls, the Dings, and the sprawling unadopted suburb of Bedminster. Some had come out of curiosity, others because they had nothing better to do with their time. Very few were fired with passionate Chartism.

There were many women and children among the crowd, too. Fergus hoped Becky might have found her way here, but he was disappointed. However, there were many faces to fill the pages of his sketchpad, and he was soon sketching away busily.

There were a number of Chartist speakers, but it quickly became evident that only Tomas Casey had the ability to rouse the crowd to great heights. The theme of his speech was that every male in the community should be afforded the dignity that was rightly his – the right to *vote*. Using this as a stepping-stone, he went on to declare that a *working*-man was worth ten of those who grew rich as the result of his labours.

There were few 'working'-men among Tomas Casey's listeners. Most were shiftless petty criminals from the slum districts of the city, but they all accepted that Tomas Casey was talking to *them* – even though fewer than half knew what he was talking *about*. What mattered was that Tomas Casey was a brilliant speaker with the ability to reach and hold the interest of every one of his listeners.

Fergus was so busy catching the mood of the crowd on the pages of his sketchpad that he hardly heard a word of the arguments being put forward by Tomas Casey and his fellow-Chartists. Even when large sections of the crowd began chanting an enthusiastic 'Yes! Yes!' he was recording their eager perspiring animation and did not pause to question *why* they were becoming so excited. Not until the word being chanted by the crowd had become 'Fight! Fight! *Fight!*' did realisation come to Fergus that serious trouble was about to erupt.

A loudly chanting section of the crowd formed ranks to confront some two hundred frock-coated police constables, each of whom was armed with a long hardwood night-stick. Many of those opposing the police carried similar weapons.

Fergus worked furiously to sketch the scene of policemen opposing Chartists, but events were already moving too fast for him.

The superintendent of police had been forced to listen to a series of inflammatory speeches, all castigating a government he supported, and espousing the aims of an organisation he personally despised. When Tomas Casey made the waiting constables the target for his wrath, calling them 'tools of an oppressive State, bent on suppressing the just aspirations of the working man', the superintendent had heard enough. He called on his men to break up the meeting and arrest the Chartist ringleaders.

Some of the crowd tried to flee from the advancing policemen but others, seemingly eager for the prospect of a fight with the forces of law and order, forced their way against the tide of retreating onlookers.

Still attempting to record the increasingly hectic scene on paper, Fergus stood his ground for as long as possible – and suddenly discovered he had left it too late to escape the imminent clash.

A stone curved through the air, knocking off a tall black

hat worn by one of the advancing policemen. An instant later their ponderous ordered advance became a charge, and Fergus found himself trapped in the midst of a shouting, brawling mêlée, unable to fight his way clear. As staves and truncheons thudded with increasing frequency upon heads and bodies, Fergus clutched his sketchpad to him and tried to force his way clear of the fighting.

It was not clear whether the blow that felled him came from police or Chartist, but it was both heavy and deliberate. It knocked him to the ground and sent the world reeling about him. Then he was swallowed up in a roaring black void that exploded outwards from his brain.

The loud and insistent ticking of a clock intruded upon Fergus's unconsciousness. The sound was alien to his ears, and it was some minutes before it could be identified by his scrambled mind.

Gradually Fergus became aware of other sounds. Street noises from somewhere in the distance, a faint clattering of pans – and voices. Soft low-talking voices.

Opening his eyes required great concentration. His eyelids were heavy and unresponsive. Eventually he was successful – and became more bewildered than before.

He was in bed in a large unfamiliar room. It must have been dark outside because there was a low-burning lamp somewhere near. He could see the dull indistinct circle it cast on the sculpted ceiling above him.

The voices sounded close, and Fergus turned his head. He immediately wished he had remained still. There was just time to see two indistinct figures standing in the doorway before a headache such as he had never known before forced him to screw up his eyes in pain. When he opened them again an unfamiliar woman was staring down at him. Her face registered approval, but before he could ask any of the questions that were beginning to come together in his brain she had gone.

He heard a door open, and a voice called loudly: 'Miss Tennant ... Miss Tennant! Come quickly. His eyes are open.'

There was the sound of hurrying feet, and then Fanny Tennant was leaning over the bed looking down at him.

'Praise the Lord! I was beginning to believe you would *never* regain consciousness. You haven't even *moved* for three days.'

Suddenly Fergus remembered. The Chartist meeting on the Downs. The fight. But how had he got here? Presumably he was in the Tennants' house? He wanted to ask so many questions, but only managed to croak: 'My sketchbook?'

Fanny Tennant smiled and picked something up from a bedside table. He was afraid to move his head to see what it was.

'Still the dedicated artist! It's here, safe and sound. Ivor Primrose said it would be the first thing you would ask for when you came round.'

That was another of Fergus's questions answered. Constable Ivor Primrose had brought him here. Fergus had glimpsed the large policeman standing head and shoulders above his colleagues when they were lined up on the Downs. But why had he been brought to *this* house?

As though reading his thoughts, Fanny Tennant explained: 'Ivor didn't know where else to take you. He couldn't return you to Lewin's Mead. It was fortunate for you he was near at hand when you were clubbed down. Without proper care I doubt if you'd be alive now.' She saw him wince. 'Does your head hurt?'

'Yes.'

It came out as a painful gasp. Talk of Lewin's Mead had reminded him of a great many other things. Becky. Suddenly his head hurt worse than before.

'The doctor said you would have a very bad headache when you regained consciousness. Your skull isn't fractured, but you received a severe blow and suffered concussion. He's left something for you to take. I think it's laudanum.'

Fergus detested laudanum. It reminded him of the pain-filled weeks spent waiting for his injured ankle to heal. But he was in no position to argue; his head felt as though it might burst at any moment.

Calling on the maid to help, Fanny Tennant raised Fergus

to a sitting position and spooned a large dose of laudanum down his throat.

Fergus sank back on the pillow gasping in pain, and Fanny Tennant was concerned. 'The laudanum should take effect soon. Try to rest and I'll send a maid to fetch the doctor. It isn't right that you should be in such pain.'

Most of her words were lost on Fergus, and by the time the doctor hurried into the room he had drifted off into an opium-induced sleep.

After checking Fergus's pulse and breathing, the doctor straightened up and smiled at Fanny Tennant. 'His heartbeat would shame a drayhorse, and he's breathing well. I don't think you need worry, Miss Tennant. Your young man will suffer headaches for a while, but I don't doubt he'll make a full recovery. He'll need rest, that's all. It will be at least a week before I'll even consider allowing him out of bed, but with such an attractive young nurse in attendance it should prove no hardship for him. If he doesn't enjoy your attentions, then perhaps I should look for brain damage!'

Later that same evening Alderman Aloysius Tennant tiptoed into the room where his daughter sat reading a book by lamplight as Fergus slept.

'How is your young invalid?'

'He hasn't moved since I gave him his medicine, but he's breathing easily. Dr Harrison says all he needs now is rest.'

'He can stay here until he's well.' Aloysius Tennant shifted his glance to the sleeping figure. 'I know you're smitten with this young man, Fanny, but how much do you know of him – apart from the fact that he's living in the worst slum in the city?'

Aloysius Tennant's question was not put in an unkindly way. A self-made man who had worked very hard to earn his fortune and a place in Bristol society, his concern was solely for his daughter's happiness. Father and daughter had been very close since the death of Fanny's mother, some years before.

'I'm not "smitten", as you put it, Father. Fergus is a very talented artist who is working hard to achieve an ambition. I *admire* him. He's also an asset to the ragged school. I want to see him well again.'

'You and that school.' Aloysius Tennant spoke in mock despair. 'Charitable works are all very well, Fanny, but you can't wed a good cause.'

'I'm not looking for a husband, Father. I've told you so, many times.'

'So you have.' Aloysius Tennant looked pointedly at Fergus. 'But perhaps one will turn up when you least expect him. I'm off to a meeting now. Don't stay up all night. I pay servants to perform such duties.'

'You're a fusspot, Father.' Fanny Tennant stood up. After straightening her father's cravat, she gave him a kiss. 'But I love you for caring. No man will ever take your place.'

'I doubt whether there's a father in the land who hasn't been told the same thing by his daughters – but I love you, too. I don't want to see you hurt.'

Fergus's recovery was marginally slower than the doctor had forecast. It was ten days before he could stand, or even sit up, without feeling that his head was about to explode.

However, Fergus discovered it was possible to work in a prone position and he managed to sketch each of the servants who attended to his needs. He even made a sketch of the cook. Brought grumbling from her kitchen, she left the sick-room delighted with the likeness she clutched in pudgy hands. Word soon went around the servants' quarters of the Clifton houses that Alderman Aloysius Tennant's sick guest was a genius.

During the evenings Fanny spent much time in Fergus's room, and he made many sketches of her – far more detailed than those he had made of the servants. They talked a great deal, too. At first much of the talk was of Becky. Fergus had hoped Fanny might have learned of her whereabouts, but as time went on it seemed Becky must have left the Lewin's Mead rookery.

Whenever Alderman Tennant visited the sickroom the talk turned to Chartism, a cause with which he had a great deal of sympathy. Many of those involved in the meeting on Durdham Downs had been arrested. Some had been summarily dealt with and sentenced to periods of imprisonment ranging from one to six months. Others, looked upon as instigators of the violence that had erupted at the meeting, had been remanded for trial at the forthcoming assizes. Search was still going on for other ringleaders – chief of whom was Tomas Casey.

Aloysius Tennant declared the Chartist leader would do well to flee to the remotest hills of his native Ireland. The British government was determined to stamp out Chartist violence. If he were found Tomas Casey would face charges of sedition – a capital offence.

'*Has* he left the country?' Fergus asked.

The Bristol alderman shrugged. 'I don't know, and I must confess I don't very much care. I'm a firm believer in the aims of Chartism, but I won't countenance violence. It certainly hasn't helped the cause. By stirring up trouble at his meetings Tomas Casey has hardened official attitudes and set back Chartism by years.'

'Father, if you continue talking politics you'll have Fergus's head spinning and set back *his* progress, too.'

'You're right, my dear, of course. Quite right. But I *do* want to talk to this young man about his future.'

'Then, I'll leave you to talk for a few minutes – but don't bombard Fergus with questions. His brain has taken a severe shaking. Dr Harrison says he needs rest and *quiet*.' Fanny put down the book she had been reading and left the room.

'My daughter is very fond of you, young man. I hope you're aware of this?'

'Fanny's a very warm and caring girl. The children in the ragged school think the world of her.'

Aloysius Tennant opened his mouth to tell Fergus he had missed the point of his statement, but he changed his mind. 'I'm proud of her work in Lewin's Mead, of course, but there's more to life than what Fanny sees as "her duty". To be perfectly honest, I'd like her to spend less time in that part of the city.'

'But she's doing wonderful work. The children *need* her.'

'They need *someone*, certainly. It doesn't have to be my daughter. Fanny's proved her point. The school is a success.

There's no reason at all why she can't pass the responsibility on to someone else now. She needs to look to her own future. Most young girls of her age are married by now – or heading in that direction. I don't want to see her left behind.'

Fergus was puzzled. Aloysius Tennant was an alderman and Unitarian churchman. He preached the equality of all men, yet Fergus doubted whether he was about to suggest he would approve of Fanny being courted by a penniless artist.

But Aloysius Tennant was a man of many surprises. 'As I say, she's *fond* of you. I don't want you getting foolish ideas because of it, but folks who should know tell me you've got an exceptional talent. I'm willing to put up money to give you a studio here in Clifton. I can guarantee you'll never be short of people coming to have their portraits painted. No doubt Fanny will want to see you get on and will spend more of her time helping *you*. Time spent with you will be time away from Lewin's Mead. Are you beginning to understand me now?'

Fergus's head had begun to ache again, but he nodded.

'I thought you would. You're no fool, Fergus. You've been around – and you've got a God-given talent. Use that talent well and it'll make you a rich man, like me. Then, if you and Fanny are of a mind to wed, you won't find me standing in your way.'

Fergus's head was throbbing painfully now, but he tried to word his reply carefully. 'I think you're underestimating Fanny's commitment to the ragged school. She's —'

Aloysius Tennant held up his hand in a peremptory gesture and silenced Fergus. 'I don't want you to give me a reply straight away. Your brain's still addled from the blow you took, and I can tell by looking at you that I've been talking too long. I don't doubt I'm in for a scolding from Fanny. But I've spoken my mind because that's my way. Think on what I've said. I've made you a generous offer. You'd be a fool to reject it out of hand.'

When Fanny entered the sickroom she saw from Fergus's expression that his headache had returned. Ushering her father unceremoniously from the room, she drew the curtains and ordered Fergus to sleep.

Fergus lay back on the pillows and tried to follow Fanny's instructions, but his mind kept returning to the offer made to him by her father. It was an opportunity that most young artists would have grasped eagerly, and yet . . . Fergus was still trying to make some sense of his thoughts when he fell asleep.

He woke suddenly, aware he was not alone in the room. Turning his head, he saw Fanny with a small lighted lamp in her hands looking guiltily at him from across the room. She was dressed for bed, a dressing gown over her nightdress.

'I woke you. I'm sorry. I was in bed when I remembered you had no light. I had instructed the maids not to come into your room for fear of disturbing you.' She shrugged apologetically. 'But that's exactly what *I've* done.'

Fergus struggled to a sitting position, his head temporarily free of pain. 'It's all right. I've had sleep enough to last me a lifetime since I was brought here.'

Fanny placed the low-burning lamp on a table and made a slight adjustment to the wick before turning back to Fergus. 'I am intrigued by the interest Father is taking in you. He refuses to tell me anything of your discussion, saying only that I'll know soon enough, once you have made up your mind.'

'He's offered to set me up in a studio, here in Clifton.'

Fanny's reaction was one of undisguised delight. 'That's wonderful! You'll accept his offer, of course.'

'He wants me to give the matter some thought. But I don't have to think about it. I have to remain in Lewin's Mead. For the time being at least.'

'Why? Father is offering you a wonderful opportunity. People from this part of Bristol would flock to you to have portraits painted once they saw your work.'

'Why don't *you* open a school in Clifton?'

'That's different. There's a great need for a school such as ours in Lewin's Mead.'

'There's also a great need to record the lives of the people forced to exist in such a place. To sketch them in their rags amidst the filth of their surroundings. To show the conditions in which they are forced to live by their appalling poverty.

Their work, their homes. . . . There are millions of people in the land – many right here in Clifton – who are blissfully unaware of conditions in the slums of our cities.'

'Do you think all these sketches of yours can shake the foundations of our society?'

'Ah! Now, that's where I *would* appreciate your father's help. I'll need a gallery to put my paintings on exhibition when they're completed. We might even have some of the sketches published in a magazine. Run a series, perhaps.'

'And in the meantime you'll continue to live in Lewin's Mead?'

'I must. If my sketches and paintings are to have any authority at all, I need to be on the spot to record life as it's lived there. The residents of the rookery won't come to Clifton to pose for their portraits.'

'Is that your only reason for returning to Lewin's Mead? Or does it have something to do with a young ragamuffin named Becky?' For just a moment in the dim light cast by the small lamp, Fanny Tennant looked strangely vulnerable.

'I shall continue looking for Becky, yes. But my plans were laid before I ever set foot in Bristol.'

'Then, I hope you'll soon be well enough to succeed in your crusade – if not in your quest. Good night, Fergus.'

He wanted to tell her once again that Becky was no more to him than a young orphan he had befriended, but Fanny had gone from the room before he could even respond to her 'Good night'.

CHAPTER SIXTEEN

BECKY HAD LITTLE WORK TO DO for Rose Cottle during the next few days. One evening she followed a thin nervous young woman who borrowed clothes from the dollyshop but she brought only two 'clients' to the premises before changing back into her old clothes and hurrying off into the night.

When Becky commented on the woman's brief foray into the world of the 'dollymop', Rose Cottle shrugged. 'You'll see many like her, dearie. Her husband's out of work and she's two babies to feed. Brought up a strict moral Wesleyan, she was. But morals don't fill hungry bellies.'

Maude Garrett was absent from the dollyshop for five days, and Becky received a shock when she saw the young prostitute's face. Maude Garrett had taken a beating. The skin around one of her eyes was bruised, and a cut ran half the length of her lower lip.

When Maude Garrett left the dollyshop Becky followed at a discreet distance. Maude Garrett turned into the higher arcade, and Becky gave her a few moments' lead before she, too, turned into the arcade — and stopped in disbelief. The young part-time prostitute was nowhere to be seen! She could not have reached the far end of the arcade during the brief time she had been out of sight; but Becky had been daydreaming, more time might have passed than she thought. . . .

Becky began to run, but suddenly a foot was thrust out from a doorway and she measured her length on the hard stone paving.

Becky looked up to see an angry Maude Garrett glowering down at her.

'You bloody little nark! I ought to kick the stuffing out of you, just like Alfie Skewes did to me. How much is Rose Cottle paying you to follow me around? Or are you hoping to take my place? You're welcome to, any time Rose says so.'

'She's not paying me anything. I owe her a favour.'

'A *favour*? Rose Cottle don't do *favours*. She'd stop breathing if she thought there was a penny to be made from doing it. She did me a "favour" once; now I have to stay on the game to pay her off. She'll have you doing the same before you've finished saying "Thank you". What's she done for you so far – given you a cheap dress or something?'

'She's let me have a room.'

'Where? Above the dollyshop? God! I didn't know girls as green as you could still be found around Lewin's Mead. You're living in a knocking shop. Rose Cottle can do what she likes with you while you're there. Complain to a constable and he'll laugh his trousers off when you give him your address. The best thing you can do is run back to where you came from and keep well clear of Rose Cottle until she's forgotten what you look like.'

'Leaving you free to take men off somewhere else and tell Rose Cottle business is bad, I suppose?' On her feet again, Becky brushed grit from a grazed knee and looked at Maude Garrett sceptically.

'Do you think I *enjoy* what I'm doing? Having some slobbering man use me as though I'm a hired horse he's determined to get his money's worth from? You think I enjoy *that*? All right, so I sometimes take men to my own home to earn a few extra shillings. One day I might earn enough to get Rose Cottle off my back.'

Suddenly Maude Garrett's shoulders sagged. 'No, I'll never be free of her. Rose Cottle will keep her claws in me until I'm so poxed I'll be letting Lascars have me against an alley wall for the price of a drink. She'll do the same for you unless you get out now.'

When Becky made no reply, Maude Garrett shook her head. 'You'll learn the hard way, won't you? All right, come with me and see why *I'm* doing it.'

Without waiting for a reply Maude Garrett turned and walked away towards Broadmead. After a moment's hesitation Becky followed.

At the door beside the ironmonger's shop Maude Garrett paused. 'If we meet my pa inside, I'll say we've come from work to pick up something I left behind. You'll back me up, you understand?'

Becky did not understand, but she nodded.

The stairway inside the door smelt of dampness, and with the door closed it was dark, but Becky could hear her companion making her way up a flight of creaking uncarpeted stairs and she cautiously followed after her.

There was another door at the top of the stairs. When it opened it allowed dim light to show peeling paintwork and stained walls. It also released a confusion of noises and unwholesome smells.

A girl's voice, pitched low, spoke from somewhere beyond the doorway, and Maude Garrett replied: 'I've brought someone with me. It's all right, it's a friend. Is Pa home yet?'

'He was, but not for long. He said he was going out to look for work.'

'That means he'll come home drunk again tonight. Make sure Phoebe isn't crying when he comes in. He'll kill her if he gives her another beating. Is she any better?'

'She's been asleep most of the day. The only way we know she's awake is when she starts whimpering.'

There was a cry from somewhere behind the speaker. As Becky stepped inside the room Maude Garrett was overwhelmed by a deluge of children, their ages ranging from about two to fourteen. It was impossible to count them with any accuracy, but Becky put their number somewhere in the region of eight.

Turning to Becky, Maude Garrett said: 'These are my brothers and sisters. Lisa's the oldest and Victoria the youngest. She's two this week, I believe.'

'Where's your ma?'

'She died when Victoria was born.' Maude Garrett feigned indifference. 'We manage all right most of the time – except when Pa's on one of his drunks. They seem to be lasting longer lately. The last one went on for a month and cost him his job.'

'This one's gone on for three weeks and looks like lasting another three!' The information was volunteered by one of the small girls.

Maude Garrett spoke to Becky again. 'I hold down a job making pasteboard boxes during the day. The money doesn't go far among nine of us – and Pa. Lisa knows how I make a bit of extra money. She'll do the same when she's a bit older – but not for Rose Cottle.'

Shaking off the children who were clinging to her, Maude Garrett said: 'Talking of Rose Cottle . . . If we don't get back to her place with a client soon, she'll have her ferrets out for both of us.'

'I'll tell her there were a couple of constables in the arcades.'

Maude Garrett gave Becky a triumphant smile. 'No, you won't. You'll save that excuse for a night when I can make money out of it – I'll see you have a cut, too. But we'd better be off now. Take care of Phoebe, Lisa. If I manage to bring someone home tonight, I'll give you a couple of coppers to get something for her from the stall down the road.'

For four nights Maude Garrett took two clients a night to the crowded flat above the ironmonger's shop in Broadmead. On the fifth night she took only one there before returning with the next to the St James dollyshop.

When Becky came in after her, Maude had gone upstairs and Rose Cottle called Becky into the shop. 'Maude's been slow off the mark tonight.'

Becky shrugged. 'It's the constables. There must have been a new bunch started this week. They're being shown around Broadmead. It was half an hour before Maude dared poke her nose into the lower arcade. They'd have had her in Bridewell for sure.'

'Is that so? If that's the way it is, there's not much sense you following her around all night, dearie. Go upstairs and have an early night. You look as though you could do with a good night's sleep.'

Surprised, but grateful, Becky made her way upstairs and went to bed. She lay beneath the single threadbare blanket and thought about Fergus. She had seen Ida Stokes that day. The Back Lane landlady had told her Fergus had not been seen for some time. Ida Stokes also volunteered the information that his rent was paid up until the end of the month, so what he did and where he went were his own business.

Becky thought that if Fergus was not at the house in Back Lane, then Fanny Tennant would probably know where he was. The thought stirred an unusual emotion inside Becky. Had she been able to put a name to it, she would have called it jealousy, but Becky was aware only that it left her feeling empty and very unhappy.

Becky heard Maude Garrett go downstairs and leave the house with her departing client, then she closed her eyes drowsily. Tomorrow she would return to Fergus's room and see if she could find a clue to his whereabouts. Perhaps he was searching for her! The thought warmed Becky. It was time she made it up with him. She missed him. She must accept that Fergus did not look at things in the same way as other residents of Lewin's Mead and try to understand him. Perhaps ask him to help her. . . .

Becky came awake with a start. Some unusual sound had woken her. Then she saw that the door of her room was open and someone was standing in the doorway. She could see it was a man, and for a moment her heart leaped.

'Fergus. . . . Is that you?' Could he possibly have traced her here? To Rose Cottle's dollyshop? Then the unidentified man gave a chuckle, and Becky's hope became fear.

'I ain't no "Fergus", me dear. I don't even know who he be. But I promise you'll know as much about me, come morning, as you do of this Fergus.'

To her horror, Becky recognised the voice of Joe Skewes.

There was an echoing chuckle from another man, already in the room, and Becky sat up, deadly afraid as the man in the doorway entered the room and Rose Cottle's bulk took his place.

'I'm disappointed in you, dearie. You've cheated on me, just like Maude. Betrayed my trust in you. I gave you a good room, out of the goodness of me heart, in return for a small favour, and what happened? I'll tell you — you took advantage of my easy-going nature, that's what you did. Well, it's time you began to earn your keep. You're lucky tonight because I've found two old friends as your first clients. Treat 'em nicely, mind, or I'll be looking for men for you from that American ship that's just come up-river. Word has it that it's been slave-trading along the African coast. The men on there will know how to beat bad ways out of a young girl. They're more used to black girls, o' course, but I don't expect there's too much difference. Not in the dark there ain't, anyway.'

'There won't be no need for that, Rose. Me and Alfie know how to persuade a young girl to behave the way she should. We'll enjoy teaching this one. Alfie would tell you so himself, but he hasn't been much of a one for talking since that madwoman in the Bridewell cells choked him with her chain. You can close the door now, Rose; me and Alfie are used to working in dark places in coal-ships. We'll enjoy this more, I'll wager. Close the door now.'

Becky made a sudden bolt for the doorway. She reached it, but got no farther. A foot came out to trip her and then she was picked up bodily and carried back to the mattress. She fought for all she was worth, using fists, feet, nails and teeth, but she could not match the combined strength of the two coal-heavers. When her dress had been ripped from her body she escaped and made it to the door once again, but she was caught before she could lift the latch.

Maude Garrett heard Becky's cries when she came up the stairs with a client who was too drunk to take any notice of the noise in the room. Maude paused long enough to hear the sound of someone being slapped inside the small room, then her client pushed her ahead of him, grumbling at her tardiness.

By the time Maude left the dollyshop the only sound coming from Becky's room was indistinct low-voiced talking.

Rose Cottle was standing on the pavement outside the shop, and in a sudden burst of anger Maude Garrett said: 'Are things so bad you're having young girls raped to earn a living for you now?'

Rose Cottle's eyebrows rose very slightly. 'Oh, found some spirit at last, have we, dearie? I should save it for your clients, if I was you, they'll get a pleasant surprise – and I don't care for that word "rape". She's paying her rent, that's all. Just paying the rent. I'll have yours while we're about it, and if you don't watch your tongue you'll find the cost of renting a decent dress and a room is likely to go up. Come to think of it, I believe *you're* due another reminder that it don't pay to cheat Rose Cottle. . . .'

Becky was subjected to abuse and humiliation until the early hours of the morning, by which time her mind was registering the nightmare experience from a distance far removed from the sordid little room above Rose Cottle's St James dollyshop.

When both men left the sloping-roofed room, well pleased with their night's 'work', Becky rose to her hands and knees and crawled painfully to the door after them, only to find it securely locked. She collapsed sideways against the door-frame and rested her cheek against the door, painfully aware that Joe Skewes and his son had made free use of their fists in subduing her.

Crouching with her head against the closed door, Becky heard the sound of footsteps passing by outside. After the sound of whispered words, heavy footsteps moved away and Becky heard the stairs creaking beneath the weight of a man.

Suddenly there came a gentle tapping at the door. Fearing it was one of the Skewes men again, Becky sucked in a terrified breath and backed away.

The tapping was repeated, and this time a voice whispered urgently: 'Becky? Are you there?'

It was Maude Garrett.

'Can you open the door? It seems to be locked from the outside.'

Becky could hear Maude Garrett fumbling in the dark passageway, and then her voice whispered: 'Rose Cottle must have the key. There's no bolt or anything. I heard what was happening. Was it because you hadn't told on me?'

'Yes. I've got to get out of here. Can you help me?'

'How? Is there someone I can tell?'

Becky thought immediately of Fergus, but she could not tell *him* what had happened to her, even if he *had* returned to Lewin's Mead. She rested her forehead against the door and felt the hopelessness of her situation.

'Becky! Can you hear me? I can't stay here much longer.'

'Get word to Irish Molly. In Ida Stokes's house, in Back Lane.'

'Where's Back Lane?'

A wave of total despair swept over Becky. She had realised that by sending word to Irish Molly she was merely hoping that in a roundabout way she might bring Fergus to her aid.

There was silence outside the room, and a few minutes later Becky heard Maude Garrett's footsteps going away along the passageway and down the stairs.

CHAPTER SEVENTEEN

BECKY NURSED DESPAIR and an aching body all that day. By nightfall ravenous hunger added to her other problems.

When the sounds and movements in the passageway outside the room told her the evening activities were beginning in Rose Cottle's dollyshop, Becky crawled back beneath the sloping roof and waited for what she knew was in store for her.

She recognised many of the voices she heard passing by the room. Most belonged to older women who paid only for the temporary rent of a room, too worldly-wise to fall into Rose Cottle's dollyshop trap.

It must have been mid-evening before there was a knock at the door. Her heart beating faster, Becky crouched in the corner of the room farthest from the door and said nothing. The knock was repeated, and then Rose Cottle's voice came to her: 'I know you can hear me, dearie. It'll do you no good pretending you can't.' When Becky maintained her silence Rose Cottle adopted a wheedling tone. 'I've got food here for you. Bacon pie and taters. All you need do is show a bit of common sense. We can make a lot of money, you and me. You'll not find me greedy. Fair payment's all I'll ask for. No more, and no less. What do you say now, dearie?'

Becky wanted to shout defiance at the unscrupulous old procuress, but she remained silent, her fiercely clenched fists the only indication of the effort it cost her.

'All right, you please yourself. You'll come round to my way of thinking soon enough. Then it'll be "Yes, please,

Rose", and "No, thank 'ee, Rose". I've seen it all before. Girls like you come two a penny in Lewin's Mead, and without someone like me you'll never be worth anything more. Your friends Joe and Alfie Skewes'll be back soon to help you change your mind. I'll have words with Joe — tell him not to be so nice to you tonight.'

When Rose Cottle had gone away muttering angrily to herself, Becky looked about her in utter desperation. The thought of being subjected to another night's ordeal at the hands of the two coal-heavers filled her with terror. Joe Skewes and his son would not have her again. She would stop them somehow.

But it was as though Rose Cottle had deliberately furnished the room with the imprisonment of young girls in mind. There was nothing Becky could use in her defence. There was no ceiling in the room, only rough wood rafters to which the slates of the roof were nailed. As she turned around, Becky grazed her arm on one of the rafters — and then she saw the very thing she was seeking.

A number of slates on the roof were cracked or broken, and Becky suddenly saw a piece of broken slate about ten inches long and shaped like a dagger. It was low down where the roof touched the floor but, by lying flat and stretching out, Becky was able to work the piece of slate free.

When she finally held it in her hands, Becky felt elated. Her hope was that the two Skewes men would not return to the house — but, if they did, she was determined they would not use her again.

Becky must have dozed off for a couple of minutes before a sound from outside brought her awake with a start. She had no way of knowing what time it was, but light still showed through the gaps in the roof tiles.

When a key turned in the lock Becky gripped the piece of pointed tile tightly in her hands. Then the door opened, and Joe and Alfie Skewes entered the room. Behind them the ample figure of Rose Cottle blocked the doorway.

'Hello, me young beauty. Are you pleased to see us again, eh?'

When Becky made no reply, Joe Skewes turned to his grinning son. 'Where's that bottle you brought with you, Alfie? Offer the girl a drop of "blue ruin". That'll cheer her up. Rose says she's had no food or drink all day.'

Alfie Skewes pulled a bottle of cheap gin from a pocket of the jacket slung over his arm. Drawing the cork with his teeth, he held the bottle out towards Becky.

When she made no move to take it, Joe Skewes sighed, but his expression gave the lie to any implied sympathy. Calling over his shoulder, he said: 'She's a stubborn girl, Rose. You're right, Alfie and me must have been too gentle with her. Tonight we'll give her the full benefit of our experience. She'll be a different girl in the morning, I promise you. Away you go now; me and Alfie have "work" to do. . . .'

Becky knew she had to make her bid for freedom now. As Joe Skewes's hand reached towards her she lashed out with the slate 'knife'.

Joe Skewes let out a howl of pain and snatched his hand back, blood spurting from a gash that extended from wrist to knuckle.

Seizing her opportunity, Becky ran for the door, to find Alfie Skewes barring the way – and he was grinning at her.

Becky struck out at him with blind ferocity, her mind filled with the thought of escape. The piece of slate snapped off in her hand and she let out a scream of tormented frustration that filled the small room.

The sound remained after Becky's mouth snapped shut, and it was coming from Alfie Skewes now. He stood in the doorway with both hands clutched to his stomach, but already blood was staining a larger area of dirty shirt-front than two hands could cover. For a brief moment his hoarse screaming ceased as he took a hand away from his midriff and held it up close to his face. Seeing the blood, he began a hoarse shrieking again, and this time the sound conveyed terror as well as pain.

Rose Cottle, unable to see what was happening, entered the room and collided heavily with the wounded man. Before either could recover Becky was through the open doorway and running for her life.

She hurtled down the dark staircase, tumbling down the

last few stairs. Scrambling to her feet, she fled along the ground-floor passageway — only to be caught up in a pair of strong arms as a number of men rushed past her into the house.

Arms and legs flailing wildly, Becky was lifted clear of the ground. As she struggled and shrieked abuse a voice said: 'Well, now, I do believe we've found what we came looking for.'

It was Constable Ivor Primrose.

From the moment she dragged herself out of bed in the morning until she folded and glued the corners of the last pasteboard box in the sweatshop where she worked, Maude Garrett wrestled with her conscience.

Common sense told her it would be foolish to involve herself with the happenings at Rose Cottle's dollyshop. After all, Becky's 'spying' had resulted in a beating for *her*. On the other hand, Becky was in trouble now for turning a blind eye to Maude's more recent untallied clients. The arguments for and against raged in her mind all day.

Maude Garrett was still undecided as she made her way homewards that evening and found a crowd blocking a narrow road not far from the backstreet pasteboard-box factory. Pushing her way through, Maude Garrett came to where a knot of men were gathered about a brewer's dray. They were trying to lift the heavy wagon in order to extricate a small child whose leg had somehow become trapped between the heavy iron-bound wheel and a leather-faced brake-block. The child must have been trapped for some time, because her screams of pain had died away to a low despairing moan. The moaning reminded Maude Garrett of the sound she had heard through the door of the room above Rose Cottle's dollyshop.

Turning away from the wagon, Maude Garrett hurried away, heading for the narrow alleyways of Lewin's Mead.

When Irish Molly heard the urgent knocking at her door she was at first too frightened to answer. No client would knock that way unless he was drunk, and she did not encourage men to come looking for her here. She preferred to find *them* and bring them back to the house. Besides, there was already a man in her room. He was not a client, and Irish Molly feared the police had come for *him*.

The knocking was repeated, louder this time, and Irish Molly resigned herself to opening the door. If it was the police, they would break the door down and come in anyway. If it wasn't, it did not matter. However, it would be foolish not to take elementary precautions.

Waving the man to a place where he could not be seen from the doorway, Irish Molly called: 'Who is it?'

'You don't know me. . . .' At the sound of the voice, Irish Molly sagged in relief. It was a woman. 'I'm looking for Irish Molly with news of Becky. She's in trouble.'

Irish Molly threw open the door and saw Maude Garrett standing outside looking about her nervously. 'What sort of trouble? Where is she?'

'Can I come inside and talk?' Maude Garrett's glance went to where two Irish children from the O'Ryan room hung over the flimsy banisters looking down at them.

'You cannot. Whatever you have to say can be said as well out here as inside.' Jerking her head in the direction of the children, she said: 'You need take no notice of them. They don't understand a word of English.'

In spite of Irish Molly's assurance, Maude Garrett pitched her voice too low for the children to hear and told the older woman a somewhat garbled story of Becky's plight.

'What does she expect me to do?' Irish Molly asked the question angrily. 'If I go to Rose Cottle, she'll laugh in my face – and I can't go to the police, Becky knows that.'

'All I know is that you're Becky's only hope and it was your name she mentioned.'

Irish Molly knew well why Becky had got word to her, Becky was hoping she would send Fergus to her aid. It might have worked – had she known where to find the artist.

'Damn the girl! She should have more sense than to get herself in a mess like this. Will you be going to Rose Cottle's tonight?'

Maude Garrett nodded.

'Then, tell Becky not to do anything foolish. I'll get help somehow.'

Maude Garrett's immediate relief made Irish Molly realise this girl was herself not very much older than Becky. It was a disquieting thought. Irish Molly was only twenty-six years of age, yet she felt old and weary when confronted by Maude Garrett.

When the young 'dollymop' had gone, Irish Molly closed the door behind her and tried to marshal her thoughts. She had promised to help Becky, but where did she begin . . .?

'What was all that about?'

The voice, carrying the same accent as her own, momentarily startled Irish Molly. Thinking about Becky's problems, she had forgotten that this man, too, was in desperate trouble. Her 'lodger' was Tomas Casey, the hunted Chartist leader. Seeking temporary refuge in Lewin's Mead after the fight on Durdham Downs, he had come to Back Lane hoping to find Fergus. Hearing Irish Molly's accent, he had sought her help instead. It had not been difficult to persuade her to give him temporary sanctuary. Tomas Casey was an attractive and very persuasive man.

Irish Molly looked harassed. 'It's a young girl . . . a child, and she needs help. I know of only one person who can do anything. You stay here and read one of those books I got for you. I'm going to the ragged school to talk to Miss Tennant.'

CHAPTER EIGHTEEN

FANNY TENNANT was not one to hesitate when a situation called for prompt action. Within an hour of Irish Molly's visit to the ragged school a hurriedly assembled force of half a dozen uniformed constables led by the station inspector was on its way from the Bridewell police station to Rose Cottle's dollyshop.

Despite the inspector's protest that no genteel young lady should set foot inside a house frequented by the type of women he expected to find there, Fanny insisted upon accompanying the constables to the St James dollyshop.

She got no farther than the front door before Constable Primrose emerged holding the struggling Becky out in front of him as though she were a disgraced puppy.

Depositing his struggling burden on the pavement in front of Fanny, the tall constable retained a tight grip on her. 'I think this is what we came looking for, Miss Tennant.'

As though aware of her surroundings for the first time, Becky ceased struggling and looked up at Fanny before transferring her attention to the cobblestones beneath her feet, but she was unable to control her trembling.

Taking in Becky's wild-eyed expression, bruised face, and torn and dishevelled dress, Fanny spoke sympathetically: 'Shall I ask a doctor to come and see you, Becky?'

When Becky made no reply, Ivor Primrose shook her gently. 'It's thanks to Miss Tennant that we're here at all. You owe her – and the police – an explanation.'

'I didn't ask no one to fetch *you*. Neither of you.' Still held fast in Ivor Primrose's grip, Becky rounded on him. 'I don't want your help. All I want is to go home.'

'*What* home, Becky? Fergus said you'd run off. He searched for you for days.'

'What business is it of his? I don't have to ask him before I do anything.'

Fanny's nod conceded acceptance of the strength of Becky's argument. 'True ... but it might have helped his recovery had he not been so worried about you.'

'Recovery ...?' For a moment Becky forgot all her own troubles. 'What's wrong with him?'

'He received a blow on the head at a Chartist meeting. It would have had far more serious consequences had Constable Primrose not brought him to my house. Fergus is conscious now and will be up and about before long – but at this moment I'm far more concerned about you. What *has* been going on here?'

Becky only half-heard Fanny's words. Fergus was living under the same roof as Fanny Tennant! She remained silent.

The police inspector came from the house and paused to have a few words with a constable standing at the door. The policeman hurried away, and the grim-faced inspector came to where Fanny Tennant stood with Becky and Ivor Primrose. His first words were directed at Becky.

'I've some questions to put to you, young lady. There's a badly wounded man in a room upstairs. Likely as not he'll be dead before morning. What do you know about it?'

Becky stared silent defiance at the police inspector, and Fanny asked: 'What makes you think Becky can help you?'

'The wounded man is lying in the room where we expected to find her. He's been stabbed in the stomach. He's a nasty piece of work named Alfie Skewes, and I don't doubt he deserves all he's got – but that's not my business. I've sent for a doctor. If Skewes dies I'll need to know the truth of how he came by his wound.'

'Ask his old man – or Rose Cottle. They were both there.'

'I shall have words with them in due course. There's enough evidence inside the house to charge Rose Cottle with running a brothel, and Joe Skewes was a bit too free with his fists when my men entered the room, so I'll no doubt be charging him, too. But you'd better come to the station, young lady. There's a fair bit of explaining to be done.'

'You're not taking this child to the Bridewell,' Fanny said indignantly. 'I didn't ask for your assistance in order to have her locked in a cell. I'll arrange for her to be taken to Miss Carpenter's reformatory at Kingswood. You can question here there — but only if it is absolutely necessary.'

'It *is*. If Alfie Skewes dies, I'll need to question her in some detail.'

'She'll be better able to speak after a few nights in decent surroundings. I have told you where she'll be, Inspector. I would be grateful to have Constable Primrose accompany me. On the way I will try to learn more of what has happened here.'

It was doubtful whether the inspector would have allowed anyone else to dictate to him in such a manner, but he had been a member of the Bristol police since its inception in 1836. Long experience had taught him the dangers of arguing with close relatives of those in authority over him. He agreed that Fanny might take Becky to the Kingswood reformatory.

It was about four miles to Kingswood, and Becky and her companions travelled there in a hansom cab. Seated in the cramped interior, Fanny explained to Becky about the 'reformatory'. At the moment it was part of an experiment in the treatment of juvenile criminals. Magistrates possessed no powers to commit young people here, but many young offenders *were* being sent here with the permission of a parent or guardian.

When Becky indignantly reminded Fanny that she had done nothing wrong, Ivor Primrose said quietly: 'There's a man lying seriously wounded in Rose Cottle's dollyshop, Becky. He might well die. Inspector Treblett would be within his rights to put you in the Bridewell until he discovered what happened back there. I'd listen very carefully to what Miss Tennant has to say, if I were you.'

'Perhaps one day someone will listen to what *I* have to say.' Becky spoke with great bitterness.

'If you have something to tell me, I'll be happy to listen.

According to Miss Tennant's information, you were being held in Rose Cottle's house against your will. Is this so?'

When Becky fell silent again, Fanny said sharply: 'You must help the police in every way you can, Becky. Fergus would say the same. He *will* tell you so as soon as he's well enough to come and see you.'

'I don't want to see him!' Becky's cry startled the others, and the tortured expression on her face told Fanny that no one else would ever know what had occurred in the locked room above Rose Cottle's dollyshop. Whatever it was, Becky would not be ready to face Fergus until the memory had receded into the farthermost recesses of her mind.

Changing the subject, Fanny told Becky what she would find at the experimental 'reformatory' at Kingswood.

Becky said nothing more until they had almost reached Kingswood. Then, in a more subdued voice, she asked: 'If I stay here, it will be because *I've* said I'll stay? Not because I've been sent here like the others?'

'That's right, Becky. But there will have to be a written agreement that you'll remain for as long as it's thought necessary. You'll need to put your signature to such an agreement.'

'Will it say on this paper that I've done nothing wrong?'

Fanny looked at Constable Primrose for an answer, and he pursed his lips thoughtfully before giving Becky a reply.

'We'll word it to say you're in the reformatory because you're in need of care and protection. I think a magistrate will agree to that.'

Becky thought very hard. 'Will they teach me things? How to behave like other people? Like you?'

Fanny reached out and grasped Becky's hand. 'They'll teach you all you want to know, Becky. How to read and write, too. You'll get on well here. I *know* you will.'

When the formalities had been completed in the reformatory and Fanny Tennant and Ivor Primrose had gone, Becky was forced to take a bath, then given an ill-fitting dress of coarse grey material. She was allocated a bed in a dormitory already occupied by some fifteen young female 'criminals', most of them older than herself.

The moment the woman supervisor left the room the other girls crowded around Becky, bombarding her with questions. What had she done? Where had she come from? Had she witnessed the Durdham Downs Chartist riot? Did she know . . .?

Becky was no more communicative than she had been with Fanny and Ivor Primrose. She sat on the edge of her hard bed, unused to the company of so many other girls and feeling out of place in the unfamiliar surroundings. Gradually most of the girls lost interest in the newcomer and drifted away.

Those who remained were followers of a heavily built girl with close-cut fair hair. After a few more questions had gone unanswered, the girl came and stood in front of Becky, looking down at her belligerently.

'I'm Eva Tromp. My father was a sea-captain. He had his own ship. A Dutch ship.'

Becky knew the volunteered information was intended to impress her. It did not, and she said nothing.

'I'm in here for "rolling" seamen. I'd take 'em down some back alley, then when their trousers were about their ankles my man would come out and bludgeon 'em. We got dozens like that before we was caught. Charlie – that's my man – and me were a great team. As Charlie used to say, a bloke can't run after you when his trousers are about his ankles.'

There was polite laughter from Eva Tromp's companions, and Becky thought they had probably heard the same weak joke every time a new girl was admitted to the reformatory. She did not change her own expression.

'While you're here it don't matter how you behave with anyone who's in charge, but you'll do whatever I tell you, unless you want trouble. You got that?'

Becky glanced up briefly at the girl, then looked back at the floor, still without speaking.

'Do you hear me, Becky – or whatever they said your name was?'

The girl's manner was becoming more aggressive, but still Becky said nothing.

The Dutch girl was disconcerted by Becky's silence. Surrounded by her 'followers' the self-appointed leader of the dormitory needed to assert her authority over this uncommunicative newcomer.

'Perhaps she's deaf,' suggested one of the girls.

'Then, I'd better shout in her ear,' said Eva Tromp. She leaned over Becky to carry out her intention – and staggered back as Becky butted her in the face.

Eva Tromp shook her head stupidly and stared in dazed disbelief at the specks of blood the movement spattered on the blanket of Becky's bed. She put a hand to her nose, and it came away sticky with blood. *Her* blood.

'You poxy little drab. I'll teach you to lay one on me. . . .'

Eva Tromp fell upon Becky, and moments later the two girls were rolling on the floor, fighting furiously, spurred on by the other occupants of the dormitory.

The sound of the excited girls shouting encouragement to their champion brought an inevitable response from the staff of the reformatory. Running into the dormitory wielding canes, they swiftly broke up the ring of spectators, and Becky and Eva Tromp were dragged apart and hauled to their feet.

Esther Stott, the principal of the reformatory, had held the post for only ten days. This was the first major test of her authority. She knew the staff were watching to see how she would cope with it, and the knowledge did nothing to boost her confidence. It was all she could do to control the shaking that threatened to give away her uncertainty.

'Who began this?' Her voice, like the woman herself, was thin and high-pitched, and behind gold-rimmed spectacles her eyes blinked rapidly. She felt her nervousness must be apparent to her watching staff.

Becky, bloodied but silent, saw only a tall gaunt woman with hair drawn back in a severe style, who was looking at her as though she were something particularly loathsome.

'I asked who began this fight.' Esther Stott repeated her words, this time including the grinning bystanders in her enquiry.

Still no one said a word.

'We've never had fighting before today.' The information was volunteered by the member of staff responsible for the dormitory. 'Eva has always been particularly helpful in maintaining discipline.'

Her uncertainty gone, Esther Stott turned her full attention upon Becky. 'Did you hear that? We have never had trouble in this dormitory before, yet within an hour of *your* arrival there's a disgusting brawl. What do you have to say?'

Becky had no more to say than before.

'Very well, you'll be put in solitary confinement until you've found your tongue. Take her away, please.'

Looking about her at the faces of the staff. Esther Stott thought she saw approval there. She felt she had satisfactorily passed her first test.

Becky offered no resistance until the women escorting her took her down some stone steps and opened the door of what had once been a small coal-cellar. It had an earth floor and no window other than a small grille in the door. With the main door to the cellars closed the room would be in total darkness.

As the door slammed shut behind her, Becky felt a sudden surge of panic. She did not want to be left in the darkness alone.

'Please. . . . Don't leave me here. The fight was my fault. I'm sorry. Don't leave me. . . .'

Becky was still shouting when the cellar door slammed shut behind the last of the departing reformatory staff. She shouted until far into the night, her cries faintly audible to those she had left behind in the dormitory.

At first the girls treated the matter as a huge joke, but as the night advanced the joke wore thin and most lay in sleepless silence, listening to Becky's pleas.

By morning the shouting had ceased, and a member of staff was overheard telling Esther Stott that Becky had neither moved nor spoken when bread and water was taken to her.

Expressing satisfaction, the reformatory head declared that a few more days on her own would give the girl time to accept the wickedness of her ways and reflect on the advantages of virtue.

CHAPTER NINETEEN

FERGUS DID NOT LEARN about Becky's committal to the Kingswood reformatory until two days after she had been taken there. Fanny deliberately withheld the news until the doctor had pronounced Fergus fit enough to leave his bed for a few hours.

His reaction was exactly what Fanny had anticipated. He wanted to go and see Becky straight away.

Fanny needed to explain that the reformatory was run on strict lines. Unauthorised visits were not allowed. They could only be sanctioned by Mary Carpenter, the founder and principal of the reformatory, who was ill at her recently acquired property known as the Red Lodge.

Fanny's words made little difference. Although it was already late in the afternoon, Fergus insisted that they call on Mary Carpenter immediately and obtain her permission to visit Becky. Fanny fell in with his plans when Fergus threatened to leave the house and walk to the Red Lodge to see Mary Carpenter.

By the time the Red Lodge was reached in the Tennant carriage Fergus's headache had returned, but he said nothing as he and Fanny were taken to a first-floor room and asked to wait. Unable to sit still, Fergus wandered to a tall window that offered a view over a steep-sloping high-walled garden towards the spires and chimneys about the city-centre dock area.

The light hurt Fergus's eyes and exacerbated the pain in his head. Turning from the window, he came face to face with

Mary Carpenter. A woman in her forties, she had a strong face, but it showed signs of a pain as great as his own, and borne for much longer. Yet it was *his* well-being that was her immediate concern.

'My dear young man, your head is troubling you? I have heard all about your dreadful injury. Fanny, my dear, draw the curtains a little. Come and sit down, Mr Vincent.'

'I'm all right.' Fergus's mission was more important than a little pain. 'I've come to seek your permission to visit a girl in your reformatory at Kingswood.'

'One of my girls . . .?' Mary Carpenter looked to Fanny for an explanation.

'She's a new girl named Becky. A young orphan from the house in Lewin's Mead where Fergus has a studio. A few days ago I received word she was being held against her will in a brothel in St James. I informed the police, and they raided the house. Becky was released, but a man in her room was found to have serious stab wounds. The police wanted to take her to the Bridewell . . .' Fanny hesitated. 'You were still ill, so I took it upon myself to have Becky admitted to Kingswood. I felt you would have wished it. . . .'

'Yes, yes.' For a few moments Mary Carpenter displayed a sick woman's irritability. 'You did the right thing — but it makes me wonder what *else* has been going on during my absence, both here and at Kingswood. There's a new supervisor there. How *old* is this girl? Why are you taking such an interest in her welfare, young man?'

Mary Carpenter gave Fergus a look that hinted at an immediate visitation of fire and brimstone should he dare lie to her.

'She has no one else — and I'm fond of her.' Fergus met her question with an honest aggression.

Mary Carpenter accepted his explanation without further questioning. 'Very well. We'll *all* go to Kingswood and visit your young orphan.'

'You're no more fit to make the journey to Kingswood than is Fergus. Neither of you has been out of bed for a full day yet.'

There was a faint glimmer of amusement in Mary Carpenter's eyes when she exchanged glances with Fergus.

'The Lord never intended me to be an invalid, Fanny – and Mr Vincent seems well on the way to recovery. We'll leave for Kingswood at eight o'clock tomorrow morning. I usually walk there, but if your carriage is available I shall be most happy to ride with you. Now you must excuse me. Owing to my "indisposition" the house has been neglected for far too long. There is much work to be done. . . .'

Once back inside the carriage, Fergus sank back in the seat gratefully, his head aching abominably.

'Your Mary Carpenter is a tough lady.'

'Not nearly as tough as she pretends to be. And neither are you. You should both be in bed for a few more days.'

'Time enough for that when I've seen for myself that Becky is all right. . . .'

Becky was *not* all right. When the visitors arrived at Kingswood and Mary Carpenter announced that they had come to see Becky, the school principal displayed such acute discomfiture that Fergus was filled with alarm.

'Has something happened to her? She's still here?'

'Yes . . . but she hadn't been with us an hour before she was involved in a fight with another girl. It was necessary to punish her.'

Esther Stott found it easier to direct her explanation to Fergus than to Mary Carpenter.

Fergus was bewildered. 'You had to *punish* her? But I thought she was rescued from a disorderly house and brought here to safety?'

'This is a *reformatory*. Punishment is an essential part of discipline. Without it we would be quite unable to cope with girls of the type we accommodate here.'

'Miss Stott! Need I remind you that this is *my* reformatory? *My* policy is dictated by principles I consider to be vital. To inflict punishment is to admit defeat – and there is no room for defeat here. *I* have never found it necessary to resort to punishment. I will have a full report on your actions. It will be on my desk tomorrow morning. Now you will be good enough to bring the child to us immediately.'

Esther Stott paled before Mary Carpenter's rebuke, and she had some difficulty in voicing her reply. 'She's still in solitary. I thought —'

'*Thinking* does not appear to be one of your attributes, Miss Stott. This child has been locked away in a room in a brothel, where she was no doubt subjected to all manner of unmentionable abuses. She has come here to be helped back to a normal life – and what do you do? You have her locked away again. No, indeed, *thinking* is something you should avoid, Miss Stott. Where is the poor child now?'

'In a cellar at the rear of the house.'

Mary Carpenter drew in such a deep breath it seemed she must burst. Then the air was expelled in an explosion of anger. 'Take me to her at once. *No!* Miss Hooper, *you* take me there. I don't think I want to look upon Miss Stott again. Quickly now. ... .'

One of the reformatory staff who had been listening to the exchange between Mary Carpenter and Esther Stott hurried forward. Taking a bunch of keys from the ashen-faced principal, she led the way to the cellars.

It was dark in the cellar even though there was bright sunshine outside, and Fergus waited with growing impatience while a lantern was found and lit.

As a flustered Miss Hooper tried key after key in the lock of the heavy door, Fergus called through the grille in the door to Becky. When his calls went unheeded he rounded on the harassed reformatory official. 'Are you sure she's all right? When did you last speak to her?'

'No one has been allowed to speak to her. That's part of the punishment. ... .' The woman shook out yet another key. 'Food has been placed inside the cellar, but no one has spoken to her. She shouted a lot the first night, but she's been quiet since. I felt she should have been released. I would have said so. ... .'

A key finally turned in the lock, and Miss Hooper struggled with the stiff iron handle. Impatiently, Fergus stepped in front of her. Using two hands, he turned the handle and swung open the heavy door.

Inside the small cellar Fergus kicked over a full bowl of

cold watery gruel. Two bowls of untouched food stood nearby. Behind him someone brought the lamp to the doorway, and Fergus saw Becky.

She sat crouched against a wall, legs drawn up, her forehead bowed on knees. In spite of the commotion in the doorway she had not moved.

Fergus dropped to one knee beside her. 'Becky, it's me . . . Fergus. Are you all right?'

She did not move. Alarmed at her stillness, Fergus put a hand on either side of her face and raised her head. Her eyes stared back at him, but there was no recognition there. No emotion of any kind.

'Becky. . . . Everything's all right now. We've come to take you out of here. Can you stand up?'

There was no reaction from her and, standing behind Fergus, even Mary Carpenter seemed at a temporary loss as to what ought to be done.

Looking down at Becky's pinched face, as dirty as on the day he had first seen her, Fergus felt pity for her well up inside him.

'My poor, *poor* Becky.'

Fergus spoke in a whisper, but to Fanny it was as though he had shouted his feelings for the numbed little ragamuffin to the world.

Fergus gathered Becky in his arms. For a brief moment she tried to fight against him. Then she slid through his arms to the floor.

Mary Carpenter kneeled on the cold floor beside Becky, and her efficiency returned.

'The poor child's fainted. From lack of food as likely as not.' She nodded grim-faced towards the uneaten gruel in the bowls by the door. 'Bring the girl upstairs – Miss Hooper, send for a doctor, please. Tell him it's urgent.'

Fergus carried Becky from the cellar with ease, appalled at the lack of weight in her body, and Mary Carpenter led the way to a tiny bedroom situated behind the study. On the way they met with a wide-eyed and fearful Esther Stott. Mary Carpenter walked past the principal of the reformatory as though she did not exist. Esther Stott's brief period in charge of the wayward girls was over.

In the tiny bedroom Fergus laid his burden gently upon the bed and then he was dismissed from the room.

Fergus was in the study when the doctor arrived, but he had to wait for another anxious half-hour before he could question the physician about Becky.

'The child is suffering from severe malnutrition. It's a condition by no means uncommon among children brought here from the slums of Bristol.'

'She has also been grievously abused. . . .' Entering the study behind the doctor Mary Carpenter could not hide the anger she felt. 'Those responsible should be transported and forgotten.'

'Has Becky told you anything of what happened to her?' asked Fergus.

'No. She's conscious now, but she won't say a word.'

'Will you allow her to come back to Lewin's Mead? I'll look after her. . . .'

Mary Carpenter shook her head. 'She has agreed to stay in a reformatory. The commitment is not one to be entered into lightly by either side, and in view of her recent experiences in Lewin's Mead she's better off away from there for a while.'

Aware of Fergus's genuine concern, Mary Carpenter added: 'Don't worry, Mr Vincent, she'll recover in due course from *all* that has happened to her. I have seen similar symptoms shown by sensitive children subjected to solitary confinement. It's a barbarous punishment. That reminds me, I have something to say to Miss Stott. I don't want her here at Kingswood for one moment longer than is absolutely necessary.'

Mary Carpenter hurried from the room, her purposeful air boding ill for the reformatory principal. The doctor followed after her, leaving Fergus in the study with Fanny.

'Can I go in and see Becky?' Fergus's question broke the awkward silence that fell between them.

'She's better left alone for a while. It's been a bad time for her. Far worse than you know. Right now I would say you are the *last* person she wants to see.'

Fergus could not understand why Becky should not want to see him, but he bit back the question. Instead, he asked: 'What will happen to Becky now? She'll never settle here after what's happened.'

'Mary Carpenter is opening a new reformatory in Bristol, in the Red Lodge. She intends taking personal charge there. Becky will be the first girl to go there.'

'Will I be allowed to visit Becky?'

Fanny hesitated before saying: 'That's something you'll need to discuss with Mary Carpenter.' After a slight hesitation Fanny added quietly: 'You must not forget what Becky is, Fergus. Don't expect too much from her. She'll hurt you again – not because she wants to, but because she can't help herself.'

CHAPTER TWENTY

FERGUS RETURNED TO BACK LANE the next day. Calling at the Red Lodge *en route*, he was told only that Becky had arrived there but was not yet talking. His request to be allowed to see her was refused. The doctor had ordered strict rest and quiet. Mary Carpenter's staff would ensure his instructions were obeyed to the letter.

The brief reunion with Becky had put a strain upon Fergus's friendship with Fanny. Fergus believed that Becky's ordeal in solitary confinement might have been avoided had Fanny informed him at the time she was found and taken to Kingswood.

For her part, Fanny was of the opinion that Fergus's reaction was more emotional than mere friendship demanded. Nevertheless, she tried to persuade Fergus to remain at the Tennant house until he was fully well.

Fergus argued that it was time he began working again and declined the offer of the Tennant carriage to return him to Lewin's Mead. Arrival by carriage in the narrow streets would immediately set him apart from the other residents and destroy the *rapport* he had built with the suspicious slum-dwellers.

As he climbed the stairs to his attic studio, Fergus was inclined to question the wisdom of his own decision. The stairs were littered with rubbish and filth of every description; the stale, stomach-churning stench of cooked cabbage hung heavily on the air, and a noisy argument could be heard above the crying of children in Mary O'Ryan's room. The opulence of the Tennants' Clifton home and the squalor of the Back Lane house were worlds apart.

Thoughts of Becky were still foremost in Fergus's mind, and the first thing he saw when he entered his room was her half-completed portrait standing on the easel by a window. Fifteen minutes later he was working on the painting and the remainder of the world was temporarily forgotten.

Fergus was still painting when Irish Molly entered the attic room, an hour and a half later. She did not knock, and Fergus was so engrossed in his work that he was not aware of her presence until she stood beside him, staring at the portrait with awe in her eyes.

'What a *beautiful* painting. I've never seen anything like it. . . . But where *is* Becky? Is the child all right?'

Fergus looked at her with the abstract expression of a man woken from a particularly absorbing dream. Then he put down his brush.

'No, she's not all right — although everyone keeps telling me she'll improve with rest.'

Fergus told Irish Molly of Becky's experience after the police raid on Rose Cottle's St James brothel.

As he ended his story, Irish Molly exploded in anger. 'I knew it! All the time I was telling that Miss Tennant about Becky, something inside me was saying that no good would come of calling in the po-lice. It never does. All they're interested in is *arresting* people. Poor Becky, I should have minded my own business.'

'You did the right thing, Molly. Everyone did. Becky couldn't keep running. Things went very wrong at Kingswood, that's all.'

'Talking of people running . . .' Irish Molly dropped her voice as though they were surrounded by people. 'I believe you know Dr Casey? Dr *Tomas* Casey?'

Fergus's hand went to his head, and he said ruefully: 'Yes, I know him. Thanks to his brand of Chartism, I've spent the past couple of weeks laid up with a sore head.'

Irish Molly looked at Fergus in dismay. 'Does that mean you'd like to see him caught by the po-lice?'

Fergus shook his head. 'No. He's an honest enough man,

and he has a just cause. It's his methods I question. But what's all this about? I wasn't aware *you* knew Tomas Casey.'

Irish Molly ignored the question. 'What would you do if he came to you and asked for your help?'

'Molly, are you telling me you know where he is?'

'Would you help him?' Irish Molly persisted doggedly with her own line of questioning.

'Of course I would. If he's caught, he'll be hanged for sedition. He's done nothing to deserve that.'

Irish Molly sagged with relief, and Fergus said: 'You *do* know where he is! I think you'd better tell me what this is all about.'

'He's downstairs in my room.' Irish Molly was relieved to be able to share her secret with someone. Hiding Tomas Casey was proving a great strain for her.

Fergus could scarcely hide his disbelief, and Irish Molly added: 'He came here looking for you, but we discovered we're both from the same part of Ireland. He knew my father . . . in better days. Can I tell him you'll help him?'

After only a moment's hesitation, Fergus nodded. 'He'd better come up and see me. Tell him to wait an hour. It will be dark then and there'll be no risk of any of the O'Ryans seeing him.'

Halfway down the stairs, Irish Molly paused to call back: 'I'm sorry about Becky, truly I am. I'd hoped she might escape from the rookery through you. But there's no escaping, is there? Not for the likes of her and me, there ain't.'

Irish Molly's parting comments gave Fergus much food for thought. He would not argue that Becky was a product of the Lewin's Mead slum. It was something he had always accepted. But to suggest that she and Irish Molly had anything in common . . . He looked at the unfinished portrait and picked up his brush again. No, it was *not* true. He would not allow Becky to travel the same path.

Fergus was finally forced to accept that the light was too poor for him to continue painting any longer. After cleaning his brushes he lit a lamp and turned his attention to the fire.

Some twigs had just begun to crackle cheerfully when the door opened and Tomas Casey entered the attic studio.

The Chartist leader had not shaved since his escape from Durdham Downs, and a full red curly beard now hid his sharp features, but the bright intelligent eyes had not lost their humour.

'Well, well, well! It's nice to see you again, Fergus. It's a fine place you have here.'

'Not up to Clifton standards, perhaps, but it's home.'

'Ah, yes! I hear you've been nursed back to health by the delightful Fanny. That was a terrible blow you took on the head from a constable. Terrible. I saw it all. The way they laid into us, I swear they were out to kill someone, so they were. And you just standing there minding your own business! I hope you complained to Fanny's father, him being the chairman of the Watch Committee, and all.'

'I'm not certain it *was* a constable. It could just as easily have been a Chartist. Your men were wielding stakes with as much enthusiasm as the police.'

'It was the police, I'm telling you. Haven't I just said I saw it all?'

'Only moments before I was struck down I saw you busily engaged in sending some of your men to head off a band of constables. You weren't even looking in my direction.'

'Wasn't I now?' Tomas Casey grinned unashamedly. 'Well, I don't need to jump into the ocean to know it's wet; and tell me, why would any Chartist want to hit *you* over the head?'

Fergus ignored the question. 'Irish Molly says you have need of my help. What is it you want me to do?'

'Ah!' Tomas Casey appeared mildly embarrassed. 'Well, now, there are one or two small problems in my life at the moment – as you'll appreciate. The most pressing, and embarrassing, is a temporary shortage of funds. Molly's a good girl – figuratively speaking, of course – and more than willing to help a fellow-countryman when he's in trouble, but she's a working girl. I fear I've prevented her from pursuing her . . . "profession"? As she so rightly reminds me from time to time, she has rent to pay and food to buy.'

'Will five guineas help?' Fergus pulled out the money-pouch he kept hanging on a thong inside his shirt.

'Could you make it ten? I'll give you an IOU, of course. I'm not short of funds, you understand, but they aren't immediately to hand.'

Fergus counted out ten sovereigns and passed them to Tomas Casey.

'God bless you, Fergus. You're a gentleman.'

'Ten guineas might solve your immediate problems, but what of the future? You can't spend the rest of your life hiding in Irish Molly's room.'

'True, Fergus — but I'm hoping you might be of some assistance in this matter, too.'

Something of Fergus's misgivings must have shown, because Tomas Casey said hurriedly: 'It's only a little thing. It need hardly take any of your time at all.'

Fishing a folded piece of paper from his pocket, the Chartist leader handed it to Fergus. 'Here's a list of Irish ships trading into Bristol whose captains are known to me. If any of them is in harbour at the moment, I'd like you to take a message to the captain for me.'

'Don't you think a watch will be kept on the docks for you?'

Tomas Casey shrugged. 'Perhaps. But they'll be looking for a Chartist leader, not a bearded seaman.'

Fergus tucked the paper in a pocket. 'I'll have a look around the docks tomorrow. It will be safer than asking questions.'

'Good lad. Now I'd like to see some of these pictures of yours, and you can talk to me while you're showing them. Molly's a big-hearted girl, but she's no conversationalist. Comment on the weather, the cost of food, and how many prostitutes were arrested during the night and you've exhausted her conversation for the day.'

CHAPTER TWENTY-ONE

NONE OF THE SHIPS listed by Tomas Casey was in Bristol, nor did they visit the West Country port during the ensuing week. In the meantime Tomas Casey borrowed another five guineas from Fergus, while Irish Molly became increasingly unhappy about the effect her lodger was having on her trade. She complained she was losing regular clients to younger girls who were constantly swelling the ranks of Bristol's prostitutes, and who owed no loyalty to the loose-knit fraternity to which they belonged.

Molly suggested Tomas Casey should move to the attic room, but Fergus refused to consider the suggestion. The Irish Chartist leader was too garrulous to have in the tiny attic room. Fergus was working hard on his paintings; Tomas Casey would be a calamitous distraction.

Fergus also nursed a forlorn hope that Becky might be allowed to return to Ida Stokes's house in Back Lane, even though common sense told him Becky was likely to remain at the new Red Lodge reformatory for a long time yet.

Alfie Skewes was on the road to recovery now and had wisely refused to consider charges against Becky. However, the circumstances surrounding Becky's 'rescue', together with her mark on a magistrate's agreement, were enough to keep her in Mary Carpenter's care.

Fergus had still not been allowed to visit Becky. Mary Carpenter was in London for a few days, and on the two occasions when Fergus called at the Red Lodge he was told only that Becky was 'making satisfactory progress'.

However, she was still confined to bed and no visitors were being allowed.

Fanny, too, proved suddenly elusive. She was not at the ragged school when Fergus took his weekly art lesson, and her staff claimed not to know when she was likely to be available.

Then, nine days after Fergus's return to Lewin's Mead, he was checking the docks when he saw one of the ships on Tomas Casey's list. *Lady of Wexford* was berthed in the part of the docks that extended into the very heart of Bristol, hardly a stone's throw from Lewin's Mead.

According to the Chartist leader, the captain of the ship should be one Henry Kennedy. The vessel was moored outside two others, and Fergus boarded it with some difficulty. He could see no sign of activity on board, but when he was beginning to think the boat was deserted a man wearing a soft woollen hat, dirty corduroy trousers and a badly holed blue jersey emerged from a hatchway.

When Fergus asked whether Captain Kennedy was on board, the seaman's glance rested on Fergus for only a second before he asked: 'Who'd be wanting him?'

'A friend of mine – he's a friend of the captain, too, I believe.'

'Would this "friend" be having a name?'

Fergus looked about him quickly. There were men working on the other ships and on the quayside above them. 'It might be better if I spoke to Captain Kennedy.'

'I'm Henry Kennedy, and *Lady of Wexford*'s not in Bristol to entertain visitors. If your business can't be spoken of out loud, then I don't want to hear about it at all.'

Captain Kennedy picked up a heavy coil of rope and began dragging it towards the ship's stern. Moving along with him, Fergus tried again. 'This friend needs your help. He asked me to find you. . . .'

'It's surprising how many friends I find in foreign ports, and every one of them in some sort of trouble.'

Pulling a spliced loop from the coil, Captain Kennedy handed it to Fergus. 'Take this and put it over that bollard on your way ashore. My crew were so eager to go landside we're not even half-secured.'

As the Irish sea-captain handed the rope-end to Fergus, he said in a low voice: 'Name an inn where I can meet you this evening.'

In an equally low voice, Fergus replied: 'The Hatchet inn, Frogmore Street.'

Straightening up, the Irish captain said loudly: 'I'm sorry I can't help your friend.' With this he turned and picked his way across the deck of *Lady of Wexford*. Moments later he clattered down the steps of another hatchway and was lost from view. Limping slowly from the quayside, Fergus observed a small nondescript man taking a great interest in the dirty water lapping around *Lady of Wexford*'s bow. He remembered there were large rewards out for a number of prominent Chartists who had been present at the Durdham Downs meeting – and the largest reward of all was for the apprehension of Dr Tomas Casey.

Captain Kennedy came to the Hatchet inn soon after eight o'clock that evening. After watching Fergus at work for a while he said he would like to have Fergus make a sketch of him.

It was a quiet evening, and as Fergus sketched the two men were able to talk. Captain Kennedy wanted to know the name of their mutual 'friend'. When Fergus told him, the Irish sea-captain sucked air through his teeth noisily.

'I figured as much. I heard of the trouble at his meeting. It won't be easy. The authorities are set on bringing him to trial and making an example of him. Every Irish ship in the port of Bristol is being watched day and night.'

'So there's little chance of Tomas escaping by sea?'

'I haven't said that. The sooner Tomas returns to Ireland the better. He has more friends there than in England – yourself excluded, of course.'

'I'm no more than an acquaintance,' corrected Fergus. 'But I'll not stand by and see a man hanged for no other reason than to deter others from taking up a just cause.'

'We're more used to it happening in our land than you are, it seems.' Henry Kennedy spoke with no trace of bitterness in his voice. 'But I'm in agreement with your sentiments. A rope collar's an uncomfortable prospect for a sensitive man like Tomas. I'll do my best to see he never gets to wear one. Can you get hold of some seaman's clothes for him?'

'It shouldn't be too difficult. The local pawnshops carry on a good trade with sailors. Tomas has grown a handsome beard, too, but I'm not sure that will be enough to get him past the men who are watching your ship.'

'It won't be necessary. Only the Irish boats are being watched. My brother is captain of *Lucy*, trading between Bristol and Halifax, in Canada. His boat is lying in the dock about three ships behind mine. Tell Tomas to go on board after dark tomorrow. He'll be landed on the coast of Cork and able to take a gentle stroll home from there.'

'How much will his passage cost?' Fergus was aware that *he* would be required to foot the bill.

'Are you asking me to put a price on a man's life?' For a moment Captain Kennedy frowned angrily, then his brow cleared and he said: 'That's a fine sketch of me you're making. I'll take it as a gift and you can leave it to me to make the arrangements with my brother.'

Late the next morning Tomas Casey was in the attic with Fergus, drinking tea and chatting happily about the prospect of returning to his native land.

'You'll have to come visiting, Fergus. It's a grand country. There's no other place quite like it in the whole world.'

'Is that why so many of you live elsewhere?' Fergus's current opinion of Ireland and the Irish was coloured by the fact that Tomas Casey had just borrowed more money from him. Fergus now held Tomas Casey's IOUs for twenty-five guineas. It was more money than he could afford, and the prospect of having it returned to him looked decidedly bleak.

'I didn't say it was easy to *live* there, only that it's God's own country.' Tomas Casey refused to allow Fergus's remarks to dampen his good humour.

'Will you continue working for Chartism when you return there?'

Tomas Casey looked at Fergus scornfully. 'Can a bee stop buzzing? I'm committed to Chartism, and there's no going back. Mind you, I'll need to lie low for a while. I'll go to the west coast and set up in practice as a doctor again. I'll get by; you needn't worry about me. But the country ...! It's green, with a smell about it as though the world is renewed every morning. A man's not afraid of breathing in and filling his lungs with air. ...'

Tomas Casey's eulogy of his homeland was brought to a halt by the sound of footsteps hurrying up the stairs to the attic.

Even as the Irish Chartist looked about him for a place to hide, the door was flung open and Irish Molly stumbled into the room. Seeing Casey, she cried: 'Thank God you're still here. I was feared you might have already gone.'

Tomas Casey had told his countrywoman only that he would not be sharing her room for another night. She knew nothing of the ship that was to return him to Ireland.

'You must come with me, Tomas. Your skills are needed at the old houses down by the river.'

'*I'm* needed? I don't understand you, woman. No one knows I'm here. How can *I* be needed?'

'You're a *doctor*, aren't you? Or so you've been telling me all this time.'

'I'm a doctor right enough, but if there's someone sick you'll need to send for a Bristol doctor. I'll not risk being caught now, not when another twelve hours will see me on my way home to Ireland.'

'There's not another doctor would come within a mile of the poor souls I'm asking you to help. They're our people. Irish.'

'But they're not in Ireland now, so they've become the responsibility of the English authorities.'

'Responsibility, you say? No one will take any responsibility for these poor souls. They're outcasts. When they become a problem they're moved on somewhere else.

Anywhere else. These people – *our* people – are sick, Tomas. Desperately sick. Fergus . . . you sketched two of the children a couple of weeks ago. Show him.'

Fergus walked to the far end of his long room and picked up a canvas that leaned with its face to the wall. He handed it to Tomas Casey without a word.

Tomas Casey looked at the painting, and the faces of two undernourished and unsmiling children stared back at him from the canvas. Their eyes were sunk deep in fleshless faces, and twiglike arms protruded from tattered sleeves. It was a tragic and moving painting, but their story did not end on the canvas.

Jabbing a finger at the painting, Irish Molly said: 'I've seen both these boys this morning. One is lying dead and the other's dying on a bed of filthy straw, in a cellar that was flooded until two days ago. There are almost two hundred others who'll go the same way if they don't get help right now.'

'What's wrong with them? *Why* are they dying?'

'Have you no eyes? Look at the painting. They're starving to death. They were starving when they arrived from Ireland and they've stayed alive by scavenging. They're living in tumbledown houses down by the river. *River*, did I say? It's an open sewer. A disgrace to the city. A week ago the river rose in flood and poured inside the cellars of the houses. All those who'd been sleeping there moved upstairs to where they were already sleeping as many as twenty to a room. When the water went down many of them moved back to the cellars, even though the walls were streaming with filth and water. It's no wonder fever's broken out among them.'

'Fever?'

'Every one of them is ill in some way or another. The children especially.'

Tomas Casey's instinct for self-preservation was battling with the sense of duty he felt towards his countrymen and their children.

'How far are the houses where these people are living?' Tomas Casey put the question to Fergus.

'They're on the edge of Lewin's Mead. I doubt if you're

likely to meet up with a constable on the way. Even if you did, you wouldn't be recognised behind that beard.'

'All right, then, we'll go and see what can be done – but I'm not missing that ship, you understand?'

The stench from the river as they approached the houses was almost overpowering, and Tomas Casey wrinkled his nose in disgust. 'I'm not surprised that fever's flourishing hereabouts. Does the Bristol Council have no regard for public health?'

When they reached the derelict riverside houses, Tomas Casey's concern increased. The houses were in an advanced state of decay, and the recent floods had not improved matters. There was not a pane of glass in any of the windows, half the doors were missing, and the roof of one house had collapsed in upon the upper storey.

A cool wind was blowing by the river, yet a number of men, women and children sat or stood in the lane before the houses, or on adjacent wasteland. No one seemed to be *doing* anything. Even the children sat and stared at the ground. One or two raised their heads to gaze from sunken lacklustre eyes at the newcomers. Most did not bother. There were no comments about the arrival of the trio from Back Lane. Indeed, there was an almost total lack of conversation among the people here.

Tomas Casey stopped and looked about him in concern. 'I haven't seen people who looked like this since I was in Kerry during the famine of 'forty-five.'

'You're looking at the *fit* ones. Wait until you go inside. . . .'

Irish Molly took the lead, and the two men followed her inside the first of the broken-down cottages. The stench in here was more oppressive than outside, dampness and decay adding to other odours. They passed a number of men and women as they entered the house, but no one showed any interest in them. Then they entered a cellar, and Fergus was brought face to face with men, women and even children who had given up all interest in life itself.

He could only see those in the immediate vicinity of the stairs, the light from above penetrating no further than three or four feet into the cellar. It was enough. Bodies were packed so close together that it was almost impossible to pick a way between them, and the air in here was well-nigh unbreathable.

For a few disbelieving moments Tomas Casey just stared at the bodies lying at his feet. Then he took command, calling for a light so that he could assess the situation more fully. When nothing happened, the Chartist leader repeated the demand in Gaelic. Within a few minutes a lighted candle-stub had been produced and handed to him.

Treading carefully, Tomas Casey picked his way across the cellar floor, occasionally pausing to stoop over a still form. When he gained the far wall the Irish doctor turned, and Fergus saw the shock on his face.

'I can't believe it. Half these people are dead already!'

From the cellar steps, Irish Molly spoke with a choked voice. 'You'll believe it, Tomas. There are more of them upstairs – and it's the same in every house.'

'But . . . there are *ten* houses!' Fergus was horrified.

'That's right. *Now* do you believe these people are in desperate need of help?'

'They're all doomed unless we can do something for them right away.' Leaning over another still figure, Tomas Casey parted the front of a tattered shirt. As he did so the tiny scrap of candle disintegrated in his hand and left them in darkness.

'Unless I'm mistaken there's both cholera *and* typhus here – in epidemic proportions. It's a situation no town council can afford to ignore.'

Gingerly picking their way between prone bodies, Tomas Casey and Fergus returned to the steps. The Chartist leader stood in silence for a moment, deep in thought. Suddenly his shoulders straightened, and Fergus saw a return of the expression he had seen when the Chartist leader roused the passions of his followers at the Durdham Downs meeting.

'We can't do everything that's needed, but we can make a start. Molly, I'll need opiates, laudanum, peppermint water and flannel – lots of flannel, to make belts for those who are still free of cholera.'

'Oh! And will I be given all these things out of the goodness of someone's heart? Or do I offer them one of Tomas Casey's IOUs?'

Reaching inside the waistband of his trousers, Tomas Casey pulled out a small linen bag, and there was the dull clink of gold coins as he emptied the bag into Irish Molly's hand.

'Get as much as you can with this.'

'But it's all the money you have.'

'Don't stand here arguing, girl. Each minute you delay is costing life. Fergus . . . you know Alderman Tennant. Go to his house and tell him what you've seen here. Ask him to obtain doctors and medical supplies – and food. As much food as he can provide. Molly . . . on your way out try to bully some life into all the men you can find. I want them to help me clear this cellar. It's the only way to separate the living from the dead. If we leave them down here any longer, there'll be *no one* left alive. Go on, get moving, Fergus. What are you waiting for?'

'If the authorities become involved, they'll send constables. You're a wanted man.'

'I've always known what the consequences of my campaign might one day be, Fergus. I've controlled my own destiny as far as any man can. These poor souls have had to accept whatever fate doled out to them – and it's always been a loser's hand. If I were to walk away from them now, I'd be haunted all my life by something more relentless than the law of the land. I couldn't live with it. Go and fetch all the help you can muster. Get Fanny to help you; she's worth ten others when it comes to an emergency like this.'

CHAPTER TWENTY-TWO

ALDERMAN TENNANT WAS NOT AT HOME – but Fanny was. Fergus impressed the urgency of his mission upon the servant who opened the door to him, and minutes later Fanny hurried into the room where he waited.

'The servant said you needed urgent help. What is it? Have you lost another Lewin's Mead urchin?'

Fergus described what he had seen at the derelict cottages on the bank of the Frome river, and repeated what Tomas Casey had said about the situation.

'Tomas Casey is still here? In Bristol? But there's a price on his head.'

'He's well aware of it, and plans had been made for him to leave England tonight, but he's given all his money to buy medicines and is refusing to leave the sick families.'

After a few more brief questions, Fanny said: 'We must discuss Tomas's problems later. First we need to bring help to these poor people – doctors, food and clothes. If they have the fever, everything they own must be burned. How many of them do you think there are?'

'I don't know for certain. Probably about two hundred.'

'So many? You return to Tomas, and I'll do what I can, as quickly as possible. Take this and use it to buy anything Tomas feels he needs in the meantime.'

Fanny took Fergus's hand and dropped a number of gold coins into his palm.

Tomas Casey had been busy during Fergus's absence. The

cellars of the houses had been cleared, and their recent occupants lay on the waste land beside the houses. A few were on blankets, but most lay on the bare earth. Others, farther from the houses, lay shoulder to shoulder in neat rows, their suffering over. Most had died unnoticed in the dark and crowded cellars.

Irish Molly had bought what she could with the money Tomas Casey had given to her, and she and some of the Irishwomen were busily tearing flannel cloth into strips to make 'belts' for those not yet stricken with cholera to wear next to their skin. This was widely believed to be an effective means of keeping the disease at bay.

Meanwhile, Tomas Casey was doling out doses of a mixture of laudanum and peppermint water, all the time complaining that there was only sufficient medicine for a single dose.

When Fergus handed over the twenty guineas donated by Fanny Tennant the Chartist doctor called to Irish Molly and sent her off once more to procure all the medicine she could buy.

'How many of them are ill?' Fergus asked the Chartist doctor when Irish Molly had hurried away.

'Pretty well *all* of them, I'd say. As for a count. . . . There are people in some of the upstairs rooms I haven't seen yet.'

Wiping a dribble of medicine from the lips of a pathetically thin young girl, Tomas Casey rose to his feet and looked about him in despair.

'There are too many here for me to deal with alone. I've had seventeen bodies laid out over there, mostly young children. I'd say we're likely to lose three or four times that number before we're through.'

With a movement of his arm, Tomas Carey encompassed the people about them. With the exception of the few women who were making flannel belts they stood around in silent apathetic groups. 'Look at them. They've given up. They're so used to losing their battles with life they've stopped fighting. As they fall ill they just lie down and die.'

Gazing about him at the homeless Irish refugees, Fergus knew the bitter words spoken by his companion were true. There was an air of hopeless resignation among them that seemed to have passed beyond human help.

'Is there something I can do?'

'Go through the houses and make sure everyone is brought outside. The air here is far from fresh, but it's better than inside. Then gather the men together; I see a couple have shovels with them. Get them to clean the filth from the houses, from attic to cellar. When that's done I'll see if the money will stretch to lime-wash for the cellars. While you're about it, try to prevent them leaving this place. If cholera reaches Lewin's Mead, it will go through the place like the wrath of God.'

By the time Fanny Tennant arrived on the scene the house-cleaning operation was well under way. She brought a number of volunteer helpers and two light wagons loaded with food – and suddenly there was new-found hope among the sick and hungry immigrants. They crowded about the wagons, snatching greedily as food was offered to them.

Fanny undertook her own tour of inspection in a bid to ascertain the extent of the problem and she spoke at some length to Tomas Casey. By the time she reached Fergus she was visibly shaken by the desperate plight of the Irish families.

'It's appalling that people can exist in such conditions in the very heart of our city without anyone knowing.'

'I saw them here some weeks ago, when I was searching for Becky,' said Fergus guiltily. 'But I had no idea things would become as bad as they are now.'

Just then Irish Molly returned from her latest errand. She was accompanied by two youths from the apothecary who were helping her carry the medicines. Seeing Fergus, she made her way to him.

Nodding a brief greeting to Fanny, she said: 'I've got most of the things Tomas wanted. Where is he?'

'In the end house. I found a mother with a tiny baby in the top-floor rooms who refuses to come out. He's gone to see them.'

'I'll take some of this medicine to him there. He might be needing it.'

As Irish Molly walked away Fanny said: 'That's the girl who came to tell me Becky was locked in a room above the dollyshop. Is she a prostitute?'

'Yes.'

Fergus did not amplify his reply, and Fanny looked at him curiously. 'You have some peculiar friends, Fergus.'

'I suppose I have.' Fergus looked at her without humour. 'Some might include you among their number. It's not everyone who would come to the aid of people as sick and destitute as these.'

'It will become far worse before we see any improvement.' Fanny looked anxiously up at the clouds gathering in the sky. 'It will be raining soon. How long before the houses are thoroughly cleaned?'

'They won't be ready today. They are in a disgusting state.'

'Then I'll send someone to the barracks for marquees. Better still, I'll go myself. The Army will have doctors experienced in cholera, too. Tomas on his own can't do all that's needed here.'

'Tomas should leave if army doctors are being brought in. If he's taken by the police or the Army, he's as dead as any of those corpses over there.' Even as Fergus spoke another body was being carried to the line of corpses.

'I forgot. What should I do?' It was the first time Fergus had ever heard Fanny ask anyone for advice.

'Tomas will never leave until there's someone to take his place. Bring army doctors here if you can. Once they've arrived I'll try to persuade Tomas to leave.'

Fanny Tennant succeeded in obtaining three large marquees and the services of two army doctors by evening, but fortune did not smile upon Tomas Casey.

Fergus was upstairs in one of the houses when he heard a commotion outside. Looking from the broken window, he saw Irish Molly running. Holding her skirts high, she was already halfway to Lewin's Mead. Closer to the houses Tomas Casey struggled futilely against the three policemen who held him. One was Ivor Primrose.

Nearby, one of the army doctors was protesting angrily to a police inspector. Around them a number of Irishmen watched the scene with non-participating interest. There were town officials, too. Escorted by the constables, they had come to assess the situation on behalf of the Bristol authorities.

By the time Fergus reached the scene Tomas Casey had been handcuffed to Constable Ivor Primrose and the brief scuffle was over.

'Tomas . . . are you all right?'

The Chartist leader held up a manacled hand and shrugged. 'I'd be better if they took this off and gave me a half-mile start, so I would.'

Ivor Primrose frowned at Fergus. 'How long have you known the whereabouts of Casey?'

'Fergus knows nothing.' His voice loud and arrogant, Tomas Casey was no longer the solicitous doctor treating dying patients. He was a Chartist leader, holding the attention of a gathering. 'He wouldn't be here at all if I hadn't suddenly appeared at his door and asked him to enlist Miss Tennant's help on behalf of my poor suffering countrymen here.'

Ivor Primrose still looked accusingly at Fergus. 'You should have reported his presence to the police straight away. There's a warrant out for his arrest.'

'He's been responsible for saving many lives here today. If it hadn't been for his efforts, you'd probably have twice as many bodies lying over there.'

'I'll add my professional endorsement to that statement, Constable.' One of the army doctors spoke heatedly to Constable Primrose. 'But for Dr Casey – if, indeed, it *is* Tomas Casey – every one of these men, women and children would be dead within a week. I'll repeat my statement in open court, if necessary.'

'Your remarks will be noted, sir, and if you aren't able to attend the court I'll ensure they're passed on to the proper quarter. But I have my job to do. Tomas Casey has been recognised, and there's a warrant out for his arrest. He's now my prisoner.'

'He's desperately needed here, Ivor,' Fanny Tennant interceded on Tomas Casey's behalf. 'Can't you allow him to continue his work until all the Irish have been treated? There are more than two hundred of them — many are children, and most are desperately ill. If you release him, I'll take full responsibility.'

Ivor Primrose shook his head. 'I'm sorry, Miss Tennant. I'd be in serious trouble if I didn't take him into custody immediately. As for these unfortunate people . . . The Inspector of Health is here now, and they've become his responsibility. He'll provide all the medical care that's needed.'

Tomas Casey tugged at his curly red beard and attempted a weary grin. 'Don't worry yourself about me, Fanny. It will be a relief to have a shave and emerge from behind this foliage. I don't know why I grew the damned thing; it's fooled no one.'

Nearby, the Irish immigrants were crowded about a fire on which the contents of a huge soup 'boiler' were beginning to bubble, wafting an appetising aroma over a wide area. Tomas Casey tried to point in their direction, but the handcuffs prevented him. Lowering his shackled hands, he inclined his head towards them.

'Do all you can for them, Fanny. They're simple folk from Ireland's far west, but they feel pain, sorrow and humiliation as surely as the rest of us.'

Fanny and Fergus watched helplessly as Tomas Casey was led away, handcuffed between Ivor Primrose and another constable.

'What do you think will happen to him?' Fanny asked the question anxiously.

Fergus shrugged. 'He'll be charged, of course, but he'll probably get off. All he's done is to put into words what the rest of the country is thinking. All the same, he'll need plenty of support. I'll be visiting him in prison.'

'We'll *both* visit him. But we can do nothing for him at the moment, so I'll find out what is going to happen here.'

The pale-faced health inspector was surrounded by his officials, each of whom was compiling some form of inventory of the Irish immigrants. When Fergus asked the inspector what he intended doing, he received a curt reply.

'I'll do whatever is best for the citizens of Bristol – but what's your business here? Who are you?'

'I'm Fergus Vincent – and this is Miss Tennant, daughter of Alderman Tennant. We've been helping these people as best we could.'

Some of the belligerence left the health inspector, but he showed no inclination to be friendly. Touching his hat to Fanny, he said: 'Good day to you, miss. I don't doubt you've done much to relieve the suffering of these people – unlawful vagrants though they are – but I'm here as the official representative of the Town Council and will ensure that all necessary steps are taken.'

'Oh?' The scorn in Fanny Tennant's voice would have withered a more sensitive man. 'Have you brought doctors? Food? Medicine? And men to bury the Irish dead?'

His face reddening, the official said: 'I have only just arrived, Miss Tennant. I will do what's needed when I've assessed their needs. . . .'

'These people don't need "assessing". Any fool can do that with no more than a glance. They need food, clothing, blankets – and more doctors. When you've made all these things available I and my helpers will leave – but I don't doubt we'll still be here when darkness falls.'

Fanny was right. She and her volunteer helpers did not withdraw from the derelict houses until after dark, and there was still no aid from the Bristol Town Council. They left the Irish families in better circumstances than when they had arrived. All had been fed, and bread was left to break the night's fast. A few items of clothing had also been obtained, together with blankets. The newly cleaned rooms had been heavily whitewashed, and there was an air of cautious optimism among the Irish vagrants for the first time since the potato blight had driven them from their lands. It seemed that at last someone *cared* about their plight.

The two army doctors left at the same time, but they were less optimistic. They dismissed Tomas Casey's diagnosis of typhus among the Irish families. They identified the rash on the children as measles – just as much of a killer among the weak and emaciated children — but there was no doubt that many of the immigrants were suffering from cholera. The outbreak could be expected to worsen before it began to improve. The doctors promised to return with more medicines the next morning.

Fergus was exhausted when he returned to the house in Back Lane. He had declined an invitation to go to Clifton for a meal at Fanny's house. The emotional impact of the plight of the Irish immigrants had left him drained of energy. Even so, there were some faces that haunted his mind. Most were children. He wanted to commit them to paper before he slept.

On the landing where Irish Molly had her room, Fergus paused before knocking at her door. There was no reply, but he thought he heard a sound inside before he knocked again. This time there was utter silence. Hesitating for only a moment, Fergus lifted the latch and pushed the door open.

It was gloomy inside the room, light from a full moon barely penetrating the uncleaned panes at the small window.

At first Fergus thought he must have been mistaken and the room empty, but then he detected a slight movement in a chair across the room.

'Molly, is that you?'

'Who did you expect to find — a titled lady, perhaps? Of course it's me — and I don't remember asking you to come in.'

There was belligerence in Irish Molly's voice, but it was not as aggressive as it might have been. Crossing the room towards her, Fergus smelt the fumes of cheap gin.

'Are you all right, Molly?'

'And why shouldn't I be?'

A lamp flickered on in a window not six feet away across the narrow thoroughfare outside, and the light invaded the room. Irish Molly turned her head away, but she was not quick enough to prevent Fergus from seeing her face.

'You've been crying.'

'Prostitutes are too tough to cry. Surely you know that? Oh, what the hell! Yes, I've been weeping, I've been weeping for that red-haired idiot who'd be on a boat heading for

Ireland now if it wasn't for me. Did the po-lice take him?'

'Yes.' There was no gentle way of confirming what Irish Molly already suspected.

'Damn! Damn the po-lice. Damn those poor ignorant suffering people down there by the river. Damn you for letting me see the sketches you'd made of them in the first place. But if anyone needs to be damned it's me, for persuading poor Tomas to help them.'

She swung the bottle of gin towards Fergus. 'Here, pour some of this down your throat – but don't drink it all. I'll need more of it if I'm to go to work tonight.'

'You'll be bringing another man back here?'

'Isn't that how I earn my living? Pass me that bottle if you're not going to drink. I need it more than you.'

Irish Molly took the bottle. Raising it to her lips, she drank noisily. When she lowered the bottle again she saw Fergus silently watching her.

'What will they do to him, Fergus? What's going to happen to the poor dear man? Will they hang him, as he thinks they will?'

'No.' Fergus fervently hoped he sounded more optimistic than he felt. 'What's happened today will be taken into account. He'll be given transportation, but in a year or two the demands of the Chartists will be met and he'll be pardoned.'

'Do you honestly believe that, Fergus? Do you really believe he'll be all right?'

'I certainly don't think they'll hang him. All the other Chartists who were arrested on the Downs have been transported or imprisoned.'

'Thank you, Fergus. I'll always blame myself for causing Tomas to be caught, but you've made me feel better . . . about everything.'

Irish Molly stood up unsteadily and reached for her shawl. 'You're a kind man. I know you've been giving Tomas money during the time he's been staying here. I can understand why Becky thinks so much of you. Out of the way now; I've a living to earn. . . .'

Irish Molly paused in front of Fergus and breathed gin

fumes in his direction. Reaching out, she patted him drunkenly and none too gently on the cheek. 'If you ever feel lonely up in that room of yours, just come down and see Irish Molly. I'll find room for you in my bed any night, my love.'

CHAPTER TWENTY-THREE

FERGUS WOKE EARLY THE NEXT MORNING. Throwing off his blanket, he placed his feet on the bare-board floor and crossed to the window. It was grey and overcast outside, but at least it was not raining. He was able to fan some life into the embers of his fire, and while he waited for the kettle to boil he washed and dressed and put sketchpad and pencils in a canvas haversack. Fergus was going to check on the condition of the Irish vagrants, but this time he intended making a detailed record of their plight.

There was no sound from the remainder of the house. Few of the residents pursued occupations requiring them to rise early – and Irish Molly was unlikely to be abroad early today.

When Fergus left the house a sprinkling of men and women were making their way from Lewin's Mead to places of work outside the rookery. A light drizzle was riding the wind, and Fergus turned his coat collar up about his face and thrust his hands deep into coat pockets.

Leaving the narrow alleyways behind him, he crossed the waste ground that extended towards the river – and came to a sudden surprised halt. The area in front of the derelict riverside houses was filled with people milling about in apparent confusion. Most were Irish, but there were constables here, too – and the health inspector who had come to the houses the previous day.

Hurrying to the health inspector, Fergus demanded to know what was happening.

For a moment the health inspector could not recollect

Fergus. When he remembered, he immediately looked about him for Fanny Tennant. Failing to see her, his confidence grew.

'We're moving the Irish. They'll be on the road out of Bristol by the time most people are abroad.'

'On the road to where? These are homeless people – and they're desperately ill.'

'That's none of my business,' the health official said callously. 'The decision was taken at a special meeting of the Town Council last night. Hopefully we're in time to avoid a cholera outbreak in the city.'

'They would only have acted so swiftly upon your recommendations,' Fergus accused the official angrily. 'Did you tell the Council just *how* sick these people are?'

'My duty is to the city of Bristol. By your own admission these people are vagrants. They are also a very serious health hazard. They must go, and quickly, if an epidemic is to be averted.'

'These "vagrants" are men, women and children, driven from their own homes by starvation. They need help.'

'Then they must find a place where help is available. Preferably many miles from Bristol.'

'At least let them set off with a good meal in their bellies,' pleaded Fergus. 'Food will be here soon.' He knew Fanny Tennant and her volunteers had arranged to bring breakfast to the sick Irish families.

The health inspector shook his head stubbornly. 'I want them out of Bristol before people take to the roads. They'll leave as soon as the constables can round them all up.'

The Irish vagrants were almost ready to move off, those who had difficulty in standing being supported by others. Fergus made rapid sketches as he walked among them. Then he was attracted to one of the derelict houses by a commotion going on inside.

As Fergus reached the door a constable staggered out. His tall hat was missing, and blood flowed down his face from a gash on his forehead.

'Take care. . . . There's a madman inside!' The policeman gasped out the information as he pushed past Fergus.

The noise was coming from upstairs, and at the head of the broken stairs another constable lay on the floor, attended by his colleagues. Beyond them a number of constables crowded a narrow and gloomy passageway. Among them was the giant figure of Ivor Primrose, and Fergus pushed his way through to reach him.

'What's happening?' Fergus asked the question with difficulty as an angry and unintelligible bellowing filled the passageway and constables were forced back upon their companions.

Peering down at Fergus, the giant constable exclaimed: 'Oh, it's you. . . .' As he spoke, Ivor Primrose warded off a retreating policeman who was backing into Fergus. 'One of the Irishmen's gone beserk. He's got hold of a shovel and has downed four constables already. He's keeping us from going into the room at the end of the passage. I think his family must be in there.'

'Let me through. I might be able to reason with him.'

It was neither bravado nor a wish to aid the police in their distasteful task. Sooner or later the constables would be ordered to rush the shovel-wielding Irishman. Someone might be seriously injured, or even killed. If this happened, the Irishman and his family would suffer the penalty of the law.

Helped by Ivor Primrose, Fergus wormed his way forward, squeezing between the close-packed constables, most of whom were clutching heavy wooden truncheons.

The two constables in the front rank were hatless, and one had a bloody face. On the floor in front of them lay four tall black hats. No more than two paces away, filling a doorway, stood an Irishman, the sharp-pointed shovel balanced in his big hands as menacing as any medieval battle-axe.

The Irishman was one of those who had helped Fergus clean out the houses the day before, using the very shovel he wielded so effectively today. Fergus remembered something else. One of the smallest bodies laid out on the waste ground had been that of this man's young daughter. His wife and baby son were also ill. After they had been treated by Tomas Casey, Fergus himself had taken food to the woman. Fergus had also learned the man's name.

'Giraldus. Giraldus Reilly, is your wife in there with your child?' Fergus put the question to the Irishman quickly as the man raised his shovel threateningly, mistrustful of the movement in the police ranks.

The Irishman peered suspiciously through the gloom at Fergus. Then he moved slightly to one side, allowing more light from the room behind him to escape into the narrow passageway. Suddenly the spade was lowered to a more defensive position – and Fergus discovered he had been holding his breath.

The Irishman began talking earnestly, but unfortunately he spoke only Gaelic, a language understood by none of the men in the narrow passageway. Three times the unintelligible words were repeated in what was clearly a plea to Fergus.

When Fergus indicated that he did not understand, the Irishman eyed him uncertainly for a few moments. Then he side-stepped and signalled for Fergus to enter the room.

'Be careful!' As Fergus moved away from the assembled policemen and walked towards the room, Ivor Primrose took a pace forward to caution him. In an instant the shovel was raised menacingly once more.

'It's all right. You and your men stay here until I see what's happening inside. Nothing will happen to me.'

Having given this reassurance, Fergus ducked beneath the Irishman's raised arm – and immediately forgot the thought of any danger to himself.

A woman lay on the board floor, covered by a blanket. Her breathing was shallow and uneven, and her eyes were closed. She was undoubtedly dying, and Fergus thought she must be unconscious – until her eyes suddenly opened and she looked up at him.

Unable to endure the pain he saw in her eyes, Fergus broke off the visual encounter – and saw that the room had another occupant. There was a low fire burning in the grate, and close to this lay a baby wrapped in a ragged jacket that must have belonged to the man guarding the door. The child could not have been more than a month or two old.

The woman made a strangled sound in her throat. Turning back to her, Fergus saw she had turned her head and was also looking at the bundle that was her child. When the woman tried to speak the sound died in her throat, but there was no mistaking the plea in her dark expressive eyes.

Fergus was uncertain what to do until a shudder ran through the woman's body and he realised she did not have many minutes to live. Crossing to the fireplace, he picked up the baby, intending to place it beside the dying woman. The baby seemed unnaturally stiff, and when he looked closer at its face he realised why. The baby was dead!

Fergus almost dropped the child in that first moment of realisation, but he recovered in time. Carrying the dead child to the woman, he pulled back the blanket that covered her, laid the child by its mother's side and gently crooked her thin arm about the dead baby.

She tried to say something to him, but no words came and he found the gratitude in her eyes unbearable. Moments later a terrible tremor racked her body and Fergus crossed the room to the doorway. Touching the Irishman's arm, Fergus pointed back inside the room. The Irishman's glance went to his wife before returning to the waiting constables in an agony of indecision.

Stepping outside into the passageway, Fergus said: 'He has a wife and baby in there. The baby is dead and his wife has no more than minutes to live. I also happen to know he lost another daughter yesterday. Give him a few minutes and he'll come out quietly. He'll have nothing left to fight for.'

The uncomfortable silence that followed Fergus's words was broken by Ivor Primrose. Talking to the Irishman, he said gently: 'Go to your wife. We'll leave you in peace for a while.'

Shifting his gaze to Fergus, Ivor Primrose said: 'I'll come back for him later. We'll not have this lot moving for another half an hour or so anyway, whatever the health inspector says.'

The Irishman did not understand Ivor Primrose's words, but when the constables began to move back along the passageway towards the stairs he took a pace towards them.

Handing Fergus the shovel, he hurried inside the room to where his wife lay.

Kneeling beside the woman, the Irishman took her hand and began talking softly to her, although by now it was doubtful whether there was enough life left in her to understand what was being said.

It was this scene that Fergus committed to paper. He knew it was an intrusion on what should have been an unshared moment of tragedy, but Fergus believed it epitomised the whole sordid incident.

As Fergus sketched, Constable Ivor Primrose came to stand silently beside him and Fergus asked quietly what would happen to the Irishman.

The big policeman shrugged uncomfortably. 'Who knows? He and the others will probably tramp the shires until they die beside the road, or until there are few enough left for a workhouse to take them in.'

'What about his battle with your constables? His spade put a sizeable dent in one of them.'

'That was Tommy Cabot. He's got a wife and two young children himself. He'll not press charges.'

Fergus glanced up from his sketchpad in surprise, and Ivor Primrose said: 'Constables have feelings the same as anyone else, Fergus.'

'Of course. . . . I'm sorry.'

Fergus looked back at the tragic Irish family in time to see the Irishman gently close the eyelids of the woman. When he stood up tears were coursing down his face and he was so distraught he seemed not to know what to do next.

Ivor Primrose entered the room and took the Irishman by the arm. As he was led away the man stopped suddenly. Pointing back to the room, he said something in his own language and the big constable patted his arm reassuringly.

'I don't know what it is you're trying to ask me, but if it's about a decent burial, then you needn't concern yourself. They're digging a large plot in St James churchyard, and your wife won't be short of company. With those who died yesterday and her own child, she'll have twenty-seven companions.'

'There will be many more deaths along the road.'

'I don't doubt it, Fergus, but neither one of us can shoulder the burdens of the whole world.'

Fergus followed the other two men, and at the door the Irishman paused to grasp him by the hand before going outside to join the remainder of his people.

When Fanny Tennant and her helpers arrived at the derelict riverside houses, Fergus was sketching the macabre spectacle of the last of the Irish bodies being removed in an enclosed cart. Giraldus Reilly's wife and baby were the last to go and they were swung inside the van together in a single blanket.

One of Fergus's sketches showed the Irish vagrants being marched away, escorted by constables and health officials, and when Fanny demanded to know what had been happening Fergus handed her his sketchpad without an explanation. He wandered away to stand gazing morosely into the filthy waters of the Frome river.

It was some minutes before Fanny joined him. Handing back the sketchpad without a word, she stood beside him for a long time.

'How long is it since they were taken away?'

'Forty minutes. Perhaps an hour.'

Fanny looked to where the wagons she had brought stood loaded with foodstuffs.

'I'll try to catch up with them. They have need of food.'

'Why bother? They're doomed. They know it as well as we do.'

Fanny looked at Fergus sharply. 'You don't believe that any more than I do.'

Changing the subject abruptly, she asked: 'What do you intend doing with the sketches you've made?'

'Make paintings of some. I'm not sure about the others.'

'Show them to Lady Hammond. She'll arrange an exhibition for you.'

To have an exhibition of his works was the dream of every artist, and Fergus was no exception, but he showed no enthusiasm. 'I'm not sure I'm too interested in an exhibition right now. Besides, a lot of work needs to be done on them.'

'Then, *work* on them. You are not exactly overburdened with commissions.'

'I'll do it in my own time.'

'Will you, Fergus? Or are you enjoying living this dream of yours too much to make it anything *more* than a dream?'

Fanny waited for Fergus's reply. When none came she sighed: 'All right, tell me to mind my own business. But before you do I had better tell you of more of my meddling. I spoke to Mary Carpenter and told her how worthwhile your sketching lessons have been for my pupils at the ragged school. She would like you to hold similar classes for the girls at the Red Lodge reformatory, at a fee to be agreed. She wants to see you tomorrow morning.'

'Would I be teaching Becky?' Fergus's enthusiasm suddenly returned.

'There are no more than a dozen girls at the Red Lodge. You will be teaching them all.'

'When do I begin?'

'That's up to you. Go now, if you want to. Meanwhile I shall try to catch up with the Irish. It would be criminal to waste all the food I have collected for them.'

CHAPTER TWENTY-FOUR

FERGUS WAS PREPARING A MEAL for himself when he had an unexpected visitor. Maude Garrett entered the attic hesitantly after knocking and being invited to enter.

'Are you Fergus? Becky's friend?'

Puzzled, Fergus nodded. He did not recall having met this girl before. Drab and untidy though she was, there was a certain animation in the tired pinched face that an artist would have remembered.

'I'm Maude. It was me who came to tell Irish Molly about Becky — when Ma Cottle had her locked up in the dollyshop. I called to find out what's happened to her. Irish Molly's not in, so I came up here.'

'*You* were responsible for rescuing Becky? Come and sit down. I've just made tea. Will you have a cup?'

Maude Garrett hesitated. 'I'd really like to speak to Irish Molly. I want to ask her about . . . something. I'm on my way home from work.'

'You can spare a few minutes. I want to know exactly what happened to Becky. She's at the Red Lodge in Park Row. It was a choice of agreeing to go to a reformatory or being taken to police cells. They said she stabbed someone.'

'They've put her away for stabbing Alfie Skewes? She ought to have got a *reward*! It's a pity she didn't kill him. There's a lot of girls I know would have cheered if she had. Alfie *and* that father of his. Three months they gave Joe Skewes for assaulting a constable. They ought to have given him life for what he did to Becky.'

Her earlier reticence forgotten, Maude Garrett took the cup of tea offered by Fergus. 'Ta! I haven't had anything to drink since this morning. I upset the glue and had to work through dinner-time to pay for it.'

Taking a sip from the cup, her face lit up in sudden delight. 'It's got *sugar* in it. This is a rare treat and no mistake.'

'If you've had to work through your dinner-time, you'll be hungry. There's bread and cheese and cold meat on the table. Help yourself.'

Maude Garrett eyed the scant fare greedily, but said: 'I ought to be getting on home. My pa will be shouting for grub unless my sister Lisa's been able to earn some money. None of 'em usually has anything until I've bought it with my day's wages.'

'They'll wait for a few more minutes.' As he spoke Fergus cut off a slab of cheese, broke off a piece of bread from the loaf and set the food on the table in front of Maude Garrett. 'Before you go I want to hear all you know of Becky.'

Maude Garrett began to eat, speaking with difficulty as she did so. She glossed over her own involvement in Rose Cottle's establishment, but Fergus had no difficulty in filling the gaps in her narrative. By the time food and story had come to an end, Fergus knew exactly what had happened to Becky in the room above Rose Cottle's dollyshop.

Maude Garrett's knowledge was graphically supported by a vivid imagination, and Fergus was gripped by self-guilt. He ought to have tried harder to find Becky before she fell into the clutches of Rose Cottle. She had been out there in Lewin's Mead all the time. He should have carried on looking until he found her. Suddenly the brush he had unconsciously picked up snapped in two in his fingers.

'Are you all right?'

Maude Garrett had been looking at him curiously as he tormented himself with thoughts of what Becky had suffered. If only he had behaved differently when she had given him the stolen watch. . . .

'I'd better go now.' Maude Garrett stood up, studiously avoiding looking at the broken brush. 'If I'm not home soon, Pa will think *I've* been kidnapped. Not that he'd care about *me* overmuch. If it wasn't for the money I give him, he wouldn't notice if I went home at all. I used to think the kids would miss me, but since Phoebe died the rest seem to have been running wild. Still, Lisa's getting money most days now.'

Maude Garrett seemed to be talking largely to herself, but looking up at Fergus she asked: 'Do you know how long Irish Molly's likely to be?'

'No, but if you want her urgently she can usually be found in the White Hart when the docks are as quiet as they are right now.'

'Ta! When you see Becky tell her I hope everything goes well for her....' She hesitated uncertainly for a moment, then nodded towards the painting on which Fergus had been working. 'Could you paint a picture like that of me?'

'I'd be happy to sketch you any time you have a few minutes spare.'

Maude Garrett beamed at him. 'Would you ...? And let me take it away? I'll come in one evening, on my way home from work....' She suddenly became serious. 'I can't pay for it....' She looked at Fergus speculatively. 'Not with *money*, I can't.'

'The sketch will be a present because of what you did for Becky.'

'You don't have to pay me for *that*. Seeing Rose Cottle put away for six months is payment enough — even though it *has* left me short of money.' Maude Garrett shrugged. 'But that's *my* worry. I'll come and see you one of these evenings.'

Fergus presented himself at the Red Lodge the next afternoon. After being made to wait for some minutes he was taken upstairs to an airy wood-panelled study. It smelled of polish, and every speck of dust seemed to have been banished from the room.

Mary Carpenter was seated behind a large desk. Its vast polished surface was empty except for a slim vase containing three carnations, and a slim writing-folder.

The reformatory-school pioneer greeted Fergus unenthusiastically. It would be some time before Fergus learned that the stern austere spinster reserved her smiles and the hidden warmth of a caring personality for the girls sent to her by the courts.

'So you wish to share your talents with my girls, Mr Vincent?' She managed to make it sound as though he had come to the Red Lodge begging a favour.

'Fanny seems to think they would benefit from sketching classes.'

Mary Carpenter sniffed almost imperceptibly. 'Miss Tennant speaks very highly of your work. Have you brought any sketches with you?'

Fergus handed over his sketchpad and sat waiting as Mary Carpenter turned the pages. Occasionally the reformatory-school founder drew in her breath sharply and an expression of distress would come to her face. More than once she looked up at Fergus as though seeking the answer to an unasked question.

When she reached the last sketch Mary Carpenter closed the pad and placed it carefully on the desk before her. She sat in a deep brooding silence for long moments before fixing her gaze upon Fergus.

'You have a great talent, young man, but it carries with it an equal responsibility. These sketches provide a stark record of the plight of the more unfortunate members of our society. What use do you intend making of them?'

'When I've made paintings from the sketches I'll probably hold an exhibition. . . .'

'I'm not talking of the furtherance of your career. You are a young man; you can afford to wait for recognition. Many of the subjects of your sketches cannot. The wretched Irish vagrants; the slum-dwellers right here in our own city; children like Becky. I see you have a great many sketches of the girl, including a number of her sleeping. . . .'

There was disapproval and a question in the statement, and Fergus found himself telling Mary Carpenter of his first meeting with Becky, and of her use of his room as a refuge. Mary Carpenter's eyes never left his face during the whole of the time he was talking.

'There are other sketches of her, too. On a ship?'

'For a treat I took her on a day-trip on a paddle-steamer. It ended in disaster when the ship ran aground on its return passage up-river.'

'I seem to have heard something of the incident.' Mary Carpenter's fingers tapped the desk in front of her abstractedly, but there was nothing abstract about her expression. 'What exactly is the relationship between you and this girl? The truth, if you please, Mr Vincent.'

'There is no "relationship". Becky is hardly more than a child. She was the first person I met when I came to Bristol. We became friends. She has no one else, and I suppose I feel a certain responsibility for her in a strange way. I am also rather fond of her.'

The movement of the fingers on the desk ceased, and Mary Carpenter stared hard at Fergus for some moments more.

She nodded suddenly. A short, sharp and positive movement. 'Becky is a young *woman*, Mr Vincent, but young women are as needful of the *right* kind of affection as are young girls – more so, perhaps. I'm happy to know Becky has *someone* to care for her. She's a strangely lonely young lady. You are aware of course that she has not said a word since coming to the Red Lodge? The physician assures me there is no medical reason why she doesn't talk. It is simply that she chooses not to.'

Rising to her feet, Mary Carpenter said: 'You may have a few minutes alone with Becky in the garden, if you wish. Perhaps she will talk for you. Then, as you're here, you can give the girls their first art lesson. I don't believe in wasting time. Becky is not well enough to take lessons yet, but she should be present at your next class. Shall we say the same time every week? A two-hour lesson at a fee of two shillings and sixpence. I will provide pencils.'

The tone of Mary Carpenter's voice ruled out all discussion of the matter, and there was nothing for Fergus to do but nod his agreement.

'Good. I'll have you shown to the garden while a room is prepared for your class. If you have trouble with any of my girls, you will discuss the matter with me personally. Good day to you, Mr Vincent.'

Mary Carpenter bustled from the room, and a few minutes later a maid arrived to show Fergus the way to the garden.

Surrounded by a high stone wall, the well-kept gardens sloped down sharply from the house to give a view across the rooftops and the masts of tall ships tied up to the quay in the heart of Bristol.

Fergus had to wait a while before Becky joined him in the garden. She came from the house alone, and Fergus stood up to greet her as she walked slowly down the steps towards him.

When she reached him the words of greeting died on his lips and he took one of her hands in his, greatly concerned at her appearance. Becky was clean – cleaner than he had ever seen her – and was wearing a neat grey frock of a serviceable coarse material. Her hair was pulled back and tied neatly behind her neck. She was painfully thin, but it was her eyes that held his attention. Dark dull expressionless eyes that dominated her pale drawn face and stared at him with a total lack of expression.

'It's good to be with you again, Becky. I've been worried about you.'

Still holding her hand, Fergus led Becky to a garden seat. Sited beside a bed of perfumed French roses, the seat was in full view of the house, as were all the other garden seats.

'I'll be seeing you quite often in the future. I've been asked to come and take a sketching class, once a week.'

Becky sat down, her hand still held in his. She had not tried to pull it away, but neither had she responded when he squeezed her fingers affectionately.

'Are you eating well? If there's anything you particularly fancy, I'll bring it for you when I come to take my sketching class. Miss Carpenter won't mind.'

It was a lie. Fergus never doubted that Miss Carpenter *would* mind. He was merely trying to provoke a response – *any* response – from Becky. It was possible she was being given something to calm her, but her total silence was unnerving. For a few more minutes Fergus tried without any encouragement to provoke a reply from Becky. Finally, aware he would be allowed only a few more minutes alone with her, he grew desperate.

Gently pulling her around, he forced her to face him.

'Becky, I know what happened at Rose Cottle's dollyshop. Maude came to see me. Maude Garrett. She's told me everything. What you were doing at Rose Cottle's, and why she went to Irish Molly.'

'She couldn't tell you *everything*. I'm the only one who knows that.' Becky's voice was low and strained, reflecting her long silence.

Overjoyed that she had broken her unnatural silence, Fergus said: 'None of it matters now, Becky. All that's important is for you to recover and begin looking towards the future.'

'It *does* matter. . . .' The words came out as a wail of anguish, and Fergus gripped her hands tightly until Becky pulled them free. Clasping them in her lap, she looked down at her tangled fingers.

'I'd never done it before. . . .' Suddenly she said fiercely: 'Did I kill Alfie Skewes? I wanted to. I wanted them both to die for what they did. . . .'

Fergus gripped her hands again. 'Alfie Skewes didn't die, and it's all behind you now. I'm so very, very sorry I didn't understand how much the present you offered me meant to you. I looked for you after you'd gone. I searched *everywhere*.'

'You weren't searching for me on the night I saw you going out dressed up to the nines. You were on your way to see Fanny Tennant, I expect.'

'Why didn't you speak to me then, Becky?'

'I told you, you was on your way to see *her* and her fine friends up at Clifton. You wouldn't have wanted anything to do with me. Not *that* night, you wouldn't.'

'Becky, if I'd seen you, I'd have given up all thought of going *anywhere*. I was worried sick about you.'

Becky looked at him doubtfully. 'Honest?'

'Honest. I'd have given a reward of everything I owned to have found you again.'

It was some moments before Becky spoke again. 'I've been stupid, haven't I? Running away, I mean. If I hadn't done that, I wouldn't have ended up in Rose Cottle's dollyshop.'

'It's all over and done with. You're on the mend, and everything is going to be all right again.'

Becky managed a wan smile. 'I'm glad we've had this talk, Fergus. Do you think they'll let me go home now? I mean, to Lewin's Mead? To your room? I'll be all right, honest I will. You can tell that Miss Carpenter —'

'I don't think you understand, Becky. You've signed an agreement before a magistrate that you'll stay here. There's no going back on that.'

Becky looked at Fergus, not comprehending. 'But I've done nothing wrong.'

'You stabbed Alfie Skewes nigh to death. You'd have been charged with attempted murder if you hadn't agreed to come here.'

'Attempted murder? After what he'd done to me and was trying to do again?'

'There were *two* of them to deny all you said about them, Becky — Rose Cottle, too. You *might* have got off, but more likely you'd have ended up being transported. Fanny Tennant thought this was a better way out for you.'

'*She* would. How long do I have to stay here? A month? Three months? How long?'

'I don't know. Until Mary Carpenter thinks you're ready to go out into the world again, I suppose.'

'How long is that likely to be? I could be here for a year. *Two* years, even.'

'It won't be that long — and you're better off in here for a while. You'll be out of the way of Alfie Skewes — Joe Skewes, too, when he comes out of prison.'

'I'll be out of *everybody's* way, yours included. Do you think a couple of years spent in this place will make me more like your precious Fanny Tennant? Well, it *won't*. I'm Becky, and I'll still be Becky, no matter how long they keep me in here.'

'I don't want you to change, Becky, and if it were possible to take you off with me this minute I'd be the happiest man alive, believe me.'

Becky's eyes searched his face for the slightest hint of a lie. 'Cross your heart?'

Fergus made the sign of a cross over his chest. 'Cross my heart and hope to die.'

Becky's glance fell from his face to her lap once more and remained there for a full minute. When she raised her head once more he saw she had reached a decision.

'All right. I'll stay here for as long as they make me, just so long as I know you really want to have me home with you. While I'm here I'll work hard at learning to behave more like your Fanny Tennant. When I come out you'll be able to take me anywhere, I promise.' Just for a moment her lip trembled. 'I won't shame you again by having to take me somewhere barefoot.'

Fergus's smile hid the pain he felt on her behalf. 'I wasn't ashamed of you on that day, Becky, and I never will be.'

'It's easy to say that now, Fergus Vincent, but one day you're going to be famous. You won't want a Lewin's Mead brat hanging round you. Mary Carpenter's right. I should stay here. There's no other way to shake off the dirt of Lewin's Mead. I'll learn everything she can teach me, and I'll learn it well. You'll never have to be ashamed of me, I promise you.'

'Cross your heart?' Fergus managed a grin, although he felt closer to tears.

'Cross my heart and hope to die.' Becky grinned, too, and it cost her even more.

The woman who had brought Becky to the garden was advancing down the garden steps towards them now. It was time for Becky to return to the house.

'I'll need your help sometimes, Fergus.'

'You'll have it, I promise you.'

Becky nodded briefly but she was unable to prevent tears from welling up in her eyes. Cuffing them away angrily, she said: 'It's all right. I don't cry ... never.' Then, as her eyes filled again, she whispered: 'But I still wish I was coming home with you.'

CHAPTER TWENTY-FIVE

TOMAS CASEY was never brought to trial to answer the charges laid against him. Forty-eight hours after treating his homeless countrymen he was himself struck down with cholera.

Irish Molly gave the news to Fergus when he returned from the Red Lodge to the house in Back Lane. Tomas Casey had sent word from the Bridewell that he wanted to see her.

'I'll come with you.'

Fergus realised guiltily he had been so preoccupied with Becky that the plight of the arrested Chartist leader had been pushed to the back of his mind.

'I can't go anywhere near the Bridewell. The po-lice are looking for me.'

Irish Molly sounded genuinely distressed, and Fergus remembered how quickly she had taken to her heels when the police arrived at the derelict riverside houses to arrest Tomas Casey.

'Why should they be looking for you?'

'I spent an evening in a beer-shop with a drunken seaman, then he complained I'd stolen his purse. He said it had his pay from a two-year voyage in it.'

'Was he telling the truth?'

'He was not.' Irish Molly spoke indignantly. 'There was no more than two guineas there. The man was a boastful liar.'

Feeling that Irish Molly's indignation was perhaps not entirely justified, Fergus asked: 'When did all this happen?'

'Almost a year ago.'

'And the police are still looking for you? Surely they could have picked you up at any time, had they wanted to?'

'I've kept well out of their way.'

'Well, we can soon find out the truth of it. Here, take these upstairs to my room. I'll be back in a few minutes.'

Fergus passed his sketching satchel to Irish Molly and hurried from the house. He had spoken to Ivor Primrose not five minutes before. The big constable was trying to sort out the traffic chaos on a steep hill just beyond Lewin's Mead, caused by a wheel collapsing on an overladen wagon. He would know whether Irish Molly was still wanted.

When Fergus found him Ivor Primrose was wiping perspiration from his forehead with a large spotted handkerchief, having just played a considerable part in manhandling the broken wagon off the road.

'Irish Molly wanted? No – but I remember the complaint well. The seaman in question tried to obtain money from the Sailors' Relief Fund on the strength of his loss, but they discovered he'd never been farther than Ireland on his "round-the-world" voyages. He was given a month's hard labour and then he disappeared from Bristol. Are you telling me Irish Molly's thought for all this time that we were after her?' The constable grinned. 'No wonder she legged it so fast when we arrested Tomas Casey.'

'It's because of Casey that she needs to know whether she's still wanted. He's gone down with cholera, and we want to visit him in the Bridewell.'

'I'm sorry to hear about Casey. He's worked hard to help his people. But it's probably for the best. There's been talk that he would swing for his part in the rioting on the Downs. That's no way for a man to end his life – especially an educated man like Tomas Casey.'

Fergus had learned what he wanted to know but, as he turned to go, Ivor Primrose asked: 'By the way, how is that young friend of yours? Has she told you what really happened in Rose Cottle's place?'

'Not everything, but the gaps have been filled in for me by one of her friends.' Fergus told Ivor Primrose all he had heard.

'I thought it must be something like that when Alfie Skewes refused to lay any charges, even though he was close to death. He and his father are bad villains, Fergus. Beware of them. They won't know Becky is in Mary Carpenter's reformatory, and one of these days they're likely to come to Ida Stokes's house looking for her. Don't let anger lead you into any foolishness. They'd as soon stick a knife in you as look at you.'

'I'll try to remember your warning — but I can't promise anything.'

The sight of constables entering and leaving the Bridewell police station, just across the road from the prison, reduced Irish Molly to a state of abject fear. She had yet to be convinced that Ivor Primrose's assurance was anything more than a trick to bring her out of the narrow-streeted safety of the Lewin's Mead rookery. She became doubly nervous when she entered the damp dark confines of the Bridewell prison and she clutched Fergus's arm fearfully every time a heavy iron-clad door clanged shut behind them.

'It's all right, Molly. We're just *visiting*. There's no need to be nervous,' Fergus reassured his companion for the umpteenth time.

'So you keep telling me. Just you make sure you don't leave here without me, that's all.'

Eventually they were led to a small dark-walled cell, the gloom relieved by the faint light from a lamp hanging from the ceiling. A wooden bench ran the length of one wall, and on this Tomas Casey lay covered by a coarse grey blanket. There was no one in the room with him, and the gaoler did not enter. Locking the door behind Fergus and Irish Molly, he remained outside in the corridor.

Tomas Casey's breathing was shallow and rapid. He still had his red curly beard, and above this his face was bathed in perspiration. Fergus thought the Chartist leader was either asleep or unconscious, but he had heard them enter the cell. In a cracked voice he begged to be given water.

Her own fears forgotten, Irish Molly lifted a battered pewter jug from a small rough-board table in a corner of the cell.

The jug was empty. Striding to the door, Irish Molly banged on it noisily, adding a few new dents to the jug.

When the door swung open she thrust the jug at the gaoler. 'Here, fill this — and make sure it's good sweet water, or you'll feel the weight of the jug about your ears. Quickly now, before I forget I'm a lady and give you what you deserve for leaving a sick man without water or attention.'

By no stretch of the imagination could Irish Molly have been mistaken for a 'lady', but her anger was real enough. The gaoler took the jug from her and, grumbling to himself, hurried off to do her bidding.

The floor of the cell was filthy, and Irish Molly hitched up her skirts before crouching by the side of the crude and uncomfortable bunk. Wiping Tomas Casey's face with a silk handkerchief, purloined for her by Becky many months before, Irish Molly asked gently: 'How are you, me darling? Can I give you something to eat? I've brought some ox tongue, and a couple of bananas, given to me by a sailor. . . .'

Weak though he was, Tomas Casey shook his head with enough vigour to silence her. 'No. Just a drink . . . and talk.'

'Save the talking until you've had some water. Your voice is rough enough to take the hide off a Belfast dog. Here, I've brought you a drop o' "blue ruin". I'll not have you saying "no" to it, neither. It's the best thing you can possibly have inside your belly in your state.'

Putting a strong arm beneath Tomas Casey's head, Irish Molly raised him without any visible effort. Pulling the cork with her teeth, she placed the bottle to Tomas Casey's lips and tilted it.

Not until the sick man began choking did she remove the bottle. Fergus looked on in alarm as the sick Chartist leader threshed about on the narrow bunk, fighting for breath, his body writhing and contorting as though he were having a fit.

Irish Molly looked up at Fergus and shook her head sadly. 'He's on his way out, poor soul.' She spoke in a 'whisper' that carried to the gaoler, approaching along the corridor. 'It's always been his favourite tipple. I've known him knock back a half-bottle with hardly a pause for breath before now.'

When the gaoler entered the cell Fergus took the jug from

his and hurriedly filled a cup. Taking over from Irish Molly, he fed water to the choking man while she berated the gaoler, demanding that he bring a bucket and mop and clean up the cell floor.

Before the gaoler left the cell Fergus slipped a half-guinea into the man's hand. It was sufficient to stop the man's grumbling, but Irish Molly voiced her disapproval loudly.

'Anyone who needs to be given money before he'll tend to the needs of a dying man is a robber. Away with you – and when you return bring something to make the poor man half-comfortable.'

As the door banged shut behind the hurriedly departing gaoler, Tomas Casey beckoned for his two visitors to move closer. Whether it was as a result of the gin, or of the water, his voice was stronger, although he was still breathless.

'Molly, you're a fine girl. You'd make a good wife for a man. I'd marry you myself . . . but I've nothing to offer a girl now. I've little to offer anyone.'

'You haven't brought me here just to listen to your old blarney, Tomas. If you've something to say, then let's be hearing it.' Irish Molly's brusque and businesslike words were tempered by the fact that she had taken his hand and was patting it affectionately as she spoke.

Instead of replying, Tomas Casey arched his back in sudden pain. For more than a minute his two visitors looked on helplessly as disease and Irish tenacity fought each other for control of the wasted body.

When the bout was over Tomas Casey needed to wait until he was breathing more easily before he spoke again.

'I've made a will. . . . The prison chaplain has drawn it up for me. He's sent it to my executors . . . in Dublin. I don't own much. A small cottage. . . . A few pounds in the bank. . . . They're all to be yours when I die, Molly. . . . All but the money I owe to Fergus.'

'Hush now, we'll not be having any talk of dying. While you've God-given life left in you there's always hope.'

'I'm dying, Molly. You know it . . . and so do I. If only I could have lived to see the Chartists win the day. They will. . . . Ah, Fergus! If only you could put some of the power you show in your sketches into Chartism. . . .'

Suddenly it seemed as though the effort of talking became too much. Tomas Casey fell silent. As his eyelids drooped slowly the noise of his laboured breathing filled the tiny cell.

For many minutes Tomas Casey's breathing was the only sound in the cell. Then the distant clanging of heavy doors heralded the return of the gaoler.

As the sound came closer, Irish Molly said to Fergus: 'There's nothing more you can do for Tomas. Go on home: I'll stay with him for a while.'

She still had hold of her countryman's hand, and looking down at him she added quietly: 'It won't be long now. I've seen too many like him to hope for a miracle. Once they've sunk this low they go quickly. It'll be the kindest thing, too. Tomas has lived his life as a proud man, but a man with cholera is better knowing nothing at all of pride.'

The gaoler's key rattled in the lock, and Irish Molly repeated: 'Go now, Fergus. I'll be all right. No man should die alone, especially in a place like this. I'll stay here with him to the end.'

Fergus knew he could do no good by remaining in the evil-smelling Bridewell prison. Tomas Casey had lapsed into a sleep that bordered on unconsciousness. If he ever recovered his senses, Irish Molly and her bottle of 'blue ruin' could provide such comfort as might help the Chartist leader.

Sadly, Fergus left the Bridewell prison.

It was midnight when Fergus heard footsteps climbing the stairs to his attic room. He knew who it must be, and by the time Irish Molly pushed open the door he was filling a tumbler with Hollands, a somewhat superior gin to the 'blue ruin' she had served to Tomas Casey — but it was no less potent. Fergus handed the tumbler to Irish Molly without a word. He had already been sampling the contents of the bottle.

'God bless you, Fergus. I have need of this. I stopped off at the White Hart, but I couldn't take the good humour there tonight. Not after those last few hours with Tomas, God rest his soul.'

'He's gone, then?' Fergus realised he must have drunk more than he had realised. His voice sounded unusually slurred.

Irish Molly appeared not to have noticed. 'Sure he's gone, but he fought it to the end. Tomas was a fighter, and I dare anyone to say anything to the contrary.'

She emphasised her words by banging her already empty tumbler on the table, causing everything else there to jump and rattle.

Fergus refilled the tumbler, adding a splash of gin to his own half-empty glass. 'He was a good man,' he agreed.

'Good? He was a *saint*, I tell you. A real, live, God-fearing *saint*. Didn't he give his life for others? He should have been sailing back to his home instead of tending to his fellow-men. Back to Ireland. . . . Have you ever been there, Fergus?'

Fergus shook his head sadly.

'You must. You must. It's a lovely land. You'd love it.'

Irish Molly downed another glass of Hollands and stared morosely down at the empty glass until Fergus leaned across and refilled it.

'I've got a house there now, you know? *He* left it to me. He was a dear man. A dear, *dear* man.'

'You'll be going back to Ireland now you have a house there?'

'It's something I dream about, Fergus. To return and live the sort of life I can hardly remember any more. But that's all it is. A dream. I know that.'

Fergus shook the last few drops of gin from the bottle into Irish Molly's tumbler, and she looked down at it with an expression of dismal resignation.

'My room feels empty, not having Tomas there at all hours of the day and night. He was a great one for chattering. Half the time I didn't understand him, but he never seemed to mind. It's going to be even worse next week when Iris leaves the house. She's getting married, you know?'

'She's what . . .?' Fergus could not hide his surprise. Iris was the prostitute who occupied the room next to Irish Molly. Older than the Irish girl, she would pass the time of day with Fergus whenever they passed each other on the stairs, but he had never held a conversation with her. She appeared to pursue her 'profession' quietly and efficiently. 'She's marrying a Dutch captain. He's taking her to Holland with him.' Irish Molly stood up unsteadily. 'I'll go back to my room now.'

She set off across the attic studio, walking as though she carried a heavy weight suspended from her left hand.

By the time Fergus intercepted her she had strayed well off course and was heading for the wall a few feet to one side of the doorway.

'I'll help you down the stairs. They're a bit cranky, even when a body's sober.'

Fergus held Irish Molly's arm and took her down the stairs with exaggerated caution.

Leaning heavily on him, she said: 'You're a good boy, Fergus. A good *man*. Becky was foolish to run off and leave you the way she did.'

They were still a couple of stairs short of the first landing when Irish Molly pulled him to a halt.

'Will you stay with me tonight, Fergus? I don't like being on my own at any time. It'll be worse than usual tonight.'

'I'll see you safely back to your room, that's all. I don't think you'll have any trouble getting off to sleep.'

'Are you thinking I'm too old for you, Fergus Vincent? Is that what you think? Ah, well, you could be right. Perhaps you'll be more interested in the girl who's taking Iris's room when she's gone. Her name's Maude and she's not much older than Becky. . . . But you already know her. Maude Garrett. . . ?

CHAPTER TWENTY-SIX

THE FUNERAL OF TOMAS CASEY was well attended. The service was held in Bristol's Roman Catholic cathedral, and the large modern building was filled to capacity for the occasion. In spite of the events of the weeks preceding the Chartist leader's death, many civic dignitaries attended the service, as did numerous Chartist supporters. The large number of mourners overawed Irish Molly. She had been Tomas Casey's only visitor while he was in prison. Fearing his body was destined for a pauper's grave, she had made a tentative offer to pay for a simple funeral. To her surprise, she had been informed by the prison authorities that 'arrangements were in hand' for Tomas Casey's burial.

Fergus accompanied Irish Molly to the service and they occupied seats well to the rear of the building. At the graveside, too, they stood well behind the 'official' mourners, and Irish Molly's small posy was lost amidst the more ostentatious floral tributes contributed by the city elders.

Nevertheless, Fanny saw both Fergus and Irish Molly. Indeed, it would have been difficult to overlook the Irish prostitute, even in such a crowd. Irish Molly had put on her very best dress for the occasion, but the bright-green full-skirted velvet and silk creation had been purchased from a dollyshop to attract sailors, not for attending a funeral.

Aware of Irish Molly's way of life, Fanny disapproved of her easy familiarity with Fergus, even though she tried to keep things in perspective. Fergus lived in Lewin's Mead, Bristol's most notorious slum. It was hardly surprising if his friends were from there, too. She told herself that Fergus was pursuing a goal, one that no one else could achieve. Yet the nagging conviction persisted that it might as easily be achieved from Clifton.

When the Catholic priest began saying a prayer over the grave of Tomas Casey, Irish Molly broke down in tears. Fergus would have led her away, but the Irish prostitute refused to allow him to leave.

'Please stay, Fergus. Tomas would have wanted one of us to stay until the end. I always make a fool of myself at funerals. They're almost as moving as weddings. I'll go, but you stay. Please!'

The next moment Irish Molly had gone, slipping away easily through the loosely knit crowd.

Fergus remained until the ceremony was over. Then, with the others, he stood back respectfully to allow the official mourners to leave first.

Fanny would have walked past without acknowledging him, but Lady Hammond was with her, and the elderly philanthropist recognised him.

'Why, it's the young Scots artist – but of course you met poor Tomas at one of Fanny's parties. You should have joined us . . . Fergus – isn't that your name?'

'*Mister* Vincent came to the funeral with a friend from Lewin's Mead.' Fanny's voice was icy enough to cause Lady Hammond's eyebrows to rise in amused surprise. 'Where has she gone? Lady Hammond would have enjoyed meeting her.'

'Irish Molly was so overcome with grief she had to leave.' Fergus was puzzled by Fanny's unprovoked hostility, but he thought she deserved an explanation. 'She knew Tomas well. She was with him when he died. I believe she is also the sole beneficiary in his will. It was she who persuaded him to come out of hiding and treat the sick Irish families. Because of what happened, Molly feels responsible for his death.'

'Poor girl. I would have liked to meet her. It's time you and I met again, too, young man. Call on me some time soon – and bring your sketchbook with you.' With a smile and a nod of her head, Lady Hammond moved on.

Fanny remained behind for a moment longer and seemed

about to say something to Fergus. Instead, she turned and hurried after Lady Hammond, and the two women walked together to a waiting carriage.

A few nights later a large number of ships docked in Bristol from the West Indies. Fergus took advantage of the increased business at the Hatchet inn. There were more seamen in the inns about the docks than there had been for very many weeks and they were willing to pay for sketches. Fergus did good business, and it came as a great relief. Loaning money to Tomas Casey had left Fergus with little to spare after paying for rent, food and fuel.

It was about eleven o'clock at night when a man made his way to the table where Fergus had just completed a sketch of a black-bearded Welsh seaman. Fergus had seen the man earlier that evening. Seated at a table just inside the door, he seemed to be taking a great interest in Fergus and his work.

Setting his drink on the table, the man sat down facing Fergus. Looking up at him, Fergus smiled and turned to a fresh page of his sketchpad. 'Is it a sketch you're wanting? Well, you've come to the right place.'

'I'm in the right place all right, but what I want to know is the whereabouts of a friend of yours.' The man spoke hoarsely, as though he was suffering from a severe sore throat.

The smile left Fergus's face. 'A friend? If it's Tomas Casey, you're too late. He was buried today.'

'It's not Casey. I want to find a girl. Becky's her name.'

'Why do you want Becky. . . ?' Sudden enlightenment came to Fergus. 'I know you. You're the son of Joe Skewes.'

'Names don't matter. It's Becky I want. I've been told that if anyone knows where she is it's the crippled painter who works the Hatchet inn. I don't see any other crippled painter in here.'

'I'll tell you nothing – except that she's beyond your reach.'

Fergus felt a great rage growing inside him. This was one of the men who had brutally raped Becky. He felt frustration, too. He ought to give this man the beating he deserved, but Fergus realised he would be no match for Alfie Skewes. More than a head taller, the coal-heaver must have been at least four stone heavier, and his face bore the scars of a lifetime of fighting.

Ashamed of his inability to deal with Alfie Skewes as he deserved, Fergus gathered up his sketchpad and made a move to rise from the table. Alfie Skewes leaned across the table and, placing a great hand on Fergus's shoulder, pushed him back in his seat again.

'You'll go when you've told me where I can find the girl. I know she's not living in Back Lane any more. I've been there.'

Fergus struggled to break free, but the grip on his shoulder tightened painfully. In a sudden burst of furious desperation Fergus lashed out with his fist. The blow caught Alfie Skewes over his left eye. There was sufficient force behind the blow to cause Alfie Skewes to release his grip, but before Fergus could make his escape the bullying coal-heaver was on his feet and towering over him.

'I'll teach you to hit me. . . .' Alfie Skewes swung his arm in a backhanded blow and knocked Fergus from his seat to the floor.

As Fergus struggled to sit up Alfie Skewes threw the heavy table to one side. Moving surprisingly quickly for a big man, he leaned down intending to drag Fergus to his feet.

Alfie Skewes was brought to an abrupt halt when a hand as large as his own gripped the back of his jacket collar and hauled him upright.

'I'll have no brawling in my inn. If you've a difference with someone, you'll settle it with words or go elsewhere.'

'Keep out of this, landlord. This is between me and the crippled artist.'

Not until Alfie Skewes had tried unsuccessfully to shake off the hand gripping his collar did he turn around to look at the landlord of the Hatchet inn. He saw a bald-headed man, burly but past his prime. The sight reassured him.

Meanwhile, Charlie Waller was talking to Fergus. 'What's this all about? It's not like you to become involved in any trouble.'

'This is Alfie Skewes. He and his father take their pleasure attacking young girls. The last one fought back and left Alfie with a scar to remember her by. He's trying to make me tell him where she is, so he can teach her a lesson.'

'Oh, you'll tell me all right. By the time I've done with you you'll be singing like a lark.'

Once again Alfie Skewes tried to break free of Charlie Waller's grip, but the landlord screwed the collar tighter. 'It's not singing but *dancing* we'll have here tonight, my beauty — and *you'll* be dancing to *my* tune, make no mistake.'

Alfie Skewes dug back with his elbow, at the same time throwing all his weight behind an attempt to break the landlord's grip.

Charlie Waller was ready for the ploy. The elbow missed him, and he released his grip on Alfie Skewes's collar. As the coal-heaver turned towards him the landlord of the Hatchet inn stepped in close. Two short vicious jabs landed flush on Alfie Skewes's jaw, dropping him to the floor, his senses thoroughly scrambled.

The brief action brought howls of glee from the patrons of the inn. Before the sound died away, Charlie Waller's big voice boomed out: 'I think he's a bit dazed, boys. He's more used to beating young girls who can't fight back. A good dowsing should bring him round. Will you give it to him?'

A loud chorus of 'Ay!' gave Charlie Waller his answer. Putting up only a feeble resistance, Alfie Skewes was picked up bodily. Encircled by a couple of dozen seamen, he was hurried out through the door to the street.

'You saved me from a beating.' Fergus spoke to the landlord as he recovered some of his pencils from the floor beneath the upturned table.

'You ought to pick on someone your own size, me lad, otherwise you'll end up with worse than that — especially if the Skeweses are involved.' Charlie Waller touched a graze beside Fergus's eye, where a ring worn by Alfie Skewes had broken the skin.

'I'll need to watch my step,' agreed Fergus. 'The Skewes family are slow to forget a grudge.'

'You don't need to worry overmuch. When Alfie Skewes

climbs out of the dock he'll find Ivor Primrose waiting for him. Ivor was in the back room enjoying a drink when the trouble began. He'll warn Alfie what to expect if anything happens to you. Ivor's too well known around Lewin's Mead for anyone to want to cross him. Come into the kitchen now and let my wife put something on that cut, or you'll bleed all over your sketches.'

Becky was concerned when she saw the bruising on Fergus's face and learned he had come to blows with Alfie Skewes. However, it was necessary to keep her feelings largely to herself. Because the girls in the Red Lodge reformatory were of dubious morals, the authorities insisted that Fergus's lesson be conducted with the classroom door wedged wide open. Even with this precaution a suspicious official put her head round the doorway every five minutes or so. Yet it was still possible to conduct a conversation while pretending to be criticising a sketch, and occasionally Fergus would enclose Becky's hand in his and guide her pencil over the paper, aware of the knowing grins and elbow-digging of the other girls in the class.

Becky was less understanding when Fergus told her Maude Garrett would soon be moving to Ida Stokes's house in Back Lane.

'Why is *she* going to live there?' She hissed the question at Fergus. 'She's got her own place in Broadmead, and a family to look after.'

'Maude's sister has taken on more responsibility for the family so that Maude can branch out on her own.'

The statement needed no explanation. Becky knew well enough how young girls living alone in Lewin's Mead earned a living.

'You know a lot about it. Who told you?' Becky's quick guarded glance was filled with suspicion.

'Maude has been to the house to talk to Irish Molly a couple of times. I've thanked her for her help in rescuing you from Rose Cottle.'

Becky snorted. 'She's talked to you more than she has to me. Has she been up to your room?'

'Yes. She admired the sketches I've made of you.'

'Are you going to paint *her* picture?'

'I haven't thought about it,' Fergus lied. He was aware that the other girls were taking an increasing interest in the conversation between Becky and himself.

Fearing one of the staff might look into the room while Becky was in such a smoulderingly explosive mood, Fergus took her hand and attempted to move the pencil over the sheet of paper on the desk in front of her. 'We'll talk about it some other time.'

'When? After the lesson's over when I line up with the other girls for my tea? Or during the two hours afterwards when we're all having "religious learning" together? No, I've just remembered, it's *bath* night tonight. This is the night when the staff watch us undress and bath, and make us wash out our mouths with soap if we've been caught swearing during the week.'

Becky pulled her hand free angrily. 'There's *no* way you can talk to me in here. Not without someone listening to every word we say, there isn't. They even walk around our rooms at night to see if they can find out what we're *dreaming* about. I *hate* this place. I hate everyone in it – and I hate *you*, Fergus Vincent.'

Becky's voice became shriller as she gave way to her anger, and as two members of staff hurried into the room the class erupted in pandemonium. Fergus was bundled from the room clutching his sketchpad, and more members of staff arrived to help restore order.

Fergus was left in a small room by himself for more than twenty minutes before the uproar gradually subsided.

Eventually a tall grim-visaged woman entered the room and informed Fergus that Mary Carpenter wished to speak to him.

As he followed the tall member of staff up the stairs to Mary Carpenter's study, Fergus felt depressed. Coming to give sketching lessons to the Red Lodge reformatory inmates provided him with an opportunity to meet and talk with Becky. No doubt the riot in the classroom would put an end to such meetings.

Much to Fergus's surprise he found Mary Carpenter in a cheerful frame of mind. When he tried to apologise for the disturbance, claiming it was his fault, she waved him to silence.

'I have no doubt you *precipitated* the trouble, Mr Vincent, but we have been expecting something like this for quite a while.'

The pioneer reformer smiled at his bewilderment. 'It doesn't surprise you, surely. You are well acquainted with Becky. She's a lively spirited young girl, used to leading a life of almost total independence – as are most of my girls. Confinement in this house, with all the discipline it entails, is totally alien to her. We've been waiting for just such an explosion of temperament. It happens to *all* girls of her type who come here. It's a *good* sign, believe me.'

'But . . . does it mean I'll be able to continue to come here teaching? That was a near-riot in there. . . .'

Mary Carpenter smiled once more. 'No, Mr Vincent. It was the pricking of a fester. The opportunity for some of the wickedness that's in all of us to escape harmlessly. It was a *noisy* incident, nothing more.'

Greatly relieved, Fergus asked eagerly: 'May I speak to Becky before I go?'

Mary Carpenter shook her head. 'I don't think that would be wise. Nor will she attend your next couple of lessons. This is not a punishment, I hasten to add, but Becky is very fond of you. She will feel foolish and ashamed of her behaviour today. She will not *want* to see you for a while. We'll keep her away until she asks if she can resume sketching again. I'm quite certain you understand. But I have much to do – I don't doubt you have, too. Good day, Mr Vincent. We will see you again at the same time next week.'

In spite of Mary Carpenter's reassuring words, Fergus left the Red Lodge with a feeling that he had somehow failed Becky.

He would have felt far worse had he known that from the window of a room, high in the Red Lodge, Becky watched him making his way home to Lewin's Mead. She hoped he might turn and see her, and yet she remained poised to dart away from the window if he *did* turn round. She could see by the set of his shoulders that Fergus felt miserable and the knowledge was a solid painful lump deep inside her.

CHAPTER TWENTY-SEVEN

BEFORE IRIS LEFT IDA STOKES'S HOUSE to marry her Dutch sea-captain the prospective bridegroom threw a party that would be remembered in Lewin's Mead for many months to come.

Fergus was busy painting in his attic studio when the drinks began to arrive. Hearing a noise, he went down the rickety stairs and peered over the banisters to the first floor. A number of firkins of ale were being manhandled up the stairs by cheerful Dutch sailors.

Not wishing to join in the celebrations, Fergus returned to his room and resumed painting. He was nearing completion of the series depicting the plight of the Irish immigrants, and it was an emotionally exhausting task. Committing the tragic figures to canvas conjured up many memories and mental images that he thought he had forgotten.

Fergus soon became totally engrossed with his painting. Although aware of an increasing noise in the remainder of the house, it had no part in his work and he was able to exclude it from his mind.

When the light was beginning to fade he heard footsteps on the stairs to the attic and then there came a hammering at the door. Before he had time to rise from his chair the door opened and Maude Garrett entered the room carrying two battered pewter tankards in one hand.

'I thought this was where you'd be. Aren't you coming downstairs to join in Iris's party? Everyone else in the house is there. I'm going to have a hell of a job clearing up when I move in tomorrow.'

Fergus shrugged apologetically. 'I've got a lot of work to do. I want to complete the paintings of the Irish. . . .'

'I knew you'd have some excuse for not coming down, that's why I've brought a drink up for you.'

'That's very thoughtful of you, Maude.' Fergus had been so engrossed in his work he had paused for neither food nor drink since breakfast. He took a full tankard from her hands and raised it to his lips, believing it to contain ale. The fumes that rose to his nostrils told him of his error, but by then he had already taken a deep gulp and was coughing out his mistake.

'I thought you was going at it a bit greedy.' Maude Garrett put down her own tankard and began thumping his back as she spoke. 'That's real good brandy, that is. Captain Gobius brought it in a barrel specially for his wedding.'

It was some minutes before Fergus could breathe normally once more and take another sip from the tankard. He nodded appreciatively. It *was* very good brandy.

Meanwhile Maude Garrett was inspecting the paintings lined up against a wall to dry. As she crouched down to look more closely at one of the paintings her thin dress was stretched taut across her back and Fergus saw that she was pitifully thin. Skinnier even than Becky.

Straightening up suddenly, Maude Garrett turned to look at Fergus with an expression of new respect. 'These are beautiful paintings, Fergus. But they're so *sad*. They make me want to cry.'

'That's exactly how I felt when I made the sketches.' Acutely aware of the brandy warming his empty stomach, Fergus studied a painting depicting the afflicted Irish families being escorted away from the derelict houses. 'They were a doomed people.'

'Do you always feel something for the people you're painting?' Maude Garrett had moved on and was examining a number of completed paintings, among them some of Becky.

'That depends on the subject.' Fergus made a guarded reply.

'I hope you haven't forgotten you've promised to paint me.'

'I've promised to *sketch* you,' Fergus corrected her. 'There's a difference.'

'All right — to *sketch* me, then. When?'

Fergus shrugged. The brandy was taking effect and he felt at peace with the world. 'Any time. *Now* if you like.'

'Yes, do it now. What do you want me to do?'

Fergus drained his tankard and handed it to her. 'You can go and get me another drink while I look out a good pencil.'

Maude Garrett's face had a fine bone structure, but she was not a good model. She insisted on adopting unnatural facial poses that could not be transferred to paper. Nevertheless, by persuading her to talk to him as he worked, Fergus caught her unawares often enough to produce a good likeness. However, Maude was not happy with the sketch.

'I don't look like *that*!'

The sketch showed a certain sharpness of expression that was not immediately discernible on Maude Garrett's face.

'The light isn't too good right now,' he pleaded. 'Besides, it takes more than a single sketch if I'm to get a true likeness.'

The explanation seemed to satisfy Maude Garrett. Still looking at the sketch, she suddenly smiled. 'I expect you're right. It isn't too bad really, although it looks as though I'm wearing what my sister Lisa calls my "someone's-going-to-suffer-for-this" expression.'

'How is your sister? Will she be able to care for the family when you've moved out?'

Maude Garrett's smile disappeared. 'She'll *have* to. Pa's giving her a hard time, but I've put up with him for long enough. It's her turn now.'

Her voice died away as they both heard someone noisily negotiating the stairs outside the room. There was a crash and mumbled cursing as the unseen visitor slipped. Then there was a noisy hammering at the door.

Fergus lifted the latch, and as he opened the door a large man with greying hair and an unkempt beard fell into the room.

The bearded man blinked in the sudden light of the oil-lamp, a luxury Fergus had recently acquired. Rising to his feet, he extended a large hand to Fergus. 'You must be the artist. I am Pieter Gobius. I am to marry Iris. You have not come to our party. Do you not wish us happiness together?'

Then the Dutch sea-captain saw Maude Garrett standing in the shadows at the far end of the long attic room.

'I am sorry. You have *other* reasons for not coming to my party. No matter, you will come. She will come, too. *Everybody* comes to my wedding party. You must bring this.' Captain Pieter Gobius picked up a sketchpad and waved it drunkenly in front of Fergus's face. 'You will make a picture of Iris and me.'

Fergus did not feel inclined to argue with the sea-captain. In any case, the brandy brought to the attic by Maude Garrett had put him in the mood for a party.

'All right. I'll give you a sketch as a wedding present. Lead on. You, too, Maude.'

Maude Garrett scowled as she left the attic. She had planned to spend much of the evening in Fergus's studio.

The party was in full noisy swing when the trio from the attic room arrived, but Captain Gobius's voice was capable of carrying to men in the rigging of a ship at the height of a North Sea storm. He needed to call for silence only once before the noise faltered and died away.

'You will clear a space for me and Iris to have a drawing made of us.' Turning to Fergus, Pieter Gobius asked: 'Where would you like us to be?'

As Fergus looked around the dingy overcrowded room, the voice of Irish Molly called loudly: 'Let Fergus sketch you both in bed together. It'll remind you of when you first met.'

When the ribald laughter had died down, Fergus said sheepishly: 'Actually, the bed *is* the best place in the room. If the two of you can sit on the edge together. . . .'

His words were greeted with cheers, and Irish Molly could be heard shouting jubilantly: 'There, what did I tell you? It's the natural place for the pair of 'em.'

Iris and her husband-to-be settled themselves self-consciously on the edge of the bed, but they grew more relaxed when Fergus brought them closer together. When he ordered Pieter Gobius to put an arm about Iris's shoulders the good-natured bantering began again.

Fergus sketched quickly, used to working in the Hatchet inn. When he eventually ripped the page from his sketchpad and passed it over, the not-so-young couple beamed their delight. Fergus had been kind in his portraiture, carefully playing down the defects of both parties.

'It is good. It is *very* good.' Pieter Gobius's voice boomed out his approval. 'Give the young artist a drink. A large brandy.'

Moments later Fergus had another huge brandy in his hand. It was his third of the evening, and things became increasingly hazy thereafter. He remembered repeated requests for sketches, and he executed them at a rapid rate, but his pencil could not keep up with the demand – or the amount of brandy being forced upon him.

He kept going until he suddenly found himself sitting on the floor, sketchpad and pencil gone, and with only a half-empty tankard of brandy for company, while the stamping feet of 'dancers' shook dust from the floorboards beside him.

'Come on, it's time I got you back to your room.'

It was Maude Garrett's coaxing words rather than her doubtful strength which brought Fergus to his feet after he had rescued his sketchpad from beneath the bed. She guided him through the crowd and past a couple embracing at the foot of the stairs to the attic. Fergus thought the woman looked like Ida Stokes, but he dismissed the identification immediately, attributing it to the poor light and the effects of the brandy he had consumed.

Fergus never knew how he negotiated the stairs, remembering only that at one stage he gave up the steep climb, declaring that if he had wanted to climb mountains he would have remained in Scotland.

He *did* eventually reach his room because he could remember unsuccessfully trying to focus his bleary eyes on the lamp. He also had a vague recollection of indignantly protesting when he lay on his bed as someone undressed him. . . . But he remembered nothing more of that night.

Fergus came awake with a sudden start. Opening his eyes he saw the ceiling above him and raised his head as he always did, to gauge the time from the light coming through the attic window. The move set loose the hammers held poised above their anvils by a dozen blacksmiths – all gathered and waiting in Fergus's head.

His head dropped back on the pillow, and a groan of self-pity escaped from between lips that felt like dry leather to the touch of his furred and bloated tongue.

The sound had an echo from nearby, and there was a movement in the bed beside him. Then a body came into contact with his own – and both were as naked as newborn babies.

Battling successfully against pain and the nauseous swinging of the room about him, Fergus struggled to a sitting position and peered down at Maude Garrett.

Fergus leaped from the bed, his self-induced ailments forgotten. By the time Maude Garrett stretched spindly arms above her head and opened one brown eye to gaze in his direction, he was hopping awkwardly in a clumsy circle, trying to thread a second leg inside a pair of trousers.

Maude Garrett sat up, and her skinny chest settled into an undernourished semblance of womanly form.

'What time is it?'

'Late. Past nine, certainly.' His voice emanated from deep within his throat.

'Christ! I'm hours late for work. I'll have the sack. . . .' Her urgency ebbed away as suddenly as it had sprung into being, and Maude Garrett lay back on the bed again. 'Oh, what the hell! I move into Iris's room today and begin a new life.' She turned both her brown eyes on Fergus. 'Do you think the party is still going on?'

Fergus groaned. 'I don't even want to think about it. I feel too ill.'

'Poor Fergus.' Maude Garrett threw back the blanket, exposing her thin body as far as her knees. 'Come back to bed. I'll make you feel better. . . .'

Fergus had his trousers on just in time. His stomach was heaving, and the communal privies were in the backyard. He fled barefoot down the stairs, determined to reach the yard in time.

When Fergus returned to the attic room, ashen-faced and wan, Maude Garrett was dressed and the kettle rattled merrily on the fire.

'Sit down. I'll make you some tea. Would you like any breakfast? No, I didn't think so.'

Fergus sat down shakily and followed Maude's movements about the room. When she put a mug of steaming tea on the table in front of him he put his hand around the mug gratefully, avoiding looking up into her face.

'Are you sure you know what you're doing? The life you intend leading ... ?'

Maude Garrett snorted derisively. 'That's a funny question after last night. Yes, I know what I'm doing. Irish Molly's going to take me to the White Hart with her and show me the ropes. It'll be good to be working for myself and not having to hand over most of my money to the old man, for him to spend on drink. I'll make sure the kids don't go short, though.'

Fergus winced, not because of the life Maude Garrett intended leading, but because of her references to the previous night.

'Did anything happen last night? I mean ... between you and me?'

'Don't you remember? I'll need to work harder if I'm to have my regulars, like Irish Molly.'

Fergus groaned. 'I'm sorry.... I was so drunk I don't remember a thing.'

'If you wanted to go back to bed again, I could remind you.'

Maude Garrett was enjoying his discomfiture, and Fergus rose to his feet unsteadily. 'I'm going out. I need some fresh air.'

'I expect I'll be in my own room when you get back. Call in and see me, Fergus ... *any* time.'

Crossing the first-floor landing, Fergus thought Maude Garrett was being unduly optimistic. It looked as though a battle had been fought in the room she was to occupy. Bodies, bottles, barrels, tankards and all manner of rubbish extended as far as the front door of the house. There was even a man dressed as a seaman lying in the gutter in the street outside, the linings of his empty pockets ominously displayed to the world.

Fergus wandered disconsolately about the quays, watching ships being loaded and unloaded. The rattle of block and tackle vied with the creak and clatter of horses and wagons, and wagoners cursed their horses as shod hoofs slipped and slid on cobblestones wet from the light drizzle that fell on the city.

It was autumn cold, and Fergus shivered. He had come out without a coat, but he did not want to return to Back Lane just yet. He found a small coffee-house on the quayside and for twopence bought a large mug of weak but sweet coffee. He sat in the dismal coffee-house warming his hands about the mug.

Fergus wished he could remember more of what had occurred the previous night. There were brief recollections of tripping on the stairs while someone tried to steady him, and of lying on his bed while someone else undressed him. He cringed at the thought. He was very self-conscious of his crippled leg and rarely allowed anyone else to see it. Fergus tried to stretch his memory, but it was a total blank. He would never know what had happened after he had been put to bed by Maude Garrett.

Sitting in the coffee-shop feeling cold and ill, Fergus came close to abandoning his dream of recording the life of those who lived in the slums of Bristol. He could move on to London, perhaps. Begin again.

Just then a young urchin came into the coffee-shop wearing a dress consisting of a slip of sacking, stitched up the sides and with holes for head and arms. Her face was as dirty as he had once seen Becky's.

The urchin was begging, and the coffee-shop proprietor waved a cloth in the air, ordering her to get out. Expressionless, she had turned to obey when Fergus called her back.

Reaching in his pocket, he pulled out a fourpenny piece. He had once given a coin of the same value to Becky. The urchin's face lit up with delight, and she ran from the coffee-shop as though afraid Fergus might change his mind. Behind the counter at the far end of the coffee-shop the proprietor dried a cup with the dirty cloth and shook his head in disapproval.

Rising to his feet, Fergus limped to the door. Hunching his shoulders against the drizzle, he stepped outside on to the wet cobblestones of the quayside.

He would not leave Bristol. He would continue painting children like the one who had just left the coffee-shop and he would put together an exhibition that would bring their plight home to the world.

He owed it to Becky.

CHAPTER TWENTY-EIGHT

IT WAS THREE WEEKS before Fergus saw Becky again. Mary Carpenter had sent a message to him, suggesting that he cancel his lessons for the two weeks following the trouble at the Red Lodge.

When Fergus did return he found an unrepentant Becky who refused to apologise for her behaviour on the occasion of their previous meeting. Indeed, she hardly spoke to Fergus during the whole time he was there.

For the next few weeks Fergus showed great patience, and the rift between them healed slowly. Then, one late autumn day, when the first frost of the year had put a silver sheen on the grass of the park sloping away up the hill from the Red Lodge, Fergus entered the reformatory to a welcome from Becky that was warm enough to dispel the chill from the high-ceilinged room. The unsmiling classroom supervisor passed her charges into Fergus's care and had hardly left the room when Becky suddenly hugged Fergus and planted a happy kiss on his cheek.

Hastily waving her classmates to silence, Fergus asked what he had done to deserve such a welcome.

'It's because I'm happy to belong to you.'

'*Belong* to me? I don't understand.'

'Well, I do. Fanny Tennant said so. She brought a lady to see us. A *real* lady. . . . Lady Hammond, I think her name is. Fanny Tennant called me to the front of the class and said: "This is Becky; she's Fergus Vincent's *protégée*."' Becky said the word slowly and carefully, as though she had been practising. 'I asked Selina what it meant, and she said it means you belong to someone.'

Selina was the brightest of the girls in the reformatory, placed there for her part in a banknote fraud that had netted hundreds of pounds and resulted in two counterfeiters being gaoled for life.

Becky looked at Fergus anxiously, afraid she had made a fool of herself. 'That *is* what it means?'

Fergus smiled. 'I guess it does – and, yes, you are certainly my *protégée*.'

'There you are, then!' Becky beamed triumphantly. 'If I'd known I was your *protégée* . . . if you'd *told* me, I wouldn't have caused you half the trouble I have.'

She frowned. 'How did I become your *protégée*?' She was enjoying the use of her new-found word.

'It happened when I became fond of you and began to feel responsible for you.'

'Does that mean you're my *protégé*, too?'

'Not exactly. . . .' The other girls were following the conversation with great interest, and Fergus was aware that the lesson should have begun. 'We'll discuss it some other time. You'd all better begin sketching now.'

'All right, if you say so.' Becky smiled happily at him, and Fergus wondered whether Fanny Tennant had any idea how her simple introduction had brightened Becky's young life.

Fergus worked hard at his paintings until a shortage of money sent him back to the Hatchet inn. However, he still took his sketchpad about with him whenever he went out during the daylight hours. The cold weather heralded an early winter, and beggars, vagrants and the desperately poor had already donned their winter 'fashions'. Every available form of covering was utilised to protect thin bodies from wind and weather. Tattered blankets, sacking and even newspapers were brought into use, but even such primitive protection was beyond the means of a few orphaned urchins. Fergus sketched them as they sheltered in corners and doorways, angry red chilblains flourishing on their dirty hands and feet.

Fergus had seen little of Fanny Tennant since Tomas Casey's funeral. It was as though she was deliberately avoiding him, even when he gave his weekly lesson in the ragged school. It came as something of a surprise, therefore, when Fanny walked into one of his classes at the ragged school. After greeting Fergus politely she went to a corner of the room where pupils squatted on the floor sketching a quite ordinary pitcher. After inspecting their half-completed drawings she returned to stand beside Fergus and looked down at the sketch he was making of the class at work.

'We always seem to have a full class for your sketching, Fergus.' She spoke quietly, so as not to disturb the working children.

'It's warmer in here than out on the streets.' This at least was true. Through the high rounded windows the sky was a sullen snow-filled grey.

'I believe it's something more than that. Whatever it is, I wish we could bring it into our other lessons. The numbers of our pupils are dropping quite dramatically.'

'Perhaps the school is suffering as a result of your absence.'

'Because I don't often attend the school on the days *you're* here doesn't mean I am not here on the other days. . . .' Aware of the possible interpretation of her words, Fanny explained: 'I help my father one day a week, but he is in London on business for a while.'

'I wasn't being critical, merely making an observation. I realise you lead a very busy life . . . but I also believe the ragged school needs you.'

'I wonder. Indeed, I sometimes wonder whether it might not be better for everyone – especially for *me* – if I gave up the whole wretched idea. Perhaps I should take my father's advice and spend more time in London, or seeing something of the Continent.'

Fanny's words rocked Fergus. He had always looked upon her as being totally dedicated to her 'good causes'.

Fanny saw his bewilderment and she shrugged apologetically. 'I'm sorry, Fergus. I am feeling particularly depressed this morning. I was called to the Bridewell police station last night. One of our pupils is in trouble. She is involved with an

233

unsavoury young man who has been in and out of prison regularly since he was eight years old. Last night they entered a house, threatened an old lady and stole some silver. They ran from the house straight into the arms of two constables.'

Fanny shook her head sadly. 'I cannot understand her. She is such a bright young girl. One of the school's best pupils. I had great hopes of setting her on the path to a decent future, perhaps using her as an example for others to follow. Now she'll receive ten years, or more, in prison. When she comes out, thieving or prostitution will be her only means of earning a living. Before long she will be back in prison again – and that will be the pattern of her miserable existence. It's a tragedy.'

Fergus was about to make a trivial remark about life being simple were it not complicated by people, but he could see that Fanny was deeply upset.

'We mustn't expect too much of people, Fanny. Especially those brought up in Lewin's Mead. Things that seem everyday to us appear frighteningly strange to them – and, God knows, the familiar is frightening enough.'

'I seem to remember suggesting you should apply such splendid logic to your relationship with Becky.'

After only the slightest hesitation, Fergus said: 'I do, but I'm always willing to help her improve *herself*.'

Fergus's hesitation had nothing to do with the reply he made. He was wondering why, whenever he was talking with either Becky or Fanny, each seemed disproportionately interested in the other.

'That wasn't a fair comment, Fergus. I'm sorry. I really came here to remind you of your promise to show your sketches to Lady Hammond. I met her a day or two ago. She said if you don't soon bring her some of your work she will be forced to visit your studio, in Back Lane.'

For a moment Fergus contemplated the stir a visit from Lady Hammond would cause in the squalid and overcrowded slum. He dismissed the thought immediately. Ida Stokes's house was no place for Lady Hammond.

'I haven't forgotten. I'll show them to her.'

'When?'

'I have a lot of paintings to do that I haven't even begun yet. . . .'

'Lady Hammond isn't asking to see all your work. She would like to see a sample. Some sketches and one or two paintings, no more.'

'I do have *some* paintings completed. . . .'

'Good. When can I tell her to expect you?'

Fanny was forcing Fergus into making a decision. There was no way he could wriggle free without appearing churlish – and no *real* reason why he should. Ironically, the true reason for his prevarication was the one he had given to explain the behaviour of those who lived in Lewin's Mead. He was as reluctant to move on into the unknown as were they.

Fergus had spent many months sketching the Bristol slum and had built up a remarkable pictorial catalogue of its people and their way of life. There was still much work to be done before he would be satisfied with his self-imposed task. It would *never* be fully comprehensive, but the time was fast approaching when others would need to judge whether his work was worthwhile. Fanny was pushing that time closer.

There was some justification for Fergus's apprehension. Lady Hammond was an acknowledged art expert. Her comments about Fergus's paintings and sketches would be accepted by the art world, of which she was a formidable part. If she were to be critical of his paintings, his dream of showing them to the world at large would be over.

Fergus was not certain he would find Lady Hammond's approval any easier to accept. He would then come under pressure to complete his project. There would be exhibitions, discussions of his work, and no doubt commissions, too. The simple life he had been leading in Back Lane would be over. He would become part of the larger world once more.

'If you don't want to take your sketches and paintings to Lady Hammond, I will willingly take them for you. I'll come to Back Lane and collect them, if you wish.'

'No.' The word came out unintentionally abruptly, but Fergus would not entrust his completed paintings to anyone else, especially if they were to be carried through the narrow thief-infested alleyways of the Lewin's Mead rookery. 'I'll take them myself.'

'When?' Fanny was relentless.

'Next week, some time.'

'What day next week – and at what time? I'll come with you and show you the way.'

By the time Fanny left the classroom Fergus had committed himself to taking a sketchpad and two completed paintings to show Lady Hammond. He would bring them to the ragged school at six o'clock the following Tuesday evening, and Fanny would be waiting with a carriage to take Fergus and his work to Lady Hammond's Clifton home.

CHAPTER TWENTY-NINE

LADY SARAH HAMMOND'S HOME was sumptuous, even by Clifton standards. A liveried butler opened the door to Fergus and Fanny and escorted them to the room where Lady Hammond sat with a number of her friends. Fergus was disconcerted by the company. He had expected to be showing his work only to Lady Hammond. He was not dressed to meet the guests he found in her house.

Lady Hammond saw his discomfiture and guessed the reason immediately. Advancing across the room, she took his arm and led him to the large table where a servant had placed the paintings and sketches, waving for her other guests to follow.

To Fergus, she said: 'You can meet the others later. They're here because they have been *dying* to meet you and see your work. Actually, the only one you need take any notice of is Ferdinand. Ferdinand Lascelles. Of course, if he *really* likes them, he'll probably refuse to say anything at all, for fear you'll put up the price when he tries to buy them.'

Now Fergus was more certain than ever that it had been a mistake to bring his work here. Ferdinand Lascelles was a famous art critic and dealer. One wrong word from him this evening and any future Fergus might have had as a painter would be ruined.

They reached the table with the others close behind, and Lady Hammond released Fergus's arm. 'You can begin by showing us some of your sketches. Fanny speaks of them as though they depict life in another world, so let us inside this world of yours, young man.'

Fergus had brought his personal sketchpad, not the one he took to the Hatchet inn. It commenced with sketches of Becky and life in and about Back Lane. It also included sketches made on board the ill-fated paddle-steamer. The polite murmurs of Lady Hammond's guests turned to silence when the pages began to show ragged urchins seeking food amidst the rubbish piled in the Lewin's Mead alleyways.

The unfolding of the drama of the Irish vagrants on the pages of Fergus's sketchpad provoked gasps of horror, and Lady Hammond asked Fergus to explain the series of harrowing sketches.

The guests listened in shocked silence until Fergus revealed that the subjects of the sketches were Irish. One of the men snorted derisively: 'You should have told us that in the first place, young man, and we need not have wasted our sympathy.'

'Why? Does dying come easier to *Irish* children?' Fergus's voice was deceptively quiet as he tried hard to control the anger he felt.

'I think *I* would like to hear your answer to that question, General.' Support for Fergus came from Fanny.

The general looked from Fergus to Fanny and he smiled condescendingly. 'Ah! The innocent compassion of youth. Such sentiment is sadly misplaced where the Irish are concerned. As a race, they have scant regard for life. Why, I've known instances where women and children urged their menfolk to murder captured British soldiers, then fought each other to be first to strip the clothes from the murdered men's still-twitching bodies.'

'I could introduce you to a hundred women and children right here in Lewin's Mead who would do the same – and men who'd kill and rob an old woman for sixpence. *They're* all English. I can also name an Irishman who forfeited his own life to help others – and another who grieved as deeply for his wife and children as any Englishman. Fanny, will you hand me that top canvas?'

When Fergus had the wooden-framed canvas painting in his hand he turned it over and held it up to view. It was a painting of a dying woman lying on the rat-gnawed floor-boards of a room in one of the derelict riverside houses. Her arm was about her dead baby, and her tearful husband knelt helplessly by her side.

When Fergus eventually lowered the painting, only the general remained unmoved.

'It's an artist's business to use his imagination. He must paint a picture capable of moving prospective purchasers. It's something you do well, Mr Vincent.'

Fergus placed the painting back on the table. 'I wish I could say that scene existed only in my mind, General. Sadly, it was painted from life – and death – right here in Bristol.'

'Minutes afterwards that man was driven out of the city, leaving his wife and two children lying dead behind him. The order came from you, I believe, General?' asked Fanny.

'They were moved out of Bristol on my instructions, yes. As chairman of the Health Committee I still believe I made the correct decision,' the general bristled angrily. 'I've never been one to run away from a difficult decision, young lady.'

'What an interesting evening this promises to be.' Lady Hammond smiled disarmingly at her guests before moving closer to the table, where Ferdinand Lascelles was turning the pages of Fergus's sketchpad.

'What do you think of them, Ferdinand dear?'

'They are quite good,' replied the art critic cautiously.

'Come now, Ferdinand. You can do better than that. Give us an *honest* opinion – as an art expert, not as a prospective buyer.'

Ferdinand Lascelles seemed more amused than embarrassed by Lady Hammond's remarks. 'Very well. You are an extremely talented young man, Fergus. *Exceptionally* talented. Your paintings – the sketches in particular – display a rare sympathy with your subject. You also have the ability to transfer that sympathy to canvas. Technically, too, you are extremely skilful. If I were to make any criticism at all, it would be that the colours in your paintings are perhaps a little *too* delicate – although this does serve to make them quite distinctive. There, does that satisfy you, Lady Hammond? It should, it's more fulsome praise than I have ever given to an unknown artist before. As a result I have probably priced myself out of the market for this second painting – the young urchin looking out of a window. It is quite delightful.'

'That one's not for sale,' said Fergus hurriedly. The painting was of Becky looking out of the attic window at the family of sparrows. 'I've promised it to the model . . . when she returns to Lewin's Mead.'

Lady Hammond peered at the painting. 'Why, it's that young *protégée* of yours. The girl in the reformatory. I hope she will appreciate such a gift.'

'I believe she will.'

'Good. Shall we dine now? You'll sit next to me, Fergus. I have a proposition to put to you. . . .'

In the dining room Lady Hammond sat at the head of the table, with Fergus on her right and Fanny beside him. Fergus was relieved to see that the general had been given pride of place at the far end of the table, where he happily dominated the conversation about him.

During the meal Lady Hammond unfolded her suggestions for the future of Fergus and his art. She would provide him with a studio and accommodation in Clifton where he could produce paintings from the many sketches he had made of Lewin's Mead and the people who lived and worked there. He would be free to accept commissions during this time and, as Fanny pointed out, Bristol 'society' women would flock to him when the comments made by Ferdinand Lascelles were repeated and it became known that Lady Hammond had become Fergus's patron.

'I'm not certain I *want* to paint portraits of society women,' asserted Fergus. 'I came to Bristol to paint the people of Lewin's Mead.'

'Nonsense!' Lady Hammond spoke sharply. 'You've sketched *hundreds* of characters from this dreadful slum. Do you want to sketch them all over again? Or do you wish to become a well-known and respected painter? Besides, what are you doing with the paintings of your slum-dwellers? Is your way of life a crusade to make Bristol's more fortunate citizens aware of the plight of their fellow-men? Very well, I will arrange an exhibition of your work – and I promise that every alderman and councillor in the city will attend. How long will it take you to produce enough paintings for such an exhibition?'

'I don't know. . . .' The unexpected and generous offer took Fergus by surprise. 'Probably the best part of a year.'

'Ferdinand!' Lady Hammond's voice cut through the conversation around the table. 'If Fergus produces enough paintings of his precious slum-dwellers, could an exhibition be arranged in Bristol – say, in a year's time?'

'Of course. I know many men who would be delighted to be associated with such an exhibition. It will prove one of the most important for many years, you have my word.'

'There! Does that suit you, my young artist friend? Will you agree to have one of Ferdinand's friends make you famous?'

'You are most generous, Lady Hammond.'

'It is a wonderful opportunity, Fergus.' Fanny added her own quiet persuasiveness to the discussion. 'It's the chance to have your talent recognised, and the fulfilment of your dream. Why are you hesitating?'

'I don't know.'

Fergus tried to find words to explain his confused thoughts – words that would make sense to the others seated about the table. Becky would have understood. . . . And suddenly he knew the cause of his doubts. If he left the house in Back Lane, it would feel as though he was abandoning Becky. She belonged to Lewin's Mead. It was not the reason he gave to Fanny.

'Perhaps I'm worried that I won't capture the true essence of my subject if I live outside Lewin's Mead.' The excuse sounded feeble and ungrateful. 'If I moved away and things didn't work out, it would be a disaster for me.'

'Unless you give it a try you'll never know.' Lady Hammond's manner became suddenly brisk. 'You could keep your room in the slums – and return there occasionally if you found it necessary to recapture this "essence" you consider to be so important. I have offered you my patronage, Fergus. The decision whether or not to accept must be yours.'

Peremptorily dismissing the subject with a brief movement of her hand, Lady Hammond raised her voice to carry above the chatter. 'Shall we adjourn? Ferdinand has found a delightful new painting for me. I must show it to you. It's a hunting scene — rather more to your liking, I fancy, General.'

As they left the dining room Fanny walked beside Fergus. Without glancing at him, she asked: 'Have you thought of the effect any decision you make will have upon Becky's future?'

Fergus looked at her sharply. 'In what way?'

'Unless I and the staff of the Red Lodge have misread the situation, Becky is going to want to be near you when she is eventually released. Do you *really* want her to go back to Lewin's Mead and all that Mary Carpenter is trying to put behind her?'

Fergus was still pondering Fanny's words when he climbed the stairs to his room in Back Lane. Fanny was right, of course. Becky could never escape from her past here. Where would she live? *How* would she live? Sleeping in the overcrowded room occupied by Mary O'Ryan and her succession of 'paramours' had always been fraught with danger for Becky. When she left the Red Lodge she would be a couple of years older — and even the most innocent of observers could see she had already left childhood behind. To think of her sharing a room with Irish Molly or Maude Garrett was equally unthinkable. That left only Fergus. Becky had slept in his room before, and he knew she would expect to again, but was it only for this she was learning to read and write and to be 'more like Fanny Tennant'?

Clutching his paintings and sketchbook, Fergus pushed open the door to the attic room and fumbled for matches and a candle on the shelf where he kept them. As he did so his foot kicked against something on the floor. Fergus was puzzled. He had left the room tidy before going out. As he shifted his foot he trod on something that broke beneath his shoe. Reaching down, he felt the broken frame of a prepared canvas.

Groping in the darkness, Fergus finally located the candle. Striking one of the long matches, he produced a flame and applied it to the candle – but by then he had already seen the mess about him. Canvases and pages from the sketchbooks he had left in the room were strewn about the floor. His expensive lamp was smashed. So, too, was the easel made by Henry Gordon. There were paint-smears on the walls, and broken brushes were strewn about the floor.

The room was a shambles. Fergus stood amidst the debris and gazed about him in utter dismay. Whoever had wrecked the room had done so in an unsystematic manner. Many of his sketches had been screwed up, or torn beyond redemption. Others could still be used. Nevertheless, the damage caused to his prepared canvases and painting equipment was serious. If Fergus had not taken his most important sketch-pad to Lady Hammond's house, the vandalism would have proved disastrous.

Outside the room one of the stairs creaked beneath a stealthy footstep, and Fergus looked about him for a handy weapon. He settled for the iron poker that stood in the grate. Snuffing out the candle, he took up a position in the shadows close to the door. If the destructive burglar was returning, he would receive a shock.

'Fergus . . .? Are you in there?' Maude Garrett's nervous whisper came through the door.

Fergus relit the candle, and Maude Garrett entered the attic room cautiously, gazing wide-eyed about her at the damage.

'Do you know anything about this?'

Maude Garrett nodded. 'It happened this evening, as me and Irish Molly were getting ready to go out. We'd left it late because there aren't many ships in —'

'Who did it?'

'Joe Skewes. We heard someone coming up the stairs and thought it was you. There was a bit of noise, but we thought you might have been drinking. But when we heard things being smashed up Irish Molly came up here and found Joe.'

Maude Garrett looked at Fergus and shrugged helplessly. 'He'd have made a better job of it if she hadn't stopped him when she did.'

'But why should Joe Skewes want to smash up my studio?' As he asked the question Fergus remembered his first encounter with Joe Skewes, and the sketch he had made for Constable Ivor Primrose. But that had been too long ago to provoke this.

'Joe Skewes was after Becky. He's been drinking since coming out of prison yesterday and came looking for trouble.'

'Where is he now?'

'Irish Molly took him off to the White Hart and got him so ginned up he couldn't remember his own name. She said to tell you he wouldn't be back tonight. She also said she'd expect you to foot the bill.'

Fergus began to pick up sketches from the floor. 'I hope she also told him Becky's not living here any more. There's months of work in these sketches, and most of them are irreplaceable.'

Maude Garrett began to help Fergus with his task. 'It's no good telling anything to Joe Skewes. When he's full of drink he'll not remember a thing he's told – but he won't forget that he's going to get even with Becky. He'll come here again. If he doesn't find her, he'll take it out on you instead.'

'He's mad. Someone ought to have him locked away.' Fergus's anger flared as he found a half-completed painting with a hole kicked through the canvas.

'He's not all there,' agreed Maude Garrett. 'And Alfie's no better, but it would take a brave man to try to have either of 'em put away. Oh, look at this beautiful lamp of yours. It's smashed to bits.'

Maude Garrett placed the pieces of broken oil-lamp on the window-sill and turned to watch Fergus for a while.

'Leave it until morning. Come down to my room and I'll make you a nice cup of tea. I'm not working tonight. . . .'

Fergus shook his head. He did not want to have to listen to Maude Garrett's chatter – or to go along with whatever else she might have in mind. He needed to think.

Maude Garrett's shrug did not hide her disappointment. 'Please yourself, I'm sure. I must be poor company compared with all your swanky friends.'

She waited a few more moments, hoping for a reply, but Fergus was lost in thought. He hardly noticed her departure, noisy though it was.

244

Fergus slept very little that night. He lay on his bed gazing up at the ceiling for a long time and he was awake when Irish Molly returned home. She was not alone, but the voice of the man with her was not that of Joe Skewes.

Fergus was still awake when the first dull grey light of dawn filled the attic windows. By then he had made up his mind. He would continue to pay rent to Ida Stokes for the attic. It would form a base for his sketching forays into the maze of the Lewin's Mead streets. But he would accept Lady Hammond's offer and move his studio to Clifton.

It was the only sensible thing to do. His sketches were too valuable for him to risk another visit from Joe Skewes. Sooner or later the Skewes men would go back to prison. When this happened he would consider returning to Back Lane.

Belatedly, Fergus dozed off. His last waking thoughts were of Becky. He hoped she would understand.

CHAPTER THIRTY

BECKY did *not* understand Fergus's decision to move away from Lewin's Mead, and she greeted his news with dismay and bewilderment. They were in the garden of the Red Lodge, Fergus having wrung permission from Mary Carpenter to pay Becky a private visit.

'But *why* do you want to leave Back Lane? I thought the attic was ideal for your painting. You've told me so yourself, many times.'

'It *is* ideal, and there's no question of my *wanting* to leave,' Fergus explained patiently. 'But from now on I'll be painting for an exhibition, and that costs both time and money. I can't risk having Joe Skewes or his son come there while I'm out and destroying everything I've done.'

'Joe Skewes was drunk when he went there. He won't have remembered a thing about it when he sobered up. It won't happen again.'

'Are you saying Joe Skewes won't be drunk again? Or that Alfie Skewes won't come looking for me when Constable Primrose's warning isn't quite so fresh in his mind?'

'This is all my fault, isn't it, you having to leave Lewin's Mead and being threatened by the Skewes family? If I hadn't been so stupid, everything would be all right. You'd still be in your attic – and I'd be there, too.'

'Things *would* have been different,' Fergus admitted, 'but you mustn't blame yourself. We all do foolish things and most of us get away with them. You were unlucky enough to fall foul of Rose Cottle and her friends.'

Becky sank into an introspective silence for a while, then she raised her head and looked directly at Fergus. 'None of it would have happened if I didn't care so much for you. When you took me on that boat you gave me the most wonderful and exciting day of my life. I *had* to give you something in return. That's why I took that watch for you. I wasn't to know I was taking it from Fanny Tennant's old man, was I? Anyway, he could walk into a shop and buy another; I couldn't – and neither could you. I wanted you to have a watch. When you said you didn't want it I thought it was because it was coming from *me*. . . . That you didn't want to feel . . . *beholden*.'

'Beholden' was another new word in Becky's rapidly expanding vocabulary. Fergus had seen it written on the blackboard in the classroom where he gave his sketching lessons.

Fergus was deeply moved. Becky was not given to expressing her true feelings. He took her hand in a sudden gesture of affection. 'Becky, you don't *need* to steal for me. There's no one in this whole world I would rather be beholden to. I'm more fond of you than of anyone else I know.'

'Honest? Even after what's happened?' Becky searched the recesses of her mind for the most sacred oath she could find. One to which Fergus would not dare lie. 'God's truth?'

'God's truth, Becky.'

'I think more of you than anyone else, too.'

From the corner of his eye Fergus saw one of the reformatory supervisors advancing determinedly down the steps of the house towards them. 'You won't do anything silly because I'm leaving Lewin's Mead?'

'I'll try not to. Where will you live?'

'Clifton.'

'At Fanny Tennant's house?' All the happiness disappeared from Becky's face.

'No. Lady Hammond is to become my patron. I'm to live in a studio in the grounds of her house.'

The smile returned. 'Then, I don't mind, and when you're famous I'll be proud of you. I'll make you proud of me too. . . .'

'*Mr Vincent!* You will release this girl's hand *immediately*. Physical contact of any kind is strictly forbidden between girls and their visitors – even their closest relatives. It disturbs them.'

'Miss Carpenter needn't worry. She'll not have a harder-working girl than Becky. One day she'll be more famous than any of them because I've painted a portrait of her that will live for ever.'

Leaning forward, Fergus kissed Becky on the cheek. Then he walked away, leaving the outraged reformatory supervisor glaring after him.

Lady Hammond was a generous patron. Fergus was installed in a small cottage in the grounds of her Clifton house, and she ensured he wanted for nothing. Although small by Clifton standards, the cottage was palatial compared with Fergus's Lewin's Mead room. The living quarters were on the ground floor, and the whole of the upper floor had been made into a studio that was in itself four times the size of the Back Lane attic. Fergus brought most of his surviving paints, brushes and canvases with him, but they were not necessary. Lady Hammond understood the requirements of a painter, and the studio was liberally stocked with equipment far superior to any he had used before.

Servants from the main house did his cleaning, washing and cooking, and Fergus was expected to take his evening meal in the main house. When Lady Hammond had dinner guests – which seemed to be most evenings – Fergus would end the evening by showing them his work. He also became used to Lady Hammond calling at the studio during the day, frequently accompanied by friends. Such visits were disturbing at first, but Fergus quickly learned he was not expected to join in their conversations and he would continue with his work, leaving Lady Hammond free to put her own interpretation on what he was doing.

At first, Fergus was embarrassed about accepting Lady Hammond's generosity, but when he mentioned it to her she brushed it aside as being of 'no consequence'. She suggested that, if he painted her portrait and presented the painting to her, she would consider it more than ample repayment for all she was doing for him.

Soon the weekdays fell into a regular pattern. On Monday he would spend an hour working on the portrait of Lady Hammond; on Wednesday afternoon he took a class at the Red Lodge, and on Thursday at the ragged school. On Saturday evenings it became the custom for him to dine at the Tennants' home – but always the paintings of Lewin's Mead and the tragic record of the Irish immigrants dominated each working day.

For the first few weeks Fergus paid a regular visit to Back Lane whenever he went to teach at the ragged school, paying the rent for the attic room with money given to him by Lady Hammond. On these occasions he renewed his friendship with Irish Molly, and sometimes spoke to Maude Garrett, but as winter settled upon the city Fanny would give Fergus a lift back to Clifton in her carriage after school, and his visits to Back Lane became less frequent.

During the worst of the weather Fanny's carriage was usually waiting for him outside the Red Lodge, too, and Fanny was a frequent guest at the home of Lady Hammond.

Meanwhile, Becky was keeping the promise she had made to Fergus. She could read tolerably well now and, although her spelling was atrocious, she would write long notes to Fergus in a bold even hand and pass them to him secretly during the sketching lessons. She seemed content with life at the reformatory and eager to learn all she could.

A few days before Christmas, Fergus was painting in his studio when a maidservant came to tell him he had a visitor.

'Is it one of Lady Hammond's friends?' Fergus was painting in details of Lady Hammond's portrait, hoping to have it completed as a surprise Christmas present. He did not want any of Lady Hammond's circle to have a preview of the painting.

'It's *not* one of m'lady's friends, sir. It's a . . . a "lady".' Accompanied by a loud sniff, the word was more polite than descriptive. 'The butler told her to go and wait by the garden gate, and he's sent me to inform you she's there.'

Fergus was intrigued. Servants were the most broad-minded of people, but clearly the maidservant did not approve of his visitor.

There was a thick frost on the lawns, and Fergus shivered as he walked to the gate. He wished he had slipped his coat on before leaving the warmth of his studio. However, when he opened the solid-wood door set in the high stone wall that surrounded Lady Hammond's garden, he found his visitor was very much colder than he.

Irish Molly stood as close to the door as was possible, taking advantage of what little shelter the shallow doorway afforded against the icy wind. Wearing a thin lined coat more suitable for warding off summer sunshine than the blast of a winter wind, she had forsaken warmth for 'fashion' on this her first visit to Clifton. She had also gone to a great deal of trouble with her heavy make-up, but her experience in this field was with sailors and not with the butlers of large Clifton houses.

'Molly! What are you doing here? Come to my studio and get warm.' Irish Molly was shivering violently, and Fergus bundled her through the doorway and hurried her to the cottage.

Although she was so cold, Irish Molly looked about her with great interest. She had not seen gardens such as this since her childhood days in Ireland and she had not imagined Fergus to be living in such surroundings.

Once inside the cottage Fergus led Irish Molly to the tiny ground-floor sitting room and pulled a comfortable chair close to the crackling log-fire.

'Sit down and warm yourself while I fetch you a drink. I've got some brandy here that I've been keeping for a special visitor. It was brought from France by one of Lady Hammond's dinner guests and is much to good too be drunk when I'm alone.'

By the time Fergus returned with two half-filled glasses Irish Molly had her shivering under control. She was holding chapped hands out towards the fire, rubbing them together occasionally to ease the pain of returning circulation.

Handing her one of the glasses, Fergus raised the other.

'Cheers! This will warm you from the inside, I don't doubt.'

Taking a swig of the brandy, Irish Molly belched appreciatively.

'This is a very pleasant surprise, Molly. What's brought you to Clifton? Is business so good you're thinking of moving up here now?'

Irish Molly snorted, and brandy fumes rose to the back of her nose. When her coughing and spluttering came to an end, she croaked:'I'd never get within a mile of a place like this if I stayed on me back for a hundred years.' She snorted again, more cautiously this time. 'I'm not so sure I'd want to, either. Is everyone as stuck-up as that feller in the house who's dressed up like an organ-grinder's monkey? Would he be the *Lord* Hammond, or something?'

Fergus grinned. 'He's the butler. But what's brought you here today, Molly? You haven't come to tell me that Ida Stokes wants to let my room to someone else?'

'No – although she could. Iris has come back.'

'Iris . . .? The one who got married?' Fergus was still embarrassed by the memory of the night of the wedding party in Back Lane. 'What's happened?'

'Her husband was lost on the very next voyage he made after taking her home with him. His folks in Holland were as kind as they could be, so she said, but Iris couldn't understand what they were talking about, so she caught a boat back to Bristol.'

Fergus was at a loss for words. Iris had left Lewin's Mead with the hopes and dreams of every Bristol prostitute nailed to the mast of her new husband's ship. She was proof that even the lowest among them could pull herself free of her profession and move on to lead an ordinary decent life.

Irish Molly, warmer now, was hauling something clear of the bodice of her dress. It was a small linen bag. Clasping Fergus's hand, Irish Molly poured the contents of the bag into his palm. Bewildered, Fergus looked from the pile of gold sovereigns to Irish Molly and awaited an explanation.

'There's twenty-five guineas there, and it's all yours.'

'For what?'

'It's the money owed to you by poor Tomas – God rest his

dear soul. I had a letter from a solicitor, right here in Bristol, asking me to go and see him – "in connection with the estate of the late Tomas Casey, Esquire", his letter said. Well, I went to see him and he told me Tomas had left me his house, as he promised, but there was some money, too – *a hundred and seventy-two guineas*, no less. I knew twenty-five guineas of it was yours, so here it is.'

Fergus was deeply touched, not only by Irish Molly's honesty, but by her willingness to sally forth from Lewin's Mead on a bitterly cold winter's day to bring the money to him.

'I thought you might have need of the money, you not being able to get down to the Hatchet to work. I thought that might be why you haven't been down to see me lately. I needn't have worried; you're doing all right here, Fergus.'

'Not for ready money, Molly. Lady Hammond gives me bed and board and pays all my bills, but I don't think she realises that people like to have money in their pockets – and I can't bring myself to ask her for any. She's already been very generous. I've even thought of sneaking off to the Hatchet some night to sketch sailors again.'

'Well, you won't have to worry about that for a while now. You're better off here, Fergus, I'm telling you. The weather's that bad out at sea we haven't had a ship in or out for a whole week. The sailors we do see have been in Bristol so long they've spent all their money. When I go to the White Hart these days it's *me* who's buying *them* drinks. I'm taking home men these nights just to warm up me bed. No, Fergus, you stay here – but I'll have another of those brandies, if you don't mind. It's putting a glow like summer inside of me.'

Fergus filled Irish Molly's glass and handed it to her. As he splashed some brandy into his own, she said: 'You know, I've never had so much money in all me life before, and it's all thanks to poor Tomas, who I talked into going to his death. It hardly seems right.'

'You mustn't think like that, Molly. Tomas was grateful to you for looking after him when he had no one else he could turn to. But what will you do with the money . . . and the house?'

'I was hoping you might give me some advice, Fergus. What do *you* think I ought to do?'

'Where is the cottage?'

'County Wexford. Tomas would talk about it sometimes. It sounds beautiful there.'

'How far would your money go in such a place?'

'Far enough to let me plant the land with praties, buy a couple of pigs and a cow, and live like a queen with what I'd have left.'

'It's a wonderful opportunity for you, Molly. Any of the girls would give ten years of her life for such a chance.'

When Irish Molly made no reply, Fergus asked: 'What does the future hold for you here? How many years before you're reduced to beckoning to sailors from alleyways too dark for them to see what you look like? Or until you're performing in dark doorways with Lascar seamen?'

'You've got a cruel tongue, Fergus Vincent. Hurtful, too. Poor Iris had her first Lascar last night – and only a few months ago she thought she'd given up this life for good.'

'Tomas Casey has given *you* a chance now, Molly. Take it. Get out of Lewin's Mead as soon as you can. This week. *Now!*'

Irish Molly held up her glass again. As Fergus filled it he could not tell whether she was thinking of what he had said, or whether the brandy was having a dulling effect on her senses.

As though aware of his thoughts, Irish Molly said: 'I'm thinking, Fergus. Thinking that I'd likely die of boredom within six months.'

'There are worse ways to die, Molly. If you are in any doubt, then come with me. There's something I'd like you to see.'

Rising to his feet somewhat unsteadily, Fergus led the way up the stairs to the studio. Many completed paintings hung on the walls. Others, unframed or not completed, rested against the walls around the room.

Fergus went to a stack of unframed paintings and picked up one of them. Thrusting it towards Irish Molly, he asked: 'Do you remember her?'

Irish Molly took the canvas from him and gazed at the painting for some minutes. Suddenly her eyes filled with tears. 'It's poor old Meg. She worked out of the Hatchet years ago. Long before you set foot in Bristol. She's dead now, poor soul. Been dead this five weeks since.'

'Look again, Molly. She died inside *years* ago.'

Reluctantly, Irish Molly gave the painting a sidelong glance. It showed old Meg, diseased and filthy, sitting in the rain among the rubbish behind a dockside warehouse. She was dressed in rags, an old piece of sacking about her shoulders. With an empty 'blue ruin' bottle clutched in her hand she gazed open-mouthed and glassy-eyed at a world that had overtaken her, leaving her far behind.

'Is that how you want to end your days?'

Irish Molly thrust the painting away and shook her head. Turning away, she headed back towards the stairs. She was brought up short by a painting hanging on the wall. It was one of Fergus's Irish series and showed Tomas Casey kneeling on the ground beside a sick child.

'He was a good man.' Irish Molly spoke as though to herself. 'He tried to save them with his skills. Now he's trying to save me, with money and his own home.'

Turning to face Fergus, Irish Molly said: 'All right, Fergus. I'll return to Ireland. I'll go out in the mist every morning to weed the praties and drool over the size of the backsides of my pigs. I'll milk the cow and shake my head at the weather when I meet up with my neighbours. If that's what you think Tomas wanted for me, then I'll give it a try.' Her glance dropped to the empty glass clutched in her hand. 'But right at this moment I'll settle for another of those brandies. . . .'

When Fergus returned with the brandy-bottle Irish Molly was standing in front of a portrait of Becky. When her glass was full, she asked: 'Do you still see Becky?'

'Every week.'

'I was hoping you did.' Irish Molly produced a small wrapped package from within the sleeve of her dress. 'Give her this from me. It's for Christmas. It's only a handkerchief, but it's a silk one. I wasn't sure what they would let her have in there.'

Fergus took the present from her. He had been so involved with his paintings he had forgotten how near Christmas was.

Suddenly Irish Molly said: 'Do you know, Fergus, I must be the only one in the whole of Lewin's Mead who's never been sketched by you.'

'That's easily remedied. . . .' Picking up a sketchpad and pencil, Fergus sketched Irish Molly as she stood with a full brandy-glass in her hand, not daring to raise it to her mouth while he worked.

Fergus stopped working and shook his head. 'It's no good, Molly. Your expression's all wrong. Come back here and look at this painting of Tomas again.'

Irish Molly obeyed, and when she looked at the painting of the Chartist leader her expression softened immediately.

'That's better! *Much* better. This is the Irish Molly I want to remember.' Fergus worked furiously as he chatted. A few minutes later he led her to another painting. This one showed a dying Irish child, and here he sketched Irish Molly again.

For half an hour Fergus led her from painting to painting, sketching as he chatted ceaselessly. Occasionally he paused to refill her glass, usually topping up his own, too.

He sketched Irish Molly in tears. He sketched her laughing . . . angry . . . and sad. But not once did he sketch her as she appeared to Fanny when she came to the studio that evening.

Accompanied by a small, round-faced, middle-aged man Fanny entered the studio and saw a heavily made-up woman dressed in a gaudy outmoded dress, with strings of glass beads at her throat. Irish Molly's hair had been carefully pinned up for her visit to Clifton, but in moments of excitement or uncertainty she had a habit of putting her hands to her hair. The result was that during the course of the day it had become increasingly dishevelled. She had been drinking heavily, too, and was lying back on a sofa, urging Fergus in a loud voice to sketch her in an exaggerated posture of repose.

Belatedly aware of the two visitors, Irish Molly struggled to her feet. Her hand flew instinctively to her hair, but by now it was beyond redemption.

Fanny recognised Irish Molly immediately. Had they met in the vicinity of the ragged school, she would have engaged her in conversation, but Fanny did not approve of the prostitute's presence here.

Pointedly ignoring Irish Molly, Fanny spoke to Fergus in a voice as frosty as the lawns outside. 'I've brought someone to meet you. I wasn't aware you had ... *company*. We'll talk over dinner tonight.'

Fanny's assumption that he would be where *she* expected him to be annoyed Fergus almost as much as did the manner with which she had snubbed Irish Molly.

'I'm sketching. It will go on until late. When I've finished I'll probably take Irish Molly to an inn for a meal.'

Fanny Tennant paled. 'Fergus, this is Mr Stern. He's here at the request of Ferdinand Lascelles. He's travelled a long way just to see you. . . .'

'I'm an artist, a *working* artist, not some zoological specimen – and I happen to be busy right now.'

As Fanny and Fergus stood in the middle of the studio glaring angrily at each other Irish Molly struggled to her feet. Relying on the back of a sofa for support, she said: 'I must go now, Fergus. I promised to meet Maude in the White Hart. . . .'

'You're in no state to meet anyone, Molly. I'll get a hansom and take you home.'

'May I suggest a solution?' Unnoticed by the others, the man brought to the studio by Fanny had wandered over to examine the sketches of Irish Molly, scattered haphazardly on a table. Now, advancing across the room, he held out a hand to Fergus. 'I'm Solomon Stern, an art dealer and critic. Both occupations stem from a passion for art coupled to a sad lack of talent. I am pleased to make your acquaintance, young man – and I believe you called this charming lady "Molly"?'

'*Irish* Molly.'

Solomon Stern was not a tall man, and Irish Molly beamed down at his balding head as he bowed extravagantly low over her hand.

When he straightened up, the art dealer spoke to Fergus once more. 'I have a light carriage outside. May I instruct my driver to take the young lady home?'

'I'm going to the White Hart to meet Maude,' insisted Molly. Relinquishing her supporting grip on the sofa, her determined expression dared Fergus to suggest she was incapable of taking care of herself.

Fergus knew better than to argue with the Irish prostitute after she had been drinking. She had a sailor's vocabulary and could hold her own with any of her kind in the dockside taverns.

'As you wish. Don't forget to take your sketches with you.'

Solomon Stern said quickly: 'Not *all* the sketches, I beg you. I've just been admiring them.' He picked one from the table. 'This one is particularly good. If you hold it back for me, young man, I'll commission you to make me a painting from it.'

The sketch was one Fergus had made when Irish Molly was looking at a painting of the sick Irish children.

'You can have that one,' said Irish Molly generously. 'I don't need a picture to remind me of the times I've cried. I like these happy ones. I'll take them to show Maude and the others, to prove I really *have* been here today.'

She scooped up half a dozen sketches, leaving twice as many lying on the table.

'I am grateful to you, Molly. Now, if you two young people will excuse me, I will escort Molly – I beg your pardon, *Irish* Molly – to my carriage and give my driver his instructions.'

As they walked away across the studio, Solomon Stern held out his arm to Irish Molly. 'Perhaps you'll do me the honour of taking my arm, dear lady. I fancy the stairs are a trifle steep. . . .'

CHAPTER THIRTY-ONE

WHEN THE ILL-MATCHED COUPLE had passed from view down the stairs, Fergus smiled. 'Where on earth did you find *him*? He's an absolute charmer. He's got Irish Molly eating out of his hand. I doubt whether any man has achieved *that* before.'

'Fergus Vincent! You owe me an apology – or at the very least an explanation. Solomon Stern is a famous man in the world of art. Most artists would sell their soul for an introduction to him. I bring him here for you to meet over dinner and find you cavorting with a . . . a common *prostitute*. Did Lady Hammond know that creature was here?'

'That "creature" has just inherited Tomas Casey's estate. She came here to return some money I loaned to him. She's also the "creature" who told you Becky was being held against her will in Rose Cottle's house. Irish Molly also brought our attention to the plight of the families in the houses by the river – *and* helped them while the rest of the city quaked at the very thought of coming in contact with cholera. She was a friend to me while I lived in Lewin's Mead. A *good* friend. Now she's got a chance to return to Ireland and forget her past. I'm happy for her, and I wish her well. But if she were staying in Bristol I'd *still* be pleased to have her for a friend – *and* welcome her into my home. If I can't do it here, then I'll need to go back to Lewin's Mead.'

'Are you telling me you would give up a chance to establish yourself as a painter . . . for a prostitute?'

'I'm telling you more than that, Fanny. I'm grateful to you

and Lady Hammond for what you're doing for me, and I'll work like hell to succeed – but I'll not give up my freedom and my principles to do it. I'm vain enough to think my talent will be recognised eventually. I'll just go back to Lewin's Mead and wait for it to happen.'

At that moment Solomon Stern returned to the studio. He saw Fergus and Fanny standing facing each other. Neither had fists raised, but the art dealer was immediately reminded of two prizefighters shaping up to each other in a prize-ring.

Beaming benevolently at each of them in turn, as though unaware of anything amiss, Solomon Stern said: 'The young lady is safely on her way. My driver is a reliable man. He'll see she comes to no harm. "Irish Molly" . . . what a charming name.'

'No doubt Fergus is suitably grateful to you, Mr Stern, but we mustn't keep him from his work. "Working like hell", I think, was his expression. We must not stand between an artist and his destiny. I presume we *shall* see you for dinner, Fergus?'

'You might.'

'I sincerely hope we *will*, Mr Vincent. I look forward to talking to you.'

With a cheery and vaguely apologetic wave of his hand, Solomon Stern followed a stiff-backed Fanny Tennant from the studio.

'*Damn* Fanny Tennant. Just *who* does she think she is?'

Angry at what he considered to be Fanny's unpardonable arrogance, Fergus lifted the brandy-bottle from the table. There was no more than a spoonful remaining in the bottom of the bottle. Cursing his luck, Fergus raised the bottle to his lips, swallowed the brandy dregs, then flung the bottle petulantly at the far wall of the studio.

The sketch of Irish Molly chosen by Solomon Stern stared up at him from the table, beside the present she had given into his keeping. Fergus picked up the sketch and gazed at it for some minutes. Then he found a new canvas, set it up on his easel, and began painting.

Meanwhile, on the way to the main house, Fanny walked in silence until she and Solomon Stern were almost at the door, when she said: 'I really must apologise for Fergus's behaviour. . . .'

'Hush, young lady. Why should *you* apologise? Why should *anyone* apologise? You have just introduced me to a very nice young man. One who does not make excuses for his friends. He is also a very talented artist. Very talented indeed. You are fond of him, Fanny?'

The unexpected question caught Fanny off guard.

'Fond of him? I *like* him. I can recognise his talent. But he's a *difficult* man. Unpredictable, too. . . .'

Solomon Stern took advantage of the darkness to hide a smile. 'You have found a true artist, my dear. A rare animal indeed – and, like all rare beings, he needs more love and understanding than the rest of us.'

Fergus was late for dinner. It was not intentional. He became so engrossed in his painting that he was unaware of the passing of time until a servant came from the main house to tell him it was time for dinner – and Fergus had still to change.

Fergus murmured his apologies to Lady Hammond and the dozen or so guests seated about the table, aware of Fanny's disapproving look. Lady Hammond waved his apology aside. 'It doesn't matter a jot. Solomon has been entertaining us with his amusing stories. He tells me you are working hard, and even had a model in the cottage. A "lady of the streets", if my butler is to be believed. Was it the woman I saw at Tomas Casey's funeral?'

Fergus nodded, not daring to look at Fanny.

'How absolutely *fascinating*! You really should have brought her to meet me.'

'She is an interesting lady. Her face has a very attractive bone structure.' Solomon Stern came to Fergus's rescue. 'Fergus is going to paint a portrait of her for me.'

'I trust you're charging Solomon a hefty fee, Fergus. When Solomon Stern commissions a painting you can be quite certain he expects to receive a huge return on his investment.'

'I most certainly will,' agreed Solomon Stern. 'But in order to increase the value of a painting it is first necessary to bring the artist to the attention of the buying public. In the case of Fergus it should not prove difficult. But tell me, young man, why have you chosen the slums as the subject for your paintings? Have you made this your mission in life?'

Fergus skimmed over his own background in the slums of Edinburgh and told his listeners of Henry Gordon and how he had wanted to record the life about him. Gordon had chosen Bristol because the poverty of Scotland was too close to him.

Lady Hammond's guests fell silent when Fergus spoke of arriving in Bristol, only to learn that Henry Gordon had died friendless and alone in the studio flat at the top of Ida Stokes's house.

Embarrassed by what he saw in the eyes of his fellow-guests, Fergus tried to shrug off the emotion he felt when speaking of the man who had been his friend. 'When I first began painting in Lewin's Mead I thought I was doing it because I owed it to Henry Gordon. This isn't true any more. I'm painting the Beckys, the Irish Mollys and the old Megs, the sailors, beggars and urchins, because I believe others should know these people exist. A mission? Well, I didn't have that in mind when I began, but, yes, it has become that for me.'

Looking about him at the other guests, Fergus added apologetically: 'It sounds hypocritical to talk of people who have nothing, when I'm eating and drinking my fill in such pleasant surroundings.'

There were sympathetic murmurs from his fellow-diners, but with one or two exceptions it was a polite response, no more. However, he could see by Fanny's face that he had her on his side once more. Solomon Stern, too.

'Have you ever been to London, Fergus? We have slums there the like of which you will never have seen. Veritable warrens of vice, and pits of indescribable poverty.'

'I haven't been there, but Henry Gordon had. He described them to me many times.'

'It may interest you to know that many people of note in London are becoming aware of the shame of their slums, too. For years they have ignored the problem; now they accept that something must be done. Your paintings could help *them* to face up to their problems, too. If I arrange an exhibition, will you bring your paintings to London?'

'Of course!'

For Fergus the prospect of having his paintings exhibited in London was very exciting, and not only because it might help to improve the appalling conditions existing in the slums of Britain's cities. Such an exhibition would also establish Fergus as an artist of some stature.

'It's a wonderful opportunity for Fergus,' agreed Lady Hammond, 'but I want to see his paintings exhibited in Bristol before he goes off to London. Once he samples the flattery of your London friends he might never return.'

'Of course,' Solomon Stern concurred. 'And once the good people of London see his paintings he will find himself in great demand to speak of his experiences to the reform societies.'

'I'm a painter, not a speaker.' Fergus was genuinely alarmed at the prospect of facing an audience and telling them about Lewin's Mead. 'I couldn't do it. . . .'

'There is someone here who *can*.' Lady Hammond looked to where Fanny was sitting. 'Fanny, you've given talks on ragged schools and the effect of the slums on the young people who live there. How would you like to talk to London audiences supported by Fergus's paintings and sketches?'

'I would welcome such an opportunity.' Fanny spoke eagerly. 'But you'll need to ask my father whether I might travel to London for such a purpose.'

She spoke loudly enough for Aloysius Tennant to hear, and attention at the table immediately focused upon the Bristol alderman.

Aloysius Tennant had been enjoying Lady Hammond's hospitality and was in a genial mood. 'I've yet to meet the father who can prevent an only daughter from doing *anything* she really wants to do.'

There was general good-humoured agreement around the table, and Aloysius Tennant spoke to Fanny again.

'You can talk to whoever will listen. Something *has* to be done about the problem of our cities' slums – and it should be done quickly. I'll even help arrange some of the talks for you. A number of Unitarian societies are involved with such matters. When you have a date for the exhibition, I'll write and have them organise talks and meetings for you. While you're there you can stay with my sister – your Aunt Agnes. She'll be delighted to have you as a guest. Fergus, too, I'm sure.'

'It sounds a most satisfactory arrangement.' There was a note of triumph in Lady Hammond's voice as she rose from the table.

Leaving the dining room, beside his hostess, Solomon Stern said in a low voice: 'I do believe you are match-making, Lady Hammond.'

'Nonsense. I merely took an opportunity to bring two very busy young people together and give them the chance to learn more of each other. Doubtless you, too, were fully aware of Fanny's talents as a speaker when you suggested that a rather shy young man might enjoy public speaking?'

'True, but my motives lack the romance of your own. Your young artist associates too much with those he sketches. He feels their pain. True, his sympathy reaches out from the canvas of his paintings, but Fergus must learn to paint them seething in their miserable pit – and still be able to walk away from them at the end of the day. If he doesn't, he might one day slip into the pit with them and find there is no escape.'

'And Fanny? What of her?'

'Ah! She, too, is passionate in her championing of the poor, but she is a practical young lady – and fond of Fergus. She will not allow him to throw away his talent.'

'Then, we are working towards the same end, Solomon, but I fear they are both strong-willed enough to confound us.'

'Indeed, dear lady, so we must keep them busy. Give them no time to fall out with each other. Can you arrange the Bristol exhibition? Make it soon and keep Fergus working hard on his paintings. Shall we say . . . in the spring? Meanwhile I will plan a London exhibition for early summer. You have discovered one of the most exciting young artists I have met for many years, but he needs to be prised away from his conscience and brought into the *real* world.'

*   *   *

Christmas came around more quickly than Fergus wished. It was almost upon him before he realised he was expected to exchange presents with Lady Hammond, with Fanny – and with Becky.

The news that Becky had a present for him was given to Fergus when he went to Mary Carpenter's office to sign for the fee he received for giving sketching lessons to the girls of her reformatory.

As he was signing the scrupulously kept receipt-book, she said: 'I trust you'll be spending some of this on a small present for Becky?'

When he looked up in surprise, she said: 'It seems I was quite right to remind you. Christmas is only a few days away, Mr Vincent. It's a time when friends and family give small presents to each other. Becky has been working for weeks on a present for you. More than that I will not say. It is to be her surprise for you.'

'But what can I give her? I mean, what will you allow her to have?'

'Anything sensible, Mr Vincent. I have no doubt you will think of something.'

'How about a painting? A small one to hang on the wall by her bed, perhaps?'

'That will be splendid. But it must not be a portrait. A portrait of Becky would only encourage vanity, while a portrait of yourself would cause jealousy among the other girls. I don't doubt you will think of a suitable subject.'

Fergus painted Becky a group of sparrows standing on the roof outside an attic window of the room in Back Lane. He took it from the sketch he had made of the young birds that had so enchanted Becky. He was well satisfied with the small painting and put it aside to dry. He would take it to her on Christmas Day, when he had been invited with other staff to enjoy afternoon tea at the Red Lodge.

For Fanny, Fergus made a painting from a sketch she particularly liked. The sketch depicted a smiling child, one of the few 'successes' recorded in the tragedy of the homeless Irish immigrants. The child had been starving when Fanny first saw him, but a couple of good meals had worked wonders, a his smile and full rounded belly showed clearly.

For his third gift Fergus was obliged to paint well into the night of Christmas Eve to complete the portrait of Lady Hammond, but he was well pleased with his work. With the exception of a portrait of Becky it was the best painting he had produced to date. It was fitting it should be a present for his benefactress.

Because of his late night Fergus overslept on Christmas morning. He was awoken by Fanny when she made a noisy entrance to his cottage. He sat up in bed as she threw open the door of his room and strode purposefully to the window to pull open the curtains.

'Come along, Sleepy Head. It's Christmas Day and you've already missed your breakfast. Look what else you're missing by lying in bed all day.'

Large white snowflakes floated down outside the window and had already settled in a sloping white mass on the sill. In the dull grey light Fergus could see that Fanny's hair and the shoulders of her coat were sequined with slow-melting snowflakes.

'It looks cold out there.'

'Nonsense! It's marvellous. A merry Christmas, Fergus. I must return to the house now or I'll lose my reputation. Hurry and join us. Lady Hammond is impatient to see you.'

Despite Fanny's plea Fergus took his time dressing. He did not enjoy Christmas. Somewhere in the farthermost recesses of his mind he could vaguely remember seeing others enjoying good things at Christmas-tide, but could never recall sharing any of them. The Christmas days he remembered were bleak cold days when his father nursed a hangover. They grew worse with the passing of the years, despite all that his mother tried to do.

All these memories returned to Fergus as he washed, shaved and dressed, but he could not put off joining the others for ever.

Only the occasional snowflake drifted down outside as Fergus carried his two gifts to the house. The paint on Lady Hammond's portrait would not be fully dry for a day or two yet, but it would dry as quickly in the main house as in his studio.

The door to the house stood open. It was hung with a large holly wreath, and as Fergus stepped inside the rear hall he saw that holly also bedecked the paintings hanging on the panelled walls.

There was a great toing and froing of servants in the corridor. As the maids passed they dropped Fergus a curtsy and wished him 'A merry Christmas, sir'. A buzz of conversation came to him from the large drawing room, and as he drew closer he could see a great many people inside.

Fergus had expected only Lady Hammond, Fanny and perhaps her father to be in the house, but there must have been at least fifty others here. Taken aback, Fergus hesitated, reluctant to enter the room bearing his gifts.

The decision was taken out of his hands when Lady Hammond saw Fergus standing uncertainly in the doorway and advanced upon him, arms outstretched.

'My dear, we were all becoming concerned about you. We thought you must be ill. No one is *ever* tardy about rising on Christmas morning. Come along, poor Fanny is too excited to take a bite of food until she knows you approve of her present to you.'

Reluctant to admit he knew little of how people were meant to behave on Christmas Day, Fergus seized the opportunity to give his present to Lady Hammond, pointing out that the paint was not fully dry as he had been working on it during the night.

'So *that's* why you are late joining us this morning. My dear Fergus, that was very, very noble of you. I must see the portrait immediately.'

Calling to her butler, Lady Hammond had him hold the painting up for her inspection. Slowly she backed away until she felt she was viewing it to the best advantage.

She remained silent for so long that Fergus became concerned. 'Do you like it? I think it's rather good. . . .'

'Good?' The words came out as though Lady Hammond had been holding her breath. 'My dear boy, it's *marvellous* This one portrait alone justifies *all* my faith in you. What car

266

I say but . . . thank you! Thank you for a truly wonderful Christmas gift. It must hang in pride of place. . . .'

Lady Hammond led Fergus and the butler across the drawing room. Conversation gradually fell away, and by the time the small procession reached the fireplace the eyes of everyone in the room were upon them.

Acting upon his employer's instructions, the butler substituted Fergus's painting for one of an earlier Hammond dressed in the fashion of a courtier of Charles II, who struck a heroic pose above the fireplace.

Holding up her hand to still the sudden buzz of interest, Lady Hammond said: 'You are the first to see the portrait Fergus has painted of me. You will understand how privileged you are when you come closer and see it in more detail. You are looking at a major work by a young man who will one day be recognised as one of our foremost artists.'

The guests surged forward and crowded around the fireplace to view Fergus's 'masterpiece'.

Fergus himself backed away until he found Fanny at his side.

'Lady Hammond is right, Fergus. It is a wonderful portrait.'

'I've a painting for you, too.' Self-consciously, Fergus handed over his second painting. It was smaller than the one he had presented to Lady Hammond.

Fanny took the painting and held it up to view it better. An expression of great pleasure crossed her face as she recognised the subject. 'The Irish child. . . .'

Suddenly and unexpectedly her eyes filled with tears and she said in a whisper: 'Fergus . . . it's beautiful, truly it is. Thank you.'

Before Fergus guessed her intention, Fanny kissed him on the cheek. Lady Hammond's eyebrows rose as she pushed her way towards them through the guests gathered about her portrait.

When she reached the couple, she said: 'I am pleased to see the Christmas spirit is reaching you at last, Fergus.'

'Fergus has just given *me* a painting. Look, isn't it wonderful?'

Lady Hammond looked at the painting critically and nodded agreement. 'It's a very fine painting, Fanny – but I am afraid I cannot look at any painting but my own today. I am *so* thrilled with it. . . . But what do you think of Fanny's present to *you*, Fergus?'

'I haven't given it to him yet.'

Fanny was clutching a small package tied with a thin blue ribbon. Handing it to Fergus, she said almost shyly: 'A very happy Christmas, Fergus.'

Fergus stripped off the wrapping clumsily, aware that both women were watching him with an almost proprietary interest. When the last of the paper fell away Fergus held a small draw-neck chamois-leather bag in his hand. As he turned it upside down a silver watch fell into his hand, the case heavily decorated with elaborate scrollwork.

He stared down at the gift for so long that Fanny asked anxiously: 'Don't you like it. . . ?'

Fergus shook his head as though he was emerging from a daydream. 'Of course I do – but it's far too generous.'

'Look inside. I've had something inscribed there.'

Fergus pressed a tiny catch near the top of the watch, and the back sprang open. Inside was inscribed: *Fergus Vincent from Fanny. Christmas 1854.*

'It is a lovely present, Fanny. Really lovely. Thank you.'

Others began crowding about them now, demanding to see the painting Fergus had presented to Fanny. Within minutes they were separated by Lady Hammond's Christmas guests.

Later, in a quieter moment, Fanny looked across the room to see Fergus gazing down at the watch in his hand and she smiled happily. She could not know that Fergus's thoughts were neither of Fanny nor of the watch he held in his hand. He was thinking of another watch. That, too, had been a gift – a gift that had resulted in disaster for the giver.

In one of Clifton's most luxurious houses, surrounded by Bristol's most influential citizens, Fergus stood at a window and his gaze shifted to the snow-covered garden. He saw neither watch nor garden. He was thinking of Becky, wondering what manner of Christmas she was enjoying at the Red Lodge.

CHAPTER THIRTY-TWO

FERGUS OUGHT NOT to have been surprised when he learned Fanny was also invited to tea at the Red Lodge. He knew she sometimes took classes of girls in the reformatory, but he was taken aback when she informed him they would both be travelling to the Red Lodge in her father's carriage and going on to the Tennant home afterwards.

'You *do* know you are dining with us tonight?'

Fergus shook his head.

'Lady Hammond should have given you my invitation. Fergus, you *will* come? I have told all my friends you'll be there.'

Fergus realised he had been built into something of a celebrity among Fanny's friends. This had become apparent when she introduced him to some of them during the morning.

He nodded. 'It's a very kind invitation.'

He would have preferred to spend the evening painting, but it *was* Christmas. It would be churlish to decline the invitation. Fanny's relief and delight told him he had made the right decision.

They set off together from Lady Hammond's house soon after three o'clock in the afternoon. It was snowing again, and the noise of the carriage and the horses' hoofs was heavily muffled in the snow-covered streets. Clifton was situated on a hill above the city, and enterprising ragamuffins had organised themselves into snow-clearing gangs. Armed with shovels, twig brooms and buckets of sand and cheap rough salt, they negotiated a deal for helping coaches down the steeper sections of the road into the city.

Fergus carried no money with him, and it was left to Fanny to find the wherewithal to guarantee their safe arrival at Mary Carpenter's reformatory.

The speed with which the boys worked was impressive. While some shovelled and swept away the snow, two boys strewed salt and sand in an economical ribbon in front of each wheel, thus enabling the coachman to drive his horses forward in cautious safety.

Meanwhile other boys worked equally hard behind the carriage. Fergus was not certain if they were trying to recover the salt and sand, or whether they were spreading snow over the tracks to prevent other coachmen from taking free advantage of their labours.

On a sharp bend the Tennant coach strayed from the narrow twin tracks. Immediately a great deal of shouting went up and a dozen or more youngsters clung to the carriage until it slid back to the hard-won safety of the wheel-width paths. Then a horse lost its footing on the hard-packed snow and went down. This time the boys called upon the help of passers-by, and with much slipping and sliding the snorting horse was raised to its feet.

The Red Lodge was decorated on a more modest scale than Lady Hammond's house, but a neat holly wreath adorned the door, and inside the building holly, ivy and mistletoe were tucked behind every picture.

Becky's face broke into a relieved smile when she saw Fergus, but her happiness was marred momentarily when Fanny followed him through the doorway.

'I was feared you wouldn't come ... what with all the snow we've had.'

'It would take more than a bit of snow to stop me coming to see you on Christmas Day. Here, I've brought a present for you.'

Becky took the small painting from Fergus. Memories returned to her as she looked at it, and her delight was evident. 'It's the sparrows outside the window ... when you sketched me, the first time I came up to your room.'

'That's right. I've finished the painting of you, too. It's the best painting I've ever done, Becky.'

Eyes shining, Becky shook her head. 'No, *this* is the best.'

Reaching inside the wide front pocket of her pinafore dress, Becky handed Fergus a small, badly wrapped package and just managed to maintain an air of exaggerated indifference. 'Here's something for you.'

It felt very light in Fergus's hand, and he said: 'You shouldn't have bought me a present, Becky. You can't get much money in here.'

'I didn't buy it. . . .' She grinned suddenly and was once more the cheeky young urchin he had first met only some eight months before. 'I didn't pinch it, neither. I *made* it.'

Fergus unwrapped his Christmas gift, wondering what it could be. Then it cleared the paper, and he saw it was a tapestry bookmark, embroidered with his name. The letters were somewhat uneven, but it was apparent that a great deal of effort had gone into its making.

'It says "Fergus". I did it all myself.' Becky's pride in her accomplishment overcame the air of indifference.

'Becky, you're a *genius*. It's a present I shall always treasure.' Fergus kissed Becky on the cheek, something he would never have dared to do in Mary Carpenter's reformatory had it not been Christmas.

There were other guests at the Red Lodge, and more were arriving all the time. Many were local dignitaries, councillors, teachers and preachers, and most had arrived on foot.

'Come along, girls; it's time we showed our guests what splendid cooks you are.'

Mary Carpenter marshalled her girls, and soon there was a steady stream of food arriving from the kitchen. Remembering Becky's earlier attempt at cooking, Fergus could not hide his astonishment when she passed him a plate of cakes and whispered: 'I made these.'

It was an afternoon of surprises. After tea the guests were entertained by a choir of the girls, Becky among their number. Four of the girls recited poems – Becky was one of these, too, and she glowed with pleasure at Fergus's enthusiastic applause.

Afterwards the girls were allowed to mingle with their guests. On their best behaviour, they earned the approbation of the reformatory founder and her guests.

When the assembly was beginning to thin, Fergus was talking to Becky when Fanny called to him: 'It's time we left, Fergus. I promised Father I would be home early to greet our guests.'

Unthinkingly, Fergus asked: 'Is it that late already?'

Fanny smiled. 'You have no need to ask such a question now. Look at your watch.'

With this parting remark, Fanny moved away to find Mary Carpenter and tell her that she and Fergus were departing.

Becky's face was ashen when she asked: 'You have a watch now?'

Fergus nodded.

'Did *she* buy it for you?'

'It came as a complete surprise. . . .'

'But you took it? You didn't ask *her* where it came from?'

'It isn't a stolen watch, Becky.'

'Have you asked *her*? No, of course not. *She* wouldn't need to steal to get you a present.'

'Becky, it's been wonderful to spend a couple of hours with you. Don't let's quarrel now.'

'Why? Will it spoil your dinner with her? I bet you never even think of me when you walk out of here. Well, that's all right. I don't think of you, either. So if you only come here because of me you don't need to any more.'

With fists clenched tightly by her side, Becky fought hard to prevent her hurt gaining ascendancy over anger. She succeeded, but the remaining guests were looking at her curiously.

Deeply hurt, Becky's whole being strained to rebel against the strict discipline of the reformatory. She hated the regimented routine and missed the independence she had enjoyed in Lewin's Mead. Above all, she fiercely resented the privacy that had been stripped from her when she entered the house in Park Row. Not for a moment was she allowed to enjoy the luxury of her own undisturbed thoughts or her own company. Even at night she had to endure the ribaldry, the whispered conversations and surprise inspections in the dormitory. Becky put up with all these things only because she believed she was becoming the sort of woman Fergus wanted her to be. Someone more like Fanny Tennant. But, while she was in here trying hard for Fergus's sake, Fanny Tennant was out there with Fergus and buying him expensive presents.

As Becky choked on her thoughts, Fergus took her arm and led her to a quiet spot close to the great fireplace. When she tried to pull away from him he gripped her more tightly – so tightly that, had she not been quite so determined to keep her feelings from him, she would have winced.

There were fewer people at this end of the room, and when he released her Fergus said quietly: 'You're talking foolishly, Becky. I'd swap all the fine things I have now for a breakfast cooked by you on the attic fire in Ida Stokes's house.'

In spite of her present mood, Becky found it hard not to smile. Now she had learned to cook she realised how dreadful had been the breakfast she had cooked for Fergus.

'What's more, I value the bookmark you've made for me above all my other possessions, including the finest painting I've ever made – a portrait of *you*.'

'Honest?'

It took a long time for the one-word question to come out. There was no anger in her now, but her feelings were more confused than before.

'Honest.'

'Why? Why does it mean so much to you?'

'Because *you've* worked hard to make it for me. I've told you before, Becky. I'm very fond of you.'

More used to expressing his emotions in paint upon a canvas, Fergus felt tongue-tied and awkward. But it did not matter. Becky was looking at him as though he had just made a dazzling speech.

'Fergus ... I *love* you. I really do.' Suddenly Becky was hugging him close.

The display of overjoyed affection was brief, for suddenly Mary Carpenter was standing before them.

'Any physical contact between the girls and their visitors is *strictly* forbidden, Mr Vincent, as well you know. Becky, Mr

Vincent is leaving now. Say goodbye, then go to the kitchen and help the other girls with the washing-up.'

Becky hesitated, rebellion welling up inside her once more, but Fergus said hastily: 'Go on, Becky. I'll see you again when I come for my next sketching lesson. Thank you again for a wonderful present – and hang the painting somewhere nice.'

Before reaching the doorway Becky turned twice to smile and wave.

When she had gone, Fergus said to Mary Carpenter: 'You mustn't blame Becky for what happened. . . .'

'Blame her? For what? For being happy? No, Mr Vincent, I am *grateful* to you. You have let Becky know she matters to someone. Today she feels she is a *special* person. This is the most wonderful Christmas gift you could possibly give to an orphan girl from Lewin's Mead. Unfortunately, it also burdens you with a heavy responsibility. A young girl's love is a very fragile thing.'

The new year was a week old when Constable Ivor Primrose came to the house to speak to Fergus. He was shown to the studio by a disapproving butler. Uniformed police constables were among the lower orders of a class-conscious society and not welcomed in the homes of the well-to-do.

Ivor Primrose was not a man to allow the butler's disapproval to upset him. Shaking snow from his cape, he hung the heavy garment behind the studio door. Then, warming a glass of Fergus's Christmas brandy between his hands, he wandered about the large studio admiring the paintings that adorned the walls and naming many of the Lewin's Mead residents portrayed in them.

'You didn't come here just to admire my paintings, Ivor. What can I do for you?'

'For me . . . nothing. I'm here at the express wish of a friend of yours. She's landed herself in a spot of bother.'

'She?' Fergus could only think of Becky, and she was in the Red Lodge.

'Irish Molly. She and another prostitute named Iris were convicted of being drunk and disorderly in St James Square, yesterday. Unless she can find a surety of twenty pounds she'll go to prison for six months – with hard labour.'

'You must be mistaken, Ivor. I saw Irish Molly off on a boat from the Docks the day after Christmas. She went back to Ireland with more than a hundred and fifty pounds to begin a new way of life.'

Ivor Primrose shrugged his shoulders. 'All I know is that she's in the Bridewell now with not a penny to her name, and six months' hard ahead of her – unless she can find a surety of twenty pounds to guarantee her good behaviour for the next six months. It's not necessary to produce the money right away. You need only satisfy the magistrate that you'll be able to pay the money if Irish Molly misbehaves again – as she probably will.'

'When do I need to see the magistrate?'

'The sooner you sign a surety, the sooner Irish Molly will be released. There's little comfort in the Bridewell in this weather. The river runs beneath the gaol, and last week it rose and flooded the cells. They haven't dried out yet.'

'Then, I'd better go now.'

Ivor Primrose downed his brandy and looked regretfully at the empty glass. 'It isn't every day I have a drink of such quality. You've come a long way from Back Lane, Fergus.'

'It was one of half a dozen bottles given to me by Lady Hammond.' Picking up the two-thirds-full bottle, Fergus handed it to the tall constable. 'Tuck this beneath your cape. You've had a cold walk up here.'

On the way to the Bridewell, Fergus tried to learn more about Irish Molly's unexpected return to Bristol and her subsequent arrest. Ivor Primrose knew little more than he had already told Fergus. He had not been the arresting officer, but he was in court when Irish Molly and Iris were convicted and sentenced. Iris had been convicted of a similar offence before and was given six months' hard labour without the option of being bound over.

After Fergus had signed the surety guaranteeing Irish Molly's future behaviour, a gaoler took him to the communal cell where the Irish prostitute was lodged.

Irish Molly looked dreadful. Usually clean and tidy, her clothes looked as though they had been worn day and night for weeks. Her hair was uncombed, and her face was mottled and bloated.

On the way from the Bridewell to Back Lane, Irish Molly told Fergus what had happened to her.

The ship carrying Irish Molly to Ireland had been beset by bad weather from the moment it cleared the Avon river. For three days the captain battled against storms in the Bristol Channel, being gradually forced far to the south of his intended course. Finally, with crew and passengers verging on total exhaustion, the captain turned his ship about and ran before the storm.

More by luck than by any navigational skill, the vessel arrived off the north Cornwall port of Padstow. Blissfully ignorant of the infamous 'Dumbar', the sandbank that barred the entrance to the port during all but the highest tides, the ship rode in with the storm and made the safety of the small harbour.

It had been a nightmare experience. As soon as the ship was safely moored alongside the harbour wall passengers and crew abandoned the vessel. Reeling as though already drunk, they made their way to the nearest inn. Here they quickly learned how lucky they had been to reach safety. On the first day of the storm a schooner had grounded on the Dumbar and not one of the crew had been saved. Not a single vessel had entered or left port since that time. The safe arrival of the Irish-bound vessel was declared to be a miracle.

Relieved to be alive, Irish Molly had bought drinks for the crew, most of whom had spent the money earned on their previous voyage. By the end of the evening Irish Molly was buying drinks for anyone willing to raise a tankard and drink to her safe return to shore.

The party lasted for three days and nights, until the wind dropped and the sea calmed. The vessel departed from Padstow leaving behind it memories of a riotous seventy-two hours – and Irish Molly.

Vowing she would not tempt the Devil again, Irish Molly returned to Bristol by coach, arriving with just enough money to secure her old room in Ida Stokes's house for two weeks and spend four nights celebrating her safe, if unexpected, return.

Having told the story of her adventures, Irish Molly ended lamely: 'The rest you know. Jesus! By the time the po-lice picked me up I hardly knew my own name. I've never been on such a glorious hooley in my life.'

'And now you're back where you started from.'

Irish Molly shrugged. 'Ah, well! Can you really imagine me living among the landed gentry, mistress of my own house?'

'You'd be enjoying a much better life than picking up sailors in the White Hart.'

'I doubt it. Some sailors are quite nice, really. Anyway, I don't expect too much from life here, so I shan't get disappointed the way I probably would if I were to return to Ireland.'

Irish Molly touched Fergus's arm. 'Besides, I've got some good friends here. Your twenty pounds is safe, Fergus. I'll have the lawyer sell the cottage and I'll give you the money to keep for me. Now, come up to my room with me. I've got a bottle of good stuff hidden away for a special occasion – if Ida hasn't found it already.'

CHAPTER THIRTY-THREE

FOR THE FIRST THREE MONTHS of 1855, Fergus worked harder than ever before in his life, producing a remarkable series of paintings from sketches he had made during the previous year.

As more and more paintings were hung on the walls about his Clifton studio, the number of interested visitors increased. Fanny was the most frequent, and with Lady Hammond's help hung the paintings in the order she felt would prove most effective in Fergus's forthcoming exhibition.

Solomon Stern also called in whenever he was in Bristol. His ideas did not always coincide with the views of Fanny and Lady Hammond, and they would argue about the relative merits of each painting as though Fergus was not there.

One day their arguments became so heated and distracting that Fergus put down his brush, cleaned his hands and walked out of the studio unnoticed by the three quarrelling art experts.

Fergus went to Back Lane. Here he found a pencil and pad and made his way to the Hatchet inn. He was greeted by landlord Waller as though he were a long-lost friend. After sketching a few patrons, Fergus returned to Back Lane with money in his pocket and a gait that was less than steady.

He spent the night in the attic room and was woken by Ida Stokes. Fergus had arrived back at the house from the inn during the early hours of the morning, but the landlady had heard him, and much of his earnings changed hands by way of rent for the attic studio.

Ida Stokes also told Fergus what was happening in the rest of the house. Mary O'Ryan, in the room beneath Fergus's own, had found yet another 'protector' for her large family. He was the fourth since Fergus's move to Clifton, according to the knowledgeable and garrulous old landlady.

He also learned that Irish Molly had taken to spending nights on board the boats in the harbour. It seemed her recent experiences had given her an even closer affinity with the men who earned their living upon the unpredictable seas.

'What about the latest of your tenants – Maude Garrett?'

Fergus had just found a half-full bottle of gin in the small cupboard where he kept his cups and plates and he asked the question as he poured some into a cup for Ida Stokes.

'I've a feeling in my bones that I'll rue the day I let *that* one into my house,' came the surprising reply. 'She's a wrong 'un, and no mistake.'

Accepting the cup from Fergus, the old landlady continued: 'She's mixed up with that Alfie Skewes. He's not a month out of prison and he'll be back there again before long – and her with him, I shouldn't wonder.'

'Why, what are they doing?' Fergus was surprised that Maude Garrett was involved with Alfie Skewes. If either Alfie or his father learned it was Maude who had tipped off the authorities about their treatment of Becky, her life would be worth nothing.

'That young girl's greedy. More greedy than most. She's not content to earn her living like Irish Molly and poor Iris – yes, and me, too, in my time. Encouraged by Alfie Skewes and his drunken father, she's found a way to get easier money. You'll find her up around Wine Street on most nights, dressed up to look like a child's nurse with a night off and looking for a good time. She'll pick up with a gent old enough to know better and lure him down some dark alleyway, to where Alfie Skewes is waiting. Afore he knows it the gent's bludgered over the pate. When he wakes up he's lucky if they've left him so much as a stitch of clothing. One day the gent won't wake up at all. Then it'll be the gallows for Alfie Skewes *and* Maude Garrett, make no mistake.'

'Have you tried speaking to her?'

'Not me! It's none of my business what she does – but I make sure she pays her rent on time every week, I can tell you!'

When Ida Stokes returned downstairs after a second cup of gin, Fergus wondered whether he should try to speak to Maude Garrett, but decided it would not be wise. She was unlikely to take notice of anything he said, and if Alfie Skewes happened to be with her Fergus would be walking into trouble. After cleaning and tidying up the attic room, Fergus set off up the hill to the very different world of Clifton.

Solomon Stern and Lady Hammond were apologetic for their part in driving Fergus from his studio, Lady Hammond generously declaring it was unforgivable that they should have carried on such an argument in his presence.

When Fanny came to the house that evening she was more hurt than apologetic. She pointed out that they all had Fergus's interests at heart and wanted to display his talents in the best possible manner. Fergus said nothing. When the time came, he was determined that he alone would decide the order in which his paintings should be displayed.

The Bristol exhibition of Fergus's work was held in Wine Street, in a fashionable enough part of the city, yet only a short distance from the slums which had provided inspiration for so many of the paintings on show.

Lady Hammond ensured the exhibition had a grand opening. The mayor attended with many aldermen and councillors, and a great number of the city's wealthiest citizens. Many expressed their reservations about the *subject* of Fergus's work, but none criticised his talent.

Fergus found the opening night a nerve-racking experience as he was introduced to one dignitary after another. Unused to being the centre of attraction in such company, he would have been totally overwhelmed by the occasion had Fanny not been at hand to support him. She succeeded in parrying the more difficult questions, guided the more important of the guests to particular paintings, and came to Fergus's rescue when an aggressive art critic tried to interview him.

At the end of the evening, Lady Hammond, Fanny and a few of their friends remained behind to congratulate Fergus on the great success of his first exhibition. It *had* gone well. Yet Fergus felt something was missing, although he was unable to put a finger on what it was.

When he expressed his thoughts to Fanny she smiled understandingly and patted his arm in a rare gesture of affection. 'It's a perfectly natural reaction, Fergus. Tonight you've become a celebrity. Everyone has wanted to talk to you. Now they've gone you feel deflated. That's all it is.'

'Yes, you're probably right.'

'Of course I'm right.' Fanny slipped her arm through his. 'But you can relax now. Lady Hammond and I have arranged a small champagne-party to celebrate your success. Come along. I think Lady Hammond is almost as proud of you as I am.'

The following day the exhibition of paintings was opened to the general public. Much to Fergus's delight and surprise, a sprinkling of Lewin's Mead residents were among the viewers, most wearing the clothes they usually kept for Sundays.

Fergus went out of his way to speak to them all, pointing out paintings of people and places he thought would be of particular interest to them. Without exception every one of them stopped before his first portrait of Becky, marvelling at the manner in which he had captured her rags and the pinched and dirty face – and suddenly Fergus realised what had been missing the previous night. Everyone there had come to meet him not because he was a painter, but because he was Lady Hammond's *protégé*. Some had recognised his talent, it was true, *but no one had expressed shock or sympathy for the subjects of his paintings*. It had been left to those for whom such conditions were a familiar part of their daily life to show compassion.

Looking about him, Fergus saw how the well-dressed viewers studiously avoided those paintings which attracted groups of chattering excited men and women from Lewin's Mead. Not all of Bristol's citizens viewed the city's less fortunate residents with the benevolence of Mary Carpenter or Fanny Tennant. The revelation should not have come as a surprise to Fergus, but it did.

'What thoughts are capable of bringing such a serious expression to the face of an artist with such a highly successful exhibition?' Solomon Stern asked the question as he moved to Fergus's side and shared his view of the crowded gallery. 'You should be beaming, my boy.'

'The only people who are really *seeing* what I've painted are those who live in the Lewin's Mead slum – and they can change nothing. Anyone with any influence is here solely because I'm being sponsored by Lady Hammond and they wish to be seen at my exhibition.'

'Ah, yes! I had forgotten that you are not content to paint the world as it is. You also wish to *change* it. My friend, you have a talent – a *great* talent – to paint the pathos and the sadness you see about you. Now these paintings are exhibited for all to see – and not everyone is here with a cynical motive. There is far more compassion in people than you seem to believe. Many women think as do Fanny, Lady Hammond – and this Miss Carpenter. Let *them* fight poverty and all that goes with it, while you continue to paint what you see. They can take your paintings to show to those who will never visit a slum and see the wretchedness for themselves.'

'No doubt you're right. But I need to feel *I'm* doing something more for those I paint.'

Solomon Stern rolled his eyes to the ceiling. 'Artists! All my life I have either had to encourage good artists who are convinced they can't paint, or discourage bad ones who believe they are Michelangelo reincarnated. Now I find the best of them all – and he wants to be a social reformer! All right, I humour the others – why not you? Have you kept the sketches you made for these paintings?'

Fergus nodded. Except for those he had sold to sailors at the Hatchet inn, and some destroyed by Joe Skewes, he still had every sketch he had made since coming to Bristol.

'Choose the best and bring them to me. I have a friend who owns a magazine. He, too, is a reformer. Will it satisfy you for a while if he takes some of your sketches and uses them to illustrate his articles?'

'It will ease my conscience when I begin selling the paintings these people have made possible.'

'Good. But I need to talk to you about this. You must sell nothing until after your London exhibition. That will be the most important exhibition of your career.' With a movement of his arms, Solomon Stern dismissed the gallery in which they stood. 'This is merely a rehearsal. Your future depends upon your success in the capital, so any exhibition there needs to be carefully planned —'

Solomon Stern's words were interrupted by the sound of a loud voice coming from somewhere close to the entrance of the long art gallery. Then viewers were roughly pushed to one side and a burly figure lurched in through the doorway.

With a sudden chill of apprehension, Fergus recognised Alfie Skewes weaving his drunken way along the gallery towards them, causing men and women to scatter before him, all interest in the paintings forgotten.

Without taking his gaze from the unwelcome new arrival, Fergus spoke urgently to Solomon Stern: 'Send someone for a constable – *quickly*! We've got trouble.'

Alfie Skewes was stopping to examine the paintings now, pushing his unshaven face to within an inch or two of the canvases. Fergus broke into a limping run towards him. He thought he knew what the drunken bully was seeking.

Fergus was right. Pride of place in the exhibition had been given to the portrait of Becky. When Alfie Skewes reached the spot where the picture hung he stopped and peered at it for a while. Then, taking an unsteady pace backwards, an expression of drunken triumph crossed his face and he reached for the painting.

Fergus's shoulder slammed into Alfie Skewes before he could pull the portrait from the wall, and he was sent sprawling to the floor.

Alfie Skewes got up slowly, and the look he gave Fergus was more sober than it ought to have been – and it was filled with malice.

His glance flicked to the portrait of Becky, then returned to Fergus. 'What I did to her is nothing compared with what I'm going to do to you.'

Mention of Becky's ordeal at the hands of this man angered Fergus beyond all reason. Instead of retreating from Alfie Skewes he stood his ground and aimed a blow at the bigger man's face as he closed in.

Alfie Skewes brushed the blow aside as though it were a curtain and retaliated with a punch that knocked Fergus to the ground, his senses reeling.

Fergus had no defence against the larger man, but as Alfie Skewes closed in to boot him a small figure leaped between them. White-faced, Fanny tried desperately to reason with the Lewin's Mead bully.

Alfie Skewes pushed her aside as easily as he had blocked Fergus's blow, and she crashed heavily against the wall.

Fanny's plucky intervention gave Fergus time to climb to his feet. The sensible thing now would have been to flee to the street and shout for help. Instead, he delayed long enough to tug Becky's portrait from the wall, leaving Alfie Skewes between him and the door. Clutching Becky's portrait to him, he backed slowly away towards the rear of the long art gallery, occasionally stumbling over the feet of terrified onlookers who were slow to clear his path.

'Leave him alone, Alfie. He's done nothing to you.' The plea was made by a woman from Lewin's Mead, but she never expected her words to be heeded. When Alfie Skewes was dangerously drunk someone invariably suffered the consequences of his violence.

'Stand still and wait for me, cripple. There's no way out for you at the back. I should know, I've done more than one of these places in my time. I know every way in – and every way out. Stay still, and take what you've got coming.'

As he retreated, Fergus was fully aware of the danger he was in. Alfie Skewes was a dangerous man, violence a familiar part of his life. Fergus tried to think of a means of escape, but he knew there was none. Behind him there was only an office and, as Alfie Skewes knew well, there was no back door. But Fergus was more concerned for

Becky's portrait than for his own safety.

Behind Fergus someone was slow in moving from his path and he tripped, falling awkwardly to the floor. Alfie Skewes reacted swiftly, kicking Fergus's legs from under him as he tried to rise. Alfie Skewes kicked out again, but now the kicks were aimed at Fergus's body, and Fergus squirmed in pain, still attempting to keep Becky's portrait clear of the coal-heaver's boots.

Fergus was vaguely aware of the shouts of the onlookers, but no one dared tackle his assailant until the angry crowd standing behind Alfie Skewes suddenly erupted and men were flung aside. The man who carved a path between them took only two more paces to reach the unequally matched combatants.

When Alfie Skewes turned to deal with the unexpected threat he found himself wrapped in a massive 'bear hug'. As his arms were pinned to his side his breath escaped in a shout that was half pain, half anger. Then, still struggling in the powerful hold, he was propelled across the room and his head brought into violent contact with the wall, the force of the blow rattling Fergus's paintings against the plaster.

Alfie Skewes slumped in the arms of Fergus's rescuer, and his sagging body was dumped unceremoniously to the floor.

'Are you all right? By Jesus, he was wiping his feet on you as though you were an old piece of sacking. Have you been upsetting him at all?'

The words were those of a man unfamiliar with the English language. Looking up at the big man who had come to his rescue, Fergus searched his memory for a name. He came up with Giraldus Reilly, the big man who had once kept the Bristol police force at bay in the derelict house by the River Frome.

Helped to his feet, Fergus bit back a groan of pain and handed the painting of Becky to Solomon Stern.

'Is Fanny all right?'

'Yes, I'm all right. But *you* wouldn't have been had that brute not been stopped. He would have killed you. Who is he?'

'Alfie Skewes. He's the man Becky stabbed when she was being held in Rose Cottle's place.'

'So *that's* why he was after Becky's portrait. The man's insane, Fergus. You should have let him have the painting and made good your escape.'

'I'm safe enough now, and so is Becky's portrait – thanks to Giraldus Reilly.' Fergus gripped the hand of the large Irishman. 'I'm deeply in your debt.'

While they waited for the police to arrive and take Alfie Skewes into custody, Giraldus Reilly told Fergus he had been working on the railway, building a new branch line to the north of Bristol. By working hard he had made good money and learned to speak the language of the country.

The police station was close at hand, and in a matter of minutes three constables arrived with an inspector.

When the inspector had taken details of what had occurred, he declared: 'Alfie Skewes will be transported for certain this time, and Bristol will be a safer place. Had the Irishman not come to your aid, he'd have been on a murder charge. Where is Mr Reilly, by the way?'

Fergus inclined his head to where Giraldus Reilly stood before one of the paintings of the Irish vagrants. Oblivious to the admiring crowd about him, the big Irishman stood with tears coursing down his cheeks and occasionally shaking his head in anguish.

'I sketched his wife and child when they were in one of the houses down by the river. They both died shortly before you moved him and the others on.'

'We were merely carrying out the orders of the City Council, our employers,' said the police inspector defensively. 'If he's still here for the trial, I'll see that the city gives him a generous reward for his help in arresting Skewes.'

'If he *is* still here, you'll find him in Lewin's Mead. I've told him he can have the room I rent there for as long as he wants it.'

Alfie Skewes had regained consciousness by the time he was taken from the art gallery. Darkness had fallen outside, but as the Lewin's Mead bully was led away Fergus saw a face he recognised among the large crowd gathered outside. It was a pale-faced Maude Garrett. Fergus called to her, but by the time he reached the place where she had been standing she had gone. All that remained was the memory of the look she had given to Fergus just before he called to her. There had been an expression of sheer hatred on her face.

CHAPTER THIRTY-FOUR

INSIDE THE POLICE STATION Alfie Skewes went beserk when his handcuffs were removed. He floored two constables and was breaking up the furniture when Ivor Primrose entered the charge office. For the second time that day the Lewin's Mead bully met a man who was more than a match for him. Carried unconscious to the cells, Alfie Skewes was secured in heavy chains and leg-irons.

When he appeared before the Bristol magistrates, Skewes was committed for trial at the quarter sessions, charged with causing damage to the police station and assaulting Fergus and Fanny. All the witnesses, including Giraldus Reilly, were ordered to attend the hearing at the high court, and there was no doubt that the Lewin's Mead bully would be sentenced to a long period of transportation on board one of the prison hulks moored in various ports around the country.

Giraldus was quite happy to remain in Bristol, where his wife and children lay buried. Helped by the police inspector, the Irishman obtained work on the quayside, loading and unloading ships. It would prove useful to him when he decided to return to Ireland. No captain who watched him work would refuse the Irishman a place among his crew. As strong as two men, Giraldus Reilly seemed never to tire.

The big Irishman was in no hurry to return to his native land, and Irish Molly ensured he lacked nothing during his stay in Bristol. She would always be haunted by the memory of their first meeting, and when she visited Fergus's room and found Giraldus weeping over a sketch of his wife and baby son her big heart went out to him. She took upon herself the task of cooking his meals, even turning 'clients' out of her room at an unheard-of early hour in order to cook breakfast for her countryman before he set off for work.

In return, Giraldus Reilly treated Irish Molly with a quiet courtesy that no man except Fergus had ever shown to her. Sometimes in the evening he took her out for a drink or two – but he would never accompany her to the White Hart. That was strictly for her 'business'. Instead, he took her to the Hatchet inn, or to one of the smaller alehouses dotted around the dockland area.

On one occasion Giraldus remonstrated with some newly returned sailors who were singing bawdy songs in Irish Molly's hearing. Afterwards, as they walked towards Back Lane, Irish Molly asked him if he really knew how she earned her living.

'I do,' was his terse reply.

'Yet you stopped those sailors from singing a song to which I probably know twice as many verses as any man there!'

'Molly, how you earn your living is no business of mine – and certainly none of theirs. When you're out with me you'll be treated as a decent woman, or I'll want to know why.'

'You're a strange man, Giraldus – and a good one. You deserve more than life has given to you.'

'I can look back on very many happy years. To times when I've walked down a sweet-smelling lane at dusk, with a tiny hand holding tight to mine. We'd return to a snug little cot and a fine woman. She needed only to look at me to say more than all the words ever written by the Irish poets. . . .'

Giraldus Reilly's voice broke, and Irish Molly's hand gripped his arm in a gesture of silent sympathy.

'I've enjoyed all those things, Molly. They were good years. Wonderful years. Years that no one can ever take from me. Do *you* have such memories? How many good years have you known?'

Irish Molly was silent for a long while. When she did speak it was in a voice so soft her companion needed to lean close to catch her words.

'I've known poverty and shame . . . plenty of shame. There *have* been days when I've walked from an inn with cries of "Good old Molly" to warm me on my way – but, God knows, it gets cold again pretty quick when you sit down and ask yourself how much it all means.'

She fell silent again until, looking up at Giraldus Reilly, she asked: 'Will you stay with me tonight, Giraldus? I can't give you back what you've lost, but I *can* promise to make you forget for a while.'

'And what of tomorrow? Will you be back at the White Hart picking up sailors?'

'That's how I earn my living, Giraldus.'

'Then, I won't be coming to your room tonight, or any other night, Molly. I hope I'm man enough to accept what any woman has been forced to do, through no fault of her own, but once I take a woman I won't share her with any other man.'

'You're asking me to give up my living? For what? To share a dockie's money? Is this what you're asking?'

'I'm not asking anything, Molly. I'm telling you why I won't be sharing your bed.'

'You're a strange one, Giraldus. I can't ever remember meeting a man like you before.'

'Does that mean you'll come for a drink with me again, even though I won't share your bed or let you listen to bawdy songs?'

They had reached Ida Stokes's house now, and Irish Molly said: 'It means I'll be upstairs to cook your breakfast before you go out in the morning. Away with you now, before I'm tempted to come up there after you.'

Irish Molly waited outside her room until Giraldus reached the head of the next flight of stairs.

'Giraldus!'

'What is it?'

'You've given me a fine evening. One I *will* enjoy remembering. Thank you.'

Before Giraldus could think of a reply Irish Molly had gone inside her room, closing the door behind her.

*   *   *

The trial of Alfie Skewes was one of the shortest of the quarter sessions. Once the prosecution case had been presented, the recorder hurried impatiently through the evidence of the witnesses. He had made up his mind that Alfie Skewes was guilty, and there were many more cases on the calendar. Within thirty seconds of being pronounced guilty, Alfie Skewes was clattering down the steps to the cells to begin a sentence of ten years' transportation.

There was a disturbance in the courtroom as Alfie Skewes disappeared from view, and when the witnesses left the building they were confronted by Joe Skewes, incensed by his son's sentence. Joe Skewes made a lunge for Fergus but he was restrained by two constables who quickly bundled him inside the building. As he went, he shouted: 'I'll get you, artist. You've been nothing but trouble to the Skewes family since you came to Bristol. I'll get you and you'll leave – feet first. You *and* that ragged-arsed urchin of yours. I'll get you both, even though I take the drop for it. . . .'

'That one's a dangerous man,' commented Giraldus Reilly. 'Be careful of him, Fergus.'

'He's more likely to bother you than me. When he's stupid with drink he has a habit of pitching up in Back Lane.'

'He'll have a surprise when he finds Mr Reilly in your room,' commented Fanny. 'But you would be wise to keep well clear of the man.'

Fergus made no reply. He was remembering the menace in Joe Skewes's voice when he spoke of Becky as Fergus's 'ragged-arsed urchin'.

By the time Fergus's Bristol exhibition came to an end it was acknowledged that it had been a great success. Solomon Stern was well satisfied, Bristol's art critics had praised Fergus's talent, and the city's newspapers used such phrases as 'this exciting and greatly gifted young painter'. There had also been a few tentative enquiries from well-to-do Bristolians. If the London exhibition proved equally successful, Bristol society would flock to Fergus to have portraits painted.

Fergus now had a month in which to complete as many additional paintings as possible before setting off for the capital. In London he would first make a tour of Unitarian churches. A display of his sketches would illustrate Fanny's talks on the work being carried out among the children of Bristol's slums.

Solomon Stern's magazine-owning friend also wanted to select a number of the sketches for publication. It promised to be a busy time for Fergus.

Becky was very unhappy when she learned she would not see Fergus for at least six weeks. Her unhappiness turned to dismay when she learned Fanny would be with him for at least two of the six weeks.

'Why, Fergus? Why does *she* want to go to London with you?' Becky asked the question for the third time in as many minutes.

'Hush! Keep your voice down.'

They were talking during the only opportunity that would present itself before Fergus went away, their heads bent low over the sheet of sketching paper on the table in front of her. The special relationship that existed between Fergus and Becky was accepted, but it was an acceptance that depended entirely upon their own discretion and the goodwill of the staff.

'Then, tell me why you're taking *her* with you.'

'I'm not *taking* anyone. Fanny is going to London to talk to members of her church about the work she's doing in the Bristol slums. She wants to use my sketches to illustrate her talks – and at the same time help to promote my exhibition.'

'Couldn't she have gone some other time?'

'Not if she wants to use my sketches. I won't let them out of my possession, you know that.'

Becky was not satisfied, but lacking any argument that might effectively change the arrangements, she asked: 'Where are you staying while you're in London?'

'With one of Fanny Tennant's aunts. It's all perfectly respectable.'

Becky's derisive snort attracted the attention of one of the staff, who appeared in the doorway on one of the regular inspections. When the woman showed no sign of leaving, Fergus was forced to leave Becky scowling down at her sketch and return to his table in front of the class.

He did not have another opportunity to talk to Becky again until the end of the lesson, as the girls were preparing to leave the classroom.

Placing a sheet of paper in front of her, he said: 'Here, I've been sketching you as you worked. It's very different from the first sketch I made of you. You've grown into quite a young lady.'

Successfully hiding the pleasure his words and the sketch gave her, Becky asked stiffly: 'As much of a "young lady" as *her*?'

'If by "her" you mean Fanny Tennant, then the answer is yes.'

'Honest?'

Suddenly, by the use of that one word Becky contradicted all he had just said. She became the uncertain Lewin's Mead urchin once more.

'Honest.'

Becky screwed up her face, and for a moment Fergus feared she was about to dissolve into unprecedented tears, but with a visible effort she regained control of herself.

'Fergus, *I want to get out of here*. You must help me!' She whispered the fierce plea.

'Becky, I'm about to go to London for six weeks. It isn't a good moment to make a statement like that to me.'

Becky made no reply, but stood looking down at the floor at her feet.

'I'll write to you – and send you sketches of the things I see in London.'

Becky nodded, but she did not look up at him.

Fergus hesitated. He did not want to leave Becky while she was in such a dejected frame of mind, but anything else he said was likely to involve him in a commitment. A responsibility. He was not certain it was one he was ready to assume.

'Come along, girls, it's time Mr Vincent left. Becky, take the things from your desk with you, please.'

As Becky obeyed and gathered up the papers on the table, Fergus made up his mind.

'When I return from London I'll speak to Mary Carpenter

and discuss your release with her.'

The papers dropped back to the small table, a couple of them falling to the floor as Becky swung around to face Fergus.

'Do you mean that, Fergus? *Really* mean it?'

He nodded, aware of the tight-lipped disapproval of the member of staff.

Becky could not contain her excitement. 'I'll try very hard not to mind you going to London . . . but I'll be counting the days until you come back. Oh, Fergus. . . . Thank you!'

Suddenly, Becky kissed Fergus. Then she fled, before the scandalised class-supervisor could think of words strong enough to express her disapproval.

CHAPTER THIRTY-FIVE

FERGUS AND FANNY travelled to London by train, on the broad-gauge railway line constructed by Isambard Kingdom Brunel and his gangs of 'navigators' only a few years before. It was the fastest, but by no means the most comfortable journey Fergus had ever made.

It was a hot day, and by a majority decision the occupants of the carriage decided the windows should be opened. Unfortunately, they were close to the fussy little engine which belched a continuous stream of black smoke from its tall chimney. Twice Fergus removed small pieces of sharp cinders from Fanny's eyes with his handkerchief, and by the time the train jerked to an uncertain halt at Paddington station both their faces were heavily streaked with black.

They were still chuckling over each other's appearance when their horse-drawn cab drew up at the door of a tall narrow terraced house in a not-quite-fashionable street in Kensington.

The house might not have been as impressive as Fanny Tennant's Bristol home, but Agnes Spoure, widow of a Church of England clergyman, had inherited the same disconcerting bluntness as her brother.

Confronting her guests at the door, she stood with hands on hips and said: 'Before I show you to your rooms I want to know if there's anything between the two of you. Are you betrothed or do you have any . . . "understanding", I think, is the word you young people use today?'

'Aunt Agnes!' Fanny Tennant's face was scarlet. 'Fergus is

here to help me with a series of lectures I'm giving. In return I am helping to prepare his exhibition of paintings. We are *friends*, nothing more.'

'Is that the way you see it, young man?' Agnes Spoure turned such a fierce eye upon Fergus he doubted whether any mere mortal would *dare* to tell her a lie.

He nodded.

'In that case I'll put you both in rooms on the first floor. It will save me work, and you won't need to drag that lame leg of yours up an extra floor.'

Ordering the cab-driver to bring in their bags, she led the way inside the house, saying: 'I'll expect you both to make your own beds and keep your rooms tidy. Aloysius Tennant may be my brother, but *I* don't have the money to pay servants.'

As she walked up the stairs behind her 'no-nonsense' aunt, Fanny threw an apologetic glance at Fergus and he smiled his understanding.

Fergus's room was the first one they came to, and Agnes Spoure proved she was also a thoughtful woman. Throwing open the door, she said: 'You'll be comfortable enough in here. It's the room with the largest window in the house. It's south-facing, so you should have plenty of light if you wish to do any painting – but I'll not have paint spilled all over my carpets.'

Fergus tried to thank her, but she cut his gratitude short. 'What sort of paintings do you do? None of those nude women, I hope. They're disgusting, all of them.'

Before Fergus could reassure the straight-talking woman, Fanny said quickly: 'Fergus paints *life*. His exhibition will consist mainly of paintings of Lewin's Mead – the worst of the Bristol slums. There are some wonderful paintings, Aunt Agnes. You must come and see them for yourself.'

'Good gracious me, girl! I have better things to do than waste my time at art exhibitions. Besides, there's enough misery in this world of ours. I don't need to go to an exhibition to see it for myself.'

Fergus settled himself in his room before going downstairs, and for the remainder of that first evening most of the talk was of family matters. It seemed the Tennant family were indifferent correspondents, and the two women had a great deal of trivial news for each other. As soon as he felt it was polite, Fergus excused himself and returned to his room. Here he sat down and wrote a long letter to Becky, telling her of the journey and illustrating the letter with many 'thumbnail' sketches of people and places he had seen along the way.

Later that evening Fergus was looking through the many sketches he had brought with him, placing them in order for Fanny's talks, when there came a soft knock at the door. In answer to Fergus's call, Fanny entered the room.

'You're not working already? The journey itself is wearying enough for one day. I ache from head to toe. I *swear* I have ash and cinders ground into my skin. It will be at least two days before I'm ready to think of work. I was hoping I might show you something of London.'

Fergus had always regarded Fanny as being over-serious, but since leaving Bristol she seemed to have shed both years and her air of authority. He had never seen her so relaxed. The mood was infectious, and Fergus agreed to let her show him London.

The London weather favoured the two visitors, and they were able to enjoy many of the sights of the capital. Together they visited the Tower of London, the British Museum, the Houses of Parliament and the London palaces, and they explored the bazaars of Soho Square, Pantheon and Baker Street before going on to the more fashionable Burlington and Lowther Arcades.

Along the way Fergus sketched many of the London scenes, putting aside a couple of the more interesting sketches to send to Becky. Fanny proved herself to be a good companion. During the two days spent in her company, Fergus found himself growing increasingly fond of her. But as each new experience came his way he never failed to wonder what Becky's reaction to it would have been.

The two days of sight-seeing passed quickly and it was time to get down to the more serious side of their visit to London. The talks arranged by Fanny were sell attended. The audiences asked intelligent questions and seemed to take a very real interest in the problems of organising a ragged school in a slum area. Fergus's sketches came in for a great deal of attention, and he, too, was closely questioned about his subjects.

Meanwhile, arrangements for Fergus's exhibition were going ahead. Solomon Stern had found premises in Pall Mall where gas lighting would prolong the viewing hours into the late evening and show the paintings to best advantage. Somehow Fanny found enough energy to spare to help in the décor of the impressive gallery and take a close interest in the exhibition.

One evening, after a particularly happy day, Fanny returned to her aunt's house, leaving Fergus hanging the last of his paintings in the gallery. When Fanny entered the house Agnes Spoure was flicking imagined dust from the highly polished rosewood table in the hall, her expression as dour as ever.

Acting on a sudden happy impulse, Fanny planted a kiss on her aunt's cheek.

Startled, Agnes Spoure put a hand to the cheek and a number of conflicting emotions fought for possession of her face. 'And what was that for, may I ask?'

'Because you've made these last couple of weeks the happiest I have known for a very long time.'

'I can hardly take the credit for *that*. You'd be content to be locked in a prison cell if Fergus Vincent were there with you. And to think I believed you when you blushed and told me there was nothing between the two of you!'

'I just enjoy being with Fergus and seeing the exhibition of his wonderful paintings take shape. Solomon Stern says it's the most important exhibition of paintings seen in London for many years. It's all very exciting.'

Agnes Spoure snorted. 'There's a letter for you on the table. Take it to your room and read it. I'm busy down here.'

Refusing to allow her aunt's words to dampen her high spirits, Fanny picked up the letter from the table. She did not recognise the bold handwriting and, tearing open the letter, she read it there and then.

Looking up from the much-dusted table, Agnes Spoure was alarmed to see the blood drain from her niece's face.

'What's the matter? Is there bad news from home?'

Fanny read in silence for a few more moments before looking up at her aunt. 'No. . . . It's from Mary Carpenter.'

'Has something happened to her?' Agnes Spoure had once met the reformatory-school pioneer and took a keen interest in her projects.

'No, nothing. She's all right. Everything's all right.' Turning away, Fanny fled up the stairs to her room, leaving Agnes Spoure frowning after her.

The art gallery in Pall Mall was destroyed on the eve of the grand opening of Fergus's exhibition. Word of the calamity reached him soon before dawn, when a runner sent by Solomon Stern woke the whole household.

Fergus received the news standing shivering on the doorstep because Agnes Spoure refused to allow a stranger inside her house at such an unheard-of hour.

At first Fergus was unable to comprehend the scale of the disaster. 'What do you mean? Is the hall badly damaged?'

'There was a great explosion. It must have awakened half of London. I'm surprised you didn't hear it right out here. They say it was gas as caused it. My pa has always said he wouldn't have it in the house. . . . Mr Stern says you ought to come at once.'

'Of course. Tell him I'm on my way.'

At the top of the stairs, with rag curlers peeping from beneath a night-bonnet, Agnes Spoure sought to protect Fanny's nightdress-clad body from Fergus's gaze, but he had no eyes for Fanny or for anyone else. He was stunned by the news he had just received. It *couldn't* be true. All his work. . . .

'I mut go to the gallery. Solomon's there. . . .'

'I'll come with you.'

'You'll do no such thing. . . .'

Agnes Spoure's indignation was wasted. Neither Fergus nor Fanny heard her. As Fergus went into his room shaking his head in total bewilderment, Fanny hurried off to get dressed. She was determined that Fergus would not leave the house without her.

Agnes Spoure did not keep a carriage, and there were no cabs to be found at such an early hour. It was about two miles to the exhibition premises in Pall Mall, and Fergus and Fanny walked. So anxious was Fergus to reach there quickly that Fanny found it difficult to keep up with him, despite his limp.

'How much damage do you think has *really* been done to my paintings?' Fergus asked the question for the umpteenth time as they passed Green Park. He was convinced Solomon Stern's messenger had exaggerated the damage to the gallery. Surely nothing short of an act of God was capable of destroying a whole building?

'We shall soon know. It's only a couple of minutes now.'

Dawn was far enough advanced to silhouette London's buildings against the skyline, and there were all manner of illuminations in the city. Then, as Fergus and Fanny rounded St James's Palace they saw a great many lamps hanging about the premises where the exhibition was to have taken place.

The messenger *had* exaggerated – but only a little. The front of the building had been blown outwards, blocking the road. Inside, floors sagged crazily towards the ground floor. They had acted as funnels, carrying tons of rubble from falling walls and chimneys, sending it cascading towards the main exhibition room.

'Oh, Fergus, it's *disastrous*!' Fanny saw the shock on Fergus's face and she gripped his arm tightly.

He seemed not to notice. Without once taking his glance from the scene of devastation he freed his arm and limped towards the shattered building. In spite of the early hour a large crowd had gathered in the street, and Fergus had to force a way through them, Fanny staying close behind him.

At the front of the crowd a metropolitan constable extended an arm to prevent Fergus from advancing any farther.

'My exhibition is in there. My paintings. . . .'

'It's all right, Constable. Allow him through.' Solomon Stern was one of a knot of men standing amidst the rubble.

He gripped Fergus's hand and nodded a mute greeting to Fanny.

'My dear chap ... I don't know what to say to you. Nothing like this has ever happened before. It's a *tragedy*. An absolute *tragedy*.'

'What happened?' Looking about him at the devastation, Fergus felt numbed. Beneath the rubble lay not only the sum total of his Bristol works, but also his future. This was to have been the exhibition that would make him famous.

'It was the damn fool of a caretaker. It seems he spent much of the evening in a beer-house around the corner. He must have somehow blown out one or more of the gas-lamps without turning the gas off. Then, perhaps when he sobered a little, he probably took a candle to check whether he'd locked up properly. A constable standing in a doorway some distance along the road saw a small light in a bedroom window shortly before the explosion.'

'Where is the caretaker now?'

'Dead. He was blown to pieces.' Solomon Stern looked guiltily at Fanny. 'I'm sorry. It's not a subject that should be discussed before a young lady.'

'How many of Fergus's paintings have been lost?'

'All of them ... save one. I've got it here.'

Solomon Stern walked to the premises next to the picture gallery. All the windows had been blown in here, but the building was intact and the owners were inside, sweeping up glass and plaster.

Solomon Stern returned carrying a painting with a broken frame. 'If I'd had to choose one painting to save, it would have been this one. It survived because it was in pride of place, well back inside a deep alcove.'

Turning the picture towards him, Fergus saw it was the painting of Becky looking out of the Back Street attic window at the family of sparrows.

'I expect you had an insurance that will cover you for your loss ...?'

Fergus shook his head, not trusting himself to speak.

'Neither had the gallery. The paintings *would* have been insured, of course, but the insurance was due to take effect only from the time the exhibition was opened.'

'You still have your sketches, Fergus,' said Fanny. 'You can produce more paintings from them. Lady Hammond will allow you to keep the studio. It will be all right. You'll see. . . .'

Fergus could see nothing with any clarity. Almost all his work had been destroyed and his future placed in jeopardy. Yet he felt an absurd relief that the painting of Becky had survived. Fanny was right, he probably *could* use his sketches to produce the paintings again. They would not be the same, of course – but they *would* be good. Only the painting of Becky could never have been produced again – and it had survived. It was fate. . . .

So great was his sudden relief that he felt like breaking down and crying. Instead, he turned away from the scene of devastation. Still clutching the painting of Becky, he limped away.

He was fifty yards along the road before Fanny caught up with him.

'Fergus. . . . Where are you going?'

'Home.'

'That's very sensible. Go straight to bed. I'll have Aunt Agnes call in a doctor. He'll give you an opiate. This has come as a great shock to you.'

'I'm going home to Bristol. There's nothing for me in London now. I need to begin working again. My paintings have to be replaced.'

'You would do better to rest at Aunt Agnes's house for a few days. I'll send word to Lady Hammond and she'll have your studio ready for you when you return to Bristol.'

'I won't be returning to Lady Hammond's house. I'm going to Lewin's Mead. To Back Lane. It's the only hope I have of re-creating what's been lost. It *has* to be Back Lane.'

Fanny was silent for a long time, then she suddenly ran ahead of Fergus. Confronting him, she brought him to a halt.

'Are you serious? About returning to Lewin's Mead?'

'Absolutely serious.'

'Then, there's something I think you should know. It's about Becky.'

Fergus looked at her blankly, and Fanny winced. He looked so tired. Far too weary to hear the news she had to give him now.

'A friend of Becky's, a girl named Maude Garrett, was picked up by the police and sent to the Red Lodge reformatory. She and Becky had a dreadful fight, and afterwards Becky broke out of the Red Lodge and ran away. Mary Carpenter believes she's returned to Lewin's Mead.'

CHAPTER THIRTY-SIX

BECKY TRIED VERY HARD to come to terms with the knowledge that Fergus had gone to London with Fanny Tennant. She told herself he was an artist, a *great* artist, and his art must come before all other considerations. Becky looked at the painting of the sparrows he had given to her for Christmas and she felt little squiggles of pleasure inside her. Fergus *was* fond of her, she was certain of it, and he had promised to write to her. Very well, she would wait for his first letter and try not to think of what he and Fanny Tennant might be doing in far-off London town.

For three days Becky was a model of patient reasonableness to everyone about her. If she felt despair — as she frequently did — she had only to look at her painting and think of Fergus. Somehow nothing else mattered very much then, for a while.

On the fourth day, Maude Garrett was brought to the reformatory. Hers was not a serious offence. Stopped in the street by one of the new police 'detectives', who had seen her soliciting, she had hit him in the face with her shoe and attempted unsuccessfully to escape. The magistrates offered her the choice of prison or Mary Carpenter's reformatory. Having spent three nights in the Bridewell cells, Maude Garrett had no hesitation in choosing the latter option.

Becky expressed her sympathy with Maude Garrett at being committed to the reformatory, but she was secretly delighted to see her again. Maude brought with her a breath of Lewin's Mead. A reminder that a *real* world still existed beyond the walls of the Red Lodge.

Becky took it upon herself to guide the 'new girl' through the disciplined routine of the reformatory, punctuating her explanations with a barrage of questions.

Most of Becky's questions went unanswered. Others brought only short replies. Maude Garrett's churlishness was hurtful, but Becky made excuses for the girl she regarded as her friend. Maude Garrett's freedom had been taken from her, and she needed time to adapt to her new and strange surroundings.

In a bid to make her friend feel more at ease, Becky said: 'Don't worry, you'll soon get used to it here. It's not so bad really.'

'I won't be here long enough to get used to anything,' retorted Maude Garrett. 'I'm not having some bossy old spinster telling *me* what to do every minute of the day and night.'

Becky was about to say that every girl in the Red Lodge had expressed similar sentiments upon arrival, but she said nothing. Maude would learn for herself. Instead, she asked: 'How are your family. Do they still live in Broadmead?'

Maude Garrett shrugged her indifference. 'I suppose so, unless Pa's drunk himself to death. They're Lisa's responsibility now, not mine. I had to look after them for as long as I can remember. Now it's her turn.'

'But what of the babies?'

'They're both dead. Phoebe couldn't have lasted long anyway, and Lisa said Victoria died in her sleep. I expect the truth of it is that Pa smothered her one night when she was crying. She cried a lot after Lisa took to going out and earning money.'

'You don't really believe that? That your father killed her?' Becky was used to violence and brutality, but the thought of a father smothering his young daughter because she cried horrified her.

Maude Garrett shrugged. 'You asked about the babies, and I've told you. I don't suppose I'll behave any better towards mine when it's born.'

'You're having a baby? When?'

'I dunno. Probably about five months' time, I reckon, but

they'll let me out of here soon enough when they find out, that's for sure.'

'Who's the father?'

Maude Garrett threw a scornful look in Becky's direction. 'What sort of a question is that? I was one of the most fancied girls in the White Hart. I was kept busy, I can tell you, until I found an easier way of getting money – like taking old men who ought to know better down alleyways to where my man was waiting to tap them on the head and empty their pockets.'

Maude Garrett looked at Becky maliciously. 'The baby's father could be any one of hundreds. Sailors, gentlemen. Even a certain high and mighty artist – him who had my man thrown into gaol.'

Becky paled. 'You're not trying to tell me that Fergus knocked you up? You're lying.'

'Am I? Next time you see him, you ask him who he woke up in bed with the morning after Iris's party.'

'Liar! *Liar!*' Becky screamed the words at Maude Garrett.

'Call me as many names as you like. I'm telling you what happened. Not that it's worth remembering. I expect he's better at knocking women like that Miss Tennant who works at the ragged school. Women like her don't know what *real* men are like.'

Becky fell upon Maude Garrett screaming obscenities learned from a lifetime in Lewin's Mead, her fingernails raking the older girl's face.

The other girls quickly gathered round, shrieking encouragement, and within minutes the staff of the Red Lodge were struggling to contain the worst riot that had ever occurred in the Park Row reformatory.

When order was eventually restored neither girl would tell the reason for their fight and eventually both were sent to separate dormitories. They would be taken before Mary Carpenter the next day and their future decided.

That night Becky slipped out of the Red Lodge, scaled the high garden-wall, and disappeared into the darkness of the Bristol streets.

Fergus made the return journey to Bristol alone. Fanny

remained in London in the hope that more paintings might be salvaged from the ruins of the picture gallery. She had urged Fergus to remain with her, but the loss of his paintings had numbed his mind. He did not want to stay in London for one day longer than was necessary. There was also the problem of Becky's escape from the Red Lodge. Fergus was philosophical enough to accept that, given time, his paintings could be produced again. Rebuilding Becky's life was likely to prove rather more difficult.

Mary Carpenter's letter to Fanny had made mention of Becky's fight with Maude Garrett. Fergus believed it had been caused because of his part in the arrest and conviction of Alfie Skewes. Maude had been associating with the transported man and had been in the crowd outside the Wine Street art gallery when Alfie Skewes was taken away by the police.

Fergus was hopeful he could find Becky quickly. She had nowhere to go but Lewin's Mead. What he would do when he found her was another matter. It was a problem that occupied his mind for much of the bone-shaking train-journey to Bristol, taking his mind off the tragic London 'exhibition'.

On the platform at Bristol's Great Western Railway station, Fergus was cheered to see Constable Ivor Primrose. A visiting dignitary had travelled on the same train as Fergus, and the largest and most impressive member of the Bristol police force had been detailed to meet the visitor and escort him to a waiting carriage.

Waiting until Ivor Primrose's official duties came to an end, Fergus walked with the tall constable from the station to the centre of Bristol, a distance of almost a mile. Along the way they spoke of Becky.

Ivor Primrose was able to provide the answers to most of the questions Fergus had formulated on the journey from London, and in return Fergus told the constable of the decision he had taken.

They had reached one of the old toll-houses guarding Bristol Bridge, and Ivor Primrose stopped and looked gravely at Fergus.

'Do you think you have given this matter sufficient

thought? Wouldn't it be better to leave it to me to see Becky is returned to the Red Lodge? She won't be punished. Mary Carpenter doesn't believe in punishment, as well you know. Go back to your studio in Clifton and think things over for a while. The explosion in London and the loss of your paintings have been a great shock for you. This isn't the time to be making decisions.'

'I've made up my mind, Ivor. I know what I'm going to do. The only question is whether or not you'll help me.'

Ivor Primrose shook his head despairingly. 'I doubt whether Fanny Tennant will ever forgive me for this, but, yes, I'll help you.'

'Thanks. Now all I need do is find Becky.'

Clutching the painting of Becky, his sketches and a few personal belongings, Fergus made his way through the darkening streets of Lewin's Mead. A few loafers eyed him speculatively, wondering whether he carried anything of value in his bag. Many more recognised him and nodded a greeting.

By the time he reached Back Lane, Fergus had begun to think about the reception he would receive from Becky. She would no doubt be anticipating his disapproval. He had a lot to say to her. Away from the supervision of the reformatory staff they should be able to discuss Fergus's plans for her without any interruption.

There was a light showing beneath the door of the attic and the sound of someone moving about inside. Fergus threw open the door with barely concealed excitement — and was confronted by a startled Irishman holding a cup of steaming hot tea in his hand.

'Fergus!'

'Giraldus.'

Fergus had forgotten that he had turned the room over to Giraldus Reilly.

'What are you doing here? I thought you were finding fame and fortune in London.'

'It's a long story. I'll tell you about it some other time.' Disappointed at not finding Becky here, Fergus suddenly felt very tired.

'Here, have this tea. I was taking it downstairs to Molly. She enjoys a cup before going out to work.'

Fergus took the cup gratefully. He had neither eaten nor drunk anything that day.

'I was expecting Becky to be here. While I was in London I heard she had run away from the Red Lodge.'

'You must be talking about Molly's friend. A young girl. Pretty, but not a lot of flesh on her.'

'That's her. You know where she is?' The description was not altogether flattering, but it fitted Becky well enough.

'She's moved into the room next to Molly. The one that Maude used to have. But she's not in at the moment. I passed her on the stairs not half an hour since. She was on her way out to work.'

'Where would she be working at this time of night? I need to find her.'

Giraldus Reilly hesitated before replying. 'I think you'd best be asking Molly about that. She told Becky you'd not be happy with what she's doing.'

'What *is* she doing?'

'Come downstairs and see Molly. Bring your tea with you. I've another here for her.'

Carrying a cup of weak tea, liberally sweetened with sugar, Giraldus Reilly led the way to Irish Molly's first-floor room.

Irish Molly's pleasure at seeing Giraldus quickly gave way to dismay when she saw his companion.

'Fergus! We ... I ... thought you'd be away for much longer.'

'So did I. Where's Becky?'

Irish Molly sought support from Giraldus Reilly. From the corner of his eye Fergus saw the big man shake his head and shrug away any responsibility for answering Fergus's question.

'She's at the White Hart, working.'

Fergus frowned. 'That's dangerous. The police visit the inns. If she's found, she'll be taken back to the Red Lodge.'

'You don't understand, Fergus. She's picking up and bringing them back here. Becky's on the game.'

For a moment the room seemed to reel about Fergus.

'Are you all right?' Giraldus gripped Fergus's arm anxiously.

Brushing the Irishman's arm away, Fergus spoke angrily to Irish Molly. 'I don't believe you. It's a trick to stop me from looking for her. It won't work. . . .'

'It's no trick, Fergus, so help me. I tried hard to stop her. I knew how you'd take the news when you found out. I begged her to think about that. She said you wouldn't care. She said you might even become one of her regulars, like you were with Maude Garrett.'

Fergus's mouth dropped open. So *that* was why she and Maude Garrett had fought. It had nothing to do with Alfie Skewes, after all. Suddenly all Fergus's other problems were forgotten.

Irish Molly watched Fergus struggling with his guilty thoughts and there was disbelief in her voice when she asked: 'You *didn't* cop with that little shabroon?'

'I don't know, Molly. I woke up the morning after Iris's wedding party and found Maude in bed with me, but I have no idea what *happened* there.'

'You poor soul. You mean that since that night you haven't known whether you gave it to her or not?' Irish Molly tried hard not to laugh, but she failed and for a full minute she was unable to speak.

When she eventually regained some control of her voice, Irish Molly said: 'No, you wouldn't have known – and Maude certainly wouldn't have told you. She'd *want* you to believe there was something between the two of you. But I *saw* you on your way upstairs to bed that night. You couldn't have had it off with her, or with anyone else, the condition you were in.'

'Do you really think so?'

'*Think?* I *know*. Many's the time I've listened to a man snoring his head off all night, then sent him on his way in the morning believing I'd earned every penny he gave me. I can tell by looking at a man whether or not he'll make it – and after Iris's party you couldn't have even raised a smile.'

'But Becky must think I did. That's why she fought Maude Garrett and ran away from the Red Lodge. I'm certain of it.'

'I know nothing about that, but if you think it will help I'll go down to the White Hart and tell Becky she's let Maude Garrett make a fool of her.'

'I'll come with you,' said Giraldus Reilly unexpectedly. 'It's time I was off to work, too — but first I'll bundle up my clothes and get them out of Fergus's room.'

'There's no need to do that. You can stay for as long as you wish.'

'No, I'd have moved earlier if I hadn't been so lazy. I'm working at the Hatchet as a cellarman now. A room goes with the job. Wait for me, Molly.'

When the Irishman had gone from the room, Irish Molly asked: 'What will happen to Becky? You know she'll be sent back to the reformatory if the po-lice get their hands on her?'

Fergus nodded, but the carefully thought out plans he had made for Becky were in total disarray. On the way from London he believed he had resolved Becky's future. Now he was more uncertain than ever.

'Becky's not a bad girl really, Fergus. She could have gone on the game years ago when she was a hungry ragged little urchin, but she didn't, and if it hadn't been for Rose Cottle she wouldn't have started now. I've done what I can for her since she's been out of the Red Lodge, Fergus. Kept her clear of men she might have trouble with. I couldn't do more.'

Irish Molly shrugged philosophically. 'After what happened with Joe and Alfie Skewes she had nothing to lose any more.'

Fergus said nothing, although he knew both he and Becky had a great deal to lose. He had returned to Lewin's Mead to ask Becky to marry him.

CHAPTER THIRTY-SEVEN

WHEN IRISH MOLLY AND GIRALDUS REILLY left the house Fergus returned to the attic studio and waited. It was not long before inaction became intolerable. He tidied up the studio, then began to sort through the sketches brought back with him from London, putting them in the order in which he intended making new paintings. When this was done he took the portrait of Becky, recovered from the London gallery explosion, and set it up on the easel, placing it where it would be immediately visible to Becky when she entered the attic room.

The painting stood in its place for two hours before Fergus finally accepted that Becky was not going to hurry home to see him.

He contemplated going to the White Hart and having a confrontation with Becky, but reluctantly discarded the idea. Becky was a very stubborn girl. If Irish Molly had not been able to persuade her to return to the house, it was doubtful whether he would succeed – and certainly not in the presence of others. She might also fear he would try to persuade her to return to the Red Lodge. Fergus was not prepared to risk another misunderstanding. This time everything had to be right.

Looking at the painting of Becky, Fergus had a sudden idea. Lifting it from the easel, he carried it downstairs to the room occupied by Becky. The room was sparsely furnished, and there were few personal belongings in evidence. There was nowhere to hang a painting on the bare walls and after some deliberation Fergus stood it on the mantelshelf above the fireplace.

Although it was not exceptionally large, the painting dominated the whole room, and Fergus was satisfied it would not be overlooked when Becky returned to her room.

Back in his attic room once more, Fergus left the door open and settled down to wait, hoping to hear Becky when she came back to the house.

He had forgotten the night noises of Ida Stokes's house. People seemed to come and go the whole time, and the many occupants of Mary O'Ryan's room contributed in no small degree to the traffic on the stairs.

Fergus had almost persuaded himself that Becky was spending the night elsewhere when he heard voices in the downstairs hallway. He was on his feet in an instant. There were two voices – and one belonged to Becky. The other was a man's voice, and his loud laughter and slurred words made Fergus feel physically sick. Fighting back an urge to go downstairs and confront Becky and her companion, he forced himself to remain in the attic room. Tackling her now would do far more harm than good. The very fact that Becky had returned to the house with a 'client', knowing Fergus was there, was an indication of her defiant mood.

When the sound of Becky and the man became unbearable Fergus closed the door. Walking to the farthermost window, he looked out at the night sky. He should not have come back. Everyone else was right, and he was wrong. There was no returning to the past. Too much had changed. Before he left London, Fanny had told him he was trying to live out a foolish dream. She was right. He had come to Lewin's Mead to recapture something that had probably never existed outside his own mind. The only certainty now was that he could no longer live here. He could not listen to Becky's voice on the stairs night after night, knowing what was happening in her room, in her bed. . . .

Fergus was bundling up the last of his sketches when he heard footsteps on the stairs to the attic. They were followed by a soft knock on the door.

Thinking it was Irish Molly coming to explain her failure

with Becky, Fergus called: 'Come in.'

He finished tying the tape on the last bundle as the door opened and looked up to see Becky standing in the doorway. In her hands was the painting he had left in her room.

He straightened up, and for what seemed long minutes they looked at each other in silence.

She looked tired, her eyes wide and dark in the pale face. She had grown since she was last in this room, but they had confronted each other then, he remembered.

'I heard you come in. . . .'

It was not what he had intended saying. It sounded as though it was an accusation. 'I'd hoped you'd come home earlier. To see me.'

'Why did you put this in my room?' She held up the painting.

'It's yours. I painted it for you.'

'I've still got the other one you painted for me for Christmas.'

Fergus had not seen the painting in Becky's room. Her next words provided the reason.

'I keep it hidden. It's the only thing I own that's worth anything.'

'You brought it with you when you ran away from the Red Lodge?'

Becky's chin came up. 'Should I have left it there for Maude Garrett? Yes, perhaps I should have. She's got more right to anything of yours than I have.'

'Maude Garrett has no claim to anything of mine, Becky.'

'Are you denying you slept with her?'

'No.' It was useless to try to evade the question. 'But sleeping was *all* I did. Ask Irish Molly. She saw the state I was in when Maude helped me up here to bed.'

'What about the other times?'

'There were no other times.'

Becky lowered the painting to the floor and held it upright with two extended fingers. 'That isn't what she says. She told me you're probably the father of the kid she's having.'

Fergus was startled. 'Maude Garrett's having a child? Well she'll need to look elsewhere for a father; it's nothing to do with me. Is that why you fought with her?'

Ignoring the question, Becky looked to where Fergus had made bundles of his sketches. 'Are you moving your things out?'

'Yes, I'm leaving.'

For just a moment Becky looked vulnerable, but the moment passed quickly.

'I suppose you're going back to Clifton, to that Lady Something-or-other? I thought you were supposed to be in London with Fanny Tennant for some important exhibition. That's what you told me.'

'I'm not going to Clifton, and there'll be no exhibition. There was an explosion at the gallery. Your painting was the only one saved.'

'Oh! I'm sorry, Fergus, really I am.' Becky's sympathy was genuine. 'I know what the exhibition meant to you. And your paintings. . . . All the work you did on them.'

'I'll make other paintings, of other places. There will be other exhibitions.'

Turning away, Fergus began blindly stuffing the remaining sketches into his bag. He found Becky's sympathy harder to take than anger or indifference.

'You're leaving Bristol? Where will you go?'

'That's *my* business.' Fergus hoped abruptness would cloak the abject misery he felt. 'You've got a client in your room. Shouldn't you be down there looking after his needs?'

Becky winced as though he had struck her a physical blow, but it gave him no satisfaction.

'He's almost as drunk as you say you were the night Maude Garrett put you to bed. His money will buy him a good night's sleep, nothing more.'

Fergus was packed now. A few sketches protruded through the opening of his bag, but they did not matter. Nothing mattered very much any more. Fergus felt utterly defeated. Becky had achieved what an explosion and the loss of his paintings had failed to do.

Lifting the bag and tucking it beneath his arm, Fergus took a last look around the attic room. It was now part of the past. Only Becky stood between him and a new life.

Becky did not stand aside for him when he reached the doorway, and he was forced to stop and face her.

'Are you leaving because of me?'

He wanted to say no, but the lie would not come out. He said nothing.

'Why *are* you leaving?'

'There's nothing here for me now.'

This, at least, was the truth.

Becky had been watching him closely, and now she said: 'I've made a mess of things again, haven't I? Just like I did when I pinched that watch for you.'

She looked more like an abject and friendless waif than a prostitute who had a drunken man lying in her bed.

'Why did you run off from the Red Lodge and begin . . . what you're doing now? You've never done it before. You were getting on so well at the Red Lodge. Everything was working out right for you.'

'Was it? Or was it what everyone *else* wanted for me?' Becky's aggression flared up for a moment, but it subsided as quickly as it had appeared.

'I tried, Fergus. I tried very hard because I knew it was what you wanted me to do. Then, when Maude Garrett arrived and said you might be the father of her baby, it all seemed a waste of time. . . .'

Becky looked up at him, and he could only guess at the desperate struggle going on inside her. 'But I'll go back to the Red Lodge . . . if you'll stay in Bristol.'

As Fergus looked at the unhappiness on her pinched face, some of the anger and frustration bottled up inside him bubbled over. 'Why the hell did you have to become a *whore* the minute you got back here? Why couldn't you have done something else? On the way from London I thought of a way to stop you *ever* returning to the Red Lodge. . . .'

Becky's shrug hid the hurt she felt at his words. 'I was a whore *before* I went to the Red Lodge. Joe and Alfie Skewes saw to *that*. It wouldn't have mattered very much, but for you. I'd have ended up on the game one day. What else is there for a girl like me to do in Lewin's Mead?'

'You could have *married* me, Becky. That way I would be

responsible for you and could have had a magistrate rescind the order committing you to the Red Lodge.'

Becky did not even hear the second part of Fergus's statement. Looking at him open-mouthed, she gasped: 'You'd have *married* me? Why?'

'Because you're one hell of a worry to me and it's the only way I know of having some control over what you do.'

'You'd have married me . . . just for that?'

'Not entirely. I'm very fond of you . . . but you already know that. I have been since I tripped over you when I first arrived in Lewin's Mead.'

Becky's eyes filled with tears and, as though her legs had suddenly become incapable of supporting her, she sat down heavily on the top stair.

'I *have* made another mess of things. An even *bigger* mess this time.' The words came out as hardly more than a whisper. And then Becky, the girl who had once said she never cried, began to sob, and she sobbed as though her heart was breaking.

Fergus put out a hand to touch her head uncertainly. She knocked it away violently.

'Don't touch me. Go away. Just *go away*!'

Fergus brushed past her . . . then he stopped. He could not leave her like this. Putting down the bag, he sat beside her on the stair and put an arm about her, ignoring her protests. He turned her towards him, and suddenly all her resistance came to an end and she clung to him, scrubbing her eyes against the front of his shirt.

It was a long time before her sobbing subsided enough for Fergus to become aware of other sounds in the house. The murmur of Iris's voice from her room, a man's voice with her, laughing. There was a baby crying in the O'Ryan room and the shrill sound of Ida Stokes berating someone from the street-door.

When Becky spoke again it was in a voice so soft that he needed to put his ear close to her mouth before he could hear her.

'I love you, Fergus. I love you more than I ever thought I would love anyone.'

Fergus felt an absurd lump rise in his throat. He said fiercely: 'I think I love you, too, Becky.'

'Honest?'

'Honest.'

In the attic behind them a candle began spluttering as the flaming wick burned close to the hot wax, swimming in the saucer in which it stood. Downstairs another voice began hurling abuse back at Ida Stokes.

'What am I going to do with you, Becky?'

'Just holding me is enough for now. It's what I thought about you doing all the time I was in the Red Lodge. I'd listen to the other girls talking of what they'd done before, and what they'd do as soon as they got out. I'd say the same things sometimes, just to be like them, but really I just wanted *you* to hold me.'

Behind them the candle gave a final splutter. After a momentary flare-up of yellow light the attic was plunged into darkness.

'Fergus, can I sleep with you tonight? You don't need to do anything except hold me close, like this.'

'If that's what you want.'

'I do. Very much.'

Fergus stood up awkwardly. He had cramp in his lame leg. Forced to lean on Becky for a few moments he grimaced in the darkness as he suffered a moment of self-appraisal. He was a crippled artist with nothing to offer a bride but a sparsely furnished attic in the heart of Bristol's dingiest slum. He was hardly the most eligible man in the world.

CHAPTER THIRTY-EIGHT

FERGUS WAS AWAKENED in the morning by a commotion coming from somewhere in the house. He tried to move, but a weight was pressing down on his outstretched arm. When he turned his head he saw Becky looking at him . . . and he remembered.

The commotion ended abruptly with the sound of footsteps clattering noisily down the stairs to the street. Then there was a noise outside the door, and Irish Molly entered the room. Dressed in a wrap, her heavy make-up was badly smudged, her hair was in disarray and she looked about her from bleary eyes.

'Fergus, have you seen . . .? Oh, there you are!' Irish Molly answered her own part-spoken question as she saw Becky's head resting on Fergus's arm, half-hidden by the bedclothes. 'I wish you'd make up your mind which bed you were meant to be in. I've just had a seaman come barging into my room demanding to know where he was, and how he'd got here. Lucky for all of us the man in bed with me was the first mate from the same ship. He remembered they were meant to be sailing on the early-morning tide. Shall I be making up the fire and putting on the kettle for you?'

Becky looked at Fergus apprehensively, wondering how he would react to being reminded of her way of life. But he was looking at Irish Molly.

'Yes, put the kettle on, then Becky can get up and make us all some tea. She'll need to get used to it. We're going to be married.'

'That won't come as a surprise to anyone except the two of youse. I saw it coming the first day you walked into the house together, so did Ida Stokes. Don't tell *her* too soon. The minute she knows, she'll be putting your rent up – or will you be moving off somewhere else? Clifton, perhaps?'

'We'll be staying right here. I've a lot of painting to do and I work better in Lewin's Mead. Now, get that fire going while I dress.'

As Fergus donned his clothes he told Irish Molly about the destruction of his paintings, at the same time filling in some of the details for Becky's benefit.

Irish Molly clicked her tongue sympathetically. 'Now, isn't that a terrible thing? I've said many times that these new inventions will be the death of all of us. Gas, indeed. My grandmother raised ten children by candlelight, and my great grandmother twenty-two! What are we needing to see more for anyway? As you grow older you realise that darkness is one of the Lord's great blessings. We'd all be better off for not seeing so much of what's about us.'

Irish Molly used a foot to push the blackened kettle farther into the crackling fire. 'Mind you, I believe all these things happen for the best. If it hadn't been for the explosion, you might not have come back here and got together with Becky again. It was the same with me, when poor Tomas left me all that money. If I'd gone back to Ireland on me own, I'd have made a mess of me life for sure . . . and I'd never have met up with Giraldus.'

Fergus had finished dressing and he said: 'Do I scent romance in *your* life, Molly?'

Irish Molly turned around and peered at him from between puffy eyelids, the surrounding skin marbled from years of heavy drinking. 'Look at me! Would *you* marry me if you'd once been married to a decent woman and had children by her? No, of course you wouldn't. All the same, don't be surprised if I take Giraldus back to Ireland one day, to see what might be done with that cottage of mine. . . .'

The kettle slid sideways, sending a cascade of water hissing among the hot ashes, and once again Irish Molly used her foot to restore the kettle's balance.

When it was steady once more, she turned to Becky. 'Never forget how lucky you are, young lady. The "girls" in the White Hart may talk of marriage with scorn, but there isn't one of 'em who doesn't dream that the right man will come along and take her off, one day.'

The kettle had not boiled, but Irish Molly decided it was hot enough. Wrapping the trailing hem of her grubby nightgown about her hand in a manner that defied modesty, she lifted the kettle from the fire. Pausing to look across the room to where Becky had her feet to the ground, she said: 'Mind you, if I hear you repeating one word of what I've just said I'll swear you're out of your mind, you understand?'

The wedding of Fergus and Becky took place in a small Baptist chapel on the edge of Lewin's Mead. The venue had been suggested by Constable Ivor Primrose. The big policeman could not become personally involved with any of the wedding arrangements because Becky was still officially 'a wanted person', but he ensured that no obstacles were placed in the way of the young couple.

The Baptist preacher was a man who worked hard to ease the lot of those who lived in the poverty-afflicted streets about his church. He was concerned about Becky's youth and her lack of a surname, but when Fergus visited the chapel and explained the situation honestly and frankly the preacher set aside his doubts. He promised that nothing should put the wedding in jeopardy. After many years spent working for the poor he accepted that success and happiness were elusive goals. He would not stand in the way of a Lewin's Mead urchin who had the opportunity to improve her meagre lot in life.

The marriage took place three weeks after Fergus's return from London. It was a quiet affair, with only Irish Molly, Giraldus Reilly and, surprisingly, Ida Stokes attending from Back Lane. There were also a few curious members of the regular Baptist congregation in the chapel, and all added their loud Amens to the blessings called down upon the married couple.

Afterwards Fergus, Becky and their friends adjourned to a

private room at the Hatchet inn to enjoy a wedding breakfast provided for them by Charlie Waller. Fergus had resumed his evening work at the inn, and during the course of the celebrations many of the inn's regular customers looked in to wish the newlyweds health and happiness.

Later that night, as Becky lay in bed in the attic room in Back Lane she thought she had never been so happy in all her life. The moon cast a soft light into the room through the windows, there was a comforting glow from the low-burning fire in the grate, and Fergus slept at her side.

Fergus . . . her *husband*! She was now Becky *Vincent*. She had a surname for the first time in her life. Becky snuggled closer to Fergus. As the rhythm of his breathing broke, his arm reached out across her body and Becky warmed to his touch. At this moment she would not have changed places with anyone in the land.

Fergus met Fanny for the first time since returning from London when he visited the Red Lodge reformatory to speak to Mary Carpenter about Becky. Fanny was leaving the building as he entered, and her face lit up with pleasure at seeing him.

'I've been very worried about you, Fergus. Nobody here seemed to know where you were. Had I heard nothing by this weekend, I intended coming to Back Lane to look for you.'

She gripped his arm in a gesture of warmth. 'I realised you needed time to think about your future after the tragic loss of all your paintings. There is no chance of compensation, I'm afraid. Has Solomon told you? No, of course he hasn't. None of us has seen you since your return.'

'Fanny . . .' Fergus attempted to halt her chatter, but she seemed not to hear him.

'Why haven't you called on Lady Hammond? It's very naughty of you, after all she has done. But never mind. Come to dinner tonight. Lady Hammond will be there and she has a forgiving nature. She's certain to ask you to return to the studio. . . .'

'Fanny, I'm married now. To Becky.'

Fanny's mouth dropped open in utter disbelief. 'You are ... *what*?'

'I've married Becky. That's why I'm here now. I want to see Mary Carpenter and have Becky's committal order revoked.'

'Fergus ... how *could* you? What of your talent? The plans we made for the future? You've thrown them all away!'

Fanny seemed dazed and unable to put her thoughts together.

'No, Fanny, my paintings owe their very existence to Lewin's Mead. And I had Becky to think of. . . .'

'I've always known you felt some absurd responsibility for the girl, but I never dreamed you would go so far as to *marry* her. Why, she's hardly more than a *child*!'

'She's no child, Fanny. Lewin's Mead has never allowed her to be one.'

'But ... to *marry* her. . . .' Suddenly, Fanny gathered her wits together with a visible effort. 'I wish you well, Fergus, Becky, too.'

'I'll see you again soon. At the ragged school, perhaps?'

'Yes. . . . No! I won't be there. Not for some weeks. I have some work to do for Father. Goodbye, Fergus.' Turning away from him, Fanny hurried off along the street.

Inside the Red Lodge, Fergus was kept waiting for many minutes before being shown into Mary Carpenter's study. The reformatory pioneer was brusque to the point of rudeness.

'I am told your London exhibition was cancelled in most unfortunate circumstances, Mr Vincent. I am very sorry, of course, but I feel unable to make use of your services again for a while. Since the unfortunate incident with the girl who absconded we have revised our thinking on using men tutors. It seems to unsettle the girls. Becky's actions came as a great disappointment to us all.'

'It's Becky I'm here to see you about.' Fergus knew from experience that if he did not break in on Mary Carpenter's flow of words he would be outside the study and on his way again before he had an opportunity to explain the purpose of his visit.

'You know where she is? Have you told the police? Or would you rather I came with you to bring her back? She will not be punished. I accept the fight was the fault of the other girl. Sadly, she has now been committed to prison. I have had few failures here, Mr Vincent, but I regret to admit that Maude Garrett was one. However, she is expecting a child and would have had to go elsewhere anyway. We have no facilities for babies here.'

'Becky is not coming back, Miss Carpenter. I've married her, and so she is now *my* responsibility. I want to rescind the magistrate's order committing her to your care.'

Mary Carpenter looked at Fergus without saying a word for at least ten seconds, then she asked: 'You have proof of this marriage?'

Fergus handed over a marriage certificate without comment.

Mary Carpenter read it carefully before passing it back to him. 'I see. Unfortunately, I can do nothing about the committal order. It was made by a magistrate. Only he can change it.'

'I realise that, but now you know the circumstances I would be grateful if you would inform the police that Becky is no longer wanted by you. I don't want to run the risk of having her locked up and put away while I sort out the whole business.'

Mary Carpenter nodded. 'That makes good sense. I will send word to the police immediately.' She looked accusingly at Fergus. 'I must confess I find your news surprising. I was not aware you had such deep feelings for this girl. *Had* I known, you would not have been allowed to teach here. I trust you did not abuse your privileged position as a member of staff. I would view that as most improper.'

Fergus smiled inwardly at Mary Carpenter's indignation. 'I did nothing you need be concerned about, Miss Carpenter. I conducted myself as one of your tutors should.'

Mary Carpenter gave him a brief nod. 'Then, it only remains for me to offer my sincere best wishes to both of you. Not all the girls who leave here can look forward to marriage with a respectable young man.'

Mary Carpenter stood up and extended her hand.

Fergus was halfway to the door when her voice brought him to a halt. 'Is Miss Tennant aware of your marriage?'

'I told her a short time ago. We met as I was coming here.'

When Fergus left, closing the door behind him, Mary Carpenter sat staring down at the empty desk in front of her for a long time. Then she stood up and, walking to the long window, looked out across the city towards Lewin's Mead.

CHAPTER THIRTY-NINE

FERGUS'S REQUEST to have the magistrate's order set aside was granted with a minimum of fuss, and married life quickly settled down to a pleasant routine for the young couple.

Fergus would paint for most of the day in the attic studio, occasionally sallying forth to make new sketches of life in the Lewin's Mead streets. In the evenings he went to the Hatchet inn, where Charlie Waller had framed a number of Fergus's sketches and put them up around the inn walls. Soon Bristolians were coming to the Hatchet inn especially to have Fergus sketch them.

The money Fergus made at the inn was his sole source of income. It was more than most Lewin's Mead residents earned, but there was little left at the end of each week. There were painting materials to be bought for Fergus, furniture and fittings to turn the attic into a reasonably comfortable home, and clothes for Becky, who had never before possessed more than a single dress at any one time.

Much to Fergus's relief, Becky had learned to cook well during her months at the Red Lodge and there was no repetition of the breakfast she had once made for him.

On Sundays, Fergus and Becky left Lewin's Mead to mingle with families from other parts of the city on their weekly excursions. They never repeated the trip on a steamer, but the city had many other delights on offer. One day they went to Bristol's zoological park where Becky's wonderment at the strange animals on view equalled that of the children about them. She was charmed by a bear cub frolicking in its enclosure, and shivered in fearful excitement as the sensitive tip of an elephant's trunk took a bun from her hand.

That night, lying in bed together, their room lit only by the glow from the fire, Becky declared it had been the most enjoyable day she had ever known.

'Better than our trip on the paddle-steamer?'

'I think so,' Becky admitted, after giving the matter due thought. 'Mind you, I was only a child then.'

Fergus smiled and tightened his arm about her. 'We'll have to go again, one weekend.'

'Why? I've got my *own* shoes now.' Becky giggled mischievously. 'Do you think that girl would recognise me if we met again?'

'No. As you said, you were a child then. You're a woman now.'

Later that night Becky lay cradling her sleeping husband in her arms. She heard Iris return to the house and stand arguing in the hall with a man who objected to paying in advance for what she had to offer. Later still Becky heard the nervous laugh of a young man and Irish Molly's practised reassurance.

Becky hugged Fergus more tightly. Had he not loved her enough, she, too, would have been bringing a stranger back to the house in Back Lane at about this time at night, wondering what demands he would make on her body, hoping he would not turn out to be one of those men who vented his anger on a prostitute in a bid to repay the world for all the wrongs it had done to him.

Becky vowed she would try hard to ensure that Fergus never regretted his decision to marry her.

Fergus was restless. The weather had something to do with the feeling. There was a thunderstorm building up, and the air was heavy and oppressive. From the attic window the edge of a thick black bank of cloud could just be seen edging its way towards the city.

Irritably, Fergus put down his brush. 'I'm going for a walk down by the docks to get some air. You coming with me?'

Becky shook her head. Fergus had recently taught her to

make picture-frames, and she was working on one now. 'I want to finish this. You go; it will do you good to get out for a while. You haven't left the house for three days.'

It was true. After weeks spent making new sketches and painting Becky, Fergus had returned to his earlier works. He had completed about twenty paintings and hoped to have produced enough for a new exhibition by the late autumn.

Most of the doors in the house stood open, and Fergus saw a scantily clad Irish Molly lying on her bed. As he passed the room she called to ask if Becky was in the attic. Fergus grunted that she was.

'Good. I'll take up a cup of tea when I find the energy to make one. I suppose she hasn't got the kettle on?'

Outside in the narrow confined streets it was almost as hot as inside the house. Not until he arrived at the dockside did Fergus feel the first stirring of cool air about him.

Fergus wandered aimlessly about the docks for almost an hour but when the bank of cloud he had seen from the attic obscured the early-evening sun he decided it was time to go home.

Picking his way through the maze of narrow streets that linked Lewin's Mead with the docks, thinking of his work, Fergus was suddenly startled to hear anguished screams coming from a nearby house. Moments later someone began hammering against the street-door from the inside.

A woman squatting on the step of a neighbouring house rose to her feet and called through the door: 'What's the matter? What is it, me darling?'

'Jeannie's on fire! She's all alight!' There was terror in the child's voice.

'The Lord help us! Haven't I said many times that a woman shouldn't go off and leave her children on their own? Five girls in the house and the oldest no more than seven. We'll all be burned out, so we will. . . .'

Fergus tried the latch, but the door was locked. The screams were now continuous, and someone on the other side of the door began sobbing.

'Stand back from the door. I'm going to break it down.' Fergus shouted a warning to the children inside the house, but the deed was more difficult than the intention. He was not a heavily built man, and the door resisted all his attempts to shoulder it open.

By now a crowd had begun to gather, and a man pushed to the front, signalling for Fergus to stand aside. The man wore heavy leather boots, and at his second kick the door crashed open, allowing smoke and three tiny choking figures to spill from the house.

As the heavy accumulation of smoke billowed away flames could be seen along a passageway towards the rear of the house.

'Fetch water – and call out the fire-engine.'

As the man who had kicked open the door shouted his orders Fergus entered the house. The neighbour had said there were five children in the house, but only *three* had come out through the front door.

He found the missing two children close to the door of the blazing kitchen, guided to the spot by the screams of one of the two small girls.

The eldest of the family, she had been trying to drag her badly burned sister to safety when the opening of the front door had caused the flames in the room to reach out and engulf them both.

It took only a moment for Fergus to reach the children, but the older girl's clothing was already well alight. Fergus beat at her with his bare hands, spurred on by the child's agonised screams.

The girl was wearing a surprising amount of clothing, and Fergus beat at it for what seemed many minutes before the flames from the kitchen caught up with them and he was forced to drag her farther along the passageway, away from the heart of the fire. He tried to bring the other child with her, but as he took a grip on her charred dress it disintegrated in his hand. Then the flames reached out towards him, and he was forced to return to the first girl. He dragged her to the door only to be trampled for his pains as firefighters rushed into the house carrying buckets of water.

Then other hands reached out and pulled Fergus and the child out to the street. Someone poured a bucket of water over the blazing clothes of the seven-year-old girl, and her screams died away as she fell into a merciful faint. Not until someone repeated the process with Fergus did he realise that his clothing was also burning.

The cold water brought pain, too – excruciating pain – and Fergus looked down at his blackened hands in disbelief. He, too, was badly burned.

Men and women were clapping Fergus on the back, congratulating him on his bravery, but one man, more observant than the others, suggested he should find a doctor quickly.

'No, I must get home.' Fergus's voice was barely recognisable, his throat dry and painful as a result of the smoke he had encountered inside the burning house.

'Come, I'll help you. . . .' Warding off the hands that reached out to pat Fergus, the man who had suggested Fergus should see a doctor led him out of the crowd. He walked with Fergus to Back Lane, and on the way explained the cause of the fire, as told by one of the three girls who had escaped from the house.

It seemed they had been playing, dressing up in their mother's clothes, when one of the girls tripped on the long dress she wore and fell into the fire. It was the reason why the children had been wearing so much clothing. But when the helpful stranger began airing his views on parents who went out to work all day leaving their children locked in the house Fergus stopped listening. His hands were agonisingly painful by now, and he tucked them beneath his armpits in a bid to protect them in some instinctive way.

When they reached Ida Stokes's house the stranger insisted upon escorting Fergus upstairs to the attic room, and Fergus found events confusing thereafter. As the stranger explained Fergus's injuries, praising him as a hero, Becky was examining the burns to his hands and Irish Molly was insisting that he should receive treatment immediately.

When the stranger left, Irish Molly took a closer look at Fergus's hands and shook her head gravely. 'You'll not be doing any painting for a while, me darling – and you need to be treated right away.'

'Where can we find a doctor?' In common with most of the

residents of Lewin's Mead, Becky regarded the medical profession with awe.

'I'm not thinking of a doctor.' Irish Molly downed the last of a cup of lukewarm tea. 'Don't do a thing to his hands while I dress. I'll take you to someone who knows how to treat burns better than any doctor.'

When Irish Molly had gone to her room, Becky said: 'Do you think we ought to listen to her?'

'I don't care *who* I see, if they can ease this pain. But Molly's right about one thing. I won't be painting for a while. God knows where we'll get money for living.'

'My poor Fergus. I'm a burden to you already. If you didn't have me, you could go to that lady of yours — or to Fanny Tennant. They'd welcome you as a hero and look after you until your hands were well again. You can't do that now because you've got me. But don't worry. I'll get work. I *can*, you know.'

'Time enough to talk about that later. I wish Irish Molly would hurry. These hands are killing me.'

Irish Molly realised more than either of them the seriousness of Fergus's burns. She dressed quickly, forgoing the heavy make-up without which she would not usually leave the house.

The storm that had threatened Bristol had by-passed the city, and Irish Molly led Fergus and Becky northwards away from the Lewin's Mead slum, taking the road that led to Gloucester. For more than two miles they walked, until the houses of the city were behind them and fields stretched ahead for as far as could be seen.

Dazed with the pain of his hands, Fergus was beginning to think he could walk no farther when Irish Molly turned off the road to where a small stream bisected a thinly wooded copse. In the copse was a number of colourful bow-roofed caravans, and the smell of wood-smoke hung heavily on the air. Irish Molly had brought them to a gypsy encampment.

As they entered the camp a man with an outdoor tan stepped into their path.

'Are you wanting something?' His accent was not unlike that of Irish Molly.

'We've come to see Mother Whelan.'

'Who's come to see her?'

'Tell her it's Irish Molly – with a friend who's burned his hands badly.'

'Wait here. I'll find out if she's seeing anyone today.'

When the man walked away towards the caravans, Becky looked questioningly at Irish Molly, as Fergus tried in vain to hold his hands in a position that would ease the pain he felt.

'She'll see him,' declared Irish Molly confidently. 'They're *Irish* gypsies. Mother Whelan knows more about healing than anyone in Ireland – or anywhere else, for that matter.'

'I hope she hurries.' Becky put a comforting arm about Fergus. 'We should have taken him to a doctor right away, in Bristol.'

It was at least ten minutes before the man who had challenged them returned, walking as though there was no sense of urgency.

'Mother Whelan will see you, but try not to tire her too much. There isn't much strength in her these days, and she's a long journey ahead.'

Mother Whelan sat on the steps of a caravan surrounded by men and women of all ages. It was impossible to hazard a guess at her own age, but her wizened face had the appearance of uncared-for leather.

She looked briefly at Becky, nodded to Irish Molly, then turned her full attention on Fergus.

'Show me.'

Her voice was as old as her face, but it carried authority. Fergus held out his hands, and she looked closely at them, supporting his arms with a finger beneath each wrist.

'You're the artist who pulled two children from a fire.'

Fergus was startled. The news had reached the gypsy camp quickly.

'They're both dead. They should have been brought to me. I might have saved one of them, at least.'

'So he burned his hands for nothing.' Becky spoke bitterly.

'If it hadn't been for your man, the other three would have died – and half of Bristol been burned down. Not that anyone would have been any worse for *that*.'

Turning to a woman standing in the doorway of the caravan behind her, Mother Whelan spoke at some length in rapid Romany. When the one-sided conversation ended the younger woman disappeared from view inside the caravan.

'Will Fergus's hands be all right?' Becky blurted out the question when Mother Whelan returned her attention to the visitors.

'If you're asking whether he'll paint again, the answer is yes. You'll carry scars for life, young man, and some days you'll not be able to hold a brush before mid-morning; but if you'd gone to a doctor you'd never have held a brush at all.'

'That's a great relief.' Fergus grimaced with pain. 'I'll make you and your camp the subject of my first painting when my hands are well again.'

'We'll be gone long before then.'

The old woman looked up into Fergus's face. 'I'm being taken back to Ireland to die.'

Mother Whelan cackled her amusement at Fergus's shocked expression. 'I've had a good life, a useful life, and I've outlived all my friends and most of my children. I'm ready to go now.'

Gripping Fergus's forearms, she said: 'Your life is in front of you. Make the most of it. I've heard of your paintings of the cottiers – the homeless Irish you helped down by the river. . . .' She cackled again at Fergus's surprise. 'There's little goes on within fifty miles of Bristol that I *don't* know about. One of my grand-daughters visited your exhibition. She told me it was like watching the cottiers dying before her very eyes. That's *your* path in life, my young artist. To show folks what's going on about them.'

The woman came from the caravan carrying an earthenware jar and a length of clean linen. Mother Whelan took the jar and signalled for the woman to hand the linen to Becky and Irish Molly.

'Tear it into strips about three fingers wide. Use all of it. Now, give me one of your hands, young man. I need to make a good job of this if you're to change the world with your talents.'

Dipping inside the jar, the old gypsy woman scooped out a

333

handful of a thick green greasy substance.

'This will hurt for a while, but then your hands will feel as cool as a clear Kerry stream. Grit your teeth now.'

Mother Whelan's bony fingers held Fergus's wrist in a strong grip, and she began smearing the thick ointment on his burned and tormented hands. Fergus made no sound as she worked, but occasionally his teeth drew blood from his lip as he bit back the agony he felt.

The old woman worked swiftly and expertly with surprising gentleness, at the same time crooning sympathetically in the strange Romany dialect.

It took a while for the salve to take effect, but by the time the gypsy woman had finished binding his hands, making them immovable, they were more comfortable.

'Didn't I tell you so?' Mother Whelan replied when Fergus told her the pain was easing. 'Have faith in everything else I say and you won't be disappointed.'

To Becky, she said: 'Take the salve with you – but only change the dressings once a week, making quite certain you keep the air out when you bind them.'

'How long will it be before I can stop? When Fergus's hands are well again?'

'Continue with the salve for at least three months. Then use dry dressings for another three. After that he'll need to learn all over again how to hold a paintbrush.'

'Six months!' Fergus was aghast. He had barely enough money to last for two weeks, and without hands he could not paint. Trying to push such thoughts to the back of his mind for the moment, he asked: 'How much do I owe you?'

'More than you can ever repay, my young artist, so we'll not talk of money. Instead, I'll accept your promise to paint the poor and the helpless for as long as there's a need.'

Fergus had looked closely at his hands while the old gypsy woman was working on them with her ointment. If ever they were fully healed, it would be nothing short of a miracle – and no price was too much for a miracle.

'You have my promise.'

'Then, two little girls never died in vain.'

The old gypsy woman struggled to her feet, and one of the men standing nearby came forward to take her arm. Nodding to Fergus, she said: 'Goodbye, Artist. We'll not meet again. Not in this life.'

CHAPTER FORTY

THE NEXT FEW WEEKS were hard ones for Fergus. He watched his money dwindle, knowing there was no way he could earn more. He never explained the full seriousness of their situation to Becky, although he suggested she should cut down on their household expenses as much as possible.

Eventually the day came when Fergus gave Becky the last of his money to go out and buy food. When she had gone he sat in the attic staring at the completed paintings leaning against the wall at the far end of the attic studio.

He looked at the paintings for a long while before choosing two. One was a portrait of Becky, the other a Lewin's Mead street scene. After struggling awkwardly for some time he managed to secure them beneath his arm.

Downstairs he met Irish Molly on the landing. Seeing the paintings, she raised an eyebrow. 'Are things so bad you're on the way to Uncle's now?'

'Uncle's?' Fergus was puzzled.

'The shop with three gold balls hanging over the door. The pawnbroker.'

'Oh. . . . No. I'm taking the paintings off to sell them.'

'I thought you were saving them all for a new exhibition. Does Becky know you've begun selling them?'

'Is there any reason why she should?'

Irish Molly was shrewd enough to guess the reason why Fergus was selling his paintings. She said: 'It's nothing to do with me. I hope you get a good price for them.'

Fergus's intention was to ask Fanny Tennant to show the

paintings to Solomon Stern, in the hope that he might agree to purchase them. Fergus had not seen Fanny since telling her of his wedding to Becky, but he did not doubt she would do such a favour for him.

He enquired for Fanny at the ragged school, only to be informed she was in London. It was a blow to Fergus's plans, but he needed money desperately. The only other person capable of helping him was Lady Hammond. Clutching the paintings tightly beneath his arm, Fergus set off for Clifton.

Lady Hammond's butler was sympathetic about Fergus's burned hands, as were the household staff who gathered about Fergus within minutes of his arrival – but Lady Hammond was not there. She was on a tour of the Continent, and her household did not expect her to return to England for at least another two months.

Making his way homewards, Fergus felt thoroughly despondent. Unable to paint and with no income, the immediate future looked bleak indeed. He wondered how he could break the news to Becky. She seemed to be managing surprisingly well, but she was not a naturally frugal person.

Fergus took a long way home, walking down the steep and fashionable Park Street, heading towards the docks and the heart of the city. He was almost within sight of the docks when he saw three golden balls hanging above the door of one of the shops he was passing and he was reminded of Irish Molly's question. This was a pawnbroker's shop. 'Uncle's.'

Fergus stopped and gazed in at the window for a very long time. There were many varied items offered for sale, each one mute evidence of human failure, carrying price-tags that put a pathetic value on heartbreak and poverty. Wedding rings were here aplenty, with brooches and bangles. Few were of any great value, but most had meant far more than money to their late owners. There were clothes here, too, sharing the window with vases, cutlery, watches – and two small paintings.

When Fergus entered the pawnshop a small, grey-haired, grey-faced man stood up from behind the counter. He had been hunched over a small table cluttered with the workings of a watch, and a magnifying glass held in place by a frown hid one eye. The magnifying glass was removed as Fergus approached, and the liberated eye blinked furiously for a moment or two.

As Fergus clumsily deposited his paintings on the counter, the pawnbroker clucked in sympathy.

'What have you done to your poor hands?'

Fergus thought the man sounded more like a solicitous priest than a pawnbroker, but this impression was swiftly dispelled.

'I trust it's nothing contagious? I'll have only clean goods in my shop.'

'I burned my hands,' Fergus retorted. 'That's why I've brought a couple of paintings to you. I can't work for a while.'

'An artist! Ah, I'm a great admirer of talent. What it is to be gifted. Let me see what you have here.'

The little pawnbroker lifted a painting of Becky. Holding it out at arm's length for a while, he put it down again without comment and picked up the Lewin's Mead street scene.

'This is better – but who would want to buy a painting of such a place? Park Street, perhaps. Clifton, yes. But Lewin's Mead?' The pawnbroker shook his head. 'It's a *business* I'm running here.'

Clumsily, Fergus pulled the paintings towards him, and the pawnbroker looked startled.

'What are you doing? I thought you were here to raise money on your paintings?'

'But you've decided you don't want them.'

'Did I say that? No, my boy, but I want you to have no foolish expectations of them. To me they're worth very little, but I see you as a man of honour. You'll raise the money and get them back some day. In the meantime I'll keep them safe for you, and charge little more than storage. . . .'

'How much will you advance on them?' Fergus broke in on the pawnbroker's insincere patter.

'Three shillings apiece.'

Fergus could not hide his disbelief, and the pawnbroker rapidly made a new offer. 'All right, *six* shillings for the street scene and four for the other one.'

'Both paintings are worth far more. You must know this.'

'So? I am taking them as security for a loan, not buying them. Where will I find a buyer if you don't come back? You want to *sell* them, then take your pictures somewhere else.'

'Ten shillings on each painting. If for any reason I fail to redeem them, you'll get your money back a hundredfold.'

Even this was far less than Fergus had hoped for, but his financial state was desperate.

'Your name ... it's Rembrandt, perhaps? Or would it be Constable? Seven and sixpence each.'

Once again Fergus began to struggle to pick up his paintings, and the little pawnbroker sighed. 'All right. All right. *Ten* shillings each – but only because of your poor hands. I can see you have need of the money.'

Unlooping a cord from about his neck, the pawnbroker used a key hanging from it to open a drawer built into his side of the counter. Taking out four five-shilling pieces, he put them in a neat line on the counter. Scribbling a few details on two numbered green tickets, he slid money and receipts across the wooden counter to Fergus.

'There you are, my son. I charge interest of a penny in the shilling per week. Any goods not redeemed within six months are sold.'

Fergus nodded. 'Will you put the money in my coat pocket? I can't pick it up.'

As the pawnbroker reached across the counter to carry out the request, Fergus asked: 'Will you take more paintings if I have a further need of money?'

'Am I to become an art dealer now? All right, but I can't guarantee ten shillings each for all of them.'

When Fergus left the shop the pawnbroker took the paintings and pasted a ticket to the back of each. Then he looked at both paintings again, fingers stroking his chin thoughtfully. Opening a panel door giving access to the shop window, he hung the pictures at the back of the window, then went outside to study them anew.

There were some boys playing in the gutter a little way along the road, racing twig-boats in a stream of evil-smelling water that flowed from a knacker's yard behind the row of shops. Calling one of the boys to him, the pawnbroker produced a penny from a soft leather purse tucked inside his waistband.

Handing the coin to the boy, he said: 'Go across to Phillips the art dealers on the other side of the docks. Ask for Mr Phillips himself. Tell him Isaiah Rodden has something that might be of interest to him. There's no hurry, but tell him it will be worth his while to pay me a visit some time.'

Fergus believed Becky was ignorant of their financial state, but he underestimated her intelligence. Aware there was no money coming in, she saw how carefully he doled out the money he gave her when she needed to go shopping. She also knew the number of paintings in the attic studio was dwindling.

Becky tried to speak to Fergus about the situation but, although he was loving and patient with her in every other respect, he refused to discuss money matters.

Irish Molly had told Becky of seeing Fergus leave the house with paintings tucked beneath his arm, but the Irishwoman did not want to involve herself with their domestic difficulties. She had problems of her own looming on the horizon. The landlord of the White Hart was selling his inn, and the prospective buyer had declared that prostitutes would not be welcome on the premises. His pronouncement caused great concern among Irish Molly's colleagues. The White Hart had been a recognised 'hunting ground' for as long as anyone could remember.

On a day when two more paintings went from the attic, Becky told Fergus she had obtained work to tide them over the next few weeks. She would be washing-up at a good-class inn, the Great Western, not far from the Hatchet. Becky did not add that the work was conditional on her standing in as a serving-maid in the tap-room when the inn was busy. As it was, Fergus declared angrily that it was not necessary for *his* wife to wash dishes in a tavern in order for them to live.

Becky tried to make it clear she did not intend to become the family provider. She was merely helping out until Fergus's hands were healed sufficiently for him to resume painting –

and there were already some signs of improvement. There was movement in two of his fingers, although he needed to be careful with them because the thin skin cracked easily, causing him much pain.

Grudgingly, Fergus came to accept that Becky would be going out to work each day. He could hardly do anything else. His stock of paintings was desperately low, and the day was not far off when he would have none to pledge to the pawnbroker. Besides, he had sensed that Becky was becoming restless with the restrictions his injured hands imposed upon their activities.

The evenings without Becky seemed very long, and by the time she returned to the house in the early hours of the morning she was on the verge of exhaustion. At first, Fergus would wait up for her, but most nights Becky wanted only to go to bed and sleep, so he reverted to his usual bed-time.

Some nights Fergus did not even hear Becky return to the attic room, and more than once he woke in the morning to find her sleeping on the floor, as she had done when she was a homeless street-urchin.

It was not an ideal way of life for a young married couple, but Fergus promised Becky that when his hands were healed he would work hard to make up for all the sacrifices she was making.

During the evenings, after Becky had gone to work, Fergus tried to exercise his hands, willing the burned fingers to move beneath the dressings, feeling a grim exhilaration when pain in the scarred and wasted muscles of his fingers signalled success.

Fergus was assured of a welcome at the Hatchet inn, but he found it difficult to accept drinks from Charlie Waller and Giraldus Reilly, knowing he was unable to return their generosity. Yet Fergus found it difficult to settle in the attic room alone, unable to paint or even to make himself a cup of tea.

He began to spend more and more time wandering the Lewin's Mead streets, observing scenes and incidents that would one day become background scenes for his paintings.

During one of these evening excursions, Fergus heard a

sound as though an illegal prize-fight or dog-fight was being staged. Following the noise, he found himself in a courtyard shared by more than twenty houses, their jumbled outbuildings backing on the rubbish-strewn dirt space.

There must have been at least seventy people crowding the entrance to the courtyard, and at first Fergus had difficulty obtaining a clear view of what was happening. Not until he pushed his way to the front of the crowd could Fergus see it was no form of fight that had drawn such an audience. The attraction was a poor lunatic. Chained to an iron ring set in a great stone, he was being cruelly tormented by two jeering youths who prodded at him with long sticks.

Bearded and ragged, the lunatic sat hunched outside a small shelter constructed from sticks and sacking. When the goading became too insistent the poor lunatic rounded on his tormentors. Bellowing with rage, he scattered them with a rush that ended when the chain snapped taut and he was brought to a halt tearing futilely at the iron collar secured about his neck. His rage and distress brought howls of glee from the onlookers. The more he fought against his iron collar, the greater was their delight.

Ending his bout of tortured frenzy for a moment, the lunatic's eyes suddenly found Fergus. His body became rigid as he stared at him, and then the madman's hands dropped away from his throat and with a shrill scream he sprang at Fergus.

The chain snapped taut and the lunatic dropped to the ground so heavily that for a moment the crowd fell silent, fearing he might have broken his neck. Then, screaming with pain as well as with fury now, his hands went up to the cruel band of iron, and the watchers roared their approval.

Fergus remained silent. He had recognised the lunatic. It was Joe Skewes.

Fergus had more reason than anyone there to hate the violent coal-heaver, but it shocked him to see Joe Skewes in such a state, chained to an iron ring like some captive animal and tormented by those who were sane enough to know better.

'He doesn't seem to like you,' cackled a toothless old hag

gleefully. 'Let him see you again. Go on, we'll have some fun with him.'

Ignoring the woman, Fergus backed away, pausing only to ask a young boy how long Joe Skewes had been chained in the courtyard.

'A fortnight,' came the reply. 'You should have been here last night. We gave him a bath with buckets of water, and he screamed at us the whole time. I don't think water had ever touched his skin before.'

Fergus limped away from the lunatic-baiting crowd as fast as he could go, not slackening his pace until the sound of laughter was far behind him. The scene had brought back disturbing memories of his younger days, and of vigils beside his mother's bed in an asylum ward.

He was still thinking of the scene he had just witnessed when a voice from behind him called: 'Don't you speak to old friends now you're a hero?'

Fergus came to a halt, and Constable Ivor Primrose caught up with him.

'I'm sorry, Ivor, I didn't see you.'

'You weren't seeing anything, Fergus. Are your hands troubling you?'

Fergus lifted up his bandaged hands, then let them drop to his side again. 'No more than usual. I was thinking about Joe Skewes. . . .' He told Ivor Primrose of the scene he had just left.

The constable listened in silence, occasionally nodding his head gravely. When Fergus ended his account of the chained coal-heaver, Ivor Primrose said seriously: 'So Joe Skewes has finally come to the end of the road. It had to come. He's been insane for years.'

'Then, surely he should be locked away somewhere, not chained in a courtyard and treated as a sideshow? God knows, I'd have seen the man *hanged* after what he did to Becky, but this is degrading to everyone concerned.'

'We'd need an army of constables to fetch him out of the rookery – and Joe Skewes wouldn't exactly welcome us with open arms. Forget him, Fergus. Someone must have accepted some responsibility for him or he'd have starved to death by now. Talking of such things, it can't be too easy for you right now.'

Fergus shrugged. 'I manage.'

'Have you seen Fanny Tennant lately? When last I saw her she told me she had some good news for you.'

'Fanny's back in Bristol?'

'Yes, and asking after you. She'd have come to the rookery looking for you, but I warned her against it. She was safe enough a few months ago, when she was teaching regularly at the ragged school, but she's been away for too long. There are villains in the rookery now who've never heard of her. She'd be set upon before she walked fifty yards.'

'Then, I'd better go and find her. Thanks for telling me.'

CHAPTER FORTY-ONE

FERGUS FOUND FANNY at the ragged school where she had just dismissed the evening classes. She was standing in the hallway talking to a tall thin man. When she saw Fergus a guarded expression came to her face. It became concern when she saw his heavily bandaged hands.

'Fergus, how are you?' She lifted one of his hands gingerly and looked with some distress at the bandaging. 'Ivor told me you had burned your hands rescuing some children from a fire. I had no idea you were *still* bandaged. Have you been treated by a doctor?'

'Some old gypsy woman dressed the burns for me....' Fergus intercepted the looks exchanged by Fanny and the tall stranger. 'They're a lot better now. I need to keep a dry bandage on them for another couple of months, that's all.'

Again there was an exchange of glances between Fanny and her companion. Then Fanny said: 'Fergus, this is Dr Pike. He's just been examining some of our pupils. Will you allow him to look at your hands?'

'There's nothing to look at. They're healing, just as Mother Whelan said they would.'

The doctor showed immediate interest. 'Did you say Mother Whelan? I've heard a great deal about her. She has earned a remarkable reputation as a healer. Will you at least allow me to change your bandages? I have some new ones here in my bag.'

Fergus's bandages were still the strips of rags provided by the gypsies. Because Becky was working, they had been overlooked and not changed for more than a week. He nodded agreement.

'Good. Perhaps you have a room somewhere near, Miss Tennant. . . ?'

In the room that served as Fanny's office, the doctor removed the rags from Fergus's left hand, and Fanny gasped in horror when she saw the angry red scarring that disfigured the whole skin area. Fergus's right hand was no better, and when the doctor held them up to examine them together Fanny was brought to the verge of tears.

Not so Dr Pike. Turning them over and peering closer at the skin, he murmured: 'Incredible. Quite incredible.'

'I'm beginning to get some movement back in them. In three months they'll be as good as new.' In an attempt to prove the truth of his words, Fergus managed to twitch one thumb and a couple of fingers.

'I didn't realise you'd been so seriously burned, Fergus. I'm so sorry. . . .' Fanny choked on her words.

'Mr Vincent, you are a very lucky man. Had burns such as these been treated by any doctor I know, you would have lost the use of your hands for ever. As it is . . . Well, they may never be *quite* as good as before, but you'll certainly have enough use in them to lead a normal life.'

The doctor released Fergus's hands reluctantly. Opening his bag, he took out a bandage. 'If I possessed this gypsy woman's skill, I could earn a worldwide reputation.'

Fanny was unimpressed by the doctor's enthusiasm. The sight of Fergus's scarred hands had distressed her, and the shock was slow to wear off.

In a bid to take her mind off his injuries, Fergus said: 'I met Ivor Primrose this evening. He said you've been asking after me.'

'What. . . ? Oh, yes!' His ruse succeeded, and Fanny dragged her gaze away from his hands. 'I have good news for you. Solomon Stern's friend has used some of your sketches in his magazines.'

Fergus looked at Fanny blankly, and she said incredulously: 'Don't you remember? You left some sketches with him.'

Fergus had forgotten. They had not been among his best works, and so much had happened since then.

'It's a good job *someone* has your interests at heart. I have a hundred pounds here for you – and I am assured there will be more when the other sketches are used.'

Fanny nodded towards the now bandaged hands. 'I don't doubt that you have need of the money. Things can't have been easy for you, especially as you are now a married man.'

Fergus scarcely heard her. Fanny had said she had a hundred pounds for him. It was a fortune – and there would be more! His money problems were over. There was no longer any need for Becky to go to work.

'It's *wonderful* news. Yes, things have been hard – but they'll be better now. Bless you, Fanny. You're an angel. Thank you, too, Doctor. The hands feel much more comfortable now.'

He had to find Becky and tell her of the unexpected change in their fortunes. Halfway to the door he stopped and turned back to Fanny. 'I have some paintings Solomon Stern might like to buy. If I bring them to your house, will you give them to him when he next comes to Bristol?'

Fanny nodded. She knew why Fergus was hurrying away.

On his way to the Great Western inn, Fergus passed the pawnbroker's where so many of his paintings were pledged. Half a dozen of them were now exhibited in the window, one being the portrait of Becky. Eager to savour the first fruits of his newly acquired wealth, Fergus entered the pawnbroker's shop to tell the proprietor of his good fortune.

Isaiah Rodden was talking to two young men, but he broke off the conversation and made an expansive gesture of surprise when he saw Fergus.

'Gentlemen! Gentlemen! *This* is who you must speak to if you wish to buy one of the paintings. I am only a poor pawnbroker. I loan money to my fellow-men to help them weather bad times and I take good care of their property until such time as they claim it from me again. If I also sometimes act as an honest broker and both parties are generous – well, that is an unexpected reward. Speak to him, gentlemen. He is a reasonable man. An artist – with a need for money, as you can see by the bandages on his poor hands.'

This last remark was accompanied by a wink, which Fergus was not meant to see, and one of the men said: 'My friend would like to purchase one of your paintings. The portrait of the young dollymop.'

Fergus flushed angrily. The only painting that might be construed as being of a 'dollymop' was the portrait of Becky. It was evident that both young men had been drinking, but this did not render the remark any less offensive.

'The painting's not for sale. I'll be redeeming it in the next few days.'

'Come now, you're an artist. I'll give you a fair price. Five pounds? Six?'

'I'm sorry, it's not for sale.'

'Very well, then … ten. Ten guineas. Julian is so smitten with this dollymop I've promised to buy him the damned painting, even if it costs more than *she* did.'

It was a situation Fergus had hoped would never occur. That he would one day come face to face with one of the men who had known Becky when she was taking men home from the White Hart.

'I'll not sell the portrait for a hundred guineas. Good day to you both.'

Fergus turned to the pawnbroker, but one of the young men took Fergus's arm and pulled him back roughly to face him.

'You're being offensive, sir. *Damned* offensive. I've offered you my money and you've refused to take it – and for no good reason that I can see.'

'Oh, come away, Henry. Who wants a picture anyway? We'll go and see the real thing, and I'll let you buy me a drink there. I might even let *you* take her off tonight. Then you'll know what it is I find so special about the girl.'

With a last defiant glare at Fergus, the young man released his arm and walked from the pawnbroker's shop with the stiff-legged gait of a tom-cat who had just asserted his authority over another.

Fergus stared after the two men as they walked off arm-in-arm, their laughter gradually fading in the distance.

'They offered a fair price. Most artists would be delighted to sell a painting for ten guineas.'

'I'm not *most* artists.' Fergus's reply was abrupt. He was puzzling over the conversation between the two young men. They had gone off as though they were expecting to meet up with Becky. But that was not possible.

'I'll tell you what I'll do. I'll take *all* the paintings you've left with me, for seven pounds apiece! It's a fair offer. It should set you up until you're able to paint again.'

Fergus shook his head. Perhaps one of the two young men had seen Becky in the Great Western inn. She might have been sent out to collect his plates or glasses, and he had made up a tale about her when talking to his friend. . . .

'Very well. Seven *guineas*.'

'No.'

Fergus decided he would go to the Great Western inn right away and tell Becky there was no longer any need for her to work. A hundred pounds would tide them over until his hands had healed. Once he began painting again everything would be all right. He would be able to provide Becky with all the things he knew she yearned for, and she would never have to work again. . . .

'All right, I'll give you what the young gent offered you. *Ten guineas a picture* – and I'll take the lot. No argument about whether or not they're worth the money. . . .'

'My paintings are not for sale. I came here to tell you I'd be redeeming them some time during the next day or two.'

Disinclined to discuss the matter any longer, Fergus turned away abruptly and left the pawnbroker's shop. He was anxious to find Becky and take her home.

When Fergus had gone, Isaiah Rodden cursed himself for a fool. He should have offered Fergus his top price of *fifteen* guineas for each painting. His art-dealer friend had seen the first of Fergus's sketches in a London magazine and offered twenty-five. Fergus was arousing considerable interest as an artist. Prices for his paintings could be expected to rise rapidly.

Fergus entered the Great Western inn and stood inside the

door of the tap-room, looking about the crowded interior. There was no sign of either of the men who had been in the pawnbroker's shop. Neither could he see Becky, but he had not expected to find her here.

Suddenly Fergus saw Giraldus Reilly sitting at a table. The big Irishman saw him at the same time and came across the room to greet him with a big grin of welcome.

'It's good to see you, Fergus. I'm enjoying my night off by seeing what the other inns are like. But let me buy you a drink. What is it – a large brandy? I know the cellarman here. He has a nice barrel tucked away specially for his friends. There's no Customs stamp on the barrel, but that adds to the flavour of the brandy.'

'I'm not stopping for a drink, Giraldus. I came to speak to Becky. To tell her she doesn't need to work here any more.'

A puzzled expression came to Giraldus Reilly's face. 'Becky doesn't work here any more. The cellarman told me that Becky was here for only three evenings before she left. I can't say I blame her; it was work for a drudge with no mind for thinking of what she *might* be doing instead. Not for the likes of a young girl married only a few months. But are you telling me you didn't know she'd left?'

Fergus shook his head, thoroughly bewildered. 'She leaves home at the same time each day. I thought she was coming here. Perhaps Irish Molly knows where I can find her.'

'No, she'd have told me – but wait a minute. The cellarman here mentioned seeing her the other day. I'll go and ask him where it was. . . .' The big Irishman hesitated. 'That's if you're really sure you *want* to know where she might be.'

Fergus would dearly have loved to say no, but he could not.

Giraldus Reilly was away for what seemed a long time. When he returned he would not meet Fergus's eyes.

'Where is she?'

'Ah, well. . . . You see, the cellarman wasn't certain at all, you understand. He only thought it *might* have been Becky he saw. I don't suppose it was really her. . . .'

'Where was it he *thought* he saw Becky?'

'Going into the Cabot Arms – but he only saw her from the

back. He was probably mistaken; he admits that himself.'

Now Fergus understood Giraldus Reilly's embarrassment. The Cabot Arms was notorious as an inn frequented by young men of the town. They went there to pick up 'dolly-mops' – servant girls, millinery assistants, nannies and other young girls who sought to supplement the meagre wages they earned in their unexciting occupations.

As Fergus turned to leave the tap-room, Giraldus Reilly said: 'If you're going to the Cabot Arms, you'd best hold your fire for a minute. I'll come with you as soon as I've downed this pint. . . .'

'There's no need.' Fergus held out his bandaged hands. 'I won't be starting any wars.'

Fergus was not clear what his intentions were as he limped through the gas-lit streets, heading for the Cabot Arms. He felt hurt and confused. He had believed Becky's brief foray into the world occupied by Irish Molly and Iris would never be repeated. He *still* believed it. There had to be some other explanation for the circumstantial case building up against her.

As Fergus neared the Cabot Arms he slowed his pace and tried to think things out logically. What would he do if he found Becky inside the tavern? What would he say if she refused to return home with him?

The Cabot Arms was busy. The noise and laughter from inside reached him when he was still fifty yards away. He stopped for a moment in the shadow cast by an overhanging upper storey – then he saw one of the two young men he had last encountered in the pawnbroker's shop. On his arm was a young girl. She was on the side farthest from Fergus, but he did not doubt it was Becky. She was the reason they had come here. . . .

Fergus ran awkwardly along the pavement after the couple. He did not know what he would do when he caught up with them. He did not know what he *could* do, but Fergus would not stand back and watch Becky go off with another man.

'Becky . . .!' Fergus caught up with the couple as they

turned off the thoroughfare into a narrow gas-lit alleyway. Brushing the man aside, Fergus grabbed the girl's arm and turned her towards him – and discovered it was not Becky.

'What do you want? I don't know *you*.'

As the girl drew back from him in alarm her companion recovered from his surprise and pushed Fergus roughly to one side.

'Well I'm damned! It's the artist who won't sell his paintings. The man's mad!'

Shaking a fist at Fergus, he shouted: 'Clear off, or I'll forget you can't defend yourself and give you what you deserve. . . .'

CHAPTER FORTY-TWO

FERGUS KNEW IT WAS BECKY when he heard her foot-steps coming up the first flight of stairs from the hallway. She was very late. The last time he had looked at his watch in the dim glow from the fire it had showed ten minutes after two. Now, hunched in a corner of the attic room, he dreaded the confrontation that was only moments away.

There was no way Becky could disguise her progress up the final decrepit flight of stairs to the attic. An inconsequential thought crossed Fergus's mind: Ida Stokes would soon need to do something about the stairs and would no doubt put up the rent to pay for the repairs. . . .

Becky opened the door to the attic studio slowly and quietly, as though trying not to wake him.

She crossed the room towards the fire, but there was insufficient light for him to make out her face.

'You're late.'

His voice, thick and momentarily unfamiliar, startled her.

'Fergus! Where are you? Are you all right?' She sounded alarmed.

'Where have *you* been?'

'I've been working. You know that.' The brief hesitation before she replied was barely discernible, but it was there. 'Have you been drinking?'

'Yes, but I'm not drunk. I've been out looking for you.'

'Oh! Then, you'll know I'm not working at the Great Western inn any more.'

'Giraldus Reilly told me. I'd rather have heard it from you.'

'Would you have approved had I told you I was now working at the Cabot Arms?'

'You know I wouldn't.' Fergus struggled to his feet in the darkness. He had sat hunched up for so long he had cramp in his good leg. 'Why have you gone back to *that* sort of life, Becky? For God's sake, *why*?'

'*What* sort of life? I'm a serving-girl at the Cabot Arms.' The hesitation was there again, but more noticeable this time. 'It's a sight easier than washing-up, and it pays more. I knew you wouldn't like me working *there*. That's the only reason why I've said nothing about it.'

'I met two men today who wanted to buy a portrait of you because one of them had slept with you. When I wouldn't sell they went off to find you – so the second man could share his friend's experience.'

For a long time there was silence in the room. Then the coal on the fire shifted. In the brief light of a short-lived flame, Fergus could see anguish on Becky's face.

'I know the man you're talking about. I only went with him once, Fergus. He came to see me tonight, with his friend. I wouldn't have anything to do with either of them.'

Fergus knew she was lying. 'How many men have there been, Becky? Why have you done this to us?'

'For you, Fergus. For *us*. I've watched you getting more and more worried about money. I know you've been pawning your paintings and they're all you have in the world. It's all so ... *unfair*. I know how much your paintings mean to you. Perhaps you should go back to Clifton, to Lady Hammond – or Fanny Tennant. If you'd done that instead of marrying me, you wouldn't have burned your hands and you wouldn't *need* to sell your paintings.'

'You mean more to me than all my paintings. I married you so you'd never need to do anything like this again – and now you're saying you did it for *me*?'

'It means nothing to me, Fergus. Honest.'

'It means something to me – and to the man I met today, too, otherwise he'd not have wanted to buy your portrait.'

'We needed money....'

'Making money is my responsibility, not yours. That was

why I came to find you. My sketches have been published in a London magazine. I can redeem my paintings and we'll be left with enough to live on until my hands heal.'

Becky was silent for a very long time. Then she said: 'I won't ever do anything like this again, Fergus. Honest, I won't.'

'You promised me the same thing when we were married. What excuse will you find for breaking your promise *next* time?'

'Do you think I *want* other men, Fergus? Is that what you really believe?'

'I don't know *what* to believe any more. I thought that once we were man and wife there would be no one else for either of us.'

Fergus was rubbing salt deep in his own wounds, but he had been nursing the hurt to himself for too many hours. It had to come out.

'Am I asking too much? Perhaps I am. You've grown up accepting prostitution as a way of life. Irish Molly, Iris, Maude Garrett. No doubt it's an easy way to earn money. I don't know.'

'That's right, Fergus. *You don't know*. You paint pictures of life in Lewin's Mead. Life in a slum. But scratch the paint off one of your pictures and what's underneath? I'll tell you. *Canvas.* You're a painter, Fergus, a *fine* painter, but it doesn't mean you understand all there is to know about life. Not my life, or anyone else's in Lewin's Mead. Yes, I've grown up with women like Irish Molly and Iris about me. I've watched them and believed that one day I'd need to do the same. When you came along I thought a miracle had happened. I didn't ask *you* to marry *me*. That was your idea. I'd have cooked for you, worked for you – done *anything* just to be with you, to be *your* woman. If it hadn't been for Rose Cottle, there would never have been any other man. . . . But it's no good talking about what *might* have been.'

'That was in the past, Becky. Before we were married. To do it again now . . .' Fergus choked on his words.

'I told you why I did it. To get money for us. Now I'm asking you to forgive me. Fergus . . . please.'

Fergus made no reply. He had tried to think ahead, to what life would be like when this nightmare was over. But he was afraid. If he closed his eyes when he and Becky were making love, would he see the faces of the young men who had been in the pawnshop? And when Becky went out in the evening would he always be wondering what she was doing?

'Please, Fergus. I beg you.'

'I don't know if I can.'

He wanted to say he would *try* to forgive, *try* to understand. The words would not come – and then it was too late. Becky had gone.

Fergus hardly noticed the dawn arrive, or the grumpy squabbling sound of Ida Stokes's house waking to face another cheerless day. Even when a heavy storm broke over the city it failed to shake Fergus out of his numbed apathy.

There had been other tragedies in Fergus's life. He had survived the loss of his mother, and the injury that had left him a cripple, but this time it seemed fate had dealt him a whole series of shattering blows. First the destruction of his paintings in the London explosion, next the burns to his hands – and now Becky's return to prostitution. For the first time in his life Fergus felt too weary to fight back. He accepted defeat.

It was after noon when Irish Molly and Giraldus Reilly climbed the stairs to the attic studio and found Fergus still huddled in the corner where he had remained since Becky left him.

He might have been dozing, or perhaps his exhausted brain was too tired to function. Whatever the reason, he never heard them arrive and did not turn bleary red-rimmed eyes on them until Giraldus Reilly touched him, concerned at Fergus's stillness.

'What do you think you're doing, sitting there all night and half the day, too?' Irish Molly fussed about Fergus as the big Irishman lifted him to his feet and helped him to the bed.

Fergus made no move to help himself. He felt drained of all energy.

'Becky *was* at the Cabot Arms.' Fergus spoke to Giraldu

Reilly. 'She was one of the dollymops. . . .'

'Was she there because she *enjoyed* what she was doing?' Irish Molly spoke scornfully. 'Or did she have other reasons . . . like thinking she was helping a damned fool of a husband who got his hands burned minding someone else's business? Oh, yes, I meant to tell you before. One of the three surviving children you rescued died a couple of days ago. Knocked a pot of scalding water over herself while her mother was out at work. *That's* what you damned near lost your hands for. There are only two sorts of people in Lewin's Mead – fools and survivors. No heroes. If you live here, you learn to mind your own business and look after your own. It's something you can't put down on canvas – but it's what Becky's been doing. She's looked after *you*, in the only way she knew how. You ought to be damned grateful to the girl.'

'I can forgive what she did before. Not now. Not having other men. . . .'

'You're a fool, Fergus Vincent, like all men. So damned conceited that you believe five minutes in bed with a man makes him unforgettable. A woman *will* give heart, soul and mind to a man, but only if she really loves him – and Becky loves you, I'm sure of it.'

Giraldus Reilly was listening to Irish Molly with great interest, but she sent him to make some tea in her room. The fire had gone out in the attic grate.

When her fellow-countryman had gone, Irish Molly said to Fergus: 'There wouldn't have been any other men for Becky if she hadn't seen the world falling about your ears. She *had* to help, but what could she do? All she had to offer was her body, so she sold it – for *you*. If you think that came easy to her, then you know nothing about women.'

When Giraldus Reilly returned to the attic Irish Molly helped Fergus to drink a mug of tea, then she ordered Giraldus to light a fire in the grate. Meanwhile she began to clear up grey ash, scattered about the floor by fierce storm winds blowing down the chimney.

More than once as she worked Irish Molly cast a glance in Fergus's direction, but when she spoke it was to Giraldus Reilly.

'Were you very fond of your wife, Giraldus?'

'I was. I couldn't have wished for a finer wife. She was a darling woman.'

Giraldus Reilly's words recalled a memory for Fergus of the big angry Irishman standing off the might of the Bristol police force in defence of his wife and family.

'If she were here now and told you she'd done what Becky's done – and for the same reasons – what would you do?'

Giraldus Reilly was not a fast-thinking man. Squatting on his haunches by the grate, he gave the question his undivided attention. Suddenly his eyes filled with tears. 'Ask any man that question of his wife and he'll tell you straightway that he'd kill her. A year ago I might have said the same myself, but if only I had her and the children back again I'd forgive her *anything*, so help me, I would.'

Irish Molly crossed the room and gave Giraldus Reilly an affectionate hug. 'I believe you, Giraldus. You're a fine man.'

To Fergus, Irish Molly said: 'It'll be too late to have regrets when Becky's gone. You think about what Giraldus said.'

Fergus's mind began to work in a rational manner for the first time in almost twenty-four hours. He thought of Becky, of her past life and of the girl she had become. Then he made an honest appraisal of himself. A crippled, helpless, near-penniless artist. The wonder was that Becky thought enough of him to want to do *anything* for him. Things could never again be quite the same between them, but his life would be empty without Becky.

When Fergus put his feet to the floor both Irish Molly and Giraldus Reilly swung around to look at him.

'And what do you think you're doing?' Irish Molly was the first to speak.

'I'm going to find Becky.'

'Why?'

'To ask her to come back. She's still my wife.'

'You just stay right where you are. Giraldus, go and tell Becky her husband wants to see her. I'll be down as soon as I've swept up and thrown the sweepings out of the window.'

'You know where Becky is?'

'Her sniffling kept me awake for half the night. I'll be pleased to be rid of the girl.'

At the first sound of low voices on the stairs, Irish Molly whispered: 'Remember now, be kind to her. She needs you.' Then the Irish prostitute was gone. Fergus suspected she would pause on the stairs to repeat a similar message to Becky.

Fergus was shocked when Becky walked into the attic room. Her eyelids were heavy and swollen, and her face blotched and streaked as though she had tried to wipe away her tears with a grubby hand.

They both looked at each other uncertainly for a few moments, then Fergus held out his hands.

'Come here, Becky. Come back to me.'

CHAPTER FORTY-THREE

THE NEXT MORNING Fergus removed the bandages from his hands and began exercising his scarred fingers in earnest. At first he despaired of ever bringing life back to them, but by the end of the day he could grip a paintbrush in his fingers for a couple of seconds. The next day he tried again, and the next. He persisted even though each movement brought pain, and the new skin tended to split if he worked too hard.

His painful doggedness was rewarded a week later when he stood at his easel and made his first tentative brush-stroke. He had returned to the world of painting.

It was harder than he had anticipated, and at first he found it frustratingly difficult to control the movement of the brush, but he persevered and three weeks later he walked into the Hatchet inn armed with pad and pencils to spend the evening sketching the patrons.

It was an evening for celebrations. Giraldus Reilly and Charlie Waller kept Fergus liberally supplied with drinks, and at one stage of the proceedings he was called to a back room where a uniformed Ivor Primrose had come in off the streets to raise a glass to his recovery.

At the end of the evening Giraldus Reilly helped Fergus home to Back Lane and up the stairs to the attic. As Becky put him to bed she thought she must be the only wife in Lewin's Mead who was happy to have a drunken husband come home to her.

Fergus worked at his paintings during the days that followed sketching at the Hatchet inn most nights. He worked as though determined to make up for the time he had lost. He still needed to stop work frequently in order to rest his fingers, as the muscles were not as well developed as before, but his hands had healed astonishingly well.

Fergus had built up an impressive array of paintings by the time Fanny paid a surprise visit to the Back Lane studio when he and Becky were there together. Fergus had not resumed his sketching classes at the ragged school and he had not seen Fanny since receiving the hundred pounds from her in payment for his published sketches.

Fergus told Fanny she was foolhardy to walk through Lewin's Mead on her own, but Fanny brushed his fears aside, saying: 'I was walking through Lewin's Mead before you came here, Fergus Vincent. I doubt if it's any worse now than it was then. Anyway, you should be grateful to me. I've brought you this.'

She pulled something from inside a sleeve and handed it to him. As he took the tightly rolled bundle it sprang open. It was a roll of banknotes.

'You'll find fifty pounds there. Solomon Stern's friend has used more of your sketches. Solomon says he will take any you have left, especially those of Irish vagrants. They are in the news at the moment. He wants you to go to London, so he can discuss them with you.'

As she was talking, Fanny's glance was roving around the attic studio. There was much here that was new: a larger bed, two comfortable chairs, a good table, and curtains at the windows. It was clean, too. Becky had learned a great deal during her stay at the Red Lodge.

Suddenly Fanny saw the paintings leaning against each other in the studio alcove.

'You're painting again!' Fanny's glance dropped to Fergus's hands, and in spite of her resolve she winced involuntarily.

'I've been painting for a couple of weeks.'

'May I look at your work?'

Without waiting for a reply, Fanny dropped to her knees in the alcove and began examining the paintings. She looked at every one, making small sounds of delight and occasionally lifting a painting to examine it in more detail.

Her inspection completed, Fanny remained kneeling on the floor for some while before standing up and turning to Fergus and Becky. Reaching out, she took Fergus's hands in her own. Turning them over, she looked at the extensive scarring and shook her head in disbelief.

'It's nothing short of a miracle. With hands like these the career of most artists would be at an end. Yet you've not only overcome this disaster but *you're actually producing better paintings than before*! You're a genius, Fergus Vincent. I'm proud to know you.'

Fanny's words left Fergus with a warm glow. She would never know how close to despair he had come. No one ever would. It was behind him now.

'Will you go to London, Fergus? Solomon Stern will make all the arrangements. He and his friend would like you there as soon as possible – next week, if you are able to make it.'

'All right.' Fergus made up his mind quickly. He had come so far along the road to recovery, this would be another step forward. 'I'll travel to London on Monday, and take some sketches with me.'

'Good. I'll let him know. I'll tell Lady Hammond of your incredible progress, too. She hasn't been too well lately; this will help to cheer her. You ought to pay her a visit, Fergus. She often talks of you, and always with great affection. Now I must go and write to Solomon Stern immediately.'

'I'll walk as far as the ragged school with you.'

'No, you won't. You'll remain here and continue your painting. Becky can walk with me.'

If Becky was surprised that Fanny should want her company, she said nothing. Throwing a cloak about her shoulders, she followed Fanny down the stairs.

Fergus was busily painting when Becky returned. Hardly looking up, he asked: 'Did you see Fanny safely back to her school?'

'Yes.' Becky waited for Fergus to finish the detail he was

working on and look at her, but he was too engrossed in his work to look away from it.

'It's good news about my sketches. They're proving a life-saver for us. Not that I fancy travelling all the way to London again. . . .'

'Fergus! Fanny's asked me to teach at the ragged school.'

Fergus's astonishment was all that Becky had wished for, and she looked across the room at him smugly.

'That's wonderful,' said Fergus when he found his voice. 'What will you be teaching?'

'Nothing. I told her I didn't want to teach at no ragged school, even if I would be an . . . *inspiration* to the children there.' Becky had made tremendous progress with her vocabulary, but she still had problems with unfamiliar long words.

'Why not? You'd enjoy it.'

'I'm not going there to be bossed about by *her*.'

'That's a pity. Fanny isn't really bossy, and she's right. You'd not only inspire them to work harder, but you'd understand their problems, too. Think about it, Becky.'

At that moment they both heard the sound of someone climbing the stairs to the attic, and Irish Molly entered the room.

'Hello. I hope I'm not interrupting anything between the two of you.'

'No,' said Becky. 'Fergus has work to do because he's going to London again — and I've been asked to teach at the ragged school.'

'Well! You'll be charging folk to talk to you soon. But have you heard the news of Joe Skewes?'

Becky fell silent, but Fergus said: 'The last I saw of him he was chained up in a courtyard and as mad as a weaver.'

'That's where he was until last night, living on scraps that folk threw him when they remembered. But he must have been working away at the ring his chain was fixed to. Last night he pulled it clear and ran off, dragging the chain behind him, and with half the kids and dogs in Lewin's Mead after him.'

'Is he still free?' Becky looked suddenly scared.

'Freer than he's ever been. He got as far as the dock before his chain caught in something or other and he fell back under a loaded dray-cart. It's fast becoming a joke in Lewin's Mead that drink finally killed Joe Skewes.'

'Good!' Becky was fiercely exultant. 'I've wished him dead times enough.'

'Of course you have, and he's no loss to anyone. But I've some more news for you. I'm leaving Lewin's Mead. Going off the game for good.'

'What will you do? Don't tell me you've finally agreed to marry Giraldus?'

'Marry him? No, but we're both going to Ireland together, to the cottage Tomas Casey left to me. When we get there . . . Well, we'll see how things work out. That's partly why I've come to see you, Fergus. I'd like you to write a letter to Tomas Casey's solicitors for me. To tell them I'm coming to claim my property. I *can* read and write a bit, but not well enough to write to a solicitor. Will you do it for me?'

'Gladly, and I hope everything works out for you and Giraldus, even though Becky and I will be sorry to lose two such good friends. When do you expect you'll be leaving?'

'Not for a month or two. There's the business of the cottage to be sorted out first, and Giraldus and I need to see how we'll get along together. Giraldus is moving in here with me. I've been to the White Hart for the last time.'

Irish Molly chuckled happily. 'When I told Ida Stokes she said she hopes Iris doesn't go respectable again, too, or the neighbours around here will refuse to speak to her.'

CHAPTER FORTY-FOUR

ARRANGEMENTS FOR FERGUS to go to London were completed with great speed, but Fergus was unhappy to be travelling alone to the capital.

Becky had at first agreed to come to London with him, but the night before they were due to travel she changed her mind, pleading a mild stomach upset. Fergus believed Becky found the thought of going so far from Bristol frightening. He tried to change her mind, reminding her how much she had enjoyed the paddle-steamer voyage, but Becky was adamant. She would not go to London.

A few weeks before, Fergus might have successfully persuaded Becky to come with him, but the rift brought about by her activities at the Cabot Arms had not fully healed and they were not as close as they had been before. However, Fergus finally wrung a reluctant promise from Becky that she would, after all, help at the ragged school and he left Lewin's Mead happy in the knowledge that Fanny would keep a watchful eye on Becky.

Fergus did not expect to be in London for many days. Nevertheless, he left half of all the money he possessed with Becky. It amounted to twenty-five pounds, so she should not run short of cash.

Fergus was startled to discover he was already something of a celebrity in London. Within hours of his arrival at the offices of the magazine publishing his sketches he was besieged by representatives of London newspapers. Eventually he succeeded in escaping from them and returned to the inn near Regent's Park where he was staying – only to find more of them waiting for him there.

Solomon Stern was already negotiating for the hire of a Bond Street gallery to house Fergus's next exhibition, and Fergus was brought into the negotiations. When he realised he was expected to make suggestions on the décor of the gallery, Fergus wrote to inform Becky that his return to Bristol would be delayed. He was not too concerned. No doubt Becky was being kept busy at the ragged school – and he was finding his new status both flattering and exciting.

Gradually the ranks of waiting reporters dogging Fergus thinned, but now the social reformers moved in on him and Fergus was persuaded to give talks about his experiences in Lewin's Mead. He faced his audiences not in church halls now, but in huge theatres – and he spoke to capacity crowds. His popularity resulted in a second letter to Becky, and the few days he had expected to be away from her soon stretched to twenty.

Fergus realised he had become caught up in a gigantic movement for social reform. He had not *begun* the movement; it had been there all the time. Fergus merely provided its supporters with a tangible *raison d'être*, a standard to which they could flock. Reformers who had never been near a city slum came to his meetings. Waving magazines containing his sketches, they clamoured for something to be done about the city slums.

It mattered not that many of the sketches they waved in the air depicted homeless *Irish* vagrants, victims of an entirely different set of circumstances. The reformers saw what they wanted to see – and would fight harder for the cause because of it. Before long there was not an adult man or woman in London who was not familiar with Fergus Vincent's sketches.

Solomon Stern spoke to Fergus about his popularity and what the future held for him one evening when the two men were having dinner at a restaurant near the gallery, after yet another busy day.

'It's all going very satisfactorily.' The art dealer sat back in his chair and beamed about him. 'Your success so far bodes well for your exhibition, but I am thinking farther ahead now. How many Lewin's Mead sketches do you have?'

'About two hundred. Three hundred if you include the sailors and characters I've met at the Hatchet inn. I can make plenty of sketches, of course; I simply have to walk outside the door of the house in Back Lane.'

'No, you have enough.' It was a surprising reply, but Solomon Stern explained. 'People will eventually become bored if you continue to paint nothing else but slums and slum-dwellers. It's time you moved on to other subjects.'

'But I *want* to paint slums, and those who are forced to live there. That's what I've always intended doing.'

'And you've achieved your objective admirably – but by painting too much of it you'll defeat your own ends. You can best keep interest alive by including other subjects in your exhibitions. Landscapes and scenes of other parts of your city. Portraits, too; the public will always come to look at a good portrait, and I already have an important commission that should satisfy your crusading spirit, yet at the same time take your career a giant step forward.'

'What is this commission?' Fergus had not been convinced by Solomon Stern's argument.

'To paint Lord Carterton, the leader of the campaign seeking to abolish slums like Lewin's Mead. He is also the chief Opposition home affairs spokesman in the House of Lords.'

Fergus grudgingly conceded that if it were *really* necessary to paint a portrait there could hardly be a better subject – but he was unprepared for Solomon Stern's next words.

The art dealer wanted Fergus to begin painting Lord Carterton immediately, first in London then completing the portrait in Oxfordshire. Lord Carterton was preparing to make an extended visit to India and needed to return to his country home to complete his preparations.

Fergus agreed to the arrangements suggested by Solomon Stern, but there were more surprises in store for him. As Fergus painted the reforming peer, he learned that Lord Carterton not only supported Solomon Stern's view on limiting the number of sketches Fergus made of Lewin's Mead but went much further. He suggested that Fergus should move away from the Bristol slum!

'Part of our campaign strategy is to point out how eager these people are to leave such an unhealthy environment,' Lord Carterton explained. 'It has already been pointed out to us by the Government that you live there from *choice*.'

'If I didn't live in Lewin's Mead, there would be no sketches or paintings,' retorted Fergus. 'I went there to record the slums as they really are. It couldn't be done properly unless I actually *lived* there.'

'Quite!' agreed the peer. 'And you have succeeded in everything you set out to do. We have been provided with damning evidence of the state of the poorer areas of our cities. Your sketches have done more to move government and people than fifteen years of campaigning. I don't want to run the risk of losing ground now. Think about it.'

Fergus did think about Lord Carterton's words, both in London and later, when he was staying at the reforming peer's Oxfordshire home, but he had reached no firm decision by the time the portrait was completed.

It was a good portrait, and Lord Carterton was so pleased that he paid Fergus on the spot for his work.

It was a handsome fee, and Fergus rode the coach to Bristol the next day, making plans to buy Becky a present to celebrate his sudden wealth.

CHAPTER FORTY-FIVE

THE JOURNEY from Oxfordshire to Bristol was made on indifferent roads, but the coach maintained good time and rolled into the city shortly before dusk. When they neared St James Square the coach-driver pulled up his horses and allowed Fergus to alight not far from the ragged school.

Evening classes were in progress at the school, and as Fergus passed he could hear singing coming from inside. Acting upon a sudden impulse, Fergus went inside. It was just possible that Becky would be here, taking a class.

Fergus came out of the ragged school a few minutes later frowning deeply. Becky was *not* at the school. What was more, a somewhat diffident tutor had informed Fergus that she had not taught there during his absence from the city.

It seemed that Becky's courage must have failed her without his support and was something Fergus should have anticipated. Suddenly his frown cleared, and Fergus smiled ruefully. He wondered what excuse Becky would give him for the failure to keep her promise.

When Fergus reached Lewin's Mead, a few lamps and candles were already alight inside the houses that hemmed in the narrow alleyways. Everything seemed dirtier than Fergus remembered, and he wrinkled his nose in disgust at the foul stench rising from the River Frome.

The streets of the slum were curiously deserted, yet Fergus could hear a hubbub of sound that grew steadily louder as he neared Back Lane.

Puzzled by the noise, he walked faster. Soon he could hear

shouts of anger and derision. When he came within sight of Back Lane he saw a huge crowd gathered here. They were being held back from the lane by a double line of grim-faced constables.

The policemen were the targets for the crowd's abuse – and an occasional missile. Beyond them, in Back Lane itself, more constables were gathered about Ida Stokes's house.

Thoroughly alarmed, Fergus pushed his way through the close-packed crowd towards the police line, ignoring the angry protests of those he roughly shouldered from his path.

Eventually Fergus reached the double line of policemen, but here his progress was halted. The constables were unable to hear him above the general din when he cried that he *lived* in Back Lane. In desperation he tried to force a way through them, but he was driven back into the angry crowd.

When Fergus saw the tall figure of Ivor Primrose he shouted at the top of his voice. The constable was talking to a white-faced police inspector but he turned and looked towards the crowd. Unfortunately, Fergus's slight figure was lost behind the ranks of tall high-hatted policemen. Then Fergus began jumping up and waving his arms, his antics soundly cursed by those about him as he landed heavily on their toes. But the tactics worked. Leaving the inspector staring after him, Ivor Primrose hurried to where Fergus was wildly waving his arms.

The police lines broke for a moment, and Fergus was hauled through the gap to Back Lane.

'What's happening?' Fergus put the question as soon as he could draw breath.

'It's Alfie Skewes. News of the death of his father was given to him on the prison hulk at Sheerness. Three nights later he killed one of his gaolers and escaped. He was seen today by the docks, but he half-killed a constable who tried to arrest him. Now he's holed up in Ida Stokes's house.'

Fergus felt as though a ton weight was pushing him into the ground. 'Is Becky in there? I'm just returning from London. . . .'

'We don't know who's inside. The door has been locked We're debating whether or not to break it down and go in

Alfie Skewes is a desperate and violent man. There's also a possibility that he's armed.'

'You must do *something*. If Becky *is* in there . . . Let *me* go in and talk to him.'

Ivor Primrose shook his head. 'We can't allow that. Alfie Skewes isn't a man to reason with. In his own way he's every bit as mad as his father was.'

'But you can't leave him in the house with Becky. He blames her for everything that's happened to the Skewes family. Let me go in.'

'No.' Ivor Primrose gripped Fergus's arm as he turned towards the house. 'Come and talk to the inspector. . . .'

There was a disturbance at the edge of the crowd and the sound of voices raised in argument. Moments later, scattering constables before him, Giraldus Reilly came towards them, his success in breaking the police cordon cheered by the Lewin's Mead crowd.

A number of constables charged after Giraldus Reilly, but Ivor Primrose waved them back, and he and Fergus hurried to intercept the big Irishman.

'What's going on here?' Giraldus Reilly echoed Fergus's question.

'Alfie Skewes has escaped from a prison hulk. He's in the house. Do you know if Becky's in there?'

'She was a couple of hours ago. I left her with Molly. We've only been waiting to see you before we set off for Ireland. . . .'

The Irishman broke off as an outburst of near-hysterical screaming came from the house. Moments later the door was flung open and Ida Stokes stumbled out through the doorway.

Picking herself up, she waddled towards the policemen who ran to her aid. Fergus and Giraldus Reilly went with them.

As they reached her, Ida Stokes sank to her knees, wheezing noisily.

'What's going on inside?' Ivor Primrose had to put the question three times before Ida Stokes heard and looked up at him with terror in her eyes.

Still wheezing alarmingly, she said: 'He's *killed* her! Stabbed her to death ... on the first-floor landing. Oh my God! He'd have killed me, too. He's mad ... as mad as his father.'

Fergus never waited to hear what else Ida Stokes had to say. Running awkwardly, he had almost reached the door of the house before Giraldus Reilly overtook him, with Ivor Primrose no more than a pace behind.

'Go back. We'll deal with him.'

Fergus ignored the constable's order, but the two men beat him to the doorway and were halfway up the first flight of stairs before Fergus reached the hallway.

On the first-floor landing he could just make out the other two men crouching over a still form on the floor.

Ivor Primrose stood up as Fergus reached him. 'She's dead.'

'Becky ...!'

Fergus's cry died in his throat as Giraldus Reilly turned a tortured face towards him. 'It's not Becky. It's Molly. Why should he want to kill her? Why should *anyone* want to kill her?'

Giraldus Reilly put the unanswerable questions to Fergus as blue-uniformed constables pounded up the stairs from the ground floor, a couple of them carrying lanterns. As they crowded together on the first-floor landing Ivor Primrose sent them to search the rooms off the landing, but it soon became apparent that Alfie Skewes was not on this floor.

Giraldus Reilly stood up from Irish Molly's crumpled body. Without a word, he climbed the stairs to the second floor, with Fergus and a number of policemen close behind him.

Once more the constables spread out to search the rooms, but they found only Mary O'Ryan and some of her young family, for once in their lives too scared to cry.

Giraldus Reilly did not stop here. Checking Fergus who tried to push past him, Giraldus made his way up the final flight of creaking stairs.

There was a sudden noise from the attic room, and Fergus shouted: 'Becky... ?'

His words were drowned by the bellow of the Irishman: 'This is Giraldus Reilly, Skewes. I know you're there and I'm coming in for you. It'll not be the hulks this time, nor the rope, neither. I'm going to take that knife from you and slit your throat with it, just as you did to Molly. . . .'

Giraldus Reilly choked on his words. Without pausing to check whether or not the attic door was locked, he put his foot to it and kicked it open.

Alfie Skewes was just disappearing through the attic window to the ledge outside – but he was not quick enough. Giraldus Reilly made it to the window in half a dozen long strides. Reaching out, he secured a grip on the leg of Alfie Skewes's loose canvas trousers.

Alfie Skewes tried to kick himself free, and when this did not succeed he struck back with the sharp carving-knife he carried in his left hand.

It proved to be the escaped prisoner's undoing. The knife-thrust was made at an awkward angle and caused him to overbalance. When he tried to right himself his foot slipped on the pigeon droppings that soiled the stone ledge. For a moment he balanced on the edge of the ledge, staring back at the Irishman, his arms gyrating wildly in an effort to right himself. Giraldus Reilly released his grip, and Alfie Skewes toppled over the edge to crash to the cobblestones of the lane, forty feet below. He landed with a sickening thud that brought a gasp from the crowd, which had fallen silent while the final act of the drama was being played out high above them.

Inside the attic room Fergus was far more concerned about the whereabouts of Becky than in following the final moments of Alfie Skewes.

He was still frantically searching when Ida Stokes was brought back to the house and informed Fergus that Becky had not been in the house when Alfie Skewes had burst in upon the landlady and Irish Molly.

Fergus sank into a chair, suddenly weak with an over-whelming relief, and listened to the landlady's story of her terrifying experience.

Alfie Skewes had entered the house while Irish Molly and Ida Stokes were in the landlady's front room. The two women were having a drink together to celebrate the forthcoming departure to Ireland of Irish Molly and Giraldus Reilly.

The two women were safe enough while Alfie Skewes was drinking the contents of their celebratory bottle of gin, even though it quickly became evident to both of them that he was not sane.

When the drink was gone, the escaped prisoner demanded to know the whereabouts of Becky and Fergus, both of whom he blamed equally for having him committed to a prison hulk, and for bringing about the death of his father.

Whatever retribution Alfie Skewes intended exacting on Becky and Fergus was interrupted by the unexpected arrival of the police outside the house. It took everyone by surprise. Policemen did not enter the Lewin's Mead rookery. It was part of an unwritten understanding between police and the criminal fraternity. The police kept out of Lewin's Mead. In return, the brawling, drunkenness and debauchery of the slum-dwellers was largely contained within its narrow squalid streets.

However, the police viewed the return of Alfie Skewes to Bristol with great alarm. When one of their informants followed the escaped prisoner to Back Lane and disclosed his whereabouts to Ivor Primrose, the police inspector in charge of the area had no hesitation. All available constables, and as many additional men as could be found at short notice, were ordered to enter the slum and arrest the fugitive.

During the initial confusion, Irish Molly and Ida Stokes fled upstairs, but Alfie Skewes came after them brandishing a kitchen-knife. Irish Molly told the landlady to hide while she stayed to reason with him. Irish Molly had known the violent coal-heaver for many years, and he had no quarrel with her.

Unfortunately, the mentally unbalanced man was beyond all reasoning. While they were talking he suddenly attacked Irish Molly without any warning in a sudden irrational outburst of violent temper, and Ida Stokes fled from the house.

While Ida Stokes was still telling her story, Fergus began to worry about Becky again. Leaving the crowded ground-floor room, he went back to the attic studio, hoping to find some thing that might tell him of Becky's present whereabouts.

In the room he lit the lamp and carried it to the table – and it was then he saw the package. Wrapped in brightly coloured paper, it was on a shelf where Fergus kept his pencils.

Untying the ribbon that bound the package, Fergus unwrapped the paper. Inside was a small leather box. When he opened the lid he found a watch. A *gold* watch.

Filled with trepidation, Fergus lifted the watch from the box and held it in his hand. He thought Becky must have been stealing again – but the watch-case was too highly polished. Too new. He flicked open the case. Inside, the inscription read: *To Fergus from Becky*.

It *was* new. Becky must have bought it for him – but it would have taken all the money he had left with her to buy food. How had she been living during the weeks he had been away?

Slowly, almost with reluctance, Fergus put the expensive watch back inside the box and replaced it on the shelf.

He left the house without a word to anyone and made his way to the Cabot Arms. He hoped his intuition would prove to be wrong. *Prayed* it might be wrong.

The Cabot Arms was busy, the interior heavy with smoke. It was a minute or two before Fergus saw Becky. She was on the far side of the crowded room, sitting at a table between the two young men he had met in Isaiah Rodden's pawn-broker's shop. One of the men had his arm draped about Becky's shoulders. She was laughing. . . .

Fergus was sitting at the table in the attic with the watch in front of him when he heard Ida Stokes wheezing up the stairs. She was the last person he wished to see right now, but he pulled out a chair and invited her to sit down.

'No, thank you, Mr Vincent. I won't be stopping.'

The landlady's unsmiling face and her use of the formal 'Mr Vincent' warned Fergus that this was not a social visit, but he was unprepared for her next words.

'I'm afraid I must ask you to leave my house. As soon as possible, if you don't mind.'

'We're all upset about Irish Molly's death, Ida, but no one

could have anticipated the actions of a madman. . . .'

'It's got nothing to do with Irish Molly, or with Alfie Skewes. We've had murders in Lewin's Mead before — madmen, too — but we've never before had the police come in and take over the place. Lewin's Mead folk don't like it, Mr Vincent. They don't like it at all. They say they won't sleep easy in their beds so long as you're here in case it happens again.'

'While *I'm* here? The police coming in had nothing to do with me. . . .' Fergus's voice faltered. He was too tired, too distracted to argue with anyone.

'That's as may be, but we never had nothing like it before you came.' Ida Stokes glared at him. 'There's another thing, too. It seems there's been a lot about you in the papers lately. Word's going about that you want to have our houses pulled down and put us out on the streets.'

'That's nonsense, Ida. All I've said is that people shouldn't *have* to live in slums like this. My sketches and paintings have been made to show how bad conditions are here.'

Ida Stokes was unimpressed. 'Too much has been said. Lewin's Mead is *our* home. It's where we want to be. I don't expect you to understand; you're not one of us.'

Fergus opened his mouth to counter Ida Stokes's latest statement, when the words that had once been spoken by his friend Henry Gordon came back to him with startling clarity.

'. . . In a slum an artist must observe the rules of the people who live there. *Their* code. Break it and he might as well pack up his things and leave. . . .'

Fergus felt suddenly very, very weary. Bodily and mentally drained of all energy.

'What of . . . Becky?'

Ida Stokes shrugged. 'No one's said anything against her that I've heard. She can go with you, or she can stay. She'll manage without you, the same way as she has while you've been away — and I won't have to put up with all that whispering and giggling on the stairs at all hours of the night. I might be getting old, but I've still got ears — and eyes. No, you don't need to worry about her. She's one of us. . . .'

*   *   *

Carrying a bag containing his belongings on his shoulder, and with a slim canvas satchel tucked beneath his arm, Fergus limped along a narrow rubbish-strewn alleyway that led from Lewin's Mead.

Turning to take a last look back, he did not see the urchin lying amidst the rubbish on the ground.

'Here! Mind where you're putting your bleedin' feet. . . .'

Time Warner Paperback titles available by post:

☐ Ben Retallick	E. V. Thompson	£6.99
☐ Chase the Wind	E. V. Thompson	£5.99
☐ Singing Spears	E. V. Thompson	£5.99
☐ Lottie Trago	E. V. Thompson	£5.99
☐ An Apple From Eden	Emma Blair	£5.99
☐ Flower of Scotland	Emma Blair	£6.99
☐ Time and Again	Evelyn Hood	£6.99
☐ The Silken Thread	Evelyn Hood	£5.99

The prices shown above are correct at time of going to press. However, the publishers reserve the right to increase prices on covers from those previously advertised, without further notice.

TIME WARNER PAPERBACKS
P.O. Box 121, Kettering, Northants NN14 4ZQ
Tel: 01832 737525, Fax: 01832 733075
Email: aspenhouse@PSBDial.co.uk

POST and PACKAGING:
Payments can be made as follows: cheque, postal order (payable to Time Warner Books) or by credit cards. Do not send cash or currency.
All U.K. Orders **FREE OF CHARGE**
E.E.C. & Overseas 25% of order value

Name (Block Letters) _____

Address _____

_____

Post/zip code: _____

☐ Please keep me in touch with future Time Warner publications

☐ I enclose my remittance £_____

☐ I wish to pay by Visa/Access/Mastercard/Eurocard

Card Expiry Date

_____